MW01124166

THE MATERIALIST MAGICIAN

To Bob

I hope you enjoy

and benefit

Cloyd Taylor

THE MATERIALIST MAGICIAN

CLOYD TAYLOR

TATE PUBLISHING
AND ENTERPRISES, LLC

The Materialist Magician
Copyright © 2014 by Cloyd Taylor. All rights reserved.

No part of this publication may be reproduced, stored in a retrieval system or transmitted in any way by any means, electronic, mechanical, photocopy, recording or otherwise without the prior permission of the author except as provided by USA copyright law.

The opinions expressed by the author are not necessarily those of Tate Publishing, LLC.

This novel is a work of fiction. Names, descriptions, entities, and incidents included in the story are products of the author's imagination. Any resemblance to actual persons, events, and entities is entirely coincidental.

Published by Tate Publishing & Enterprises, LLC
127 E. Trade Center Terrace | Mustang, Oklahoma 73064 USA
1.888.361.9473 | www.tatepublishing.com

Tate Publishing is committed to excellence in the publishing industry. The company reflects the philosophy established by the founders, based on Psalm 68:11,
"The Lord gave the word and great was the company of those who published it."

Book design copyright © 2014 by Tate Publishing, LLC. All rights reserved.
Cover design by Carlo Nino Suico
Interior design by Jomel Pepito

Published in the United States of America

ISBN: 978-1-63418-041-2
Fiction / Magical Realism
14.10.08

ACKNOWLEDGMENTS

I want to acknowledge those who have helped this book reach its current form.

I wrote brief pieces sporadically for decades. My interest in writing was stirred during a midlife crisis. In the fall of 2008 (I believe), Hope Chapel in Austin included writers in their arts festival. I do not recall the name of the woman who traded multiple e-mails with me to improve "The Materialist Magician" into an acceptable short story of twenty-two pages. To her and to Hope Chapel, I offer my thanks.

After three years, my dissatisfaction with the resolution of the story prompted me to begin rewriting it. John Tucker helped make signing in the story more realistic. I accept responsibility for remaining inaccuracies in those portrayals.

Special thanks go to Kirby Barker (the younger) who was the first to read through the entire original manuscript (more that 350 pages) and his critique that the story did not move quickly enough. Prompted by his advice, I reduced it to barely over 200 pages.

Many people provided much-needed encouragement for my writing. Fran Patterson, an artist, helped especially with my artistic insecurities. Nathan and Jane Bauld, Paul Brower, Cynthia Roper, and Debbie Hamby each provided encouragement.

I thank Tate publishers for working through some difficult formatting and the many ways they assisted.

My wife Kay and son Allen merit special thanks. They endured, especially Kay, far more "may I read you a portion?" than anyone else. Their forbearance and encouragement aided my writing.

Contents

Resistance

Awakening

Living

Preface

How does one become a person? How do we become benevolent humans with all the dehumanizing "demons" arrayed against us? We are warped by desires within and cultural forces and social pressures without. We are misled and deluded by sexual (and other) myths, advertising, violence, and injustices. Hidden forces in our culture, in our interactions with each other, and in our psyche limit our freedoms as persons. These vital matters arose as this book took form.

The materialist magician was inspired by *The Screwtape Letters* by C. S. Lewis. I first read it at Virginia Tech in 1970 for an honors seminar. Not until 2007 did I realize how that book woke me to spiritual realities.

This story began as a dream of a trip back to a dual perspective encounter with Jesus. The consciousness of the materialist magician scrutinized Jesus through a host. The host was a woman who washed the feet of Jesus with her tears (Luke 7). Writing this story became an odyssey.

This materialist magician believes in powers and forces beyond her but believes she is fully in control. She, like me often, is deluded. How can we not be whenever we deny central realities? She is convinced that the powers are impersonal, pursues those powers with abandon, and uses them blind to the price she pays.

She plays into Screwtape's hands perfectly as he expressed, "If once we can ever produce our perfect work—the Materialist Magician—then the end of the war will be in sight."[1*] However, Lewis reminds us: "There is wishful thinking in hell as well as on Earth."[2*] Screwtape could not anticipate God's countermoves. Nor can I.

Writing this story spurred an exploration—in the story and personally. How does a winsome identity develop? How does one become an increasingly free and consistent person, even throughout the unconscious? The writing guided me. It led to dreams and intrusions of the unconscious into her life (and mine). We are oblivious to how the hidden sways our lives. Ninety percent of an iceberg is hidden; most of myself also is. There is commerce between my conscious self and my far larger unconscious. I take wrong turns in living, wandering and meandering far off course. How can such a mass of contradictions form a coherent me? We steer a car through traffic, around curves and potholes, toward our desired destiny. We make continuous course corrections. How is my moment-by-moment living steered to connect all that is truly me together? I'm a jumble of thoughts, emotions, and desires, both deliberate and unconscious with miscellaneous bits and pieces of random and unclassified stuff mixed in. I'm a tad like that previous sentence. How is all "the mess that is me" forged into an alloy fit for living with love, joy, and wonder? It is beyond me. It cannot be, but it is.

The main character was mangled and warped deep within in the hidden places of her heart. It was done to her by clever forces who crafted her so well she presumed it was done for her. How can the unseen and unknown change? What changes free even

---

1 C.S. Lewis, *The Screwtape Letters* (New York: Macmillan Publishing Co., Inc., 1959), 33.

2 Lewis, *The Screwtape Letters*, 4.

the unconscious? Her odyssey moves toward reality and grinds her (and me) to dust—to make us more human.

There are abrupt and deliberate shifts in this work in verb tense and from first person to third person (and back). This is intended to convey how suddenly her (and our) heart shifts from other to self, from subjective to objective, and even from good to evil. These shifts likely slow down comprehension. If we become more mindful of these shifts I believe they will have been worthwhile.

The writing is complete; mysteries of the odyssey remained. Thomas Traherne (died 1674—how different was the world then, yet how alike we still are) shed light on it. He wrote:

> I have found that things unknown have a secret influence on the soul...We love we know not what, and therefore everything allures us...Do you not feel yourself drawn by the expectation and desire of some Great Thing?
>
> We must disrobe...free from the leaven of this world... Ambitions, trades, luxuries, inordinate affections, casual and accidental riches invented since the fall, would be gone, and only those things appear, which did to Adam in Paradise, in the same light and in the same colours: naturally seeing those things, to the enjoyment of which he is naturally born.[3*]

My interest in the influence of the unknown, the hidden—part of which is our own unconscious—has increased during this expedition. I plan several more books (hints of three of them are in the text) to continue this trek into how the hidden sways us. I hope you enjoy reading this story and that your story benefits.

---

3 Thomas Traherne, *Centuries of Meditations* (London: private publication, 1908), 2, 81.

Explanation: There are portions of internal struggle with opposing sides and the magician herself caught in the middle. The words of the sides are indicated with distinctive formatting and are generally positioned on the page in this manner:

the side that would control	the self	the freeing side

Part 1

Hope

Hope of Power

Hope of power fuels me, giving me an intense drive and energy to master everything needed for power—to use technology and people to empower me, and to gain control over the Life Force itself. I am creating myself with power, wealth, beauty, fame, and satisfying every desire consistent with mastery over everything and everybody around me. I am in total control of my destiny and myself since seizing control of the Life Force. I am master of aging and every bodily function, and am fully self-aware. Indeed, "All shall be mine, and all shall be mine, and all manner of things shall be mine." I am full and getting fuller of myself, expanding and pushing aside lesser souls than myself. I am a woman more powerful than any man. I am the only one to combine all the advances of knowledge and technology of this modern age with the ability to control the powers of the Life Force.

I am forging habits of heart, soul, mind, and strength to pursue power over everyone and everything. This is my theme, my anthem, my story, my destiny. My will, emotions, thinking, and actions harden and steel me for any action required for power and dominion. I am excluding all hints of compassion or love, those terrible weaknesses, and all other weaknesses that might make me vulnerable to others.

I am exercising as I often do, straining the limits of my will and all my faculties by pushing my body, emotions, and mind to their limits and beyond. I attack gymnastic with extreme vigor and creativity to meld heart, soul, mind, and strength together—I create convergence of my faculties and life. Steeling my will is the fruition of my conditioning and finely honed skills in gymnastics and acrobatics. I also have black belts in several martial arts.

Often when I exercise, I put my body on display to incite lust. Sometimes, I bring some hapless man under my spell so that he will attack me while I am running through the woods. I relish incapacitating such boys (all men are mere boys, toys for me).

My powers seem magical. I am demythologizing and demystifying magic (throughout evolution, there are vestiges of the guiding of the Life Force encoded often as archetypes in the evolutionary material). Using the Life Force, various chemical and primal linguistic keys, and the forces of my own will, I am learning to access and control both evolutionary matter and inanimate matter. My control extends to the deep recesses of the unconscious and grows still deeper. My knowledge and technology empower me to focus, fine-tune, and multiply the seemingly magical and limitless powers of the Life Force. I am close to gaining control over random quantum fluctuations, and, when I achieve that, all power will be mine. Magic! Yes, *magic* is a perfect word to describe to uninitiated, ignorant ciphers what I do. *Power*, *mystery*, *enchanting*, *dangerous*, and, above all, *dark*—that's what I am and that's what I want to overwhelmingly impress on all you nonentities.

Oh, yes, I will get into your mind. Whether you are attracted to me and fascinated, repulsed by me, or focused on being indifferent to me, I will secure your focus and gradually captivate it. In time, you will be mine! Eventually, you will confess that I am your god, your greatest source of pleasure.

Power Is My Destiny

Power is my destiny. I am confident the Life Force chose me for its next evolutionary step. Clearly, every detail of my life is being channeled toward my gaining power. For instance, when my parents were tragically killed by a drunk driver when I was six, I was devastated. But, when my aunt and uncle became my custodians and stripped me of everyone and everything familiar, I felt I had lost everything. They promptly moved me and sent my deaf twin brother away to boarding school, never to be seen or heard from, except that awful letter he finally sent.

They then rechanneled my life beginning with rigorous individual schooling in martial arts, seduction, sciences, linguistics, and making all my "play" purposeful. All was planned to drive me to my destiny. I was freed from "loving" parents who had become disgustingly joyful, generous Christians—it cost them their lives. God is an impossible and preposterous idea—at least, so far—but my destiny is to become the first and only god. I grew to resent everything about my parents for they would have made me ordinary, happy—merely adjusted. But my aunt especially rescued me from that and thrust me forcefully to power. She trained and tutored me in all forms of power; my mind has total mastery over my appearance and body.

I also had rigorous training in seduction, what she called *magic*, and all sorts of useful knowledge. I practice the highest form of meditation: mind, body, passion, and will all united in such ferocious brutish activity that the genus of the Life Force takes possession of me. They also trained me from an early age to give full expression to my sexual energy, thus magnifying it greatly. Instead of wasting energy controlling my libido, I use it to empower me. I am free of conscience, fear, pity—anything that might encumber me. I have practiced these habits so that they are my second nature and hold me to my chosen course.

My aunt was a bright Bolivian beauty, who forsook La Paz to seek fame and fortune in the USA. She got my uncle instead. He is my father's oldest sibling—spoiled by his great-grandfather for whom he is named. The elder lured the younger into his orbit with money so that the younger became both rich and a mere puppet of the elder. That the younger was rich and compliant was enough to attract my aunt. After their expensive wedding and honeymoon, her disappointment with his lack of ambition turned her to the occult, a stepping stone to the reality of the Life Force. Everything was orchestrated for my benefit.

During sleep, my dreams fortify my will, inspire me, and often provide solutions to technological impasses. From these dreams, I am developing my "trinkets." A recurrent dream, my favorite, is that I perch high above the earth on the head of the king of the dragons. I am in full command of the king of the dragons and, through him, of all his subjects (dragons, all sorts of mythical brutes, and myriads of deadly insects). My command of the Life Force and control of these nearly mindless brutes make me invincible. In my dreams, I enjoy tormenting and destroying my enemies, avenging myself on anyone foolish enough to oppose me, and especially relish the attacks of vast armies, since I am able to crush any opposition to me and the vast hordes I command.

I did have one series of impossible dreams. In them, I was an old gray-haired, wrinkled-face grandmother living in a setting that was rustic, Spartan, and unimpressive. I cooked a feast of meats, side dishes, and desserts for some family gathering. I was surrounded by a devoted, affectionate, idiotically happy family. In the dream, I was happy, even with my appearance, overjoyed with my undistinguished husband and ordinary grown children and several grandchildren. Impossible! I have never had a more unrealistic dream. I will never look old—couldn't possibly be happy if I did; will never cook for myself, much less for others; will never marry, except as an alliance for power; and certainly will never raise children to be merely happy and ordinary. Any children I have will be powerful. The insane thing is that I had these dreams six times before I was able to banish them. How could I possibly end up like that? Unrealistic! I'd have to die a thousand deaths before I would ever sink to such a life! "Indeed, in deed." What?

From a series of dreams, I developed trinkets so I can travel into the past by inhabiting a Host who lived in that time. Much trial and error were involved in adjusting the trinkets before I would risk it on myself.

I secured subjects for my experiments from the homeless, addicts, and teen runaways. The first few were in comas for several days upon their return. With my magic, I coaxed them from their coma and discovered its cause. The comas were due to the subjects being aware of far too much of the unconscious and physiological processes of the Host. My subjects were simply overwhelmed. They all recovered and spared me the bother of disposing of bodies. Though experimenting on many subjects, I gradually limited how much of the Host's unconscious thoughts were available to the subject. Eventually, I eliminated the comas, and the subjects were merely extremely fatigued.

None of my subjects ever had any conscious or accessible memories of their observations of the past. I, even with all that I am, was unable to uncover any memories. I knew from brain changes that there were significant changes. I always confined my subjects for days after their "trip" for observation and testing. I enjoyed the creativity of using my power, especially mind control, to restrain my subjects. I love power!

Each of my subjects changed after the trip. The teen runaways returned to their families or found a safe haven. The addicts gave up their addictions or entered rehabs. Even the homeless made significant changes to their lives. All my subjects became happier and more hopeful, making my manipulation and control of them a bit more challenging for me.

The clearly negative outcome was that almost all of them became more "spiritual." Far worse, most became mindless Christians who lived their idiotic convictions. That disgusted me. I consoled myself that these weaklings got what they deserved.

I enjoyed taking full advantage of the attractive males and blocked all my subjects' memories of the events before releasing them. I do regret that I couldn't safely have them retain their memories of their complete domination by me.

I was not able to determine to what time my subjects traveled or any information about their Hosts. Once I was confident of my safety, I prepared for my first viewing of past figures of power.

For a few minutes, I have been vigorously working my body as I am imprinting my superiority on your defenseless unconscious (by planting brief intrusions into your future dreams). I conclude my maneuvers of my body and your mind by rapidly running and springing across the mat, twisting and turning in the air during my flips, doing what should be impossible moves for a woman so wondrously endowed and over six-foot-tall, accelerating more and more until I forcefully crash to the floor. I badly sprain my leg. I laugh and heal my leg with a fierce crushing squeeze of my hand. The searing agony of healing myself hurt so good! Someday, oh, so very soon, I'll crush your heart curing you of self to free you to belong to me, to something infinitely greater than yourself, to serve a purpose with your meaningless life, to serve my purpose.

Seeking Power

Seeking power is always my goal. On my first trip, I observed Alexander the Great. I gained much and had little fatigue on my return. My superior powers protected me. Since then I've perfected my magic so that I know who I am going to observe.

I often "travel" back in time, always inhabiting a female Host. I suppose a male always inhabits a male Host. Too bad I don't have a male that I control enough to travel back with me. Someday, when I control some male, I will be a team. Though I cannot communicate with or affect any part of past reality, including my Host, I learn much I use to increase my power. I observed Hitler, Stalin, Nietzsche, Machiavelli, Pol Pot, and numerous others. I've learned that all great and powerful souls have an uncanny commonality—they all merge with a "one soul." They did not have the ability to absorb hapless souls, to control them fully, as I am rapidly learning. They were only able to manipulate and command the weaklings. They were rewarded for their unbridled pursuit of power by their merging into the one soul. Such is my destiny and hope.

I am currently searching for a gateway to observe Merlin. I am making great strides in finding gateways far more often. With each trip, I increase my power, so I'm always desperate for more.

When I travel back, almost no time passes in our time no matter how many hours I am in the past.

I am sure the myths about Merlin (magic and that superstitious rot) have a real basis. I will discover it and use it when I observe him. I am certain Merlin had an ability to manipulate people and even matter. The power and influence of Jesus, though they were badly perverted, certainly sprang from similar abilities.

With another trinket, I see both the power of a person and the lines of power emanating from him or her. Most people have a blue or green color about them with several black lines of power associated with them and one, usually very faint, white line of contamination. Darker colors mean greater power. As I have gained power, I myself have gone from denim blue to a dark purple—a very royal color. The multitudes of dark lines of power associated with my self have also greatly increased. The white line is most pronounced in infants and those condemned to perpetual intellectual childhood, so it must be a sign of weakness. Indeed, with most mature adults, the white line is very faint.

I easily made a fortune in real estate by reading, even better than a person is aware of, the true desires of a person's heart. I built a magnificent complex for myself to live and work in. I planted elaborate gardens with a wide array of plants with potent uses, even saturating them with bits of the Life Force for my personal enhancement and refreshment. My gardens supply me with ingredients for numerous potent uses (the ignorant used to naively call them *spells*).

Satisfying my lusts for pleasure as well as power enriches my life and is a delightful way to use my power. Saturday, soaking in the forces of my gardens, I spot my new gardener. His body is magnificent—tall, muscular, wonderfully proportioned. I lust to have him. Recently arrived from Africa, he is surely poor, unskilled, and desperate to support his parents and sisters. His power profile is light green with a white line of weakness, one of the brightest white lines I've ever seen in any but an infant.

Also like an infant, there are only a few dark lines of power, and none of them touch him. *He will do, he will do whatever I want.* He is vulnerable, naïve, has little power or resources, and needs to support others. His body will be a delightful bonus. I will control him, enjoy him, and use him for my purposes.

I prepare to have him. I read his brain, so I know the physical appearance, the aromas, the movements, the voice tones and inflections, even the words to use to make myself irresistible to him. I obtain a detailed scan of his brain and acquire samples of his hair and sweat. He struggles against my allure, though I am only in my daily seductive attire. I focus his thoughts on me and begin to bind him to me. He obsesses at not looking at me, focuses on resisting me. *Fool! I use everything, even your resistance to me, for whatever I want.*

Returning to my lab with the samples, I scrutinize the brain scans. I use the results to leverage and focus the Life Force with my bracelet. I designed the gold bracelet, encrusting it with super-conducting sensors that sparkle like jewels, aided by the dreams. I program my bracelet so I can control his brain. I will decimate his impulse control, all his higher processes, and his motor initiative; he will not be able to flee. I will amplify his sexual responsiveness and reinforce his compliance to me; he will be hopelessly addicted to me. Once he is complying with me, I will manipulate his memory and will. When I induce him to stretch his boundaries to let me in, I will gain control that I will expand. Going to my bedroom, I chose clothing, accessories, makeup, and hairstyle, and practice the movements and voice that he will find irresistible. I mold myself to his desires. I also tailored a perfume that will be the strongest sexual pheromones he will ever experience. My eagerness for Monday morning is voracious! I will consume him.

I dream of him that night. Though he briefly resists me in a most pathetic and ineffective manner, I easily conquer him. He eagerly satisfies my whims and fantasies. He is totally under my control. My gardener is now simply mine to do whatever I want with. Conquering him is almost too easy. I am going to do far better. I am going to conquer him so completely that he will think he is fully in control even of me and willfully do whatever I want.

Yes!

A Break-In

A break-in occurs early Sunday, hours before dawn. A dream makes me aware of it. Somehow, two men manage to get past all my elaborate security into my security cottage. I carefully bait the cottage as a trap, since it is the weakest link in gaining entry to the complex. Since they are only two hapless men devoid of the Life Force, I will handle them easily.

While they focus their attention on neutralizing the vital portions of my security, they do not notice my stealthy probing of their thoughts in my dream. I redirect their attention to the numerous bottles of very old brandy that are "hidden" in the cottage. Step by step, I lead them to consider, desire, and then become obsessed with having just one taste of that once-in-a-lifetime brandy. In their own minds, they only have just one taste as they drink themselves into a stupor. The duller they become, the easier I read and manipulate their minds.

They are both complete naïve materialists with no access to the Life Force. Also, they have no transcendent commitments or qualms to encumber them. They are in the blackest of black ops, some secret cell in a secret organization. I retard their metabolism of alcohol, so they pass out and will sleep for over a day.

As they pass out, I go on to other dreams. For the first time, a dream provides detailed guidance in how to use the impending challenge from the colleagues of the two men. I see the future but also get to plan and practice my response. I am finally awakened by the arrival of several men posing as policemen. They have a bogus search warrant to swarm all over my premises for some burglars. They find them drunk in the security cottage. They also secretly search for the sources of my power but aren't able to recognize them. They suspect more than I am comfortable with.

I mention to the "detective" in charge that I know all the police in our community. *Are they with the FBI or something? Is there some problem?* I also give him a very strong hypnotic suggestion that he should tell me everything.

Of course, he tells me more than he should. He justifies it to himself that he is watching my reactions. I am fascinated that people justify whatever they want. I use this self-justifying bias to bend people as I want. The more he tells, the more he wants to tell as I reinforce it with my interest and attention.

I shower him with my interest and become increasingly intriguing to him. I rapidly draw him into my orbit. We talk till dawn and enjoy it while embracing and kissing each other. His objectivity obliterated, only his strong professional commitment could be any danger to me. His heart is becoming mine. As I make the perfect probes with the right emotional nuance, my capture of his heart is nearly complete. I weave my allure into his heart, and he leaves with a deep longing for me. I will cash him in later!

Progress, such good progress!

Delighting in my successes is a tonic to me. My cook fixes me breakfast, after which I sleep deep and peaceful for a few hours, awakening refreshed. I review a recent purchase I manipulated from the heirs of an isolated rugged piece of property that is nearly useless due to the onerous environmental restrictions on its use. I will make good use of it; its large size and isolation will serve me well as a secret training ground for my "agents." Access is, even by foot, only with great difficulty. The "hermit" who cultivated its inaccessibility for decades recently died, and the heirs sold the property. It was no longer theirs—they were eager to unload it. The log structures on the property are sound and well-built but are without electricity or gas lines. It has a well and septic field. The restrictive covenants on the property prevent open fires, bringing in any utility lines, and even running gas engines, near the livable structures by the pond.

I "stole" the property. I manipulated despair in the siblings and played on their eagerness to be rid of it. I maneuvered them into begging me to make an offer on it. They settled for a fraction of its value and thanked me profusely for helping them. I achieved another of my triumphs. I congratulated myself for another fully satisfied customer—the fools!

I will forego the profit on this property. I will use it to begin enslaving various professionals. I will conduct weekend retreats there to gain control of small select groups of assets.

I sleep wonderfully that night, with exultant dreaming of my power, success, popularity, and of my conquest of my gardener the next day. I awake refreshed and eager for his arrival. After breakfast, a workout, and getting dressed up for him, I eagerly wait, wanting to watch my gardener work briefly before springing my trap for him.

Impatience grows, as he is, however, nowhere to be found. I tinker with magic a few hours. About noon, I again look for my gardener. I ask my complex manager. She tells me that he called to resign without giving a reason. How dare he interfere with my plans and my dreams for him! I tell my complex manager, "Get him on the phone for me!"

Soon, I am talking to him. I ask why he quit.

"I had a nightmare about you last night," he states. I positively gloat. After a pause, he adds, "My master wants me to quit." I offer sympathy, help, and protection, and tell him I can free him. His response offends me: "My master makes me free." He explains that he had also once been a slave to many things, but now he was free from all of them with only one master—Jesus. I groan, barely restraining my rage.

Stupid superstitious fool, I think. "And why in the world would Jesus want you to quit? You just had a bad dream."

"I'm sure Jesus wants me to quit so I would not be tempted by you," he replies. "I could tell that you were tempting me. I'm only strong enough to get away from you, not to stay near you."

I am both angered and flattered by his honesty. He recognizes my power and beauty. I begin cooing in a voice I know he finds irresistible. "I admit I am interested in you, that…"

Abruptly, he interrupts. "Even your voice attracts me too much. Good-bye. I am praying for you to be freed from this power that enslaves you." He hangs up.

How dare he hang up on me! How dare he pray for me! As if that could do anything. I will crush him. He'll beg me to take him. Plans form, and then abruptly intrusive thoughts flash though my mind: Is your desire for him in control? Are you indeed a slave to your desires, to doing their bidding? Is he right?

No! I am in control—always! Where did that come from anyway? I'll do what I want. But the making of plans is derailed, and the eruption ceased for now. It is time for serious work with magic.

Control Restored

Control restored I complete the day with good advances in a potion that I will inject in subjects to bring them under my control. Once I imprint them on me, I will maintain control with little effort. It is a next generation of mind control drug, an enhanced sedative-hypnotic. Each injection will last over a month, and I will instruct my subjects to inject themselves with more before it wears off. I head for bed after setting my security measures.

My third dream that night is ominous. A lone knight in dazzling armor, almost blindingly bright, approaches the kingdom of my dragons. Something warns me not to take him lightly. I dispatch a multitude of mighty dragons, swarms of deadly insects, command corrosive ooze and caustic vapors to come out of the ground around and under him, and prepare an earthquake to swallow his body. He is quickly totally surrounded around, above, and below. All my forces attack. I eagerly await his defeat and death.

How he survives the blue-hot flames, the battering of tons of rocks, the insects, the ooze, and vapors, I cannot fathom. I see how he survives the earthquake; the ground beneath his feet simply refuses to move. He, however, appears to be surrendering.

He reaches his hand to his helmet and removes it. I am blinded instantly by blazing light, though I am a great distance away atop the king of the dragons. The mighty dragon beneath me collapses, like butter melting in a sizzling skillet. I fall through the air blinded, helpless, fearful of the impact with the ground far below. Faster and faster I fall, further and further, far beyond where I expect to hit the ground. I fall so far and long that my eyes regain their sight. I am falling faster and faster into a black hole, until the wind is ripping my clothes, whipping through and tangling my hair, and begins to burn and chaff my skin. I wake up screaming, crying, shaking, terrified.

Never have I had such a dreadful nightmare that was so vivid. My last nightmare was twenty-one years before when I was but six. My parents had just died in that terrible crash. I had vowed to never again be vulnerable. My vow is broken. I am too badly shaken to tap into the Life Force, too trembling and too weak to walk, barely able to move, or even to think clearly. My lips and throat are parched; I cannot even make a sound. The only sound I hear is the pounding and incessant racing of my heart. My body is racked with such severe trembling that my muscles ache. Without help very soon, I fear I might die.

Exhausted, I must have fallen asleep, though I am not convinced I did. Yet, I must have—it is so confusing; I see reptilian-like things that I can see though bringing me water, potions, herbs, and tending to me. I finally calm enough to fall asleep. Before I fall asleep, I speak to my mysterious benefactors. I thank them profusely and am compelled to say, "I owe you my life. My life belongs totally to you." They seem very pleased. Wonderful, restful, refreshing dreams of power restore me.

I awoke Tuesday morning. calm and rested, without a trace of anything negative. The calming herbs and fortifying potions are still in my system so that when I vaguely recall the nightmare, it didn't seem terrifying. I am almost able to dismiss it completely. I am puzzled about the reptilian images. Surely, it was a dream.

And yet—I sense the power of the herbs and potions, so someone or something must have assisted me.

Perplexed, I speak out loud, "Surely—"

But thoughts interrupt me, "My name isn't Shirley!"

I roar with laughter and get on with my day.

Sleepwalking perfectly describes my morning. I didn't follow my normal schedule and didn't seem to plan anything. I am in the driver's seat, yet someone else is driving. I put myself into deeper and deeper dissociative trances so that I become a mere observer of a dream. Inexplicitly, I then load myself up with many more herbs, potions, and even sedative-hypnotics than I think wise to give anyone, much less myself. I can't believe I am taking any sedative-hypnotics. As I do, I think, *I won't be able to think for myself for hours with these in my system.* I hear a reply:

You had a bad dream and need help staying calm.
Your thinking will be actually far clearer—totally directed.
Life Forces will come much more naturally.
Powers you never before imagined even existed will fill you.

My work in my lab progresses more than ever. Though the sedative-hypnotics are at full force, the voice proves true. I am a mere passenger, a child enjoying a drive. The potion to neutralize a recipient's will practically develops itself. Each dose will neutralize a person's will for days and be powerfully addictive. Long before it wears off, the subject will beg for another injection.

I need a subject to try this on. I wish I could use my gardener. I am so lost in thought that I do not realize that I am stripping and injecting the potion in my own buttocks. Horrified but unable to stop myself, I watch as I inject one, two…six portions into myself. I would continue, but my thoughts are:

Now you can stop.
That's all that is safe for you now even with our help.
As you get use to it

you'll be able to have much more—
we'll be able to do much more—
we'll be able to have much more of you.

I want to protest, to resist somehow, yet an actress merely following a script is what I was now, without any control of myself or any desire to resist. I follow the script perfectly. I find myself showering, getting perfumed and dressed up in my sexiest clothes—clothes I never wore due to their discomfort, except when I was going to score some hapless man.

Dressing like this gives me a sense of power, since any man who sees me has his attention riveted on me. Most men, even without manipulation, come under my spell. Now, focusing on taking a walk in the mall, all eyes fixed on me, as a tonic and distraction for the letdown of the day before, I will luxuriate in exciting interest. I slip six needles filled with the potion in my purse and stacks of bills I leave for the mall in my racy red convertible.

This will be just the thing. We'll recruit six subjects for the next phase.

I enjoy following the script. Perhaps this is a taste of absorption into the "one soul." I have no reservations about doing whatever comes to mind.

I enjoy the power of driving my Porsche, eager to lure testosterone-laden males in with my beauty and then, instead of seducing them, to overpower them either with magic or with my brute strength. I want power, especially power over men. I want men to fear the rape of their minds, of being overpowered and helpless, of having to submit to my whims. Fitting revenge!

I spot my gardener taking a short cut through the woods. I will intercept him before he gets out of the woods, and he will be mine, fully mine. I speed around to park, and head into the woods straight for him. About ten feet away, we command, "Whisper!" He will be able to plead to us for mercy, but no one else will hear him; he will not be heard, even if he tries to call for help. Though he is eight or nine inches taller and, at least, eighty pounds heavier and wonderfully rippled with muscles, we lift him like a rag doll and throw him on the ground several feet away. I am about to pounce on him and overpower him when he whispers, "Lord Jesus, stop those evil spirits and cast them out!"

FREEZING

Freezing in place instantly, as if she is an infant strapped in a car seat—helpless. She seems totally alone with no one driving. She forgets everything, and her thoughts cease; she becomes totally passive. She merely waits for someone, anyone to tell her what to do. She loses any sense of time, of self, of feelings of any kind. She is about to faint when she hears him almost shout, "Breathe in and out, woman!" She obeys. He asks her several questions, but she gives no answers. Finally, he says, "Tell me everything that has happened."

She starts telling him everything. He guides her to tell the relevant details and not tell everything. She obeys every prompting from him. While she talks, he leads her back to her car. She tells him every detail of her nightmare, the vision of the transparent reptile-like things, about the herbs and potions, everything they said, and every detail of the new potion.

He calls several friends to meet him at a medical clinic. They take EEG and PET scans of her brain. They pray for her, giving her medicines and some shots where she injected herself with the potion. They gather around her and weep. Finally, the gardener says to her, "Tell us what you want us to do for you." She tells them to take her to her complex and leave her alone.

Beginning to awake on Thursday in my bedroom, I am only vaguely aware of any memories after the nightmare, and it is but a distant insignificant memory. My bed and I are an absolute mess, soaked in sweat and wastes. I clean up and get dressed. I open my purse. In it, there are six needles, thick stacks of hundred-dollar bills, my keys, a note from the gardener, and the other normal contents of my purse. The band around the bills is intact, so the entire ten thousand dollars is there. I am impressed, especially since he clearly needs cash. The note says that the medicines they gave me would counteract the drugs I took but would put me to sleep. I slept about thirty-six hours. I wonder what they gave me.

I do not want to remember fully about the needles, but they inspire a horror in me, so I dispose of them in the incinerator. I feel more alone than I had in decades—agonizing loneliness. I need something to refocus me. I decide to plunge into magic. I do not feel alone at all once I am in possession of my magic.

Working in my lab with no one to see me, I feel silly in my sexy attire. I follow my aunt's advice to show off as much leg, cleavage, and my curvaceous figure as the context allows. The extremely high heels and tight dress get increasingly uncomfortable and restrict me. Why not dress comfortably, like I want, instead of being a slave to fashion and impressing others? No, that's too far. This, as I admire myself in a mirror, is part of my power over others and over the lazy desire for comfort. But *slave* is uncomfortable and—my phone has an urgent message. A gateway to observe Merlin is opening 1:13–1:19 p.m. today. That's great news. That's the power fix I need—four hours to prepare.

I prepare to be hosted. My Host will have no awareness of me. I could have awareness of anything going through her brain and all my own thoughts, but I shut out almost all but the surface thoughts and reactions of my Host to focus on observing my subject.

Suddenly, an intrusion: a slave to many things. *Kill that thought!* The vehemence and intensity of the reaction startles me.

I wonder what got into me. Where did that reaction come from? Whence the determination to put it to death? "It is a weed," I retort. "A weed, or the one healthy and helpful plant in a field of weeds?"

Now I am arguing with myself. Or are there others?

The question puzzles me with its possibilities. I plunge fully into preparing for the trip to observe Merlin, devoting all my thoughts, energy, attention, and emotion—all I am and have—to that task and goal.

Again, my phone gives an urgent message, but I am so engrossed that I am not aware of it until the third buzz. Another gateway is opening today, a rare event, but never before two in a single day. The Merlin gateway will be open 1:13–1:19 p.m., and this other gateway will be open 1:18–1:22. No target for this second gateway is identified. This has not happened since I perfected my trinket to identify the target. Using the Gatewayfinder, I sift through mounds of data, gradually narrowing the identity of this second opportunity. This name above all others is one of dread to me, a mysterious dread deep within that I do not at all understand nor want to, a painful reminder, a name that had already dashed my plans earlier, the name Jesus. Words fail me. I am incensed, yet somehow also intrigued.

If you're so sure he's nobody,
dead and gone
for thousands of years,
why such deep dread?

A Dilemma

A dilemma! Staring at it, I am unsure how to make sense or react to this—this unwelcomed complication. I have a rare, no, a unique moment for me, a moment when I want guidance to do the right thing. Of course, I always want to do the right thing to gain power, but this is the first time I recall that I even consider wanting to do the right thing.

Choose Merlin, power.
Power is a sure thing with Merlin.
Take certainty and practicality.
Be real.

But Jesus?
Afraid to confront Jesus?
Mystery.
Consider Reality.

I am honestly torn between the two.
At a loss with no tactic or technique to help.

Notice the depth of your heart,
look deep within your soul.
Could you bear to have a chance
to silence all doubts,
to wrap up Jesus.
once and for all,
and not do it?

No need to choose, do both.
It's ten minutes from

the start of one to the end of the other. Not choosing is choosing.
Will you be fit
for the second after the first?
Aren't your reserves always a bit low?
That's certainly true.

You've wanted to learn
from Merlin for much longer. More mature interests
You have no real interest in Jesus. are newer than
It's nothing but a hangover from that silly gardener. infantile ones.
Don't I have any say?

Of course you do. Do what you really want. You've greatly desired to observe Merlin for a long time. Jesus is so passé, irrelevant; if the opportunity hadn't shown up so soon after those silly comments by that silly boy the interest would have died out quickly.

That side crowds you out,
cuts you off.
Look at the words,
Consider the presuppositions,
the manipulation.
Be free,
truly free,
to think, feel, act,
to seek out Reality
for your own benefit.

I hate this. I probably can't do both.
Or at least couldn't do the second one well.
The reasonable thing is to skip the first and do only the second.

Fool! That's the spirit!

Now I have less than two hours to shift my preparation to observing Jesus to dismiss once and for all that he is relevant to me. I'll master the secret of his power!

My complex manager transfers an urgent call from the police to my cell. I expect my detective, the one whose heart I carefully won, on the line. It isn't him. "We need to talk to you again about the break-in," an unfamiliar male voice says.

"Tomorrow would be good," I respond.

"Today." He insists.

"I'm preparing for an important call, could we make it after two o'clock this afternoon?"

"Sure," he replies forcefully. "But we'll be watching that you don't leave your complex. See you at two thirty." He hangs up.

I begin anew to prepare for my travel.

A complication arises. A little before one o'clock, I hear a loud knock on my laboratory door and an imposing voice—a woman's—introducing herself as a detective and demanding entry. "Open up." I make my trinkets invisible, sit at the raised desk, and release the door lock by remote.

"Come in," I say flatly. "I wasn't expecting you until two thirty."

Four stern women stride in. Each has an earpiece; several people in several different locations are also listening and will redirect our conversation as needed. Clouding and redirecting their minds is not an option. I stand behind the desk. It is on a raised platform; I am well above them.

The detective demands: "Get down here so we can question you."

I don't move quickly enough, so she barks fiercely, "Now, not tomorrow!"

I walk to the stairs slowly and then carefully walk down the steps as if my stilettos slow me down. "Isn't she the tart?" She taunts. All four laugh.

"I assume you are here on business, not to make sport of a lady," I say coldly.

"Lady." The detective switches to her softest voice. "I'm sorry." Then pausing briefly for effect, she adds, "you ain't no-o lady."

As laughter breaks out, I interrupt. "You have some questions. I have an important call very soon."

"Listen to me, you power whore. You know we're not police, but we will get whatever we want out of you." She paused for effect and then switched to a staccato voice to emphasize each word. "Whatever we have to do, and I really do mean *whatever*,

I'm sure it will take half the night, so I guess you'll miss your crummy call."

Fed up with her, resenting her tone and intrusion, I decide to get rid of them. "I'd like your badge number," I say slowly and pointedly. She flips me her card disdainfully and moves closer threateningly. I continue. "I don't like your tone. I'm not at all happy." I abruptly alter my tone to intense concern and continue. "Oh my, you look like you are getting very, very sick very, very quickly. And you also, the tall one. You look like you're barely able to walk out of here, even with help. You others better help these women get to the emergency room right away. That's right, help and support them. They might just survive if you hurry. Take them out." They leave, two very frightened women helping two suddenly very ill colleagues. That will teach them to not bother with me!

My mental and subconscious preparation disrupted, I am not as prepared as I want for my travels; I lock myself in a small room and synchronize the trinkets. On the recliner, I begin to meditate, quickly going into a trance. A few minutes later, I hear a faint countdown of the seconds, until finally I hear "Three, two, one, mark."

The Trip Begins

The trip begins. My Host is a cheap prostitute. She is used to being used, abused, and despised. She has no one's respect—not her friends', not her own, and certainly not mine. I despise her. Her life is tiresome and demeaning; she spends far too much of her time enticing customers. After only half a day of being stuck with her, experiencing her life, her degradation, I would gladly have given up the opportunity to observe Jesus. He is not likely to be worth experiencing this for almost 151 more hours. I curse the misfortune that this hosting would be more than twice as long as any previous one. I will endure it because I have no choice.

Before experiencing her inner life, I'd have blamed her surroundings, society, a lack of opportunities, and prejudices for her unfortunate state. But unimaginably, long ago, she had somehow desired the ease and glamour of this life (what a joke!), had sought it out, and had dived headfirst into it. Now she is drowning in it. What she had freely and deliberately chosen as a way to master men and earn a living now has complete mastery over her. She is enslaved by her desires and is now a slave to so many things, a victim of her own doings. I glance at the color of her power. It is a dingy gray, ugly, with a multitude of the black lines of power, and an all but invisible white line. Her power profile makes no sense; it is similar to mine. She herself is incredibly powerless, unpitiable, and unworthy of any notice or care.

Through my Host, I hear about Jesus and experience her reactions. He is a rabbi out of nowhere. She wonders how an unknown with no training could teach with such authority (she will, thus, all the more avoid him at all costs). When she hears that Jesus healed lepers and the lame, all sorts of sicknesses, freely healing all who came, even casting out demons, she is mildly curious. But her determination to avoid Jesus grows far faster than any curiosity. She wants no encounter with a man like him. She will avoid him like the plague he would be to her, unless she really needs him for healing. She decides she doesn't want to be in the same city as Jesus and makes plans to flee before he arrives. I wonder how I will scrutinize Jesus.

People are talking about Jesus. More and more often, my Host overhears comments and stories about him, and even her friends, such as they were, begin to talk of him. She wants to tell them all to shut up. Then she hears that he is headed their way. Gathering some things quickly, she starts to leave town the opposite direction he is coming. When she overhears that Jesus claims to have the authority to forgive sins, her interest rouses, and she stays close to hear more about that. Listening intently, not daring to get too near, lest she be discovered and driven away, barely daring to breathe, lest she be unable to take it all in, she overhears that some men lowered a paralyzed friend of theirs through the roof to get him to Jesus. Jesus forgives the man's sins. She can't hear it all, but she also hears that Jesus healed the man as proof that he can also forgive sins. She immediately hurries back to her house, drops off her things, and goes to the marketplace, determined to find out more about Jesus and, if possible, to see him from a safe distance.

My Host is transformed. She is desperate to find out about Jesus and any hint that he might offer forgiveness that she repeatedly risks rejection to hear more. She overhears much about Jesus and often suffers rejection. I almost find her pitiable; she is desperate for forgiveness I know she doesn't need, won't receive, and won't do her any good if she does get it. Nothing short of lengthy intensive rehab could ever help her. Without a doubt, I think forgiveness is the least of her needs. Her desperate wants interfere with her needs. Again, she is a victim of her own stupidity. Yet, pathetic as it is, her new behavior is a welcome relief to me from the tedium of her seeking men who would buy her body.

Eventually, she hears that Jesus is entering town and takes a position to see him. I've spent thirty-six revolting hours in this terrible Host before I even get a look at what I came for. I see him, yet I don't. Jesus is an altogether different sight, something totally alien. That's it; he must be an alien of some sort. He certainly isn't human. I see him yet can't make out any of his features because he appears too bright, like a photograph with far too much light that washes out all detail. I see his clothes and shape but not his facial features or his hair. As he passes by, he looks at my Host.

He looked at me and smiled. He really looked at me, at my eyes, he didn't even scan the rest of my face or body, like he cared about me and not how I looked, she thinks as she is shaken with overpowering emotion (was it something far beyond joy?).

She hears that Jesus asked a tax collector, a traitorous collaborator with the hated occupation forces, to follow him. This outcast invited other outcasts and riffraff, including my Host, to dinner at his house so they could all have dinner with Jesus. She is unsure about being in such close quarters with Jesus. Wouldn't he just draw her in, like so many of the religious types, but ultimately only to condemn her? Despair and desire clash within her. She thinks, *How can I possibly risk*...I am sure, though, she intended to not risk "it," being at dinner with Jesus. But that thought is interrupted; she continues, *How can I possibly risk continuing this death that I live every day?* She dares not take this risk; she will go to the dinner.

Good. I am eager to see how he controls a group of people.

Dinner with Jesus

Dinner with Jesus is full of surprises. My Host is astonished at how Jesus acts. Rather than lecture about the law, he laughs. Rather than find fault with these admittedly group of cheats, swindlers, traitors to their own people, and other unsavory people—these outcasts and "sinners"—he jokes with them. He is fully with them and makes them feel at long last that they are more than just tinder for hell and belong somewhere other than hell. He treats them as though they belong with him.

When Jesus refers to God, he usually spoke of him as Abba. I didn't appreciate *Abba* as a term for God until I experience the depth and richness of my Host's reaction. Her first word was *Abba*. I resonate with *Da-da*. She calls her father *Abba* to emphasize the closeness, her intimate privilege of access to him, whenever she most needs him. Wonderful memories stir even within me. My Host struggles with both the joy and clash of thinking Abba about Almighty God, he who is to be feared above all. Memories flood her soul of fearing her father, fearing his punishment and displeasure, fearing him more greatly but with a different kind of fear than she fears any others. While she feels the fear, it is awful; when she suffers his punishment or displeasure, there is anguish and pain, but later, when he reaffirms that he still loves her, the experience of the fear is tolerable; rather, even the fear is somehow good. A new light and life begin to dawn in her soul. I struggle to fight off a powerful, no, a different kind of tug on me from Jesus.

Jesus tells stories, lots of stories. He tells stories that make even me think differently. He tells stories that lead you to feel deeply, he tells stories that plant good desires even in me. He tells stories that, somehow, at least while you think about them, settle into your soul, inviting and creating deep emotions and desires, inculcating desires and motivations for good habits, growing motivations and reasons of the heart to be a better person—or, rather, a better kind of person—to live a better life, a life more joyful and free. Sometimes, unbelievably and incredibly and wonderfully, he uses the word *we*; he includes this crowd of misfits with him.

We, Jesus and us, what a magnificent thought to my Host. And it isn't just a clever and skillful use of a word. *He isn't just eating with us, he isn't just talking to us, he isn't just talking with us. He is actually with us—we are eating, drinking, laughing, joking, and sharing meaningful bits of life together*, she muses in her unconscious. This very thought somehow dignifies her, *while we, Jesus and the rest of us, are at Levi's house, we are sharing life together, sharing with him, and even with each other.* When we all finally leave and go our own way, there is—even I sense and feel it—an afterglow, belonging and a longing. Even I am drawn in for a moment. He's that powerful, he's hard to resist.

My Host finds it utterly unbelievable, as do I, that Jesus is not seizing control of the gathering. Indeed, he makes no power plays (and I know them well), uses no power tactics but rather yields control to his host and the other guests. Many of the guests compete in topping one another's jokes. He doesn't. Instead, he genuinely relishes the camaraderie of laughter and greatly multiplies everyone's enjoyment by his warmth, his affirming by laughter, gestures, expressions, and touches of his hands. He doesn't even tell us how to think, what to believe, how to act, what to desire, or how to feel. Instead, he points the way, he opens up new possibilities, planting in us new ways to think, new motives to act in radically different ways, refreshingly new desires and feelings and beliefs. I fight hard against it with incomplete success. What is happening to me? I hate what he stands for, I hate what he is doing, he contradicts what I want, and yet...

Jesus eats and drinks, joins in the toasts of wine, and is irrepressibly jovial. My Host, and increasingly I, begins to wonder when Jesus will spring his trap. He is drawing them in, he has them in the palm of his hand, and most of them are internally committing their lives to him, increasingly willing to kill or risk death for him. I see it plainly in their body language, leaning forward with faces full of desire and focus, held in rapt attention to his every word. Even my Host, despite her skepticism and doubt that he could be this real, is longing to commit herself to him.

My Host and I see his first opportunity when someone exclaims, "Jesus, you're not like the other rabbis."

He responds with a smile and a nod of approval and merely says, "Thank you."

His second chance, an even better opportunity, comes a moment later. Someone stands up and quiets the crowd by waving his arms. The room grows still. My Host recognizes him as a chief tax collector (and a dishonorable cheat). He asks, "Jesus, I want to know. We all want to know."

He pauses as if gathering courage for a response he dreads but wants to hear. The silence in the room allows my Host to hear the pounding of her heart.

He continues. "Tell us, Jesus, what should we do?" All eyes are on Jesus, eagerly dreading his response.

Jesus smiles and laughs before saying, "You already know, but you also have a vital qualification." He then pauses briefly, during which everyone there seems to hold their breath. He continued.

"You know how weak and needy you are. You don't pretend to be better than you are, unlike so many of your religious leaders."

Silence—brief and total—as what Jesus said sinks in. Then one man cries out, "As though anyone would believe that we are capable of being any better." His last words are almost laughed.

The entire gathering breaks into a riotous tension-relieving laughter. In the pandemonium that ensues, I think, *The fool, the utter fool. He knows nothing about power, nothing at all about people and their need to commit themselves*. I wish I could team up with Jesus, teach him how to properly use his power, for together we can rule the world.

Captivated

Captivated was how he affected my Host. She longs to be captured, to be free of herself, free to truly belong to another, yet without being manipulated, devalued, or controlled by the other. Her will to be emptied of herself opens her up to the possibility of a birth to an entirely different type of power.

I now understood, though I know it is a misguided waste, Jesus's will to power is a will to empower and ennoble. He seeks to empower others, their will, to free it to choose on its own, free from pressure, free from manipulation, to become a self at a deeper level, to transcend its own inherent limits, and to act ultimately in ways and with motives that begin to purify and unite the inner and outer self. Such idealistic rot!

The next days within my Host as I suffer through the changes going on within her are almost like a deep massage of my soul, a physical therapy, even torture. Once I recover from the pain and exhaustion, I will…I can't imagine how I will change or how I can keep myself from changing.

The dreams of my Host are radically different. Before the dinner with Jesus, the dreams were dark, nightmarish, filled with despair, filled with images of chains, filth, and a dark and damp prison filled with thick choking smoke in which breathing was both hard and unpleasant. She was either being eaten alive, tortured, or wasting away; she was so fearful of the continued prospect of agony that the only thing she feared more was death, which, she was sure, would multiply her agony, end any brief relief, and make it all permanent. I belittled her silly superstition that she would suffer at all after she was dead, but I must note that without that fear she could not endure her current life. I know I would not go on suffering if death were the only way to put an end to it. I guess her silly superstition gives her a kind of endurance I don't have.

Her dreams now are filled with light and hope. Her dreams include laughter, giddy celebrations, joyful dancing, and beautiful music, scenery, and aromas. In some of her dreams—my favorites—she soars though cool and refreshing air, flying far above threats and obstacles, whirling and twirling, flipping and looping though the air, a beautiful and staggering combination of the best of gymnastics, ice dancing, sky diving, and…and—it is pure poetry in motion. I envy her, and even hate that lack in myself. Inwardly, she is being set free, liberated, even though outwardly her identity is unchanged—a cheap and desperate prostitute.

My Host is being born into a far different and greater Reality than I ever imagined on my own—such a breadth of possibilities, a depth beyond my grasp, and such richness of connection with everyone and everything including herself; her true self is in the process of growing into something unimaginably magnificent. She confuses me, shakes me up, and maddens me.

Experiencing her thoughts, resultant reactions, and emotions, and observing how her will is melting, becoming fluid in anticipation of who knows what changes threaten me. Without the established masterly of my own body and emotions, my thoughts and will lack an important anchor against the strong wind and current flowing through my Host. Even with great effort, akin to rowing against the current, the ship of my soul is being carried by her current. I will not succumb, I must not.

Jesus planted a seed that was growing. He is the seed. Such growing pains! Perhaps, there were more birth pains, the birth pains of being formed into a true self, filled with something far better and more glorious than the self.

One of the pangs of my Host is shame. It is a shame commensurate with what she did, who she is, and what lay at the very center of her soul. It is a shame for having perverted her gifts, her energies, her very self to embrace a deathstyle, a living death. I can barely endure her shame; how can she? It is intensely uncomfortable; I have to defend myself against it.

Yet, she is also grateful. Jesus opens up new possibilities, a new possible identity in place of her former identity full of impossibilities. Her new identity is beginning to embrace her and enfold her into a transformation of the central desire of her heart. Her former focus, an unrelenting desperation to be loved and to fill the empty void by taking—always taking—is gradually being replaced. Her deepest longing is now becoming to love and to give. Formerly empty, now emptying of herself, she is beginning to overflow with another. It all makes me dizzy and soul-sick.

Heavily overloaded and burdened by an awareness of her own weakness and neediness, she is nevertheless heartened that Jesus considers this a qualification. Greatly weighed down by the unbearable burden of shame yet bolstered by gratitude and love, my Host prepares to express her gratitude and love to Jesus.

Jesus was invited to a meal nearby. My Host seizes the opportunity. On second thought, she will not risk it at the house of a Pharisee. Her heart impels her—she dares not risk it. She sets out, overcome with emotion, carrying a beautiful jar of costly perfume with her. Will he actually accept her? She has to be sure.

I am identifying with her! Stop it! Am I even beginning—is there a hint of caring about her? No, no, no! Is her powerlessness somehow beginning to infect me?

Simon's House

Simon's house is easy for her to enter; no one sees her. She arrives before Jesus. When he reclines at the table, she kneels at his feet. Copiously dripping off her face her tears, dripping warmly onto his feet, soak them. Embarrassed, she wipes the tears, cleaning his feet with her long hair. Kissing his feet repeatedly, she pours perfume from the jar onto his feet.

Jesus reads Simon's mind (so his powers may rival mine), dealing with Simon's judgment of the woman and Jesus. Jesus asks which of the two debtors—whose master forgave both, one ten times more than the other—will love their master more. Simon supposes it would be the one who was forgiven more.

Jesus turns toward the woman still kissing his feet. He asks Simon if he sees her. Jesus then unfavorably compares Simon with the woman Simon despised (oh, how that must have stung!). Simon provided no water for the feet of Jesus, no kiss of greeting, no oil to anoint his head. Simon was a rotten host. My Host, by contrast, washed his feet with her tears, wiped them with her hair, kept kissing his feet, and poured perfume on them. She showed great love, and, for Jesus, it proves that she is greatly forgiven. Then, Jesus addresses her, "Your sins are forgiven."

Before being hosted by this woman, my automatic reaction to the mere mention of anyone needing forgiveness would be to protest. Even now, the protest starts, but I'm now confused and unsure. While I'm around Jesus, I'm losing my struggle against him and his pesky implicit invitation to something far better than I have or am.

My Host's reactions overpower me. Her reactions, a tsunami of emotions, thoughts, and desires already embodied in her actions sweep away my basic assumptions, and even try to reform me. I swim hard against the current; I have to, lest I be swept away. But all that, as hard and unwelcome as it is, pales in importance compared with what occurs next. As Jesus's word *forgiven* soaks into her soul, as her shame and guilt explodes into joy—like dull gunpowder exploding into brilliant colorful fireworks—she kisses his feet a final time, lifting her head as she wipes away the tears. She raises her face to look into his eyes, eyes that are devoid to me of detail because all detail is washed out by his glow. To her though, his eyes express forgiveness and love.

The incalculable occurs. I see his eyes clearly and hear him speak directly and only to my soul. The eyes of Jesus—those warm, imploring, piercing, dark eyes—I see reflected in those eyes not the image of my Host but myself! Those eyes penetrate my defenses, my disguise from myself, all the technology, my prowess, my accumulated accoutrements of power, through the filter of my Host, to the naked and exposed center of my soul. The eyes arrest me, exposing a frightened little girl, then turn me fully from my innermost thoughts—turning my soul to the tender and somehow inviting greeting conveyed by those eyes. Those eyes burned into my memory, now planted in my very deepest longings. The warm, enigmatic greeting unspoken by lips but communicated heart-to-heart is: "Shalom, peace to you, Host within a Host."

Haunted now by both the image and the words, growing bit by bit in frequency and intensity until it is my incessant obsession, it allows me no peace or rest. Unable to dismiss it, I will have to battle it and put it to death a thousand times. As I triumphed over all fears and any hints of compassion and kindness, so also this dreadful beauty, this invitation to something other than myself—this too I will put to death. This, too, I will win over, I will kill it. But I no longer have any heart for it.

My Host, energized by joy and love, is a whirlwind of external and internal action. Her will, self, and soul seem supercharged to—does she make or allow?—all sorts of transformations: thoughts and way of thinking, new habits of heart and action, her passions, desires, and emotions, and, of course, her behavior. I, a pure spirit, am dizzy and dazed by all her activity and changes. Finally, her body worn-out, she, mercifully for me, goes to sleep.

PERHAPS NOT SO MERCIFUL AFTER ALL

Perhaps not so merciful after all. Then, in the stillness and quiet, I am in the midst of an intense battle.

Now, you can put this dreadful thing to death.
Pure spirit?
Maybe someday.

Do it quickly while this Host thing rests.
Slow down,
ponder carefully,

She's a terrible distraction, a horrible example for power
She's more
attractive now.

she's weak and you want to be strong,
She seems stronger now.
she getting weaker and may soon begin to weaken you.
Try on
her strength.

When she awakes she may continue to empty herself,
Isn't that
her delight?

deluding you with fantasies of love, misguided joy.
Her joy?
You don't want to be vulnerable, manipulated,
Her strength?
seduced away from power. Kill it! Become invulnerable,
Try agility,
the manipulator, the seductress,
a new leaf,
the one who always adds to her power and thus rules others.

consider Jesus
his power.

She's freer than before,
freer than you now.

Hour after hour for what seems like forever, this battle in my soul rages. I'm caught in the middle. Still attracted to power but so, so something else—that I have no appetite for it.

One does get sick
from too much of
even a favorite food.

That's it! I'm sick of it.
I'm empty and lonely,
I want a home,
not a complex,
somewhere I belong.
I long to belong,
to have someone care
more about me than
they care about offending me
I want love, not lust or fear
I need people, not power.

You can have all that, I'll show you.

Do you want
a better way?

It is yours for the asking.

One that really works?

Stop it! How do I get it to stop?
I can't take hours more of this.

Choose. You can't choose the other way,

There is a better way
than choosing.

you can't make it work for long.
This way works with minor adjustments
for whatever you want.

True.
Hard.
Richer.

Let me hear more from
this new point of view, the less wordy one,
the less pushy, the less familiar one.

I can't mislead,
won't manipulate.
Fewer words are needed.
I point to truth, Reality,
Jesus.

All lies and manipulation,
even about Jesus,
are from the other side.
This side is hard, but good.
The other side can be easy,
even fun, but final ruin.
This way is impossible on your own
or even with any help
but from Jesus.
Only Jesus can keep you
to this side,
to freedom from control.
Decide about him.
That's the best and only
reasonable way,
the only workable way.
That's it. You decide.
Open it up to
a battle about him.
The other side will do anything
to deceive and control.
Test everything you can,
by reason, by love, by life,
by where it leads,
by how it gets you there.
The best test is
the life of Jesus,
Jesus himself.
The best start is to ask for help.
Always ask for help.

Help me! Help me find relief. Can you help me
start deciding about Jesus?

The other said
he was alien, not human.

He is fully human. You won't deny that!

O, but is he merely human?

I get it.
We all agree now he's human.
Not an alien, but clearly not merely human.
He's just a man! And far more.
How did he address you?
"Host within a Host."
That's nonsense. No. Which means?
I too am a Host.
More dark lines, the darkening of my color –
I am proud of what is really my shame.
I am deluded worse than my Host.
She at least knows she's a total mess.
I am totally blind about myself,
about me.
As I gained power I was possessed by Powers.
There is a spiritual world, spiritual beings and I am possessed.
I invited them in, welcomed and embraced them.
Shame far greater than my Host's shame, sin far worse; there is sin.
I've been a spiritual whore. Jesus is indeed
NOOOOOOOOOOOOOOOOOOOOOOOOOOOOOOOO!!
God. God help me! Mercy, forgiveness, help!
Now you are freed,
forgiven.
Fill with me
or they will reenter.
Seek me above all,
love me,
do my will not yours.
Let me live my life in you.
Submit to my freedom,
the power of loving;
be full of my life,
loving,
practice loving,
make loving your aim.

Janet begins to remember Bible stories she forced out of her mind for years. She thinks, *It's true. Jesus died for me, he was raised and what's that next thing? Oh, he's been helping me all along. I've got so much to learn and change*. She is energized.

Returning

Returning, her Host's house fades. Janet is groggy—like waking from deep sleep. She wonders, *What happened? I don't remember anything after the countdown.* She realizes tears are trickling down her face, tears of incredible joy; there is a staggering sense of joy, relief, without a hint of sadness. She senses a sweet innocence that she had all but forgotten. She looks at her power profile. It's blue with a pronounced white line surrounded by swarms of dark lines in frantic motion. The dark lines no longer touch her but seem to be trying to batter their way in. She's perplexed. *It's like a good dream I can't remember*, she thinks. *Maybe the best dream I've ever had.*

Janet's thoughts promptly turn to, *What now?* Puzzled by this unique turn of events, she wants to know the right thing to do. Kicking off her heels, she goes to search for Grunde's card. She finds it, noting to herself, *Alice Grunde.* The pretentiousness of the raised desk repulses her. She makes a mental note that she will have it lowered. She calls Grunde's cell, profusely apologizing and assuring Alice that she will be fine with no need for the ER. She also apologizes to the other woman she afflicted, Ellyn O'Toole, and assures her.

Surprised by her reactions, Janet exclaims aloud, stumbling over her unfamiliar thoughts, "Sweet!" *A genuine apology is much more real, and even cleansing, than a manipulative one—ugh! I feel real for the first time in…in almost forever.* She is traversing an environment totally alien to her, and her thinking and emotions are both wonderful and awkward to her.

Changing into comfortable clothes that also seem more real, Janet washes the tears from her face. She calls Eric the gardener, expecting him to screen her call. She leaves a message, apologizing for attacking him. She thanks him for his help and the help of his friends. She confesses she needs help.

"I'm really at a loss about what has happened to me and what to do. I really want someone to point me in the right direction. Oh, and thank you for not taking anything from my purse."

Confession and need are novel to her! Refreshing. Again, she feels more real; she realizes that she is becoming more real, more human. She likes it; she likes herself in a sweet and innocent way.

At a Loss

At a loss, Janet thinks as she walks to the kitchen. *Yet I've never been this found*, she continues. *Somehow, I'm lost and liberated at the same time*, she concludes. She is amazed and a bit off balance by the torrent of different thoughts and sensations. As she rounds the corner into the kitchen, she forgets herself and exclaims rather too loudly, "Sweet!"

Once in the kitchen, she sees Marie watching her with a blend of astonishment and bewilderment on her face. Janet is only a bit embarrassed that Marie heard her last remark, mostly freed for the moment from her self-consciousness.

"Marie," she says, "your cooking smells wonderful—as always! I apologize for not commending you before. May I eat with you?"

Taken aback, Marie replies, "You look different, pleasant even. Don't you want to watch the news? Oh, um…thank you. You are the boss, you don't have to compliment me. Eat wherever you want." This is as Janet had often stressed to Marie and all her workers before.

"Oh," Janet replies, "drop the 'boss' talk. Call me Janet. I want to eat with you. May I? I want to tell you how much I appreciate you." Janet is really conversing, eating, and laughing with Marie. Janet takes it all in deeply—a breath of fresh air. She has never been so fully with another person, never been this real. She insists

Marie leave after dinner, and she will clean up, mindful she's cherishing every moment. To her, it is a delightful relief to be under control rather than desperately needing to be in control.

Now Janet is motivated with an intense drive and energy to be free of her bondage and addiction to power and herself. She is living by the power of hope.

Part 2

Resistance

Resistance Ended Gradually

Resistance ended gradually as the joy, novelty, and freshness Janet experienced slowly turned ordinary and then dull. She didn't know what to do with herself, how to tap any inner strength, or how to endure ordinary life with its solitariness when she is not engaged with "the other."

Yet, Janet is still free of the controllers she had so long hosted, and there is still positive momentum. The doorbell rings. Opening the door, her greeting is eager and warm.

"Detective Grunde! Do come in."

Grunde states, "I'm here to see Ms. Stubbs."

"I'm her. It is good to see you well. May I call you Alice?"

Stumbling over her words, Grunde apologizes. "Oh, I didn't recognize you with—de—I mean, I want to say I'm sorry for my behavior earlier tonight."

"You are fully forgiven," Janet declares with delight. "Please forgive my much greater wrong."

"Well, of course," she mutters as she glances at the dishrag in Janet's hand.

"Oh, I was cleaning up from dinner." She laughs. "Please stay for some leftovers—or some dessert?"

The warmth of the invitation is genuine, but there is also a subconscious awareness that Janet needs desperately to be with someone. Grunde declines and begins to leave.

Janet notices dirt on Grunde's shoes. Quickly kneeling, she cleans Grunde's shoes with the dishrag. "There, that's better," she says as Grunde parts. Janet is overjoyed as the pouring out of a bit of herself fills her up. Still kneeling, she takes in moments of joy before rising to close the door.

Exhaustion from the flood of emotions begins to weigh on Janet. She's alone, alone with herself. It's unfamiliar and becoming uncomfortable and intolerable.

Marie is gone, the dishes are clean and put away. As the richness and fullness of the emotions ebb away, several things happen to Janet. First, there is the inevitable letdown after a mountaintop experience. Things don't seem nearly so wonderful in the valley. Second, on the mountain looking down on the beauty, things seem so clear and so good. The view in the valley is different. Descending the steep and rocky slope, beauty is displaced by danger, clarity effaced by effort. The former ease and wonder are quickly forgotten, and even doubted.

Janet feels empty and alone. Her brief sense of reality seems like a mirage. Formerly fueled by emotions that rapidly become mere vapors, her well-established habits of thinking, willing, and doing weigh on her heavily.

I guess I'll work with the Life Force, she thinks half-heartedly. *Even though I'm not sure I want to have anything to do with it anymore, I really don't have any reason to, yet I do need to do something familiar, something I'm good at, something that comes automatically to me*, she concludes.

Janet is trying to fight for her life but has no helpful habits, no compelling reasons, and nothing to fuel her will. She stalls; it's the best she can do. She works on paperwork, e-mails, and tidying up. She makes tea but only managed to waste about an hour. Moment by moment, her boredom and emptiness grow.

I check if anything is on TV. I am disappointed. I surf the web. Boredom, loneliness, and emptiness metastasize into despair. Another hour emptied from my life. My life is becoming unbearable. I could head for the lab for a sense of accomplishment—anything to escape this void. The momentum of my life is too great to resist.

I plod toward the lab and ponder my disappointment with my weakness and with myself. What's the point anyway? Nobody really cares about me. My cook only laughs with me because I am "the boss." She's probably laughing at me now for letting her off early. But what about the gardener? Didn't he help me despite my bad intentions and my attacking him? Didn't he leave the money in my purse? But he doesn't really care about me, he can't. He only fears the consequences.

The worse I feel and the more I focus on myself, the weaker I become. I feel awful, I am awful, this is awful. It is a vicious cycle downward. I can tell what is happening, but I am merely an observer of my life, not a factor in it, like a civilian in a war. I want my old confident self back. I am ready to get to work when the phone rings. Good, a reprieve! I run to the other end of the house to answer. She wants distance between the lab and herself.

Janet eagerly picks up the phone and blurts out, "Hello!" She recognizes Eric's accent.

He asks, "What happened?"

She replies rapidly, "I don't know—probably nothing. I don't want to be involved with manipulating everything and everybody anymore, though it's all I know, but I can't help myself. It's like I am under its spell."

Eric inquires, "Could it have anything to do with God and that we prayed for you?"

A rage erupts from deep within; I bellow at him that I don't believe any of that crap, that he shouldn't insult my intelligence, and then I slam down the phone. I sprint to my lab, force aside my reluctance, and deliberately dive into my work. I see my power profile; it's nearly black. I am glad to have my confidence and my power back. She cackles as tears moisten her eyes.

I am determined to forge unbreakable chains to protect me from the weaknesses and vulnerabilities of the last few hours. I crave to be possessed by powers that transcend all mortals. I feed on despair, misery, and hatred and become invulnerable to hope and love. I see my reflection. My beauty is transformed by all that I am now filled with. I am now hideous in appearance, my true self. No one could ever possibly love me now. I feign happiness, a smile appears on my face, and I look beautiful for a moment. Many could be deceived into loving that, but it's all fake, a total lie, and any love for me would, thus, also be a lie.

I'll make a better potion to control others and turn control of myself over to my handlers irrevocably. No antidote this time! My magical powers are now so great that I will make a potion that will modify DNA so that the body itself will produce its own hypnotics and, thus, cripple the will. The freedom of the will is nearing its end.

By now, tears are flowing; a chasm of sadness and despair open up, ready to swallow me alive, if this can even remotely be considered life. I deserve misery, guilt, regret, total despair, and a living death. My possession of powers beyond all mortals is growing by the minute.

The doorbell rings. It's the gardener. He's alone. Perfect timing! With my current powers, I will have him in a moment. He will orbit me forever. I run for the door. Still a dozen yards away, I cast a spell of silence on the gardener.

I fight back second thoughts. The gardener doesn't deserve what I am going to do to him, but I will do with him whatever I want. Still undecided whether to subdue him with the Force or my own brute force (each has their delights), I reach the door and greedily fling it open.

"Ms. Stubbs," the gardener says, "You are under spiritual attack."

I am shocked he can speak. My spells never fail. I grab him and push him to the side of the hall opposite the door with myself between him and the door. I rise up to spread my arms and cast my most powerful curse at him. He should wither or double over in pain.

Simply ignoring my frantic actions and repeated attempts to cast a spell—any spell on him—he continues calmly. "You need help. You are possessed by powers you don't understand and can't resist. They control you but also have trained you to turn to them for comfort and meaning. When you chose to return to them, their hold on you deepens. Nothing can release you from their power but Jesus."

Each word fuels my anger and strength. The failures of spell after spell enflames my determination to subdue him. When he says "Jesus," I fly at him violently with all my might and fury, intent on knocking him senseless. I crash into something that gives only slightly. I am hurt terribly and fall to the floor stunned. I am dizzy and in pain from the force of the impact and the shattering of my pride. I try to spring up. I pass out from the pain and effort.

Dreaming Starts

Dreaming starts and I am high above the earth on the head of the king of the dragons. I am firmly in control. I command all creatures, and even the ground, wind, and waves follow my every whim. This is what I really want. I smile broadly, but it is a shallow empty smile, involving only my mouth. My eyes are vacant and lifeless.

I see my back. There are tentacles coming from the great Dragon into my body—a mere puppet! Ah—without the control of the Dragon, I'm only a rag doll: weak, powerless, and limp. I owe all to the Dragon. But isn't it a good puppet master, giving me everything I want?

I want whatever it has to offer because I have nothing on my own. Without it, I'm only an empty shell. It fills me, animates me, and makes me powerful. I look forward to waking to completely giving myself over to it.

After several dreams that draw me more and more into the Dragon and his schemes, I have a different sort of dream. It is ominous. I am Dr. Frankenstein's monster, or about to be. I am strapped down with tubes stuck into my body. My arms are stretched to their limit left and right and are secured with metal bands. There's a tight metal band around my neck attached to a helmet. Wires are attached everywhere. There is a terrible storm with bright flashes of light immediately followed with loud crackling explosions of thunder. The storm is above us. The lightning strikes a lightning rod, and its jolt goes through me to transform me. I am in agony; it burns me and makes all my muscles contract and cramp. I try to move or cry out but can't.

I see Dr. Frankenstein. He has a round beaming pleasant face and a great smile. With glee, he says, "That's three! Three more and my masterpiece will be complete."

I wake strapped in a hospital bed and unable to move. Tubes are in my arms, nose, and down my throat. Wires are everywhere. In a mirror, I see there is a stiff cervical collar around my neck. Every fiber of my body is wracked with intense pain and all my muscles cramped. I am in agony, even though I am heavily drugged.

A large cart is rolled in. A technician begins hooking up the machine to the mass of wires and to some of the tubes as a nurse explains, "She is fortunate that Dr. Franks has this treatment to reverse paralysis. He examined her and said she is an excellent candidate for complete recovery." She is clearly proud of her work. She pulls a dark screen over my face and continues. "The treatment makes the eyes sensitive to light. This is her third of six treatments. She'll only feel pain from the treatment in the parts of her body that aren't paralyzed. We'll have to leave until Dr. Franks examines her after the treatment. Doctor's orders."

The nurse injects a dark liquid into my IV port. As it reaches my arm, my entire body burns. A moment later, the technician turns on the machine, and excruciating current goes through every part of my body. I want out, to pass out, to get out of my body, to get out of this life. Anything, I would do anything for relief. I hear a familiar voice.

Good!
Very good!
Yes, make more room for us.

The torture lessens. There is partial relief, a drowsy drugged feeling, and a helpless stupor. Concentration is impossible. Thoughts overwhelm. *Obey…must obey…inner…voices.*

Minutes later, the visor is lifted, and I see that face, that round beaming pleasant face with a great smile. "I'm Dr. Franks. With a few more treatments, you will have what we all want."

The nurse exclaims, "Dr. Franks, you are wonderful with your patients!"

He checks me extensively. I can't move, but I feel horrible pain in every part of my body, even each muscles twitching. I want to tell him there's nothing wrong with me. I can't speak. He closes the visor over my eyes. He leaves with the nurse (I hear her squeaking shoes) sternly commanding, "You two make sure that no one disturbs her."

I hear the door bolted from inside. Footsteps approach me and stop on my right. "Hey, check this out" a voice says as two massive hands grab and squeeze my breasts. "She's got great boobs."

Footsteps approach on my left. Two hands keep mashing my breasts. A voice on my left says, "Yeah!"

The Pieces Fall into Place

The pieces fall into place. I fight back to some clarity even though I'm still in a drugged stupor. I'm doomed, to more torture, to three more of these tormenting treatments. Then, I will cease to be—free. I will be a perfect puppet. I no longer want to be at all.

Too late! Your despair is so tasty.
Now that you have given yourself to us and
there is no possibility of escape we want you to know—and despair!
We gave you what you wanted before. No more of that for you!
The only thing we will give you now is hell, a living hell.
We love your misery; it feeds us.
We grow as you shrink; it makes more room for us.
Go ahead, dare to hope so that we can dash you further into despair!

Indeed, a black hole of despair sucks me in. Anybody, help me. Can anybody still help? I hear riotous laughter, mocking, insults, and threats. My mouth and throat are parched; I'm hungry, in pain, and burning up. Desperate and drugged, my thinking still isn't clear, and then a crazed thought: I'd even pray to God if I could, if he were there and would ever help me instead of just tormenting me. More mocking and taunts. God took my parents from me, let me be adopted by my nasty aunt and uncle, took my twin brother from me, and removed all comfort from my life. When my nasty aunt and uncle were the only ones left in my life, a pastor and a priest kill them and then commit suicide.

"God, what could you do for me?" Anger rages within me. "God, just die! Do that for me!" Catcalls and filth echo through my mind.

The room becomes totally dark before I hear the door open. In dread and despair, I wonder if I can turn myself over fully to my tormentors—I long to have it over with.

Fool! You will never have it over with.
We will enjoy tormenting you and using you forever.
You'll never have anything but despair filled with more despair!

I hear a familiar voice say, "Hand me a flashlight." Eric walks in with several others whose footsteps I hear. My moment of joy deepens the following despair. I can tell him nothing; he can do nothing—doomed. I'd have shed tears if I weren't so completely dried up.

I have no one to blame but myself. I plunged headlong into this life, chose and pursued it, trained myself for it, and been proud of my progress. I am the villain; when my punishment comes, all cheer. I guess I could cheer it also. If only I didn't have to suffer it.

Eric tries several times to turn on the lights. Lacking success, he opens the blinds. He steps over and lifts her visor. "Janet, do you want us to help you?" he asks.

Janet aches to say "Yes, yes, yes, a thousand times yes!" but can say nothing. Eric catches a brief flash in her eyes and says, "Blink once for yes and twice for no." She manages to carefully and deliberately blink once. She notices two massive men asleep in chairs on each side of her bed.

The next few minutes are spent removing the tubes, IVs, wires, and metal restraints. The effects of the IV drugs began to lessen rapidly. Hope and exhilaration rise in Janet. *I'm almost free!* Only the cervical collar and the attached helmet and visor remain. They are locked in place and attached to the bed. *Thank you so much for your efforts*, she thinks, *but it's useless*. Despair takes over. She again hears hoots, howls, riotous laughter, and

We told you so!

They are in a feeding frenzy. Since being freed of her restrains, Janet has been moving her aching limbs and body ever so slightly and has been stretching and delighting in being able to move. Now she gives up and, as her last gesture, points to the door and barely mouths, "Go." Then she sinks back into motionlessness on the perspiration-soaked bed. From the exhaustion and despair and without the stimulant IV, she faints dead asleep.

Dreaded dreams overtake me and make sleep an ordeal. The dragon is eating me alive. But the proportions are reversed. The dragon is tiny and inside me, nibbling away. Body parts fall off, wounds show up from the inside out, but I am always being consumed, always in agony, always regenerating so as to give myself as food for the beasts.

I am again the puppet ruler of the dragons and in a place of honor. It is a horrific honor; ruler and food, giving orders and being ordered for dinner. A fake frozen smile is now etched onto my face. I could not unsmile.

I long for death but then remember I am already as dead as I can be. No further death available to me can even briefly interrupt my well-earned and self-chosen torment.

More dreams deepen my despair (Is there no bottom to this pit?). The downward acceleration increases.

What trick now? Suddenly, there is dim light and hope. "Right! I won't be taken in again!"

I wake in near darkness. I immediately realize it must be another dream because the cervical collar and helmet are gone.

The bedding is cool, clean, and refreshing. I seem to be in a comforting silken nightgown. Delicious fragrances waft through the air—food! I'm hungry and parched.

"Well done, little demons! Tantalize me with hope. I'm done being made a fool of by you." I speak idly in what I suppose is a continuation of the dreams. "I've made a complete and total fool of myself."

I'm startled by motion several feet away. My eyes are adjusting to the low light, and I see a woman rise to her feet and stretch.

"Oh, good, you're awake Ms. Stubbs," a pleasant young voice said. She opens the door and yells down the hall, "Ms. Stubbs is awake!" She introduces herself as Eric's youngest sister, Lela. "Would you like something to eat?"

Janet's reply is terse and sarcastic. "Sure."

After an awkward pause, Lela invites. "Come on then."

"I'm sure worms will suit me fine," Janet retorts.

"You Americans sure have strange likes," Lela comments in bewilderment. She then says, "Follow me, Ms. Stubbs."

The aromas intensify from the hall. Janet's stomach growls. Though she disbelieves any of this is real, her body obeys, following Lela into a vast open great room that once was a barn. It is clean, well-lit, and has several tables set up with chairs and a few tables filled with food. Still disbelieving her senses, she grabs a water bottle, twists off the cap, and greedily drinks it down.

It seems that everyone is looking at her. Janet catches sight of herself reflected in a large window. She is dressed in a long-flowing colorful African dress; she has been washed, and her hair is combed. She bursts into tears and sobbed, "I can't take it. This mirage is too beautiful. I can't bear hoping again."

Hapti, Eric's oldest sister, puts her arm around her, comforting her, and leads her to a seat. "Don't bother with hope just yet. Just eat and enjoy," Hapti counsels.

Still refusing to believe or hope, Janet begins to eat as slowly as she can manage. She tries various meats and vegetables and sweet potatoes. She tries goat's milk and other drinks she doesn't recognize. She visits politely with several people who tell her that they have been praying for her. Most are from Africa, and all are Christians.

After she has a chance to relax and eat, Eric comes over. "I have some bad news," he says.

"I knew it, I knew it," Janet exclaims triumphantly. "All this isn't real."

Puzzled, Eric clarifies. "No, no, Dr. Franks flew into a rage when he found you were gone. He tried to kill some of the hospital staff before killing himself."

"How did you get me out of there?" I inquire.

His phone rings. He looks at it, tells her he has to take the call, and walks away. She ate ravenously until he returns.

The Power Was Out

"The power was out when we came into your room," Eric said.

"Dr. Franks had locked you in that helmet. It's a good thing my friend is a locksmith. He got you out of that helmet. We carried you down ten flights of stairs."

"Then…" Janet laughs before starting to sob. She couldn't stop for several minutes. Tears of joy stream down her face. She hated this display of weakness but couldn't stop herself. It was a relief to give into it.

Janet struggles. She has been whipsawed by hope and despair that even a bit of hoping raises great fears.

Eric gently asks, "Why is God so painful to you?"

Anger erupts. "My parents were killed because they were Christians!" Janet bellows.

A woman turns to her with compassion, embracing her and crying. "Mine too, they were burned alive."

Janet softens. "That's exactly how my parents died. They were in an accident and were burned alive."

The woman, an attorney named Mary, inquires, "How were they killed because they were Christians?"

"A pastor and my aunt and uncle told me that God wanted my parents and took them," Janet says with anger growing again.

Saying it aloud convinces her it's pure nonsense, but somehow she believed it for years.

Mary states, "That's a lie! Were they even godly people or close to God?"

"No." Janet admits. "My aunt and uncle were atheists. Come to think of it, the pastor didn't really believe much in God either."

"How old were you when they told you that?"

"About six."

"That's a lie straight from the king of darkness, and it was intended to imprison you in darkness," Mary says forcefully. Janet knew it had, she had lived it.

There is a long pause as I recalculate what she said. I force the words from my mouth. "That's reasonable but, but I still can't believe it for some reason."

"Of course not," Mary replies gently. "Being convinced by reason is rarely just about reason. All sorts of fears, desires, and habits get in the way. You'll need help to sort it out."

So begins Janet's first friendship since coming under the authority of her aunt and uncle. As she and Mary talk, she realizes how Helena and Frank purposely cut her off from everyone but them. They cut off contact from anyone who knew her parents or who had faith. Even the pastor promoted "the reason of unbelief." They told her that her twin brother James wanted to go to a deaf school in London after they sent him. After sending him many letters, Helena finally gave her a typed note she said was from her brother (he was seven) that said he never wanted to hear from her again. The note said he resented her being able to hear. But his deafness had never bothered him. They were best friends, and their parents learned signing and taught her about it on the advice of great-great Grandma Sarah from London. They wove many lies around her. Helena and Frank never bothered to learn one sign and never showed any interest in her brother, but they were murdered protecting her from those murderous pastors.

Mary was sharp, a good listener, and asked wonderful questions. She understood Janet. Janet grew more comfortable. But a familiar craving rose within her.

Janet felt too ordinary. The clothes were comfortable but didn't accentuate her figure. These people were nobodies with nothing better to do than waste time on each other without accomplishing anything of lasting value. Her lust for power returns with a vengeance.

The attorney must have noticed the change; she is so blasted observant. She summons several others over. The gardener, one of his sisters, and several others came over. An elderly woman in a wheelchair probes. "Are you missing the power?"

I lie without thinking, *Not at all, I just want to get back as soon as I can*. I feign a smile and say, "Thank you for your trouble. Can someone *give me a ride* back to my complex now?" I embed "give me a ride" as a hypnotic command. They laugh at me! They laugh at her unnecessary attempt to manipulate them into doing what they are fully ready to do. Janet, again under the spell of her handlers, can't conceive of others with anything but malicious motives.

"That's not necessary here," the elderly woman says. "Someone will take you whenever you want."

The gardener speaks, "You were heavily drugged for no medical reason. You woke up several times in a hypnotic state and told us all about your horrible dreams, the pain of your treatment, and about your tormentors."

"Oh, all of it was a dream, a mere nightmare." I avow. "I'm perfectly all right now." I assure them, "I'm no longer paralyzed at all. I need to let a doctor check me out."

"You were never paralyzed," the ignorant gardener responds.

"And how in the world would you know?" I say pointedly. I crave power intensely now. "The doctor's treatment for paralysis worked better than he hoped for."

Someone claims, "But you jumped up after you crashed into the wall when you tried to attack Eric. When we came in, you were writhing in pain on the floor. There was no paralysis."

"Don't make up stories," I order.

"Do you want to see the video?" he asks.

Shocked

Shocked by the possibility, I recalculate my approach. In the brief pause, they set up the video, and, within minutes, I see my worst moment in the presence of these nonentities. The video was taken from outside the house and showed the gardener waiting at the door, me flinging it open, pulling him in, and then turning my back to the camera. I make wild gestures with my arms and body and then fling myself at him in such an uncontrolled rage that he merely steps out of the way, and I crashed into the wall opposite the door. All the while, the camera is moving closer. The video is showing me briefly jumping up, grimacing in pain, and then falling on the floor writhing. On camera, I see the gardener bending over me and checking me out. I feel the burn of embarrassment and anger.

"The paralysis must have started later," I conclude.

The gardener insists with stubborn witlessness. "You had no injuries that would cause any paralysis."

"You," I say emphatically, "can't possibly know that."

A woman asks gently, "Don't you know who he is?"

"Of course! My gardener who quit," I bellow.

I do not understand the looks of surprise and the shaking of their heads until one of them speaks up. "He is Dr. Eric Blanke, a visiting professor at the Medical School. He's one of the world's leading neurologists."

I feel dizzy and almost faint as I blurt out, "Why were you posing as my gardener?"

"Serious accusations were made against me. The medical board suspended me from medical practice. That's been cleared up. Seems it was a conspiracy. I needed money to stay in the country. I love gardening and I do some of my best thinking then," he explains. "Ludwig Wittgenstein spent years gardening, Jesus spent years doing carpentry. I believe God directed me your way."

I am caught too off balance to be enraged. "But...but how could I be so mistaken?" I ask myself. "You deceived me," I whisper, unconvinced of even my own words. By now, I am surrounded by about a dozen of them. How they restrain themselves from pressing their advantage, I can not fathom with my mindset. It is a turning point for me as I realize that I now respect and trust them far more than she trusts herself.

"I'm confused and a bit at a loss." Janet admits. What she thinks is, *Help! Something must be dreadfully wrong with me. I'm either going insane, or I've always been insane and I finally realizing it. How could I have been so sure and yet so totally wrong?*

The elderly woman, seeing consternation on Janet's face, speaks with gentle assurance. "You are being drawn to sanity, to true reality. The light is unfamiliar, and you have a long way to go. You mind is a battleground."

Skeptical but also very unsure of her grasp on reality, Janet murmurs, "Maybe so." With her permission, they place their hands on her and pray. She still thinks prayer is silly; how often as a little girl had she prayed without anything good happening. She has no trust in prayer and is certain there is no God, but for now she trusts the instincts of these people, even though they were all *followers*—followers of someone she is sure doesn't even exist.

Nearly silenced by her own confusion, Janet becomes quiet. Although she still hears assuring thoughts from within, she doesn't trust them. Even the allure of power is suspect to her now. She remembers the time with Marie after the fizzled attempt to view Jesus. She remembers her losing struggle against the pull of her desire for power and her own habits and how Eric's phone call—mention of God—and his arrival provoked such a reaction from her that she was clearly out of control. *Powerful? Not at all*, she thinks. *Deceived. I thought Eric would be silenced, I thought spells would work against him, I charged at him to overpower him, and he just steps out of my way.* Meekly she says softly to herself, *Help.*

They finish praying and ask her if she wants that ride to her place now or just some time alone or for someone to stay close. Janet pleads, "Please don't make me go to my complex now or be alone. Mary…and you in the wheelchair—I'm so sorry I don't know your name—can we talk?"

Francine introduces herself, and the three of them go off by themselves.

"Francine, you asked if I missed power. How come? Oh, I'm so sorry—glad to meet you. You are clearly not from Africa," Janet says, fumbling for words.

Francine laughs. "No, I was born in Oxford…Mississippi. I grew up in Memphis until I ran away at seventeen. About the power thing, I was obsessed with power myself for most of my life."

Intrigued, Janet forgets herself for the moment and asks, "How come?"

Francine makes sure she really wants to know. Her summary is that her Momma was a beautiful, bright, resourceful woman who grew up deep in Mississippi being called a "nigger" all of her life. A visiting white lecturer from Oxford University in England raped Momma, and Francine was born. They moved to Memphis hoping for a better reception than they would get in their small town. Her light brown color got her labeled as Mulotto, which meant she was excluded by almost all blacks and whites. In addition, though, she was poor and she was also well-educated, so she didn't fit in at all in Memphis.

At seventeen, she ran away to Boston and was raped by a visiting black professor and had her only child at age eighteen. She distrusted educated males and deemed uneducated males as beneath her. Momma taught her that knowledge is power; she sought it. For fifty years, she was a janitor at Harvard (and Yale, Princeton, MIT, Brown). She "stole" lectures by recording or attending them without paying. She read voraciously, tutored, and conducted study groups. Her interests were humanities and literature. She became "devoted to following Jesus" at age eighty-one. Until then, she was obsessed with accumulating knowledge for herself. Life immersed in literature and Jesus taught her to turn that on its head. Her desire for power had deformed her; Jesus turned her into a giver, one who lives by giving.

Power Deforms

"Power deforms. Yes, yes, I can see that!" Janet reflects, "My lust for power deforms my life and has to end. I can't do the Jesus thing though, unless…why did you say you became devoted to following Jesus instead of that you were born again or that you became a Christian?"

"Part of that's hard to explain," Francine begins. "The easy part is that Christian was originally a derisive turn for followers of Jesus, like Jesus Freak. Originally, Christian meant a devotee of Christ. What Kierkegaard observed about Denmark is true here. When *Christian* is used to label a preference rather than as a term for followers of Christ, no matter how imperfect, then it has lost its roots.

"As I read and lived through literature, I was reordered by a deeper and pervasive reality than evolution and science grasps. There is a grammar and morphology to living and literature that is largely learned inductively. Scientific study of people is different and ultimately inferior to getting to know a person. People aren't defined—we define ourselves by what we habitually think, feel, do, and desire. We co-author our lives. The freer we believe we are and the more we exercise our freedom, the freer we become. When I believed I had no freedom to choose, freedom slipped away. How I could be free in a deterministic world, of how there could be freedom at all, led me to curiosity. If people can be free, if they can transcend themselves, and I believe they clearly do, then something is transcendent. I became convinced Jesus helps me transcend my limits and my life. I say I follow him to stress that this is not about statements I think are true but about following him, living and loving by the life of Jesus."

Her face is lively, her eyes dancing; when she talks about Jesus, her body overflows. She continues. "Instead of pondering ideas, abstract things, I live by the life Jesus lived and imparts as I follow. I don't trust power—even or…especially my own." Tears form in Francine's eyes as she speaks of her distrust of power.

Her handlers suggest a shift, a deflection. "But I believe in evolution. Anyone who does can't believe in God, except as a symbol. Please give me any good thoughts on that if you have any." There is an eruption of smugness from below. Francine's response surprises her. "I also believe in evolution as a process of how God prepares us, but, as a myth to live by, evolution is inadequate and unreal. Social Darwinism is damaging and false. Evolutionary ethics—there's a joke—dehumanizes and provides an easy but false rationalization for almost any action. If natural selection is the center of the story, then reason itself would only have survival value rather than be true. Sometimes, rationality is even counter to survival, so evolution as a sort of 'prime mover' is self-contradictory. Oh, and that tall guy over there with the beard—he's a first-rate evolutionary biologist and a follower of Jesus."

The handlers hastily retreat, regrouping for an attack on emotion or will. A rational discussion might plant seeds of truth. Their strengths are in tempting and twisting—satisfying desires and feeding egos. They have little to offer as rational arguments against God. They know and hate him. They labor to keep what Francine said from being pondered by Janet. They want to keep it out of her mind, lest it provides a seed of truth for growth. They draw no attention to it at all, relying on Janet's ingrained habit of dismissing inconvenient truth.

Janet finds Francine fascinating, captivating, and charming. Francine is comfortable with herself, makes no effort to hide anything or impress anyone. She is alive and real. Part of her attraction to Francine is that she has something, is something that Janet lacks but only vaguely recognizes. Francine is a mystery to Janet; she thinks she's free, intelligent, personable, wise, a worthy mentor, a living real human. A thought flits through her mind, *if only she wasn't a Christian—or I was.* What she tells herself is, *She's appealing, but faith isn't rational. I can't believe something that isn't rational, I won't.* Then to shift the focus, Janet asks Francine, "May I ask how old you are?"

A wry smile appears, Francine gets a twinkle in her eye and a lilt in her voice and says, "Yes, you may ask, but that doesn't mean I have to tell you. Guess." Somehow, Francine's presence puts Janet at ease and in a good humor. "This is real," she senses.

"Oh, ninety, maybe ninety-five." Janet guesses. "Thank you! I became a follower of Jesus twenty-seven years ago." Francine divulges.

"No—no way! You've got to be kidding." Janet chortles. "That means you must be—what—one hundred eight. Impossible!"

"Ac-tu-al-ly, I'm-on-ly-twen-ty-se-ven," Francine utters slowly, overly enunciating each syllable.

The three of them burst into laughter; tears flow and their cheeks and sides hurt. It is a delightful moment of bonding, a treasured time. Defenses crumble.

"Janet, may I ask you something?" Francine asks.

Janet responds with a whimsical smile and some hoots. "You just did!" Again, the three women snort hysterically. They attract stares, but they are oblivious to the reactions of others and wouldn't care if they noticed. Their collective loss of control gives them each bonds of belonging that are real and precious to all three.

Fatigue Relieves

Fatigue relieves their joyous burden so that the riotous laughter becomes restful mirth. Unconsciously, Mary and Francine recognize it as a taste of heavenly bliss. Mary is not conscious of it, and Francine is only vaguely aware of it. Janet is clueless of it at all levels. If she could admit that she had demons within, she could easily have become aware that this extreme, wholesome shared laughter had, for a time, driven them out, banishing them to the abyss. It was her third and greatest taste of freedom because she was fully involved in obtaining this gift. When she committed her conscious mind to God, she lacked depth, and much of her response was borrowed from her Host.

Free and with no need to defend herself, Janet reminds. "Francine, you wanted to ask me a question."

"Oh, yes." She muses aloud. After recollecting her thoughts, she asks Janet, "Do you really believe that people are so rational that rationality is the primary determinant of what they believe?"

Before the bond of shared liberation by laughter, Janet would have given a textbook philosophical answer that now, in the light of the clearing away by laughter of defensiveness and the need to justify oneself, seems preposterous. "No, that's silly but…I do, of course, want to believe that all my beliefs are solely rational, even when they clearly are not." She admits. "Help me out here." Janet implores.

Francine responds, "People have dreams and desires that filter what they will pursue as rational. For instance, Armani at the Harvard Medical School showed that Freud's unbelief was motivated by his desire that nothing be over him. I stole those lectures that he wrote a book about later."

Francine coughs and gets a drink of water. Janet feels extreme discomfort. Her desires kick in powerfully. "But," she argues, "gods can't exist."

Francine responds, "That's exactly what Freud concluded. Armani showed that Freud's letters indicated his motive for that conclusion—perhaps, his own wish fulfillment. Our moods and desires often drive our conclusions. Rationally, either gods exists or not. If rationality was reliably impartial, wouldn't all reasonable people come to the same conclusion?"

Janet feels her chest tightening; her stomach gurgles. "But Christians are the ones wishing God into imaginary existence."

"That is an assumption." Francine rejoins. "Neither better nor worse than concluding that Freud's desire that God not existing proves that God does, in fact, exist."

Janet falls quiet. Something stirs deep within, unavailable to her consciousness. There is only a vague disease. Francine looks intently at Janet. Janet becomes aware that Francine is waiting on her before proceeding. She thinks to herself, *I'd never do that. I'd press any advantage I could.* Francine did not. *Why?* she poses to herself. Consciously, she dismisses that query; her unconscious reverberates with it. It is the inception of a generosity that grants greater status to people than winning. After a pause, Janet says flatly, "Do go on."

"The research of Daniel Kahneman and his associates shows that our fast mind, that we are not even conscious of, undermines rational objectivity. Our feelings, wants, desires, and values influence our decisions, even when we think we are being rational." Francine continues. "But all that was theoretical to me for years—I didn't apply it to myself until…" She confesses until she notices that Janet's attention seems to have wandered.

Battles in Janet's unconscious made her space out and stare blankly. Much of her wants to escape challenges, especially from an intelligent woman she respects. Francine's face breaks the stalemate—it is alive with a genial smile, a sparkle in her eye, and multitudes of deeply etched wrinkles that whisper persistent tolerance. Janet rouses from her reverie, imploring, "Go on."

"Years ago, I met a man," Francine says, "and we discussed challenges to faith. He explained several he had." She tells Janet that he explained that only one of the challenges to faith was primarily intellectual. The others were based in irrelevance, his emotions, his desires, and a mid-life crisis. When he has a Christian in name only, his faith was largely irrelevant, until he became a follower of Jesus. There were then intellectual challenges to his faith in college. During an emotionally hard period, he tried to shore up himself with books that had helped his intellectual growth in faith. Instead, he got angrier and grew hostile and combative; he was attacking the intellectual content of his faith in anger. He confessed that had he persisted, he'd have destroyed his faith. He realized that was happening. He addressed his emotional needs. He read Psalms and lamented to God, and the boiling emotions simmered down.

Later in an unguarded moment, he missed a sexual perversion he had escaped from. He unintentionally promised himself that he would go back to it if he decided God didn't exist. The next days, his will assaulted the basis of the faith—he was strongly motivated to decide God didn't exist so he could go back to it. It dawned on him what he was doing. As he thought it out, he knew that sin was bad for him and ruined him. That crisis abated. He had to reason through his desire for sexual slavery to stop his rebellion against faith and reason. His hardest and longest crisis was precipitated by a mid-life crisis. Neither he nor his life made sense. He remained certain of God but had no confidence in himself or his ability to follow God. Only God's palpable presence stabilized him.

Francine concludes. "Resolving his mid-life crisis was complicated, but the point he made was that all his greater challenges to faith weren't intellectual or about reason at all. He showed me a poem—not very good but intriguing. It portrayed the struggle between good and evil with himself caught in between them."

Janet asks with trepidation, "How? What?" Her interest is piqued.

Francine explains, "The words of the demons were on the left, those of the guardian angels on the right. We are caught in the middle."

Janet misses the last part; she is distracted by her own reactions that are increasingly negative. It was uncomfortably familiar, startlingly so. A thousand thoughts popped into her mind, obscuring that sense of déjà vu. Still, despite all that, Janet dives inwardly in an attempt to uncover that tantalizing possibility that could explain so much.

She tries to recall her inner dialogues, her inner battles, but something's blocking her thoughts. This exercise of her will is overwhelmed with fear, with anger at the hint that she is not fully in control of everything. She hears clearly an alluring siren voice—hers—say, "I am destined to control all."

Concerns give way to confusion and then anger that she should be challenged when she needs to be pampered ("What you have been through, you poor thing"), so unsure, so tortured…

Children Flood

Children flood the area suddenly, interrupting their conversation and derailing her coming explosive reaction. Her distress about the poem turns Janet inward to her comforters. She had, like an addict for twenty years, turned always and only to them and sex for comfort. The death of her parents made her regress to being an emotional four-year-old; her relying on them kept her there. The entry of the children, with all the chaos, pandemonium, merriment, and joy puts her on a different tack. Conversation becomes impossible, yet she hungers for more. She asks Francine for her number—another first for Janet. She gets a phone number of an old woman without money or power. Janet wants her as a friend, not as an ally or contact.

Groups form to rehearse. Janet goes to use the restroom. When she returns, the sight of a little girl wiping the feet of a boy with her long hair seizes her attention and gives her an odd sense of déjà vu. The girl looks about six. Janet sits leaning forward and introduces herself, "I'm Janet."

The girl smiles as she rises and says sweetly, "I'm Janet too!"

This girl captures Janet's heart. She was that age when her world was torn apart. Little Janet is practicing her part for "Encounters with Jesus." Little Janet explains, "This woman felt bad about what she did. She was an outcast, but she came to Jesus and was welcomed and forgiven."

Janet stuns herself with her response: "Indeed she was."

An attempt to draw Janet to rely on the host within is interrupted as little Janet, seeing a strange look on her beautiful face, runs over to hug her. Janet is seated and receives the full force of the affectionate hug as little Janet leaps into her lap. Janet smells chocolate on her breath and tastes the joy they share—another dose of reality.

Little Janet snuggles with Janet and stays in her lap. Janet notices a flood of joy and wonders, *What is this?* For the moment, she wants only this settled, happy emotion. She experiences relief also from within herself as events there, though outside her conscious awareness, provide great subconscious relief and a momentary lull in the siege.

Infernal anger erupts from the depths below, instantly disrupting the aggressive attacks of blaming between the demons. Each demon tries to flee the wrath. Punishment, however, is too swift for any escape. Instead of being consumed alive, each demon of this legion is dismembered into scores of writhing, suffering bits as a warning and to amplify their torment. Ten times as many are assigned as replacements. The scene concentrates their attention.

He speaks emphatically and deliberately. "You can certainly see and smell that failure is not an option. Setbacks will not be tolerated. Though we long to consume them for their failure, we forgo that for now both to punish them and for your, uh, benefit. Make good use of our sacrifice on your behalf, or you too will be sacrificed. Don't dare take any of what is ours. Leave them be. We are aware how hard it is to work together with each other, but certainly you see why you must. This plan has been executed for six human generations with such unbroken trends of success that even lack of progress from your work is unacceptable. You know what is at stake for each of you." With an ominous tone, he asks, "Questions?"

An arch demon is recognized. He begins. "But"—he is cut up and reassembled inside out exposing every nerve to maximum agony—"Anymore questions?"

The demons, in unity, reply, "No!"

He roars, "Am I?"

They respond, "Our Lord who alone is worthy of our devoted fear!"

After Little Janet Returns

After little Janet returns to her rehearsal, Janet wanders to drink it in. She sees children rehearsing skits that portray encounters with Jesus. Something comfortable, familiar, even attractive, tries to bubble up in her. Part of her hates it, but, knowing the risks while Janet is surrounded by many perilously real people and innocents, a suitable spark to detonate an outburst is awaited.

One skit is about encounters at the cross. A boy, perhaps ten years old, represents Jesus on the cross. He stands on a box with his arms raised as though on a cross. It's all phony. Janet takes offense. A conviction arises in her, "He deserved it." Yet, somehow, it also hurts her deeply. Unmistakably, she is drawn to Jesus, his love, his passion for people on that rough rude cross that she despises. For an instant, part of her, a very small part, almost wishes it were true, almost wants reality to have love, this cross, this man, at its center. But if he is any part of reality, she knows with absolute certainty it makes an absurdity of her passionate pursuit of power, of any such pursuit of power, of all consuming passions, save for him. If he is real, then she is the exact opposite. She can not allow that.

At once, my unbridled lust for power reasserts control. "Nonsense! Absurd! Impractical, inconvenient, unwanted! Unwanted by any who value power and its pursuit. That pitiful part of me that could ever consider any sympathy to such weakness must be put to death!" I realize my venom overflows to speaking aloud when I hear the loud hiss of Death and notice around me these sorry things silenced by me. I note some praying for me; it triggers a rage that erupts into a stream of screaming obscenities and cursing. The force of my demands that I be taken to my complex makes those weaklings comply.

Once back at my complex, my recovery precedes rapidly. I have full control of my emotions and everything and everyone around me. I give no thoughts to the wasted time with those misfits. I block e-mails and calls from them.

Hidden leavening raises humanizing desires within her. In August, an unwanted act of kindness slips out when I said an uncalculated "Thank you" to a worthless man who held the door for me, and even made pleasant eye contact with him. He smiled! I realized my error immediately.

What is wrong with me? I think. *I made that worthless old man smile by noticing him. I will root that out of myself, that weed, kill it, kill it, kill it.*

Oh, how she tries. But the seed of something not herself grows. Only by her vigilant efforts can she keep annoying acts of kindness from randomly showing up.

This new distraction takes a toll on me. Day by dreary day, I notice positive responses by the peons who receive these acts of benevolent sabotages against my power obsession. I always manipulate such positive responses by my calculated efforts. Now I waste it by not using them for myself. A seed of despair of conquering these violations of her will grows with each failure to inhibit them.

Another result, perverse and negative, is relief when I give into the good influences. The pressure of the good lets up for a while.

The good influence grows. Ominous to me is that my increasing efforts to keep these things from surfacing have less and less success. I'm holding a ball underwater that has more air pumped in. Giving in and letting it rise is more and more a relief, sometimes even something not entirely unlike joy. I despise myself, my weakness.

On October 1, this plague of kindness becomes a major crisis. I am closing a deal, a real steal I manipulated, when I simply botch the deal by inadvertently letting a scrap of truth into the open. My carefully crafted deception falls apart, and the story goes viral on the web.

I command the Life Force to help me in my dreams. "I demand an answer that will stop my self-sabotage." I head for bed early to command the dreams of the Life Force and to go through the difficult process of affixing my dream recorder. I will review and transcribe the dreams in the morning to implant their meaning and answer.

Three dreams to guide me are provided by the Life Force (and, perhaps, something else). In the first dream, I desperately want a baby girl to form in my image. I delay my pregnancy for a suitable time. I choose when to have a girl. As the child moves within, my eagerness builds. I decide I don't have time and abort her weeks before the delivery date. I do that three times and then can't stop doing it. Grief grips me. I awake wailing. I master my emotions and return to sleep.

In my second dream, I am obsessed with my appearance. I become the most beautiful and desired woman ever. All praise my face, hair, figure, and clothes incessantly, since all are obsessed with knowing every detail of my life. I retain the title "Most Beautiful Woman" for decades due to my power. I use and discard men like tissues. I have it all. I love every bit of it!

Yet, I also feel shallow, empty, alone, terribly used by myself. A horrid conviction grips me that nobody loves me nor could because I made myself an image, a mere package, instead of a person. I despair of being ever known and loved. I have nothing.

I wake to profound sadness and despair and realize that my entire life, I victimized myself, cannibalized myself. I demand the Life Force to give me a better dream, a dream with positive direction. Mastering my emotions, I fall quickly back to sleep to dream again.

My third dream starts with a previous nightmare. I am magnificent, powerful, honored, or, at least, feared by all, perching atop my throne on the king of the dragons. I command, and the Dragon King obeys my every whim, but the reality is that a tentacle from the Dragon King enters my back. I am a puppet. I demand a different dream.

The figures swirl, and next I am naked, fully exposed, and in a cage so small that I can't move. I am in a slave market with buyers leering at me, poking me through the bars. Any attempt to move results in agony. I cry out to demand another dream, but my words are mere babble. Hours of enforced passivity and helpless agony feed a desire to be bought and released from my cramped prison and public humiliation. I implore each leering face to somehow seduce anyone into buying me, but each only whistles when told my price; none even attempt to barter. My high price gives me no pride because I would give myself away for free to be a man's slave for some relief. I despair of freedom. I envy the freedom of slaves, even the ill treated ones, and am eager to be like them.

Hunger, fatigue, cramps, and especially thirst weigh heavily on me. Delirious misery and self-pity take over. Night approaches, and buyers no longer come. Darkness and blackness engulf all. I won't survive the night, I can't want to survive the night; I yearn for slavery.

A Light Approaches

A light approaches from behind me—a faint light. I hear voices and senseless conversation. I hear coins poured out and then the unmistakable and unbelievable sound of the opening of the lock. No sound is ever more welcomed or beautiful to me. As the back of my cage opens, I tumble helplessly out and resign myself to an inevitable rape. I expect to tumble hard to the ground but am instead caught by the strong hands of my unseen owner. Weak with hunger and thirst—my body stiff and sore and my spirit broken—I can not move nor even make any effort. He gives me small drinks, small berries one at a time (how wonderfully they refresh), and dresses me, massaging me and gently stretching out my limbs. Agony slips into joy and relief.

He carries me gently, troubling himself greatly to set me down often to give me again and again small drinks and more of the berries. I fall asleep in his strong gentle arms.

I wake as he sets me on a soothing bed. I wait for the expected rape. He has all power, and I none. Instead, for three days, he tenderly cares for me, refreshes me. I will not be anyone's slave. I order another dream.

I am on the Dragon King. I look marvelous. I am in total control again. The nightmare is over. I am no longer tethered to the Dragon by a tentacle. I am free!

The light increases unbearably. I see that I am filled with legions of the tentacles. I cry out for another dream.

I'm again the slave of the kindly master. I am given simple menial tasks and treated as a member of the family, like a loved child. I am clothed in beautiful silk. The other women are similarly clothed and treated. I will not be treated like an ordinary person. I order a different dream.

The Dragon King and all the other dragons and mighty brutes bow down to me and do my bidding. I expand my domain and influence with the strength and blood of the brutes. Men and women bow to me in worship.

My power and kingdom has no limits. I seize whatever and whomever I desire. This is the dream I want, the reality I will work for. I see little Janet pray for me. Incensed, I take her to raise her up and train her as my assistant and successor. I hear her say, "You were much nicer and better when you were weak. You were real."

Now, at the peak of my power, I control and define reality. I will show her reality. I make her stand before my Mirror of Reality. As the mists in the mirror swirl and clear, reality comes into focus—she a mere girl, freer and fuller than I, and I the Dragon King, terrible, hideous, vacuous. I bite my lip. Caustic fumes and liquid ooze from the wound and burn a hole in the stone floor.

I am repulsed by the price I pay for my power—but only momentarily. I am so full of power and myself that this is fitting. I am free from all limits, all restrictions, and restraints. I am totally free. Little Janet cries in pain due to my iron grip on her and from her weakness in seeing the real me. She cries out. "Jesus, free her!"

A slave again, I'm back with my kindly master and am about to command a return to the former dream when I see a brief glimpse of my future that arrests me. It intrigues me into waiting to see how this dream develops. A blend of pampering and hardship engulfs me. Far beyond exhaustion, I'm unable to resist kittens nuzzling against my face with their soft fuzzy bodies. They often comfort me. What delight! The pampering is needed recovery and preparation for the rigors of the hardships. Back and forth, back and forth, again and again. Pampering so rich, sensuous, and rejuvenating, far beyond the riches of this world to purchase, far beyond the privilege of an emperor to obtain—incomparable, indescribable, delicious. No expense or trouble is spared. The hardships are as hard and extreme in the opposite direction. There are physical rigors, far greater emotional turmoil, the exacting repetitions of the correct reactions (almost a martial arts of honorable actions, thoughts, emotions, and will), and, most difficult and rigorous of all, the breaking, tempering, and reforging of my will, the recreation of my soul. No expense or trouble is spared.

"What is all this for?" I groan.

"You are being groomed."

All this is preparation! In a flash, I see the future—am I in it?—I was a slave for decades, for the rest of my life. I die a thousand deaths and am almost ready for splendor beyond belief. The vision vanishes, anticipation arises, and my paradigm is revolutionized. I somehow embrace the idea that the hardships are vital, and I grow to cooperate with them. More and more, I even look forward to them as an athlete embraces and even learns to enjoy the rigors of training. I also have rest from the hardships and the tremendous reward of the pampering. Greater hardships are followed by greater treatments. Sore muscles, bruised egos, broken hearts, and disappointed desires are put right. My desire to bear more sufferings, to be embraced and strengthened by them, grows.

I see the gown. A stately voice declares, "Your Master, he who will be your groom made it. He infused it with his glory."

The luminosity of each thread pulses with exquisite glory, beauty, majesty, and magnificence that ennoble all who gaze on it, quiet and calm the turmoil of the soul, and focus the soul on glory. In that very act, the soul is transcended, eagerly abandoning herself. Janet puts it on. Its glory spreads to her, and it becomes her glory.

Her glory fills the room, outshining the lights—no, her glory outshines the sun. The glory of her radiance fills the room, and the walls become dazzling, sparkling, iridescent. She imparts beauty, majesty, and glory as she moves.

She sees a reflection of her in the gown—stunning, glorious beauty. The arduous hardships, once resented, now she eagerly pursues to this end. Had any narcissism lingered in her, she would have been forever transfixed, forever gazing at her image. But no, now she knows this is a gift from the groom and is for the groom. She wonders, *How soon can I go to him?*

Suddenly, the only doors—double doors—of that fabulous room rattle. She moves toward the door. With each step, as the gown and her hair moves along with her arms, head, body, majestic beauty cascades. Amazed, she twirls around, the fabric and folds of the long full gown (and her long luxuriant hair) flowing, twirling after her. An avalanche of majesty buries her shame and buoys up the best in her. She opens the doors.

There Is a Dog

There is a dog; a mere dog is rattling the doors. O, but what a dog, ever in motion. On earth, he would be worshipped as a god. One momentary glimpse of him would spawn countless myths. She remembers, wondering just moments before if she might have been mistaken for Aphrodite in all her glory. There is no doubt about this dog. On earth, he would be defied, worshipped, served. Artisans and artists would delight in their attempt to convey his raw, awesome, animal glory.

He communicates! He nudges her leg—she senses speed, power, affection, playfulness. He looks directly into her eyes—connecting, pleading, inviting. He bounds down the hall with energy and swiftness. Without words he communicates, 'Follow, Master sent, bring you.'

A lifetime of fear of being controlled, overpowered, of any authority over me, a lifetime of evasion all weigh on me in an instance. Their combined weight formerly so massive is now less than a butterfly's breath compared to the invitation from the groom to follow that dog—that enshrined and shining god—to him.

She eagerly follows. The dog speeds ahead, seemingly faster than light itself. She wonders if she will lose the dog; he doubles back in an instant. "He understands me!" While she takes one step, he bounds around her numerous times, too many to count—'Cassie, shepherd you to him.' She laughs—in this place the joy, mirth, and gladness of that laugh heals sadness.

"Correction, she is part-Australian Shepherd." Janet corrects herself with a laugh.

This laugh heals something else. Janet had been cruelly trained to obsess over always being right, to be deeply and personally wounded over making a mistake, and to despise errors and weakness in herself and others. The training served to whip her into inordinate and excessive effort but also rendered it all but impossible to even realize when she was mistaken. Whenever she was compelled to admit error, she was conditioned to explode in rage.

As she walks, the glory spreads in front making all—walls, floor, and ceiling—incandescent, with many colored, pulsing, and constantly changing luminosity that gradually and slightly fades as she passes. She wants to linger, to enjoy the splendor, but she is drawn strongly to the groom, curious and intrigued about him. She experiences desire—desire for him—a new species of desire—energizing, liberating—her reason for being herself, unique and irreplaceable. She is granted herself in her desire for him.

As she walks the hall, which is about the width of a two-lane road, the dog bounds back and forth from her to the next intersecting hall. Cassie moves with ever-increasing energy, eagerness, and excitement—'Almost there! Master! Shepherd you to him.' Cassie licks her hand. Gift from Master.' The sensation from that affectionate gesture spreads through my body, warming and soothing aches, healing cuts and cracks, transforming my body, and granting unimaginable control. The sensation is beyond sensuous or orgasmic pleasure, an entirely new genius of pleasure; I marvel. Cassie informs me that this is the first hint of my master's touch, and yet the control it confers on my body is far greater than the control I achieved with the Life Force. 'Master heal all with his touch.' She continues to say, 'Body, emotion, will, habits—all—give you full control, make you finally free and fully you.'

Janet exults, and even in (and or was it because?) that beautiful flowing gown, she expresses her joy in several beautiful acrobatic moves complete with several body rotations worthy of Olympic gold. No earthly athlete ever had a hint of that much body control. Her desire, now burning within and consuming ever more impurities still within, is ready to give herself eagerly, wholly, and with nothing withheld to the groom. She quickens her pace.

The explosion of beauty and glory and color that scatter from the movements of the gown during her acrobatic joy leaves that part of the hall shimmering and glowing with beauty and countless images. The "images" are four-dimensional scenes of the meaning of events in Janet's life. They are each overwhelmingly detailed, and, in that alone, are more beautiful than anything on earth. But that is only a small part of their beauty.

One of the images catches her eye for a moment before it rotates out of her view. Though intrigued, she will not delay her quest to see the groom to look further at it. Janet had a brief glimpse of ministers being murdered. Those ministers, after murdering her aunt and uncle as she had always been told, had committed suicide. Bewildered, she wonders who murdered the ministers. She continues her purposeful stride to see the groom marveling at the thought of what the actual touch of the groom might bring about when the mere (there was that silly word again!) lick of a dog-god grants all this.

I Wonder

I wonder why the groom sent Cassie for me. Cassie, ever attentive to me and to shepherding me, senses my musing and races back to me. She ceases for a moment her perpetual motion, save for the wagging of her tail, the constant tilting of her head, the pointing of her noise, and the speech of her eyes. I reach for her, massaging her coat. She again licks my hand, affectionately nuzzling it with the lustrous fur of her long snout. She answers; she is the answer. I'm convicted.

I wonder why a mere dog was sent to bring me. I realize the depth of my prejudice. This is certainly no mere dog—she never was. She is not *mere* anything, for she was not merely born but created by her Master. Cassie's full message—she is herself a medium of that message—is that I can not currently endure glory greater than a dog's, it is far beyond mine. Cassie's Master, the Groom, will grant transforming glory; then and forever I will be crowned with a glory immeasurably greater than Cassie's. She licks and nuzzles my hand a final time 'I love you forever.' And then she is off.

Cassie bounds around me once more, dashes into the junction with the next hall, and orients and transfixes her body and eyes on—I surmise—her Master. Perpetual motion becomes undying steadfastness. In the light of the glory of her master, I see Cassie in, at least, four dimensions. The sight transfixes me, righting even more within me. In an instant, I see Cassie born, a helpless puppy, a playful puppy, a young dog, adopted finally by her fourth family, loved and cherished even in infirmity and death.

I see all that like a series of pictures lain side by side telling a story, except that the "pictures" are 3-D video. Seeing takes an instant; understanding its depth and telling its detail require eternity. The vision results from the glorious light of the Master. I see Cassie reborn by that glory and transformed from an aged and infirmed dog with some bad habits to her current fully glorious state. Even her past changes, her bad habits and actions somehow drop out, ceasing to define her at all although still visible.

Cassie is poised and ready, every fiber of her being and every muscle taunt and ready, awaiting with eager anticipation the wishes of her Master. She sits in eager delighted obedience. 'Oh, Master, grant me something to obey!' Her crystal clear overpowering desire to fly to her Master is checked only by her far greater desire to delight him, to submit her own desires for the sake of delighting him. She lies down—stays eagerly—and races to her Master.

Awed, I receive her final message. 'My Master, your groom, awaits you with far more.' I step forward to my destiny with renewed anticipation and trembling desire.

A brief glimpse of myself arrests my thoughts. Awe grips me. Wonder fills me. Beauty as I could never imagine pours from the clothes, the body, the face, and even my voice. This can't be me; this is far beyond my beauty. Yet, this beauty is indeed imparted to me. But the approaching beautiful dread, a beauty and dread that is ever and always to be most eagerly craved, makes my boundless beauty inconsequential. A flood of transformation carries whatever is left of her old self utterly away so that what remained—her glorious, fulfilled, and destined self—appears burnishing bright like a star in supernova.

About to round the corner to where she will finally meet the groom, she is confident, full, and spilling over with glory until she rounds the corner and all that is her unravels.

She enters brightness that is unapproachable and that makes her bright glory seems dark—but only for an instant. As the extreme light pierces her clear though, piercing even to the unseen dimensions of the soul, and as the vision of the groom reaches her, she is transformed to bear the light, to be full with the light herself, transformed beyond reproach, resembling unbelievably certainly the groom himself.

"I now fully, freely, and forever belong to the groom whose likeness I bear. This very belonging is the key to unlock, liberate, and bring out of my depths my deepest longing. I awake. And so I woke with the strongest longings I've ever had." Janet, closing her journal, continues, "It was still early, but I knew sleep and dreams could not return, for every fiber of my body was energized. I asked myself, 'Could that possibly be real?' I promised myself, I swore by the dearness of that memory, the only thing I now consider worthwhile—dare I say even sacred?—that I would do anything, give up everything to know if there was even a kernel of reality in all that. I spent a few hours writing it all down and then called Francine for help."

All are silent and still. It is broken by sniffles. Tears are wiped from cheeks and dabbed from eyes. Noses are wiped and blown. Several times, someone opens his or her mouth to speak but only sighs. Someone exhales deeply.

"Of course," Janet continues, "it's probably all hogwash, the mere product of archetypes, the traumas of my childhood, and some childish wishes. I ask for your help because you are the only followers of Jesus I trust, and I respect your intellect. Come to think of it, you are the only people I respect. Before those conversations in the barn, I thought all Christians are silly. I still am convinced you are horribly mistaken."

"So what do you want from us?" someone asks.

"Your opinion," Janet replies, "about the dreams. I…"

"Didn't you say you want to know if the dreams point to anything real?" Mary interrupts. "Our opinion is beside the point. You will just continue your spiritual psychosis—your denial of ultimate reality. You need far more."

After a brief pause, Janet speaks, "The only reality I am neglecting is my own inner hurts and needs. The dreams clearly surfaced some of those. I want you to help sort those out so I can get back to what I really want to do."

"I see it clearly," Francine chimes in. "You baited, or more likely someone far above you baited the trap quite well. What you want is not what you need. What you want makes you blind to what you need and is against your own best interest."

Janet would ignore that comment from anybody but Francine. Even from Francine, she could ignore it but for the dreams. This creates a struggle for her, but she has help, an abundance of it. Her focus is drawn to the outrageous suggestion—from an old, deluded, superstitious woman—that what she wants makes her blind.

"They are the blind ones, not I! I see clearly they are trying to confuse me, bring me down to their level. That old woman is so ignorant I…" Janet blindly follows the lead until the thought that Francine is ignorant sparks a rebellion and derails that train of thought. She still believes Francine is mistaken but can not think her ignorant. What Janet says next startles Francine and even herself.

"I guess I don't know anything worth knowing. I guess, no, I know I don't even know what would be good for me. I'm not sure I want to know or that I even want it." Janet confesses. "I can't trust my own thoughts," she continues to say pensively.

"Listen! Hear this carefully," Words came slowly as Francine wrestles in prayer for the right words, the right aim and direction for the words. Others sense the momentous issue and task and also pray.

The pause allows thoughts in Janet to start closing this dangerous threat to their agenda. *This is nonsense. My needs are always ignored. A good therapist would attend to my needs and help me reach my goal without all this confrontation and judgment.* The hook is in, the thoughts begin to rapidly reel her in. *Judgment, condemnation, religious rot demand that I change, merely believe, and blindly leap into nothing.* This train of thought turns her inward and derails her resolve to know if the last dream has any connection with reality. She is almost gone, slipping away, and replaced with a scripted image—an ideal idol that was carefully constructed for twenty years.

The Shock

The shock of a full pitcher of iced water poured on her face and chest rudely reconnect Janet with her body, her emotions, her muscles, and her lungs as she jumps up from her chair gasping from the sensations and shock of the frigid water. She is livid. Thoughts of murderous magic take her over; she comes close to unleashing her fury. She turns and sees little Janet standing with her mother helping her hold the empty pitcher.

"What? Why?" Janet demands. Little Janet let go of the pitcher and runs crying to the safety of her father.

Desiree, her mother, replies rapidly with an apologetic tone, "I saw you slipping away, life and liveliness draining from your face and body like I was watching a zombie in the making. I thought someone had to do something quick when I saw my daughter struggling with the pitcher of iced water. I knew instantly that she was right, so I helped her. I'm so sorry."

Janet, surprised by her realization that she had indeed nearly been separated fully from her self and taken over by something else, savors her anger. She couldn't remember the last time she felt genuine anger. Her frequent anger and rage seem, and are, contrived and artificial, mere tools of something else. This taste of reality brought Janet joy—joy for genuine anger, disorienting.

They begin to turn her inward once again when Francine grips her arm with ferocity. Mary speaks, "You have to decide about reality. Your assumptions about spiritual reality are cutting you off from your own personal reality. Give the facts and evidence out of your comfort zone their due weight."

Somehow, despite the clamor of objections within, the jumble of reasons to reject everything Mary says, Janet manages to hold on and confess, "I want to consider all that is happening."

Most conversations that day, Janet ignores. She rejects offers of prayers. Silent prayer for her multiplies. She resents and disregards almost all of encouragement and suggestions given. The wisest and most helpful comments, but still resented, come in conversation with Francine. Before that conversation, the voices within Janet are hardening her against Christians, even these Christians whom Janet finds it difficult not to like and respect. Thoughts come into Janet's mind that all Christians want is to "score one for Jesus" and make her a Christian—a supremely disgusting thought. Francine realizes this and shatters that sneaky spell on Janet's thinking. There is a long embrace despite Francine getting herself wet and chilled. Francine calls for towels and blankets for Janet so she is quickly more comfortable. There are also touches, squeezed hands, and words of comfort. Being near Francine is itself comforting and soothing.

The greatest benefit Janet gets that day from Francine, but still resented and resisted, is the realization that Janet is barely a person. Francine's sympathetic comfort is the key. "This is going to be hard. Embracing spiritual realities is hard for you on many levels."

Janet accepts those words heartily; she silences the cynical voices within.

"I hardly expect," this wise woman continues, "it could be different for someone who hasn't embraced being a person. We need to build you up to being more human."

These words pierce the armor of her defenses. There is an eruption of protests and denials within spewing out threats, shouts, and gibberish to drown out that message. The certainty of that reality, fully though reluctantly accepted by Janet, struggle into halting words, "How can I become more human? Can you help me?" The voices within are routed and silenced for the moment.

Talking with Francine helps Janet discover that though she reads voraciously, she never enjoys it. She does not enjoy anything except power and dominating others. Her use of music, video, the web, art, exercise, and dressing up are all for effect, for how she can use anyone and everything for power. She only has useful friends and activities; everything not useful to her is a waste of time. She wastes no time; she wastes her life instead. She doesn't live her life; she does as she is rigorously trained to.

Francine takes charge. She puts a priority on helping humanize Janet. She prescribes pointless play, frivolous fun, and loads of laughter.

Janet drives to one of her labs to continue her experiments on animals. She notes a radical change: she can't do it. The memories of the kittens and Cassie in her dream create an aversion to treating animals as mere sources of data. She knows it isn't logical, those animals are clearly inferior to humans, and especially to her; she has the right to do whatever she wants with them. But her emotions won't let her. She spends the day delivering scores of dogs and cats to animal shelters with generous donations, liberating over one hundred mice at several spots far out in the country, and destroying a few animals that were badly damaged. All that work wasted; she feels good.

The next few weeks are a combination of conversations, of hikes in the brilliant fall colors of the Shenandoah Mountains and valleys, of watching children play soccer, T-ball, basketball, and of wandering aimlessly in yards and other social and frivolous activities. She usually avoids the recommended readings; internal reminders of urgent tasks interpose. She is still drawn strongly to using the Life Force and dominating men by seduction or manipulation.

Janet sometimes resists the draw of the Life Force and the appeal of using men. She occasionally even overcomes her avoidance of learning about Jesus. She slowly becomes a bit her own person; she makes a few of her own decisions. She notices this new achievement of hers and likes it, feeling a legitimate pride. Thoughts occur to her that her new balance is probably the real import of her dreams and will be useful in rehabilitating her real estate business. She feels good about her efforts, and the realization presses on her that she no longer needs involvement with these "followers." She is ready to drift from them.

Darkness still clings to the morning one Saturday when I wake. "I'll need to reward myself," I say. I dress in simple clothes for a chilly fall morning to use yard sales to get real estate listings. I promise myself I won't use the Life Force but only my own charms to acquire them.

I avoid conversation with my cook to keep focus. I'll take my big SUV—it gets a better reception at yard sales. I'll take my leather-bound folio and cheap clipboard and my high heels and flashy jewelry to put on instead of my athletic shoes to best match the setting.

I drive out; it is still dark, and I see the pavement is still damp from rain. The cold moist and delightfully clean air begin to invigorate my soul. I almost lose focus.

My Drive for Power Increases

My drive for power increases as I drive, until I am lusting for power and to dominate and use men. I am driving east and can't help noticing the beauty of the night sky and the approaching dawn. I open the sunroof, and, as the delicious air pours in, the enticing dawn begins to dissolve the devious spell. As Janet enjoys the dawn moment by moment, she comes under its happy enchantment. There are wispy clouds turning gradually from dark gray to pink and shading into fiery red. The sky displays Venus, some stars, and a harvest moon looms large as her liberator. She is out of herself and soaring into the heavens.

Her routed handlers are in the triple agony of defeat, punishment, and her intolerable harmony with nature. To her, the harmony she experiences is simple, clean, and peaceful; to them, it is horrid medicine. They curse the dawn, and a few want to impetuously mount a fierce counterattack. Before the dreams, it might have worked. A few months before, it was unnecessary because she was immune to beauty not her own. More experienced demons know that as light increases, the fall colors at peak would undermine them by distracting Janet from herself to beauty that is wholesome and good. Better to wait for the allure of nature to diminish as Janet habituates to them. A simple plan is implemented, one that peaks briefly before she arrives back at the complex.

Janet's buoyancy from the gifts of the sky, the trees, the pure air, and the rolling landscape provide the winsome natural attraction for her to gain several real estate listings. She is not tempted to use the Life Force or manipulation to sign several contracts. Her successes inflate her pride.

As Janet drives, she swerves to avoid a dog. Before experiencing Cassie, she wouldn't have altered her path for a dog. Now it's automatic. In a freakish accident, the front driver's tire blows out as she turns sharply and hits a patch of wet leaves. The SUV skids sideway, and the sides of the tires hit the curb, so the SUV gently turns over with the passenger side on the ground beyond the curb. Rage fills me, and swearing follows. But then I see young athletic men, muddy and wet from playing rugby, running toward me. I will play them well! I go limp and hang in my seat by the seatbelt. I will pose as a helpless female and let them rescue me to enslave them.

I wait for them to climb on the car, open the driver's door from above, and lift me out of the car. I pretend to be unconscious as they carry me to a dry spot. I feign coming to by writhing my body to captivate them. What man can resist a helpless female? "What happened?" I ask.

They compete to answer me. No one could plan it better. I gain control over them all! I ask for something to drink. They practically fall over themselves to offer me my choice of drinks. I stretch, protruding my chest to fix all eyes on my breasts. Feigning fear, I breathe heavily, moving my breasts and drawing them into the rhythm of my movements. They take the bait; I embed the hook, mixing confusion and commands with the tone of my voice.

"I'm okay, thanks to *you*. What would I *do...whatever...you... could I do* without *you doing anything for me*?" They are entranced with me and also for me. "*You'll do anything for me*," she whispers.

I make them get my SUV back up, change its tire, and serve me. They fawn over me as I reel them in. I notice a full beard on one of them, and I am enraged. I finger his Achilles's tendon—it will tear in minutes. I despise beards!

I notice my necklace is missing. I'll teach whoever stole it a lesson! "Oh, my necklace is missing. Help me find it!" I remark. They search frantically. I pick out the one who took it. I command him to come to me in the same tone his mother used. "Hansel, *kommst hier jetzt*!" His guilt stirs. I observe him fighting against me and the guilt. I afflict him with his memory of kidney stones. Needless to say, he restores my necklace with profuse apologies.

Something else happens for Hansel that day. He changes. He returns to being a "real man," Semper Fi—Ever Faithful—and all that. He wakes from the slumber triggered by his combat traumas. Rather than be routed by his fear, he starts getting help—that and various other changes assisted by therapy, save his job, his marriage, and maybe his life. He was thinking of suicide; the threats to his manhood of losing his job, his marriage, or both would push him precariously close to it.

His marriage, dangerously on the rocks and about to shipwreck on his drinking and anger, is rescued as his anger subsides and his drinking drops from several cases of beer each week to a few beers each week. He stops smoking around his children, and their asthma improves. He finally stops smoking after his umpteenth attempt. He returns to a radical version of the faith his mother tried so hard to train him in and his father so hard to keep him from. In reality, her faith was in a church, dogmas, and rules. The radical faith he turns to is learning to seek God himself primarily. Beginning with intense fear, he chooses to live out Semper Fi instead of increasing his drinking.

Janet is full of herself and being in control of these guys. She doesn't realize, she couldn't, that chains of slavery are refastened on her. They celebrate being in control and set her up to make further choices in their favor to increase their control. She will diminish as their control extends.

Back on My Way

Back on my way with these guys and their contact information in my pocket, I decide to blow off the T-ball game and go out and snag some guys for myself.

"I won't give up my sensuous satisfactions for those silly superstitious followers! I am free to do whatever I want. I am powerful and destined to gain all power. I must look my best!" I rush to get to the complex and change into something extremely sexy and captivating. I hit something that punctures a tire half a block from my driveway so that I won't be able to take the SUV. I let out a scream of rage and obscenities!

Getting dressed as I want proves a struggle. I curse those mindless "followers" for duping me to a lazy indulgence in the last few weeks that resulted in my gaining seven pounds! I break zippers on three of my sexiest dresses. I am now only ten pounds below my ideal body weight. There is even a tiny bulge at my waistline! I am incensed and obsessed. I will use the remedy my aunt forced on me. She trained me to control my waist and keep my stomach totally flat by lacing me tightly into a corset whenever I was sloppy. At nine, I always kept my stomach muscles extremely taut.

I command my cook to lace my corset. I admire my figure and obsess with making it better. I make her strap my six-inch heels on me and tighten the corset. It looks better, but my obsession grows. I make her mercilessly tighten it.

I love the result—bewitching and irresistible. I ask her opinion. She says my waist can be smaller by using my high bar. I cast a spell on her to strengthen her to tighten it. I pass out.

When my cook is done and I am fully dressed and ready to go out, my appearance takes my breath away. I am spectacular—irresistible! She resizes one of my sexiest dresses to make it tighter. My waist, bust, and cleavage are flawless. The heels make my legs and butt perfect.

I am finally free to appear as truly I am. I dismiss my cook and continue my preparation. I don't want to take my eyes off myself. I need to look like this. As I admire myself, my need grows into an obsession. I must always look like this.

As I head to my Porsche, my phone rings. A woman greets me. She needs me to pick them up for her son's T-ball game instead of meeting there, since she sprained her leg and can't drive. I tell her I can't take her, and her husband will have to. She explains that her husband flew to Seattle. As she says, "If you can't take us, we can't go. I can't find another ride." I hear her brat cry.

Janet can't disappoint Matt. Impulsively, she promises to be there in twenty minutes and hangs up after finding out that the coach won't let him play if he's late.

Janet rushes past the Porsche to the classic convertible, her only car available now with room for four. Rushing makes her dizzy and hot as her limited ability to breathe can't be ignored. *Oh, I'm not use to this. As long as I control my breathing, I'll do okay.* She is liberated by the fall air, the sun and sky, the smells of freshness, and someone cooking mulled cider, and the brilliant leaves entice her into the autumn pageant. The wind catches her hair and cools her face, refreshing her body and spirit. She notices a drunk driver, and my anger at him flares into a spell that causes him to crash into a police car that pulled over a speeder.

I park at the side of her house and rush toward the door on the balls of my feet to avoid the shank of the heel sinking into the grass. My oxygen debt forces me to slow down. I barely get enough air to walk. A spot in the yard collects water and is covered by leaves. I step on it, and my left foot sinks several inches in mud. Only by extreme effort and rapid stomping of my right foot to regain a footing and grabbing a branch with my arm am I able to avoid falling. My oxygen debt soars though, and only with extreme concentration of effort can I hide my distress. They evoke her trained obsession to hide weakness.

I flash a huge smile at the three and mouth a greeting. I want to avoid talking to save my breath and avoid detection of my struggle. I am in agony. She has second thoughts about how she is dressed when a glimpse of her reflection in the picture window and the reflection of some men walking by lustfully ogling me fortifies my obsession with my appearance.

The brat giggles and points at my shoes. "You look funny, and your belly is too small," he says. I look at my shoes—horror! My left shoe, with my foot to the ankle, is covered with mud, and several large leaves are skewered by the spiked heel and are bunched up near the top on the heel. My right foot lacks mud but, otherwise, looks the same.

I bend over to clear them when pain from bending at my waist forces me to stop. I laugh and say I'll remove them after I drop them off. Thoughts force into my mind but is interrupted by the brat.

"I want you to stay. Please, pretty please don't just drop me off," he bawls.

His mother explains, "She has other plans."

Weeks ago, none of this would have mattered to me, but now her heart can't bear disappointing the naïve love of a five-year-old. She never felt so unworthy of interest as she now feels.

Janet interrupts. "I'm staying. I only meant I'll drop you off to park the car," she lies. Desiree is on crutches. Janet has the ordeal of carrying Matt's car seat and pulling a large cooler with drinks and snacks for the team.

Janet lugs things to the car, puts the cooler in the trunk, and then lifts Matt into his car seat. These simple actions are an ordeal for her due to her struggle to breathe. She is barely able to get behind the wheel. Her dizziness is too extreme to drive. She stalls, "Pray that we get there safely on time." Janet doesn't hear their prayers; she is intent on recovering and praying to herself that their prayers will be long enough for her to recover. Though she blocks out their prayers, part of Matt's prayer breaks through. "Help Janet…" A crisis starts in her heart. She could have averted the inner crises had she not been so obsessed with merely breathing.

After their prayers and a pause, Desiree says, "We'd better get going."

THEY'RE OFF

They're off. Janet hides her struggles with breathing well. They arrive at the field, and Matt asks her to promise that she will come to his game. "Nothing will keep me from coming to your game. I promise," Janet declares.

Once I drop them off, I see it will be hard to keep my promise. Parking is one hundred yards off. Other than the trampled muddy grass, the only path to Matt's field is a path filled with large gravel. Walking on those large stones will be next to impossible in these heels. "I'll make up an excuse. Five-year-olds get upset all the time. He'll learn about the real world quicker this way. What's a promise to a five-year-old anyway?" But Janet rebels. She promised Matt, and she is determined to keep it.

The only parking spots Janet finds are under trees filled with birds. She sees bird droppings on the cars, so she will have to put up the top—manually. Only her pride suckers her into trying it. It almost finishes her off. Her exertion, complicated by the large gravel underfoot, makes her walking in heels difficult and unsteady. Lifting the cooler out of the trunk makes her hot, dizzy, and sweaty.

Pulling the cooler behind her over the gravel compounds the difficulty and imposition; self-pity fills her. She can't walk erect due to the handle of the cooler being too short for her height.

She tries lifting the cooler to carry it, but its weight and bulk throw her off balance and block her view of the stones in front of her. She stumbles and falls onto the cooler. She struggles back to her feet, refusing an offer of help and thinking, *How dare he think I need help!*

She settles for lowering her hand almost a foot to pull the cooler behind her. Keeping her knees bent and bending slightly at the waist allow her to pull the cooler, but they wear her down. Abruptly, her handlers throw their support behind her, making the long difficult walk to the field. They give her temporary relief. Janet begins her self-inflicted Via Dolorosa to keep a promise. They assist her in every way they can without her giving them full control. There's relief from the sun as clouds block its heat, there is a refreshing gentle breeze, and they feed her prideful confidence that she will make it. They keep her focus on rapid chesty breathing, going slow and staying calm by taking it one step at a time while carefully watching where she puts down her heels among the rocks.

When she is about halfway, they shift from assisting to hampering her. They have her trapped. She will need to call on them to either get to the field or back to her car. The breeze stops, the sun beats down mercilessly on her, and her focus is broken as she overhears kids making remarks about her funny-looking shoes and the sweat starting to soak her dress. She forgets to breathe right and strives to no avail to take in deep breaths with the result that she compounds her oxygen debt and distress. She no longer carefully picks her steps over the gravel; her ankles wobble, her legs tremble, and her confidence tanks. She tries to speed up, which makes everything far worse.

I have to stop. "I can't do this. I simply can't." Dizziness and a feeling of failure take over. "I've never failed before." But then I remember my plans for Dr. Blanke. They failed. I failed to stop those acts of kindness. The dreams I demanded weren't what I wanted. The people I sent back in time and my own trip back to observe Jesus—I couldn't recover a single memory. Now I fail to keep a promise to a five-year-old. This failure stings me even worse.

We can help you keep your promise.
Let us help you. Open up fully to us and let us all the way in.
We'll be able to help you so much more.
You need us helping you at your very center.

In desperation, I am about to obey the voices when nightmarish images intrude. The most terrifying is when I am perched high on top of the king of the dragons, gloriously attired as Supreme Emperor and Lord, crowned and holding a scepter. My face wears a broad smile of triumph, but my eyes are empty, fixed, and vacuous. I look for the tentacles from the Dragon controlling me. I hesitate.

You know you want it.
Such power and glory belong to you alone.
You deserve it, it is your destiny.
You crave it at your very center. You will pay any price to have it.
You simply must have it whatever else what might happen.

I do want it—desperately. Another memory breaks in, dispelling my intent to pursue the power, even though it would leave me empty. I want the power and glory. I am willing to pay any price. I simply must have it, but the dream of being the kindly Master's slave, and the final outcome of that dream is worth hoping for, even though it must be a delusion. Living for that delusion is saner. In the last few weeks, I experienced that dabbling in the tiniest bit of it is more real than pursuing power. I can't plunge back into it. Better to try to keep my promise to Matt and fail than give in to power lust. I wish there was any real help.

I'D GASP FOR AIR

I'd gasp for air if I could. I'm in severe distress. Sweat pours from me, soaks me, and begins to dehydrate me. I'm oxygen-starved; color fades from my vision. Dizziness disorients me. I despise weak women who faint. My obsession with appearance and seizing power over men makes me a slave to appearance, discomfort, and helplessness. Now I'm just another helpless female, unless I yield to the Life Force. Dizziness…hard to think. Matt—air—relief—faint—no choice—tentacles—trapped—help!

I hear a boy ask: "Miss, do you need help?"

My habitual response is out of my mouth before I think. "No!" I intend to bellow, but it comes out as a whimper. I don't need anything; I am complete and full—but certainly not full of air. Full of it is more like it. I look up and see Cub Scouts and a couple. Another Scout says, "Come on, Ted. She doesn't want help." They start to leave.

"Wait…please….help." It's all Janet whispers as a panic attack starts. She fears she is going to die and feels so awful that she wants to—absolute terror. She feels the corset crushing her chest, it's like she's having a heart attack, she can't breathe, is going crazy, her hands and feet go numb, her mouth is dry and her throat tight, sweat gushes from her, she can't move, she loses control, has gone crazy, is in a living hell. They catch her as she falls. She is out of her body, her only contact with her body are her terrified bulging eyes. She sees them carrying her through her eyes but can't feel her body at all—a supreme relief and terror in one.

A woman—Emily—feels the corset as she caught Janet and knows it has to be loosened quickly. Emily directs them to carry her into their tent and leave. She asks, "May I loosen your, um, your corset?" Janet tries to scream yes with her eyes. Emily sees the urgency and turns Janet's body over and tries to unzip the dress. The zipper is stuck. Emily cuts the dress off and then cuts the laces. The shock of relief from the crushing pressure also brings agony as she gasps for air, begs for something to drink, her muscles twitching and cramping.

Janet is recovering. She is given sips of a sports drink. Emotionally, she's a wreck—fearful, trembling, still panicky, fighting back tears, and almost naked with nothing to put on. She's embarrassed. For the first time, she feels ashamed of her nakedness. Her shame of herself is a good kind that is toxic to the demons within. Now they couldn't "breathe." Emily is too small to have any clothes Janet could wear but offers her husband's sweat clothes. After sufficient recovery, dressed in Bruce's bulky sweat clothes and wearing his oversized beat-up worn tennis shoes, Janet insists on heading for Matt's field looking now more like a clown than a vamp.

Tears flow suddenly, profusely. For decades, Janet rarely cried, certainly not anything like this. It feels awful and awfully good. Part of her knows that she barely averted losing total control of herself. The larger part of her suppresses that from her awareness.

I am a wreck. My emotions are stormy and raw, my hair is damp, my face is red, and I'm still catching my breath. Emily walks me to the restroom and helps me clean up as much as possible. Seeing myself in the mirror, I promise, "Never. Never, never, never again. Look at me! What a mess." I begin to curse myself, and the demons recover.

As she walks toward Matt's field, the demons draw her attention to people starring at the spectacle. She notices snickering and swallows the lie that everyone is making fun of her. She wants to run, to have revenge—both. She is almost overcome by those desires when Matt's face seizes her attention. The burst of joy from his missing-teeth-smile shatters the spell of self-concern and the budding fantasies of revenge. She smiles in return, and her pace quickens. Matt runs to her, and he jumps into her arms.

I'm greeted warmly also by little Janet and their mother. A new thought: Desiree isn't just an oppressed "wife" but is also privileged to have these precious innocent children call her "Mommy." In reality, Janet ponders, isn't she in many ways freer in her obligation and bonds of love than I am? I am such a slave to making an impression, to posturing and positioning myself for power, to having to be in control of everything and everyone around me. Deep, deep within a seed of regret sprouts for what she made of herself. She, however, remained oblivious to it but thinks "I prefer being free to belong to no one but myself!"

Janet accepts that, but deep within her unconscious, something very antithetical grows. There, secret loneliness and emptiness clamor for recognition that they are the price of accepting that lie. She needs people, love, but more vital still is she needs to get out of herself, to love others. Matt and little Janet provide easy practice for that.

T-Ball Is Pure Delight

T-ball is pure delight. Most of the children barely understand what they were doing, the rules or how to play, and certainly lack skill, but they play, really play, with wild freedom. They are fully in the moment.

I knew Desiree wanted to ask about my change of clothing. I confess I had plans she would find offensive. I also tell her that I'm eager to talk, since I want a new start. The changes Janet wants to make are superficial. They are no threat to her handlers but are considered risky because they might lead to real changes.

Janet gets used to the far greater comfort of these clothes (despite the stares of others). She contrasts them and embraces the current blend of physical comfort and social discomfort as far superior. Her handlers pushed her too far and too fast and pay dearly for their mistakes.

Watching the children play keeps her amused and lighthearted so that she is temporarily immune to attacks. She slips out of close orbit around their concerns.

She sees a ground ball homerun that rolls barely past third base. The hitter runs the bases as fast as his little legs can and never pauses. Three overthrows later, the nonstop runner scores!

During a lull in Matt's game, I also see a triple play at the next field where older children play. It would not have been a triple play with alert experienced base runners.

The sky, the breeze, the sights and sounds of happy children, the freshness of the air and its comfortable coolness, and the fall colors of the leaves again create a deeper sense of reality for Janet. She forgets her preoccupation with power, her appearance, herself. There is a sense of gentle soaring freedom, reminding her of something she can not place. It's good; she cherishes it; she prefers and chooses it over her unreal life.

A child's hug, Janet thinks, *must be one of the most genuine of all things. Matt hasn't learned to pretend he likes something*. She enjoys the genuine affection.

After the game is over, Janet does not want to go back to her complex but doesn't know what to do either. Above all, deep down, she doesn't want to be alone but is only consciously aware of a general disquiet. Desiree provides a solution when she says, "I wish I could fix you lunch or take you out for lunch. I've got to get to the house and rest. My leg is killing me. I'm so sorry."

"Oh," I seize the opportunity "I'll take you all to lunch. My treat." The biggest part of the treat for Janet is more time with these real sane people and being spared being alone with her own insanity.

I desperately want to change into better clothes but want to stay with them far more. Subconsciously, Janet fears going back to her complex, as though it's somehow haunted and she wouldn't be able to escape once she goes back in. In her haste and focus on dressing to prowl for victims, all she brought in her tiny purse are keys, basic makeup, a driver's license, and her "kit" to protect her from STDs. Her wallet and suitcase with a change of clothes are still in the Porsche.

"Since you're so tired, why don't I fix all of us something to eat at your house?" She proposes. It is a desperate move, since, although Janet is an accomplished biochemist and sorcerer, she knows almost nothing about cooking. *But how hard can it be anyway* she thought.

Janet is horrified by the prospect of fixing what is planned. Desiree, before she hurt her ankle, planned on making barbeque chicken pizza from scratch. She hadn't bought more groceries because of her accident, so it was either pizza or takeout. Janet's pride won't let her ask Desiree for money, so she would have to fix the pizza somehow.

Humiliation

Humiliation is the theme of the day for Janet. She hates being needy (actually, incompetent) at the simple task of making a pizza. The hardest part for her is making the circular crust fit the pan, "not too thick, not too thin." Desiree always stuffs the crusts of her pizzas, and the kids clamor for it until I beg off. She rescues me from the kids whining. The hardest thing for her is not erupting in anger at little Janet and Matt whom she adores but for the moment resents. Fighting her own desires, especially an overpowering one like this, is not only hard and new to Janet, but she always (since her aunt and uncle trained her to it) believed that it is both impossible and unnecessary and also harmful to resist one's own desires.

This is an onerous task to repudiate her obsession for power and control. It is a taxing burden of not cursing these kids who acted like tired hunger kids who loved being treated to stuffed crust pizza. But in doggedly persisting in actually making a pizza when she wants to run away Janet is becoming more her own person. She hates the process. Inwardly, she is begging for help to do it moment by moment. When she places the finished pizza on the table, new insights are planted deep within, beyond her conscious awareness of them.

I can control myself. I don't have to vent my anger. I don't have to be always totally in control. I really need help. The relief of the pressure of producing the pizza paired with the liberation of these new insights gives Janet a tangible and profound new sense of something she doesn't recognize but welcomes and wants. You probably recognize *peace*—she doesn't. For the moment, she tastes it; her handlers, in the full disarray of a rout, had successfully insulated her from it for decades.

She savors the moment only briefly. Desiree asks little Janet to thank God for the meal. Little Janet responds, "Ms. Janet should give thanks. She made it."

Desiree knows how awkward that is for Janet and bit her lip. Consternation and concentration show on her face. Before Desiree rescues the moment, Janet utters, "I can't." Before that day, the meaning of the words would be refusal. Now the meaning is confession. No one at the table knew that, not even Janet. However, God did, and he credits it as a great victory by Janet.

Janet enjoys eating that far from perfect pizza with those people in a modest house more than any meal in decades. She enjoys Desiree's generous "raves" of "This is great for your first pizza." She delights in the compliments of the children and that only once did Matt murmur, "I miss the stuffed crust."

Cleaning up is a challenge for Janet. She did nothing voluntarily in the kitchen since the death of her parents, except when she dismissed Marie early. She was taught that service was for slaves. Her aunt and uncle viciously punished any act of service she offered. Other times, they punished her by forcing her to serve in degrading ways or conditions. She is confused about serving.

Exhausted by the events of the day and her own confusion, Janet is about to ask if she could lie down (subconsciously, she was growing more desperate not to leave with each tick of the clock) when Desiree says, "Well, thank you for all you've done for us today. I guess we'd better let you go. I need a nap."

The implications appall Janet; thoughts intrude. *She's trying to get rid of me! After all I've done for them! She thinks nothing of imposing on me for a ride, to fix them a meal, to have to clean up because she's lazy! I'll leave and do what I want!* Janet follows like a sheep until "do what I want." She shutters. Desperation is the mother of inventing an excuse for her to tell some of the truth.

"I seem to have picked up a chill and…" she starts to say when suddenly interrupted by a sneeze, then a second one, and then a third. Her nose starts running, and she dashes across the room to grab a tissue. "I'm grumpy and sleepy," he confesses when Matt interrupts, "And sneezy too!" before he runs from the room with a coy look over his shoulder, which is a clear invitation to chase him.

Caught off guard, she hesitates until he peeks his grinning face around the corner. She chases him, grabs him, and tickles him to his delight. Somehow, the memory of her parents tickling her resurfaces and guides her. It's her first good memory of her parents. An image of her father's face and full beard intrudes and makes her sick to her stomach. Revulsion and rage at the image of his beard arises as repressed memories of it brushing against her face in the middle of the night surface. Little Janet "rescues" her brother (and Ms. Janet) by tickling Ms. Janet and joins their tickle party on the floor; they laugh to exhaustion. Janet is normally immune to tickling, but her guardedness is gone.

As fatigue sets in, Janet has an even better excuse to confess the truth. "I'm afraid to go back to my complex because it might not be safe for me, as tired as I feel." There is a pleading in her voice as she asks, "Can I please take a nap here?" When Desiree warmly agrees, Janet asks for a blanket and if she could fix some hot herbal tea.

After savoring the tea and snugly wrapping herself in a blanket (that comfort recovered another good memory about her mother) and with her insides warmed by the delightful tea and these wonderful people, she is shown little Janet's room to take her nap. There were princesses and ponies, flowers and castles, and knights and fire-breathing dragons on the wall. There are dolls and stuffed animals on a shelf and a big snow white bear on the bed. Closing the door, she gets into bed, hugging the bear. Sleep overtakes her and a dream begins.

A caldron below me is filled with Nanites—submicroscopic robots. "They will make you more beautiful! They will dress you in clothes that magnify your beauty!" Still dressed in oversized men's sweat clothes, which all but annihilate my beauty, I eagerly plunge into the pit. The Nanites swarm over my body, consuming the ugly clothes, and then envelop every part of me. The crushing discomfort is far worse than that of the corset at its tightest, and it is everywhere—my fingers and toes, limbs, face and mouth, even my tongue are quickly covered by a solid, taut covering of the Nanites. A burning heat sends agony through my body as they fuse onto my body and take control of it. They cause my body to leap up out of the pit and pose before a mirror. I look perfect and beautiful dressed in a rapid succession of seductive, demure, wholesome, coy, professional outfits as they mold themselves into different attire. They even pose my body and face perfectly for each persona. I couldn't be more pleased.

I try to move my body, but I'm encased by them and unable to. All awareness of anything is filtered through and passed on to me to experience by the Nanites. They use my contacts and people I meet to spread themselves. They remove my arms, legs, and breasts to make more room to carry more of them. They starve me so that there is still more room for them. Having made full use of my "contact list," they shut off all sense of the outside world and all perception, except for my growing hunger, pain, loneliness, and despair. Unable to do, or even alter, anything, my will atrophies. Insanity infects my thinking and impossible fantasies of anything real torment me. I retreat into a dark chaotic mass of pitch-black stormy emotions. Memory ceases in a tomb of Nanites.

Terrified and Disoriented

Terrified and disoriented she awakes with no memory of where she is. She feels the bear in her arms and sees the colorful decorations on the walls, the curtains, the dolls, and the girl's clothing in the partially opened closet. She concludes she is a little girl. She wants her mommy and wails, "Mommy, Mommy, help me!"

Janet crawls out of bed and starts to search for her mother when she sees her reflection in a mirror. Shocked back into reality, she realizes that she is a scared and needy child in a grown woman's body. Her emotions are still those of a child, a wounded and hurting little girl still grieving many losses. The dam that had been laborious built to hold back ordinary emotions is cracked and falling apart. She is an adult who never grew up, had never been permitted to grow up, to mature as a person. *Twenty years wasted!* she realizes.

Little Janet opens the door; Desiree hurries several feet behind on her crutches. Matt stands frozen at the end of the hall. Each face has its own blend of concern, fear, and bewilderment. Janet's face is wet with tears, her voice is weak, unsure, and cracks as she confesses, "I-I-I had a bad dream. I'm scared." Her body is trembling; she burst into tears again. She clings to the bear.

They surround Janet, hugging her and comforting her with pats and assuring words. As she gradually calms, she begs to spend the night, promising, "I'll be good, I will, I promise."

Desiree insists she spend the night, "We'll need to get you some clothes. Those are pretty rant." Desiree had comforted her daughter after a nightmare; she is struck by how much Janet seems like a frightened six-year-old girl.

Janet confesses she didn't have anything with her to pay for anything. Though Desiree didn't want to go back out, she offers to go with Janet and use a credit card. She accepts Desiree's offer to pay for some clothes for her at a thrift store and Walmart. It is her first time in either. Janet wants to spend more and get much nicer things, but Desiree's credit card is nearly maxed out. She opts for a pair of cheap boots, jeans, a sweatshirt since it's getting cold, and two T-shirts from the thrift store.

On the way to their house, they stop by a grocery store for a few items so Janet could fix some meals. The credit card is maxed out, so they put a roast back. Janet notes that even in their financial distress, Desiree is generous. Once back at the house, Janet struggles through fixing dinner and then watches old Veggie Tales cuddling with the kids. They watch the episodes "The Toy That Saved Christmas" and "Josh and the Big Wall."

More and more firsts for Janet pile up. The genuine affection of little Janet and Matt demolish her defenses to reality, her posturing, and even her lust for power and sex. Since Helena and Frank took charge of her and injected the demonic into her life, she had been carefully trained to rely solely on manipulation, seduction, self-gratification, and the demons within for all comfort and to assuage her magnified sense of emptiness and loneliness. They—her aunt, uncle, and demons—isolated her from all wholesome human, or even animal, contact. They planted deep within her hated and disrespect, a dismissal, of all ordinary humans and all animals, especially her formerly beloved dogs, cats, and horses. Of course, it was a trap, a vicious downward cycle. Relying on the vacuous to fill her up just made her emptier and more reliant on the abyss. Her handlers gained dominance over her by giving her comfort that drew her into an addictive orbit around them.

Glimmers of hope poison and weaken her handlers. Her twisted and stubborn will is the best defense they still have, and they will protect it until an opportune moment, for Janet is making choices contrary to her habitual desires. She resists following the rut worn of years of repetition.

They agree that Janet will drive them to church in the morning but not go in. Desiree loans her old iPad, five or six upgrades behind, to Janet. Janet would fix and eat lunch with them before leaving. Janet calls Francine, inviting her to stay a few days to visit, but it is a pretext to avoid being alone at her complex.

A sudden cold front causes temperatures to plummet, and a light snowfall begins. They huddle around a fire in the den. Though the flakes melt as soon as they hit, the lightly drifting flakes light up the world outside and Janet within with their beauty. The beauty of the snowfall, the stillness of the greenbelt and trees, the warmth and smell of the fire, and the roasting of marshmallows for s'mores entice Janet deeper into ordinary reality. Janet roasts her marshmallows over the fire and, accepting suggestions from the children, puts them on dark chocolate between cinnamon graham crackers. She has a second and third s'more. They enjoy mulled cider and storytelling by the glow of the fire.

The uniqueness of the tastes, smells, and atmosphere unlocks a treasury of good memories of her parents for Janet, but each memory of her father is tinged with revulsion, fear, and rage that envelop even memories of her mother. She concludes that the wonderful memories are but the tip of an iceberg of hypocrisy and abuse. She accepts that the death of her parents was also relief and rescue for her. That must be why I've always believed my parents were really secretly terrible to me.

Janet carries each sleeping child to their bed. When little Janet wakes, she wants her mother to pray with her. Janet listens to the prayer.

Janet and Desiree talk, heart to heart, by the fire. Janet admits that though she never wanted to remember her parents or find out anything about them, now she feels both a deep hunger to get to know them and a confusing mixture of fear and anger. A seed of suspicion that her aunt and uncle duped her about her parents was somehow planted in her soul. She talks openly about her Aunt Helena and Uncle Frank for the first time. Desiree's reactions to tales of how they treated her and the things they did to shape her validate Janet's secret misgivings that they had used her. Indeed, Janet concludes that they, their friends, and that woman ("My Mistress and Mentor") and her sons who took over for them when they died, had all badly used her.

Desiree grows sleepy and explains how to turn the couch into a bed. She apologizes that Janet would have to sleep in the den by the fire. She explains that the dog would sleep right next to her, unless she discourages it. Janet wants to put Desiree at ease, another first, by telling her she appreciates the privilege of sleeping by the fire with a dog pressed up against her. Janet muses that before Cassie, she would never have tolerated a dog anywhere near her.

Janet Is Energized

Janet is energized far too much to sleep. She grabs the iPad and logs into her e-mail. She opens Francine's e-mail about suggested readings, readings she mostly avoided. She follows the links, downloading several to her account. Fatigue, a desire to surf her favorite sites, and a temptation to just enjoy the fire, dog, and the view of lightly falling snow out the window hit her with a vengeance. Nevertheless, somehow she forges on. She reads rapidly with increasing intrigue for about three hours. She finishes two books and numerous articles.

As she gets up to take a break, the dog, pressed close to her side, grunts. She attacks the dog, Maye, vigorously kneading her coat and muscles with her strong hands. Maye looks at her with adoration and delight.

Janet puts on Maye's leash and wanders out to the backyard. The snowflakes, each larger than a ping-pong ball, lightly drift to the ground or hit her face with a cool wet kiss from nature. The trees and lawn are lightly covered with pure white snow shining in the light of the full moon, which is looming large and low in a crystal clear quarter of the sky. Before today, she would have worshipped (though she would not have called it such) nature or the Life Force at the sight of such an awe-inspiring spectacle. The readings had begun to disinfect her soul from such nonsense.

There is something good, very good, behind all this and the events of the day, the past weeks, and the dreams.

She focuses on the moon and stars in the clear portion of the sky. As she takes it in, she experiences a satisfying hunger for something. That hunger itself somehow ennobles her, invites her out of herself. She sees a shooting star, spectacular in its magnitude and duration.

Maye, snapping at and catching the large snowflakes in her mouth, nudges Janet and shakes her coat wet with melted snow. Janet is chilled and wet and needs to go in. She dries herself and the dog off, fixes herself some hot Sleepytime tea, and looks at the e-mail from Francine again. She wants to read something a bit lighter before going to sleep. She puts another log on the fire.

Janet notices that Francine wrote to encourage her to seek the origin, meaning, and destiny of things she read and experienced. Francine wrote: "Guilt especially doesn't exist for itself but is intended to prod us to turn from something, to something wholly other, to turn away from self, not on self. To turn to something that transcends self, guilt, and even fear." Janet thinks she experienced the wisdom of that several times in the last hours.

Janet is drawn to a smiley face by one of the suggested readings: *The Screwtape Letters* by C. S. Lewis. It seems like light reading. As she reads, at first she finds the premise preposterous, that a human, that she herself, might be a battleground for beings greater than her. As she reads on, the premise becomes plausible and too personal. As she is about to begin the eighth letter, she succumbs finally to fatigue and falls asleep.

The dawning sun wakes Janet with its glistening reflection of reds off the snow. The snow looks bloodstained or as if it is on fire. Only a few embers remain, and the room is cold. She stokes the fire—it returns the favor by warming her. She reads again for about two hours from the serious reading material. She looks forward to sparring with Francine on several points.

Though eating together with this family is a delight for Janet, having responsibility for a meal and clean up requires a victory over her conditioning and engrained habits. It is a wee bit easier, unnoticeably so for Janet. That it simply has to be done and she is the one best able in the current circumstances to do it is what makes it happen.

The drive is delightful. There are patches of snow in the shadows and on some trees. Janet asks Desiree how they decided to attend that particular community of faith. Desiree explains that her cousin serves there, and "he does the services in ASL, American Sign Language for the deaf. David and I agreed that we want the children to learn ASL, and Gerald, my cousin, does a really good job of encouraging and challenging us to live out our faith. His wife, Stephanie, is a delightful woman who is also deaf and from the Cameroon, so she adds to the diverse flavor of the congregation."

Janet, whose emotions are waning from fatigue, is slightly intrigued. She exclaims, "My twin brother was deaf, so I learned ASL. My aunt and uncle tried to make me give it up once my brother left, but I rebelled despite their punishments. It was hard keeping it up secretly without anyone to talk to." They pull into a high school parking lot. "But I did it because it was the only link I still had with my brother, with any of my real family."

This is new information to Janet. She never realized why she was determined to retain ASL despite punishment from her aunt and uncle. Also, she learns she doesn't consider Helena and Frank part of her real family.

They eagerly rush in. Janet watches them dash into the building and realizes that she doesn't know what time to pick them up. She pulls out her phone to text Desiree, but her phone is dead. She wants to explore various things she has been reading, so she decides to wait there and read on the iPad. She notices people going in, listens in to some greetings and conversations in ASL, and is drawn to those people by that broken link with her brother.

Janet turns on the iPad and explores, reads, and composes questions and reflections. She seems lighter, less oppressed and obsessed with herself. She doesn't know that her handlers are muted by intense prayers for her. She feels chilly and is about to start the car to warm up when she notices the gas is low, so she decides not to. After a while, she goes into the building to warm up and continue her reading.

As Janet enters the building, she sees a young woman carrying a crying infant. She recognizes the woman and, overcome by sudden excitement and surprise, cries out, "Frieda!" As Frieda turns and walks toward her, Janet fills with misgivings that Frieda might recognize her. Frieda is a runaway teen on whom Janet experimented. Frieda walks towards her only half-attentive to Janet; she is taking care of her son.

"Do I know you?" Frieda asks.

"I guess not," Janet responds as she feels a wave of relief.

"Then how do you know me?" Frieda asks.

Janet took her from the streets for experiments and held her captive for a few weeks. Frieda had been a fifteen-year-old pregnant girl who had run from her parents due to their reaction to her pregnancy. Janet decides to tell a bit of the truth.

"I met you when you were living on the streets and being ill-used," Janet explains.

Frieda interrupts her, blurting out an enthusiastic "Thank you, thank you! You must have helped me…and my son somehow! I was so angry I didn't care about myself at all, or even my son."

Janet feels uncomfortable being credited with doing good. "I did nothing to help you," Janet replies.

Frieda looks intently at Janet, and Janet feels discomfort and fear of exposure begins to grow. "I'm sure you did," Frieda states with confidence. "You somehow reminded me that Mary the mother of Jesus was also an unmarried pregnant teen who was badly misunderstood and harshly judged. How you were able to get through my rage and guilt, I can't imagine. Thanks so much!" Her certainty almost convinces Janet. It confuses her profoundly.

Frieda weeps tears of joy. Janet weeps also from a sense of awe that, perhaps, the evil she did had been turned to good. "Visit with me while I feed Joshua," Frieda invites. Janet lacks the will or power to resist.

They sit together at a table with refreshments. Frieda breastfeeds Joshua, while Janet prepares them both a hot drink. Janet is humbled by this privilege to serve someone she wronged. The memory of wiping mud from Alice's shoes comes to mind. Janet, humbled by the wrong she did, and even more so that good rather than harm somehow came from it—these things and the delights of Frieda and Joshua—put Janet into a receptive mode.

Janet Finds Out

Janet finds out that Frieda went back to her parents but was rejected by them. Her parents, especially her father, pressured her to get an abortion purportedly for her protection, but it proved that it was to protect their interests (an appointment to a plum overseas assignment) and reputation. Sixteen and pregnant, Frieda had argued for her emancipation before a judge. Her parents readily agreed that she was out of control. She lined up a family in this group of followers for a place to live while she finishes high school. Other families pitched in, promising to help her get through college and on her feet. Frieda graduates in one and a half years. They were now her family. They love and accept her.

Faith in Jesus comes up. Janet admits that she doesn't believe "any of that r- stuff." She almost says "rot" because that is her reaction to Jesus, though less and less is it based on rational objections than on habit, anger, and avoidance. Two days before, she would not be considerate to anyone, unless there was a payoff for her, especially about their faith. Frieda explains that she learned disbelief from her parents because they observed the Christian religion but did not follow Jesus. It was while living on the streets that she began to have faith in Jesus and "I'm sure you are partially to thank for that." Janet disagrees, still vehemently within, but says nothing. Frieda reads her well and comments, "I know you don't believe in Jesus or that you helped me, but you'll understand later."

Frieda explains that faith is only partly a matter of being rationally convinced about things. "For me, it is mainly about trusting Jesus and following him." She explains that following Jesus is reordering how she lives by changing her thinking and doing, by learning new emotional responses and to partner with God to reshape her will. "The leaders here especially emphasizes that we have to depend on God and each other," she concludes.

Janet is silent, her heart more opened up by this chance meeting and conversation than by all the reading. She cares for Frieda and Joshua and decides to fund education for both of them. They converse further and exchange phone numbers and e-mail addresses. Janet has mixed views about the softening of her heart.

Minutes later, Desiree and the kids find Janet and Frieda talking and laughing. Janet grows more eager to pick up Francine. Janet drives them back, fixes lunch with less trouble, cleans up the kitchen, and says her affectionate good-byes.

She uses Desiree's phone to call Francine and get directions, and then she picks her up. Her handlers, fearing a defeat and its consequences, prepare their assault, biding their time until they can exploit one of their robust footholds in Janet.

The rest of the day flies by with Janet and Francine talking and visiting, laughing and arguing, and enjoying each other's company. Janet is awkward about having a guest overnight because she has never done so before. Still haunted by fears, she is glad to have the company of a friend. They turn down the heat overnight and sleep by a fire in the den. Janet wants to be together; she especially doesn't want to be alone in her complex.

Monday and Tuesday, they talk and take lengthy drives through the Shenandoah together. Francine needs frequent rests. While Francine rests, Janet drives, soaking up the beauty and wonder of the fall foliage. New intensities of emotions are experienced as the momentum of freedom builds, and she drinks in the wonders of life. Back at the complex, they chat, laugh, and deliberate. Janet is captivated by the stories Francine tells by her recounting lectures of scholars she listened to. Francine insists that they discuss the Bible or God only when Janet wants to.

Wednesday morning, Janet drops Francine off at a friend's, agreeing to call her before five or six for dinner, and picks up a couple from Dulles who flew in to look for a house. She spends the day showing them numerous houses, and they made an offer on one. Janet is returning to the complex, mentally reviewing the readings and the conversations about God and faith with Francine. She comes to a crisis point. It presses heavily on her. She isn't ready to have further contact with Francine.

Janet, exhausted from the last days, less physically than mentally and emotionally from trying to keep the reality of God from crashing in on her, intends to rest briefly but falls quickly into deep sleep and vivid dreams. Surrounded by indescribable beauties, she twirls around to take them in, or rather to be taken in by them. Her greatest desire in the dreams is to distract herself from the most oppressive reality. She can't. She whirls around to discover to her great delight that she is in The Dress. The sensuous pleasures, the feel of the lively fabric, how it caresses and comforts and invigorates her skin, her nervous system, and all else she dares consider hers are still but a brief distraction. She is a source of beauty now; her every moment, conveyed by the dress as it moves, spreads and magnifies the beauties around her. She spins faster and faster, exponentially increasing the beauties and glories surrounding her, coming from her, in her. Glory explodes. She is center stage—but also unable to avoid the central reality. The Dress itself, because of its wonders and, well, everything about it, bears down heavily on me the deplorable notion that the dress is made by one who would be my Master. It is a gift that I cannot obtain by any means on my own and, therefore, is too costly for me personally but too precious to give up.

Creativity Born of Evasion

Creativity born of evasion flourishes as she seeks desperately to evade, escape, or, at least, ignore the relevance, the vitality of God. She sees it most clearly in Francine but also in Frieda, Desiree, in many of those ridiculous followers, and even in Matt. Anyone who follows is a fool.

She speaks confidently: "Only in my dreams could I ever believe that God exists because he is too good to be real, a mere invention of my desperate desires."

Despite her confident posing, she unconsciously knows it is all idle empty talk. She knows in the depths of her soul with laser charity the real root of her refusal to believe. It erupts in a string of obscenities, profanity, cussing, and finally in barbed complaints aimed at God.

"God, how dare you exist! I want to be the center of the universe, or, at least, the center of my own life. I want total control, or, at least, control of my own destiny. But no!" Dripping with sarcastic rage, she continues to say, "You have to exist. Stop it! How can I shine, how can I be noticed, petted, admired, and worshipped in your noonday brightness? Die already! Die for me and don't come back this time!" She represses it from any conscious awareness.

Several changes occur at once. The beauties and light all around her disappear and are replaced with a foul, sickening odor and a ghastly light. The magnificent dress melts like snow in a furnace. Her naked body, always before a source of great pride for her, develops a rash that rapidly turns into blisters and then boils that are both hideous and painful. Within seconds, her entire body is swollen and bloated. She can't bend her arms or legs. She can't breathe. Panic ensues. She is allergic to herself and needs an immediate injection of the life of God or of the dominating demons. She chooses—I choose the demons I know because I can, at least, delude myself that they, at least, allow me to stay in control.

The attack passes, and I again worship my body and myself. I am entranced, and I worshipped my image. I awake and tear off my clothes. Determination seizes me. All contact with those foolish followers will be harshly and violently rejected. I will block electronic contact and will punish severely personal contact. Since they appear immune to magic, I prepare a spray with chemicals and a virus that induces a more lasting and far more painful version of shingles.

I cannot take my eyes off of myself. I contemplate only myself. I clearly see the King of the Dragon in me. He and I are one. I am firmly in control. I give myself fully and freely without reservation. My power and beauty soar. A final tear moistens her eye…then dryness.

I am awake and alive to myself. All is well. My memory is rebooted. I am single-minded, focused fully on my power. The beauty of my body is fully bared, clearly revealed. I saunter down the hall toward the kitchen. My servants are all awestruck by my raw unimpeded beauty.

I complete my preparations to sever contact with those worthless followers. I reluctantly contemplate getting dressed. I defer, deciding instead to display my incredible beauty. A desire erupts to show off my beauty and power. Following the desire, I decide to run in a busy park.

I drive my 911 with the top down—though chilled, I manipulate the Life Force so that I am hot—and luxuriate in the many stares. At the park, I create a magnificent spectacle. Several officers converge on the park and on me. This must be the best assignment they'll ever have. I am running at full speed with earbuds in my ear and pretend I don't notice their attempts to stop me. Finally, six out-of-breath officers intercept my path and surround me. I dazzle them with my beauty and befuddle them with my powers; they apologize for wasting my time.

I return to my complex to see two of those women and two children whom I once foolishly thought of as friends. One woman pushes the other in a wheelchair. They ignored my warnings to stay away—they, not I, are responsible for what happens to them.

Seized by a wicked determination, I park in the garage, running in to get my special spray. I then run through the house, bursting through the front door while they approach it, and assail them, straying the adults thoroughly. The children, foolishly loyal to their mother, attack me, so I also spray them. They are gasping, writhing in agony, crying, and moaning. I tell them, "How dare you ignore my warnings! Stay away or something far worse will happen!"

Thoughts flow, *Now we'll see how helpful their odious faith is! We'll see how understanding they are when they are suffering. They won't*—but the thoughts are interrupted by something that neither Janet nor her handlers are prepared for.

First, Francine, though in agony and gasping, cries out, "Abba Father, help Janet!" The others also pray for Janet. Matt bawls out, "God, save Janet from herself!" They are still gasping, crying, moaning, and writhing, but they are not the ones in the deepest agony.

Janet's deep crisis, just shy of the supreme one, engulfs her as she is shocked by their responses. She hurls herself into a pit of shame for her actions, her self-delusion, her willful deception of herself, her denial of all the realities—which, for the moment when she is split open, are so obviously clear—her obstinate denial of reality himself. For this brief moment, she is freed from the decades of conditioning. She is able to decide between self-deification and self-denial, or more fundamentally between demons and deity, or a first baby step—whether or not she will admit that God exists.

Janet's window of freedom closes swiftly. Defenses are repaired, and a counteroffensive is launched. The counterattacks are numerous, rapid, varied, and, on many levels, conscious and unconscious; Janet is overwhelmed. All she admits in that instant is that maybe God does exist.

What seemed an eternity of crises and opportunity in the realm of reason and the will, mighty and momentous for Janet, is only seconds in the suffering of those thrashing about before her. Janet turns her attention to relieving their suffering. She wants to use magic to help them but has no helpful magic for them. She summons her staff to help and would have called 9-1-1, except that Francine forbids it.

Someone tosses her a T-shirt and oversized overalls left by her new gardener, a giant of a man. Janet slips them on. She looks ridiculous in them; they swallow her up. She crisscrosses the straps to keep them from slipping off her shoulders and rolls up the pant legs. Thoughts of herself or her appearance find no room in her because of her concern for others.

Janet Apologizes

Janet apologizes profusely and repeatedly; she is genuinely sorry for the suffering she caused. For twenty years, regrets for her actions are for the troubles she caused herself. She is unable to believe their assurances of forgiveness. Her aunt and uncle drummed it into her that forgiveness is nonsensical and impossible. They reinforced it by granting forgiveness coupled with reminders, punishments, and lectures that made a lie of forgiveness. They fed her shame and guilt, her grandiose sense of power, and shut off all escapes but her own desire for control. They planted a desire to inflict such forgiveness on others to gain the upper hand. They made forgiveness a ploy and trained her to be a bully. There was also constant emotional blackmail. Accepting forgiveness from anyone, or, even more so, from herself, was impossible. She politely thanks them for forgiveness she knows they can't give; the duplicity strengthens the control of her handlers.

But seeds of healing are also sown. In the following weeks, Francine and Desiree nurture those seeds. Though both women are miserable with shingles, they talk to Janet daily. They share laughter and stories, have discussions, meals, and tea together; they offer to study the Bible with her.

Francine, Mary, and Desiree are surprised when Janet accepts their offer one evening over dinner at Desiree's house. It is a ploy by her handlers. Her acceptance is riddled with insurmountable conditions. She agrees to study the Gospel of John with the three of them from the Greek text only. Each person needs a personal copy of John in Greek bound in periwinkle leather with pages six by eight inches with four inches of sixteen point text per line. If they can't start at her complex the next day at two o'clock in the afternoon, then they might start next year, since Thanksgiving is soon. Janet smiles smugly as she graciously accepts their offer to study.

All are surprised when Francine accept. "How well do you know Greek?" Janet challenges with disdain.

"I learned classical Greek eighty years ago," Francine responds. "I've read the New Testament in Greek at least twenty-seven times and read John in Greek twice that."

Janet suddenly respects this surprising woman even more. They all agree, except Desiree who can't make it, to meet at Janet's the next day at two o'clock.

Reading any part of the Bible, especially about Jesus, is what her handlers want to avoid. They fear Francine will make it weighty and significant. They are held in check, groggy, and unable to coordinate their efforts. They try to make Janet sick, depressed, panicky, or obsessed about anything that might make her back out of the dreaded study. They can't even disturb her sleep.

Janet awakes refreshed by a solid night's sleep. After breakfast, she finds an e-mail from Francine asking if Janet wants an introduction to the Gospel of John before starting. A deep-seated desire to complicate things and a willful determination to be a nuisance prompt her to write a demanding reply for an introduction to the Gospel of John. The introduction must be in Greek and contain both a general outline and its themes. The final demand that the bound copies include this introduction before the study begins is made to postpone the study that somehow terrifies her. It makes no sense to me to make these demands, to avoid so strenuously a simple reading of fantasy literature with friends. I battle against sending the e-mail. I win my battle and did not send the e-mail but can't bring myself to delete my carefully scripted demand.

After lunch, I check e-mail and, moved by my sense of privilege, send that e-mail. The time is 12:54 p.m. There can't be time to satisfy my demands. I expect Francine to plead and beg, and I relish the prospect of wielding power over her.

As two in the afternoon draws nearer, I become apprehensive that I hadn't heard from Francine. I frantically check my e-mail, my cell, my voice mail, and then all three again.

She abandoned you! She never cared about anything
except dragging you into her odious superstition!
This is the final indignity, the ultimate wound!
She claims to follow that crucified idiot and doesn't have the courtesy to even…

Janet is caught up in both the rage of rejection and her desperate hope that as she fretfully watches the driveway, tears stream down her face. As the unconscious depths of her soul grasps that, her raging despair is about to consummate in a loss of control of herself. But then she sees Mary's car coming up the driveway. *Francine must not have gotten the e-mail!* she thinks with relief as she spots Mary's and Francine's faces.

It's not your fault she didn't get it. Tell her you won't read with her since she didn't meet your requirements. She asked if you want an introduction and then ignores your response! She only asked to manipulate, she's phony, selfish…

Ludicrous, Janet thinks. *Francine is the most real person I've met.* She walks out to greet two genuine friends. She helps with the wheelchair and Francine's transfer to it. As she pushes Francine, Janet mentions, "You must not have gotten my e-mail."

"Oh," Francine replies, "I did."

"What?" Janet snaps, her jaw and cheeks tense and she over-articulates each word with rising rage at being ignored. "Then why didn't you—"

Francine interrupts her tirade, saying, "If you don't want to read, I will not manipulate you. That would show a distrust of God. What do you"—she paused for emphasis—"really want?"

Janet sees that Francine is being agreeable and reasonable, but she tries to pick a fight. "What do I want?" Janet responds with anger. "I want to be taken seriously. I will not be ignored or treated like a child!" The crescendo of her voice culminates in a yell. She is raging mad and out of control. They counted on a like response from Francine to escalate anger and increase loss of self-control by Janet.

Francine lowers her voice. "You can yell and be mad. I still love you and am your friend." Her calm response invites Janet back to sanity. Her next statements pique Janet's curiosity, completing the coup d'état that puts Janet back in control. Francine's states, "Your condition are met by the prologue of the Gospel of John an—"

Janet bursts in, "How did you know to write a prologue?"

"I didn't," Francine admits. Janet's confusion and interest increase and strengthen her control. She is put in a receptive mode by her sincere desire to fathom this puzzle.

"Please explain," Janet requests.

Francine explains that the prologue is a brief portion at the beginning that wonderfully satisfies Janet's request for a general outline and statement of the themes. "I was so shocked when I read your reply and realized that what you intended as a barrier is no barrier at all, unless you want to quibble about it," Francine concludes.

Janet is hushed and pensive. "We still don't have to read now if you don't want to," Francine repeats. The assurance of her freedom completes the captivation of her interest and undermines the forces of resistance.

I WANT

"I want to see for myself," Janet finally declares.

"Here is your copy," Francine says as she offers the thin periwinkle book to Janet. Written on the front in gold letters in Greek is, "THE GOSPEL OF JOHN," and further down, "FOR JANET STUBBS." The leather was soft, supple, and sturdy. The book is about one-quarter inch thick and easily flexes in Janet's hand. She sniffs the leather—the scent adds to the delight of her senses. She is tempted to fixate on these pleasures when Francine prompts her, "Open it." Janet flips to the last page—page ninety-one. The first word on the page is λόγος, which means "word," and the last is βιβλία, which means "book." She turns to the beginning. After the title page is "Notes for the Reader."

She reads aloud: "The first eighteen verses of the Gospel of John are called the Prologue. It primes the reader with the themes and provides a doubly stated (verses one to thirteen, fourteen to eighteen) general outline." She scans the themes: ζωή (life), φῶς (light), σάρξ (flesh, body), κόσμος (world), ἀλήθεια (truth in the sense of reality), and δόξα (glory, but also expressed thrice as ὑψόω (lifted up) and other notes about reading the Gospel of John. One catches her attention: "In my opinion, whenever Jesus says ἐγώ εἰμι—'I am' in this Gospel—he is saying the name of God 'I am' and that he is God."

Janet turns to the start of the actual text—'Εν ἀρχη'—"In the beginning…" She reads, transfixed and mesmerized by the recent events and yet another attempt to prevent her engaging her heart and soul with reality. Francine interrupts and breaks the spell.

"Janet!" she calls. Janet comes to her senses and gets Francine hot tea to warm and clear her throat. Janet joins Francine with her own cup of tea. Mary has water. The silver teapot is by Francine.

Francine begins with a prayer for open and loving hearts. Long before, Janet accepted Francine praying out of respect for her, though she is still put off by prayer otherwise. Janet enjoys hearing Francine pray—there's depth, peace, and a sense of a greater reality in Francine's prayers. They talk, Janet reads the Prologue aloud, and then they discuss it. Janet observes that the Greek is "baby Greek."

Francine responds, "Yes, it is the simplest Greek in the New Testament, which is in the Greek of commoners. The simple conveys a profound, intricate depth."

After discussion, Francine reads the Prologue aloud (somehow it sounds better, more expressive when Francine reads it than when Janet did) and challenges Janet to read the rest, if possible, in one sitting.

Francine and Mary leave after an hour. Janet is alone with no plans. Usually, she would be drawn into the Life Force or some unsavory activity to fill her void. But, instead of a void, a fullness of anticipation lifts her spirits. She decides to read a bit more. She intends to do a quick cursory reading for a few minutes, but she soon forgets everything as she is drawn deeply into the simple wonders of Jesus. She starts again at the beginning, reading slowly and thoughtfully. Her reading, always out loud, becomes more and more attentive and reflective so that by the time she reads about the Samaritan woman, her heart and soul deeply contemplate it. She refills her teacup without breaking from her reading; her occasional sips of tea are her only breaks. She wants to keep reading; other desires wilt in the light of him who looms real, tangible, and momentous to her in those words. When her phone rings, she glances at the caller ID and continues her reading.

She plunges into a depth that carries her to unimagined heights. Life and light replace death and darkness within her. The grip of her worldly nature is broken by the reality of the glory that gleams and burnishes through Jesus. Her former desperate attempts to satisfy her thirst for knowledge and power are like drinking seawater; now, the mere desire to know Jesus and to love by emptying herself of herself fills her.

She finishes with her reading and with herself. Janet calls Francine and exclaims, "I want to take the plunge into Jesus!"

A while later, Janet rides with Desiree and Francine to John's house, which has an indoor pool. It begins to lightly snow as the sky in the west turned a rich red when they arrive at John's. A crowd is already gathered. Little Janet and Matt hug her. Others welcome, congratulate, and commend her, patting her on the back. Mary embraces and holds her. Frieda hugs her tight.

Desiree's cousin Gerald and his family are there as well as many deaf followers of Jesus. Gerald speaks to her as he signs, "I understand you want to be plunged into Jesus."

Janet is silent as she nods and signs, "Yes!" She is too choked up to speak.

"Great! Unless you prefer someone else, I'll go into the water and plunge you 'to your death' with Jesus so you can rise to life with him," he continues.

"Could Francine do it?"

Gerald looks for Francine to ask her if she is up to it. Francine replies, "The water will support me, but I'll need someone to help me." Mary and Desiree volunteer.

The four women wade into the water as about fifty people surrounding the pool sing; the room fills with music and expressive signing. Janet signs as she speaks, confessing her faith in Jesus and that she wants to follow him. Then Francine plunges her into a watery grave with Jesus and raises her back up to live with Jesus. The four women hug and cry together. Then they all burst into song.

Within a few minutes, Janet is hugged and congratulated more times than in the previous twenty years, and even kissed kindheartedly a few times. She dries off and changes. Soon, food appears, and mirth, merriment, singing, eating, and conversations ensue. Many prayers are said for Janet at her request as she confesses that she is addicted to sex, power, and herself.

Soon, Janet is on the way to spend the night at Francine's after picking up one of her cars. Snow lightly drifts down, and a white blanket of snow makes the world look clean and white to Janet. It is. They and some others visit, and, after the others leave, Janet and Francine continue to pray and talk past midnight. Janet wants to know how to pray, and Francine encourages her to talk openly with God and gives her some practical pointers. Francine urges her to reflect and write about her new birth and heads to bed. Janet snuggles herself in her coat and some blankets and takes a cup of hot tea out on the porch to watch the snow drifting down in the stillness of the night. She watches and worships without words. Joy, wonder, and calm settle her soul. Janet logs on to her private journal to write.

Power Corrupted

Power corrupted me, all but destroyed me, enslaving me. Pursuing power emptied me of myself, my humanity, I sank into the quicksand of animality, ever more subject to cause and effect, ever more determined by events and powers external to myself, bit by bit frittering away my freedom and privilege as a person. Even my desires became less and less mine, they were merely played like a child's cheap toy. Instead of filling me, they addicted me to the perpetual pursuit of power and pleasure.

An image flashes through my mind. Exactly! I was like a child on a merry-go-round obsessed with getting the one brass ring to trade in for another ride. My obsession obliterated the joy of music and movement, the decorative colors, the wind, and the wonder of riding a gilded horse or a glowing unicorn. Straining to grab the ring, I was frustrated when I missed it, dismayed when I grabbed a cheap plastic one. Rarely did I get the brass ring, about every tenth time. Then I had a brief thrill followed by the futility of the rest of the ride, which now had no meaning, no more reward. I paid dearly to ride around and around, going nowhere.

Ah, but now! A different perception fills her. Submitting to the pursuing and conquering love; the love that pursues and conquers restores her humanity, fills her with freedom and joy, reestablishes her privileges as a person, and grants her a shining and serving self. A new image captivates her, elevating her above and out of herself. She soars. There is grace, elegance, poetry in motion, a symphony, and pleasures exceeding sensuality in the way she winds her way through the world. She glides through lush green valleys, ascending the peaks of mountains filled with grandeur, plunging into the hidden beauties of the ocean's floor—surrounded all the while with the explosive brilliant colors of fireworks, the rich palette of colors from the most skilled of artists.

My thoughts, my emotional responses, every trained and established habit, each perverse desire, and the full force of my will resisted. But the empowering and creative love, which loved the universe, and even me, into existence, and which retained wondrous plans for me even when I dove into a black hole of self abandoned to an unbridled pursuit of power and to desiring to be god for myself and others, had conquered to rescue and redeem me. That conquering love, liberating me from my solitary confinement in myself, gradually ended resistance.

Part 3

Awakening

Awakening to Living

Awakening to living in daily life fills the next days with wonders and joys. She spends time with other followers, and especially with Francine, Mary, Desiree, and Frieda who now holds special interest. Frieda changed radically, though her parents and circumstances did not.

The morning after taking the plunge, Janet and Francine eat a late breakfast before Janet goes to get a Bible for herself. She refused to have one before.

Janet savors the drive in the fall colors still magnificent past their peak, driving while worshipping God for the freely given beauty. Fog and shadows on the hills hint of majesty that awes her. She is waiting when John Lloyd arrives. He greets her but doesn't recognize her.

"Mr. Lloyd, I'm a new Christian and need a Bible," she says.

"Congratulations!" he says with joy. His face looks puzzled; he asks, "Have we met?"

"Years ago, and a few weeks ago at a conference," Janet replies. She relishes watching him trying to place her; she watches as his suspense turns into hope, then into an eruption of joy.

"Janet? Is it really you?" He howls and cries out, "Gail! It's Janet Stubbs here and…our prayers are answered." He hugs her off her feet and twirls her around. Gail rushes up to her and hugs her too. Janet, overcome by their reaction, sheds tears of joy. They insist she call them John and Gail.

Other customers are entering now. John tends to them, while Gail and Janet walk to the bathroom to freshen up. Janet answers Gail's questions. She's reluctant to give details without time to explain the entire story. They agree—Janet will come Friday afternoon for an extended visit, dinner, and an overnight stay. Janet unwittingly agrees to another break in her imposed isolation.

The store buzzes with customers; Janet waits for John to have a few free minutes to help her pick a Bible. "I want a good translation," she says. "And I also want a Greek version." She explains that her uncle tutored her for years in Latin and Classical Greek, steering her from, as he disparagingly referred to it, the vulgar Greek of the Bible.

John leads her to an immense computer screen. He sets it up with twelve English translations on the screen, along with the Greek Old Testament and New Testament. He suggests she browse the translations to decide which one she wants. The Greek and the translations are synchronized to show the same verses. She starts at the beginning and flips through a few pages, delighted that she can still memorize each page. After ten pages, she stops, concerned that she may be using magic and letting the demons return. She prays, and, then remembering that she memorized books at a glance before her parents died, she realizes no magic is involved. She scans the text. For the next five hours, with breaks to visit with John and Gail and a delightful lunch break, she scans the entire Bible into her memory.

He, her eventual lunch partner, walks in during a rest she gives her eyes. Seeing Greek on the screen, he asks, "Do you know Greek?"

"Only classical," she replies flatly. "My uncle and aunt kept me away from God stuff. Yesterday, faith caught me. I never wanted anything to do with God before, I hated him," Janet explains. Then realizing she said too much, she feels self-conscious.

"Great, wonderful, congratulations!" he says, observing her mood. "Anything I can do for you?" he asks.

"No, I'm okay," she replies. But something is amiss, her emotions are raw, down; she feels lonely, tired, and hungry. She says, "I need to break for lunch. Know where there's good Chinese food?"

"Sure, let me drive you," he says. "I'm Adam."

"I'm Janet," she responds. "Hey...are you trying to pick me up?"

"Oh, no way, no way," he denies. "On a scale of one to ten, you're at least a twelve on an off day. At best, maybe I'm a seven—nah, a six. You're wearing designer clothes—expensive, stylish. I shop at Goodwill, Walmart, so no—"

Taken back by his bluntness, Janet interrupts, "Your grasp of reality is refreshing and endearing. Are you safe?"

He states, "The Lloyds can vouch that I'm safe. I don't have tons of time, I've got my first lecture this afternoon. A professor had a heart attack, so I got the job suddenly. There aren't many jobs for philologists." The Lloyds vouch for him and, after he declines to drive her car, they are on their way in his old Corolla.

"How old is this car anyway?" she asks.

"Over twenty years," he responds. "It's one of the last cars with roll-down windows, standard transmission, and power nothing. It's basic. It works, and it's paid for—cheap and easy to keep running."

"Oh," she interjects. "Wasn't 2013 the last year crank windows were an option on Corollas?"

"I don't know about that," he responds haltingly. "But it is a 2013. How'd you guess?"

"I read it one time."

He shakes his head, chuckles, and asks, "Do you remember—everything you read?"

"Yes," she sighs. "And everything I hear, see, taste, experience—even things I'd give anything to be able to forget."

"Oh," he said flatly, unable to think of a response to her pain, that kind of pain.

While Adam drives, she comments, "My mother and uncle were philologists. Do you have a special interest?"

He replies, "Yeah, but I doubt you'd understand."

Irritated, Janet retorts, "Don't presume what I understand. I have diverse inter—"

"Well then," he says with sarcasm, "I focus on linguistic roots of language. Hardly anyone thinks or care…"

Janet grins and says, "Oh, like, perhaps the primacy of the verb? Are you interested in arch-language?"

"Well, yes—but—no, the verb isn't primary," he states. "And, yes, I'm interested in early languages. Do you know anything about them?" Both enjoy the verbal sparring, though neither admits it. A heated argument, eminently satisfying to both, gratifying reason and curiosity, begins and continues unabated through their drive to the restaurant, the meal, and the drive back.

Janet gradually wins Adam over to the primacy of the verb. His excitement at this distracts him from driving, almost causing two accidents, and he loses track of time. He is twelve minutes late to his own first lecture.

Her arguments touch on how an infant learns language, how languages devolve, especially with verbs (ancient Greek verb forms do more than English ones), rather than evolve to more complex and powerful forms of verb, and that language enables people to act and interact. Words, especially verbs, do things. Some nouns imply doing, say, a hunter hunts, a shelter shelters.

Janet views humans as beings who act. She is new to faith and its theology and grammar. Adam supplements her understanding of the Bible beginning with God acting—creating—and that God's name is a verb: "I am whom I am."

Both are energized by the conversation. Adam rushes to teach his class, Janet returns to scan the rest of the Bible. She buys the computer program with the multiple versions and print versions of a Greek New Testament, an English Bible, and several other books he recommends. After agreeing to a time on Friday to return, she leaves.

Janet Experiences Life

Janet experiences life without magical powers and the constant sway of beings within. Fatigue and moods come more often and readily. Depending on magic for years, she hadn't developed adaptive ways to deal with moods and the ups and downs of life. She had no healthy relationships, no friends until recently. Gradually, as God withdraws from her awareness, allowing her to experience loneliness and to come under attack from the spiritual forces on this world, she experiences far more than the normal ups and downs. God intends to strengthen and reform her.

Fortunately, by God's grace, Janet realizes her need to depend on God, others, and the Spirit's help. The help comes less "supernaturally" and more often in her prayers, reading, and following Jesus. God has a foothold in her soul and spreads his lightening and leavening effects to her daily life. He prepares her for the gathering storm.

Adam teaches his first class, all the while distracted by his time with Janet. After class, he plunges into research. He spends most of his available time the next years researching, writing, and debating others in the field. When he publishes articles about the preeminence of the verb, he becomes well-known (and controversial) in the academic community of philologists, although still unknown to most.

As Scriptures sink in, Janet is convicted to put her riches to better use. She recalls Jesus and Zacchaeus; he gives away half of everything he owned and restores four times anything he defrauded. She wants to do the same. Calculating her ill-gotten gains, she realizes it's impossible, inflicting a much-needed blow to her pride. To restore what she cheated people out of would take half her worth.

Janet decides to do just that, sell her complex, other properties, and all but one of her cars and donate all but ten percent. She donates almost all of her clothes, since they are too sensual—"Oh! And all my high heels." She talks with Desiree about upscale consignments shops and how she will shop at them.

Her appearance and comfort radically alter. Her face beams welcome and delight, her eyes are animated, her broad smile and beautiful teeth are noticed. Previously, Janet flaunted her cleavage, legs, and figure.

In a few weeks, Janet has buyers for the complex and her other properties, except for the isolated rugged property. Its difficult accessibility and rustic and rugged living conditions require someone willing to forgo comfort and welcoming challenge.

"Adam!" she exclaims. She contacts him. He isn't interested. She convinces him to look at it by telling him she would finance it.

Early Thursday, they meet at a café near the property. Adam drives them in his car. She wore a down coat, and he wore multiple layers due to the bitter cold. He parks by a barn that is part of the property. He brings his backpack.

The trees are devoid of leaves, yet they barely see the cabin due to the thick growth. She hands him a map. He takes it and climbs an oak to survey the property. Janet sees delight bud on his face then wither away in resignation.

"Good piece of property," he states flatly.

"Well," she counters, "it's nearly worthless due to environmental limits. This is the only entry—thick undergrowth and a pond hinder access to the cabin. There are no utilities, just a reliable well. No gas engines are allowed. LP gas can be lugged in for the stove. I want to get rid of it. So—"

Adam interrupts with a slight lilt, "Really?"

"Yeah," she responds, intently watching his face and body language. Janet wants, for some reason, to sell it to him. "What can you pay?" she asks.

He finally responds, "Only about five hundred dollars a month."

"Okay. Five hundred dollars for twenty years. No interest, no bank. You pay taxes, insure it—"

"I'm stealing it," he objects. "I can't—"

She interrupts, "It's not stealing if I want to get rid of it. It's yours if you want it. And"—pausing to reflect—"I think God will somehow reward me."

They Begin the Arduous Journey

They begin the arduous journey. Laboring to fight their way through the thickets, neither notices the steady drop of temperature and thickening clouds. After an hour, a dozen feet of shrubs remain between them and the cabin. A light snow begins. They celebrate together by laughing and patting each other. Janet twirls and brushes against thorns that slip inside her boots.

She barks, "I've got thorns in my boots." She struggles to loosen her boots and remove the thorns. Exasperated by the difficulty and eager to get into the clear, she pushes through the bushes without tightening her boots. Her phone signals. Pulling it out, she shrieks, "Someone's stealing my car!" Distracted, she lurches into the open. She turns her ankles and falls hard on her right arm. The ground gives way, and she falls onto a beam that knocks the wind out of her and then drops her head first into frigid water; Adam watches helplessly.

Seeing Janet headfirst in the water, he pulls a rope from his backpack and secures it to a tree. He jumps in the cistern, pulls her waterlogged coat off, and gets her head above water. She isn't breathing. He drags her up and begins mouth-to-mouth resuscitation. After an eternity to Adam (it was twenty seconds), she coughs and breathes. He sighs with relief and prays. He shouts, "We've got to get out of this frigid wind." He helps her up, but she collapses. She sprained both ankles. Her right arm is injured and useless. He carries her into the cabin; she points at the sky, "Look!" He nods; those are clearly storm clouds. Fear creates a storm in Janet that threatens to sweep all away.

They are in dire straits—freezing, soaked, and the cabin is frigid. Some windows are missing glass. Adam tells her to remove her wet clothes as he lights a fire in the fireplace. Because of her injured arm, he undresses her. He rushes out with a knife and returns with paving stones from the porch to cover the windows.

Adam explores the cabin, sheds his wet clothes, and takes stock. There's well water, no food, and no way to call for help; his cell's soaked, and hers is in the cistern. There's firewood good for an hour—not enough to dry their clothes. Her overcoat and boots are in the cistern. We're both chilled to the bone.

"Does anyone know you're here?" he asks Janet while he puts up a rope and hangs their wet clothes to make a screen between them.

"No," she quivers.

A tsunami of terror sweeps her back to habitual coping. Long-cultivated fears of abandonment, that she wasn't wanted, that she must seize control, drive her. "Hel-lo-o," she says seductively, "check out my ankles."

He resists his urges by replying, "Stick your feet under the clothes." He sees the clothes move, but, instead of her ankles, he sees her naked body slide in view. He shuts his eyes.

Incensed by his avoidance of her, Janet seizes his arm with her left hand and somehow pulls herself onto him pinning his body to the floor with hers. He's tempted by the vision seared into his mind, the situation, her body pressing against him, and his desires. He cries out to God. He struggles against her, underestimating her briefly. She's strong and determined. He wrestles free and secures her hands. Before he succeeds, she scratches his chest and face and punches him. But for her injuries, she would prevail. He ties her hands behind her with her wet jeans.

Adam is bloodied. She struggles and writhes. He dares not look at her, but he dares not watch her closely. She warns, screaming, "Untie me or I'll say you tried to rape me—you'll go to jail. I have men who will beat you to a pulp." Never had he seen anyone so wild.

He peeks outside. Everything is white. Notions flash into his mind. This she-devil insisted he park behind the barn to conceal his car. Had she planned this? No one knows they're here. He wouldn't be missed until late Monday. Images of a terrible blizzard, of dying with this crazed woman, flood his soul. You want her, go ahead because—*No! That's not what God wants!* he hisses to himself.

Janet overhears and fights with a mass of emotion and engrained habits. She isn't strong enough to free herself. She starts to pray but is stopped by a flood of guilt—*You don't deserve help…can't allow it.* Despair defeats her.

"Adam, what got into me?" she shrieks. "I'm so sorry. Look what I did," she exclaims. Tears flow, and she stops trying to get free. Focused on her survival, he remembers there's a shed—with enough wood, they might survive. He pulls out the map to locate it. In the blizzard, he'll need the rope to get back. He sneezes and realizes he needs to use the toilet. In the mirror, he inspects his face and chest. The gouges need to be cleaned. He goes to the kitchen and uses the hand pump to fill a pot to heat over the fire.

He sees that she freed herself. She grabs the fireplace poker and flings it at him; it would have skewered him in the chest if he hadn't blocked it with the pot.

"We have to work together to survive," Adam pleads. "I need to clean these wounds and see if there's anything in the shed. We don't have enough firewood."

She entices him with her voice and body, "If we're going to die, wouldn't it be better if we did so in each other's arms. I'm on the pill." It's a lie—she stopped taking them after she took the plunge, but, in her present mindset, pregnancy is easily cured. The reminder that she plunged into Jesus stirs her to pray. She is drawn from reliance on herself to put her trust in God and that he, not she, is in control.

"I'm out of control. I tried to kill you. God help us! I'll do whatever you say," Janet whimpers. Adam puts the pot on the fire and builds it up to dry his clothes some before he heads for the shed. They sit back-to-back by the fire for warmth until the water is hot to clean his wounds. He stokes the fire, dresses, ties the rope to himself, and heads for the shed. She waits by the fire praying for him.

She worries about Adam in the blizzard in wet clothes. He returns with several logs and a crank radio from the shed. He is severely chilled and shivering, his clothing partly frozen and stiff. He removes his clothes; she can't help due to her injuries. Feeling useless spurs a crisis in her that resolves by her decision to do whatever she can. He drinks hot water, and they share an energy bar. Listening to the radio, they hear that the snowstorm is expected to last through Monday and drop up to six feet of snow in the mountains.

Sitting back-to-back by the fire, they talk. Adam learns a great deal about her. She confesses being trained and conditioned to use the Life Force. She's confused; Helena and Frank were wicked but sacrificed their lives for her. She knows the Life Force is magic and entangled her with malevolent beings, yet she has no discomfort about magic or them. She is committed to avoiding magic and the demons, but they are as relevant to her as distant galaxies are to most of us.

"You got comfortable with them. It's how you lived for twenty years," he suggests. "This is out of my league. You'll need—I...I don't know. Wow—I can't imagine." He doesn't want to be involved—she's knotty and messy. The warmth and comfort by the fire, the tender pleasures of sitting back-to-back, naked and unashamed, freed of posturing and the tyranny of impressions, plant good seeds in her soul. Reality takes root and slowly grows in her.

He ices her arm to relieve the pain. He makes crutches for her, ices her ankles, and wraps them. When her clothes dry, she puts them on. Every few hours, Adam repeats the ordeal to get firewood. His clothes dry, but he is exhausted. He barely makes it back his fourth trip. It's colder, the snow is three-feet deep, and there are drifts. He hangs his outer layers by the fire to dry them. Shivering, he collapses by the fire and falls asleep. She notices him shivering. He's on his back with his head supported by his backpack. She spreads her body on top of him to warm him, supporting her weight on her left elbow to not burden him. His shivering stops, and his sleep becomes more restful. She eases off him before he awakes.

She explores using the flashlight and crutches. A hollow sound when the crutches tapped it cues her that there is a trapdoor under a throw rug in the kitchen. She discovers a cellar with jars and cans—honey, jams, vegetables, and soups. Dates on the jars are recent, just before the former owner died. She samples a jam. "Oh," she sighs with pleasure. She returns upstairs with a jar.

She tells him about the food. He brings it up. Rationing out the food to last several days, he pulls out a mess kit.

They Feast

They feast on soup, honey, jam, and vegetables sealed in Mason jars after a grateful prayer of thanks. Their spirits are buoyant. Warmed and refreshed and with provisions, relief of fear carries them to a summit of delight.

They delight in honest, deep conversation. Dropping pretenses, she is richly rewarded with warm acceptance. She describes her training, the dreams God sent, her plan to seduce Eric, her futile use of magic on him, and how she attacked him and knocked herself out. She laughs at herself and her naivety. She relates the dream with Cassie and cats and how her hatred and experiments on animals ceased. He comments that it reminds him of the Materialistic Magician from *The Screwtape Letters*. They discuss it, and she discovers she got tired just before she read that part. She wonders if her fatigue was their doing.

Janet already told most of it to Francine, but now she comes clean completely. The howl of the blizzard, the calm and relief by the fire, and the hours of nothing to do contribute to her unfolding herself to Adam.

"I was guilty of using people—teen runaways for experiments in time travel," she declares. "God benevolently trumped my evil intents, they benefited. I met one of them—Frieda. She was...

different—transformed. I'd love to know what God did for her," she says, reveling in how God redeemed her, and even her evil.

A strong gust of wind shakes the cabin; the door flies open, hits the wall, and bounces back to be driven open by the wind again. Cold and snow blow in. The view is striking—pure white and unspoiled snow adoring the branches of the trees, covering everything with a fleecy blanket, and filling the air with light, though it's midnight. Delight overcomes them, and they laugh with joy. They are drawn into the heavenly landscape.

Adam wraps her in his jacket and wraps his arms securely around her to protect her from the cold. With his cheek on hers, he whispers, "The heavens declare God's glory and the sky his handiwork."

They close the door, aglow with wonder and delight. Adam moves the table against the door. Huddled by the fire to recapture warmth, their arms wrap tightly around each other and their noses touch. Delight permeates them. There is no thought, even unconscious, of forbidden fruit.

They warm each other back up, relax, and are silent. The wind dies down. The fire glows quietly. All is still.

Restful sleep swaddles them. Hours later, a chill awakes Adam; the fire had died down. He goes to get the boards of the shelves for firewood. Problem solving is ingrained in him, part of his DNA, his training by his father, and his engineering training. "I'll make a sled and skis!" The wax from the jams would make them guide across the snow.

He takes the shelves apart and reuses the nails to make a sled. He'll use it to get wood from the shed and then to pull Janet. He also makes makeshift skis and poles.

He skis to get wood. He brings back the rest of it on the shed. The blizzard slows, visibility is decent. He explores the upper route. He prays the hill behind the cabin leads to a highway. He doesn't want anything to happen to Janet.

He crisscrosses up the hill to reach the crest. He sees a road they can sled to. He thanks God and skis to the cabin.

They huddle by the fire on Sunday. Janet talks, sorting things out verbally and unburdening herself. He listens attentively, occasionally interjecting a comment. She responds to his obvious interest by talking in greater depth and detail.

The weather forecast is perfect. A warming trend would melt the snow some. A hard overnight freeze would put an icy crust on the snow. The snow would stop at dawn Monday. By midday, the snow would get mushy. Adam figures that if they didn't make it to the top of the hill by early morning, the sled would sink into deep mushy snow. They plan to leave before dawn.

The pre-dawn landscape is breathtaking. The sky is black with a myriad of stars, which seem almost too bright and close. Icicles hang from the cabin and trees looking like diamonds shimmering in the night. The snow is perfect to support the sled and glide over it, and Adam digs the edge of his skis in the snow to aid his assent up the hill. He starts up the hill and pulls the sled up to a tree.

After lugging the shed up to the first tree, they see the first hint of dawn. On completing the second leg, the dawn turns fiery red, and the landscape glows pink. When he hauls the sled to the crest of the hill, he's spent and soaked from his efforts. The snow glistens in the morning light. He smiles from the beauty enveloping them and their success. He planned to ski down but is too exhausted. He aims the sled toward the road, pushes it until gravity takes over, and collapses onto the sled. They're off!

They pick up speed; the wind chills him cruelly. They speed under a wire that would cut a skier. He shivers violently from the fierce wind. He kicks the crude anchor off the back of the sled; they stop ten feet from the road.

Adam sees a truck approaching and jumps up waving his arms. Darkness engulfs him as he collapses onto the snow.

Janet's Broad Smile

Janet's broad smile greets Adam. He's in an ambulance wrapped in blankets and has an IV in his arm. She explains that he is suffering from exhaustion, exposure, infection, and early pneumonia. He tries to sit up, but his effort is in vain—he is strapped down.

"I feel…I'm so thankful we got you out safely," he moans between gasps for breath.

"They'll admit you for a few days. I'll take care of anything insurance doesn't," she promises. She sees he is about to object. She adds, "No, I insist. You saved my life, let me wear your jacket, and I even scratched your face." He is too tired to argue and humble enough to accept her gift.

They arrive at the ER. Braces for her ankles and shoulder further ease her discomfort. Janet implies that they are a couple and stays with him the rest of the day. While he sleeps, she arranges a rental car for her, a tow for his car, and for a delivery of things they need. She notifies the police about the theft of her car and fills out paperwork. Once clothes arrive, she showers and cleans up.

A nurse asks Janet, "How long have you been together?"

The absurdity of the question catches her off guard; she replies incredulously, "Together?" before remembering herself. "Oh," she recovers, "not long, but it's been intense." The lie bothers her, even though her intensions are better for this lie than the myriad of lies she told in her former life. She has begun to grow a conscience.

She stays by his side. When he wakes, she is at his beck and call. Adam asks her to recite parts of the Bible and relishes that he can ask for a Psalm, any chapter, or even just describe a passage "about the peace that passes understanding" or "when God was in the still small voice," and she recites it perfectly. She recites the passages in Greek or any of a dozen English translations. He listens; elation and serenity grace him with their presence. Then he slips into peaceful slumber.

Adam feels better, is in excellent spirits, and treasures their time together. Janet explains that she won't come back, since the closing on the complex is soon and she has to clear out "personal" things. She draws close to him and whispers, "I need to clear out the magical tools and technology—I don't want them to fall into the wrong hands, so I can't hire anyone else to do it."

Her closeness, the smell of her perfume, the sensation of her breath on his ear, and her breasts touching him lightly combine with his exhaustion (and sedation) to spur desire for her to slip out of control. He wants to speak, to act; he wants to ignore the impossibility, the impropriety, the certain rejection. Visions of her bare body in the cabin, of her attempt to seduce him, and the memories of their bodies in contact assault him with desires, regrets, and doubts of his manhood. Even those he withstands. But that first conversation over Chinese food, the thought that she let him in on her secrets, bared her soul to him, and let him inside her soul destroys his last defenses. He admits to himself that he is hopelessly in love with her, painfully pining for any token of her affection. Only with God's help can he break this wild lusty stallion; he gives her a gentle hug. He is spent. She kisses his cheek. It's tortuous pleasure for him. He'll buy the cabin, and she'll arrange it.

He has something more important to say to her than about his feelings for her. Telling her his feelings for her won't help either of them. Telling her this is a truth she needs.

"Janet," he exclaims to secure her attention. "You're making the same mistake I made when I came to faith."

She shifts the focus, "When was that?" She wants to go into details to evade his confrontation.

"When I was converted, I focused on learning more than living. It was easy and natural—it fed pride…it poisoned me," he admits, signaling her to remain quiet. Somehow she obeys. "What does Peter say to add to your faith before knowledge?" he asks.

She wishes she didn't know—it's too real and raw for her. She mumbles, "Virtue…moral excellence…goodness…character," recalling several translations. After a long battle within, she adds, "And I have none."

Janet Is Open

Janet is open about her need for prayers, God's sustaining presence, and help to change. Her appearance changes. Her face shows joy, her gestures are animated instead of scripted, and her expressions of affection are frequent and genuine. She's a giver rather than a manipulative taker.

There is, however, still much darkness in her and little tested virtue. As she clears her computer hard drives she finds data folders named by date. She recognizes the dates as when she sent her victims (tinges of guilt and regret begin to tear her from God and herself) to observe the past. Each trip is recorded in detail. She spots the date of Frieda's trip and skims through the files, amazed by the detail. Frieda's host was Mary the mother of Jesus late in her pregnancy. Frieda experienced Mary being treated as a pariah by her former friends.

She searches for the date she observed Jesus. She feverously opens it and quickly scans it. It distresses her dreadfully. Rage erupts at God for not allowing her to remember her conversion and sparing her suffering and angst.

"Why, O God? I believed. I was eager to obey you. I returned changed, a different person. Are you intent on torturing me? Maybe you're not good at all!" She rages, shouting at the heavens. In her rage, she flings a chair across the room. Her right arm, still recovering, is wracked with pain. She whimpers a demand, "Help me understand!" and bursts into tears from the pain of betrayal that stabs her soul.

Janet struggles. She calls Francine for prayer. Francine invites her to spend the night. She agrees eagerly. "But first, I must deal with things here," she says. "I'll destroy the drives. It can't into fall into the wrong hands. I'll save the files of my trip for later."

Spasms in her right arm results in Janet clicking a different folder and file. Her aunt hosted one of her victims. She sees her aunt and uncle prostrating themselves in abject obeisance before "my mistress" and reporting to her. When they died, Janet had to live with her. Flooded by terrible memories, Janet shudders. The pastor and priest were already dead. Shocked that the pastor and priest were murdered by Helena and Frank, who then committed suicide, she is riveted on every word of her aunt's report. Fear of "my mistress" and terrible memories of prostrating herself in abject obeisance before—shudder—*it* overcomes her. She listens to Helen's report without watching it:

> We prepared her for you to finish her training. She is fearless due to pride and narcissism; no need for courage or virtue. We planted in her unconscious distrust, damning desires, and enslaving narcissism. She loved animals, her parents, and brother. Now she despises them all, fears them; we excluded love and compassion for any creature. Her father had a beard she loved. When we took possession of her, we conditioned her unconscious without her resisting or having any memory by drugging her. For years, Frank put on a beard like her father's and brushed it against her face while molesting her, and I dressed like her mother and watched approvingly. All memories of her parents are infected with those...

Janet shut it off. She threw up until only dry heaves continued. She took a long shower as hot as she could bear and tried to scrub herself clean.

A sense of betrayal rouses: *God allowed this. He can't be trusted, resist him!* She is divided. She is repulsed by *it* and their manipulations. Her reason, will, and emotions are pulverized; she cries out to God. His Spirit helps her. Her unconscious, infected with evil, pursues terror and sabotage. The demons are confident of eventual victory. They have more in reserve.

Blind and deaf, unable to perceive the coming calamity, she prepares to save the folder of her trip to view Jesus. The files can be viewed only by a special program. A window opens with a prompt to name the archive. As a joke, she types in "The Materialist Magician" and hits Return. The screen then tells her "Archives of the Materialist Magician is being created. Please wait."

Janet dismantles her other magical tools and technologies and disposes of them. Half an hour later, she checks to find only 4 percent is complete with nine hours to go. Exasperated, she decides to check back tomorrow. She locks up and leaves to meet Francine where she took the plunge.

She drives to that delivery room where she entered this wonderful new life (except that it wasn't wonderful now). People pray for her. Then Speech in Motion, a deaf drama troupe, presents. Their drama is eloquent silence, except for outbursts of laughter from the audience.

Later, the drama troupe is introduced. The last member of the troupe is James Stubbs. Her heart races. Janet rushes up to James and asks if he has a twin sister. He signs back angrily, "No!" Disappointed, she signs an apology and explains that she was separated from her deaf brother and misses him. They discover that their aunt and uncle lied to them both. They embrace.

They converse for hours. Janet tells him all that happened to her. She finds out he trained with Navy SEALs and qualified physically but was refused due to his deafness. After hours of signing, her hands are exhausted and sore. At about three o'clock in the morning, James excuses himself to go to bed.

In the morning, Janet returns to the complex to clear out the computer. She is horrified to read that "Archives of the Materialist Magician" have been completed and moved to the Internet.

Janet destroys the hard drives and finishes moving out of the complex. "Good riddance!" she exclaims.

She drives to a three-bedroom apartment in a gated community. She took it over with three months left on the lease. She wanted a short lease because she wasn't sure she wanted to stay in the area. She wants a fresh start; the area tempts her. She isn't sure what to do with her life.

The next three weeks are a blur of activity. Her properties and her cars, except the large SUV, are all sold. She attends Bible studies and is received warmly. She starts therapy and meets daily with Francine to talk and pray.

Janet compensates those she defrauded, puts thirty million dollars in a fund for widows and orphans, and keeps about four million. For widows, she sets up reverse mortgages at one percent interest. The interest is given to communities of faith to maintain the widow's property. She appoints an administrator for the funds.

Her unconscious habits begin to take a toll. Though she dresses modestly, her behavior excites sexual interest. She keeps her breasts thrust up—her stomach extremely taut—and unconsciously flaunts, other body parts. Her tight core musculature requires her sighing often to get enough oxygen. Her sighs draw attention to her breasts. She stretches her arms backward with similar effect. She exudes sensuality and attracts interest. On an unconscious level, she hungers for attention; her behaviors elicit it and are reinforced and increased. She senses rejection from those who are put off by her sexual displays. She takes offense. She doesn't deal with her anger with God; she forces it out of her mind. It is firmly entrenched in her unconscious. She pulls away from God.

As emotions surrounding her conversion subside, her immaturity in dealing with emotions asserts itself. Her habitual ways to deal with negative emotions usually involved manipulation, but now they took exclusively sexual forms. She's committed to sexual purity but unable to maintain it. She keeps a kit to prevent STDs with her. She falls into a pattern of dates, drinking too much to lose control, sex, and then guilt feeding more negative emotions. It would be a disastrous downward death spiral, but she confesses her dreadful failures to Francine. They pray and talk about how to prevent reoccurrences. She talks with her therapist and others but doesn't realize the deep roots that undermine her best intentions.

Despair Settles into Her Soul

Despair settles into her soul. Without change, gossip and her sexual reputation will crush her spirit. "Maybe I need to get married," she admits.

"No, won't work," Francine cautions. "You lack skills for marriage. Heal first."

"I'm a failure at following Jesus," she protests. "Why can't I resist? Why doesn't God do something?" Francine grasps her hand and awaits eye contact. Janet resists looking. When she does, she sees eyes, full of forgiveness, love—warm and imploring—evoking a deep memory and longing. "Where have I seen that?" She recalls the record of her trip to see Jesus she hasn't fully viewed. She promises herself to view it. She becomes aware that Francine is talking.

"So God wants to forgive and help you. He doesn't want you punishing—you've been lost in thought." Francine observes. Janet tells Francine her thoughts.

Janet's openness about her failures, telling Francine and her therapist everything, prevents their plans from rushing to its conclusion. Plan B starts.

She finds the record of her encounter with Jesus and watches it. She views the parts about Jesus and wants to be faithful to him. Her inability to do so grieves her deeply.

An abyss of hurt, anger, fear, and despair grows in her, fed by the past, the present abysmal failures, and the prospects of an appalling future. Hope is dying. She begins to look forward to her dates. More and more, she only gets relief during sex. When it's been longer than she can stand, she goes to bars to get picked up. One guy tried to get nasty, and she hurt him badly. Her therapist and Francine warn her that she is addicted to sex. She starts to want to avoid them and view time with them as an ordeal.

One day, Janet decides not to visit Francine. She gets a call from Adam. "What does he want?" she grumbles. She hasn't given him a thought since turning the closing over to her attorney. *Oh, I never set up a mortgage account!* she remembers. She answers, "How's the cabin?"

He replies, "Great. I've moved in and been fixing it up with my father. Best thing that's happened to our relationship."

She asks, "How? I thought your father refused to speak to you."

Laughing, he says, "I know. Miracles never cease. I managed to tell Mom about the cabin. After she told Dad about it, showed him pictures, and told him that I need his help, he came around."

"What a clever way to draw him in," she says.

"No," he says with irritation. "I wasn't clever, it was true. I needed him or hired help I couldn't afford."

She remembers that Adam is vanilla and dull but also extraordinarily real and solid. He reminds her that he needs to pay the mortgage. She promises to e-mail instructions.

Somehow, hope sprouts. Janet meets with Francine and asks to stay a few days—at least, until Easter—to prevent her escapades. They chatter to her continuously. They aggravate shame, stirring it into despair. They mix in self-pity, liberally sprinkling in anger that her freedom is being eclipsed, that she was robbed of her parents, and even of her good memories of them. Doubts about and anger at God are shifted in; he let it all happen to her but prevented her remembering her deliverance by Jesus. He allows her too much freedom, enough to hang herself. She knows better but is powerless against her own lusts for power, approval, and the sexual satisfaction of seduction, of making a man crazy for her. The siren song of power and being the center of attention is deadly for her.

Self-loathing adds to the cauldron; loathing of men, Christian singles, all Christians bubble up. Francine is one of the few exempt from her fermenting hatred. They learned the folly of pushing too far and fast. Janet confesses all of which she is aware (less each day) to Francine, even that she is indulging and cherishing sexual fantasies. They talk and pray together, but, even in the midst of her prayers, Janet comforts herself with fantasies. The desires of her heart are divided. She confesses that she believes marriage is her only escape. However, in her deepest unconscious is a well-planted, deeply-defended, and fierce determination to never succumb to the slavery to a man called *marriage*. Marriage appeals to her as much as a double mastectomy followed by chemo and radiation with no quality of life. Deep in her unconscious, she'd rather die than be controlled by a man. If she married, she'd keep an unconscious promise to herself to satisfy herself with anyone she chooses. At the center of her soul is a resolve to be her own person, submitting to nobody.

Fed by her deliberate fantasies, her dreams become sexually dominated. The third night, Janet wakes from a compelling dream and sneaks out. She goes to an all-night fantasy outlet and buys clothes and boots to accent her sexual appeal and scream her eagerness. The sales staff know her well and egg her on to dress sexier. Heavily perfumed and showing far too much flesh for a chilly spring night and wearing heels high even for her, she teeters two blocks to a bar, gets plastered, and, for the first time, wakes up in a cheap motel with a guy she doesn't remember. She didn't use any protection, and she worries that she could be pregnant or infected. She is devastated and has a terrible hangover. The repeated dashing of her hopes turns into a terrible despair. She knows the Bible cover to cover. She knows what to do but doesn't do it. It looks like she—*like I don't even want to.*

I quietly get out of bed and dress in the bathroom. It takes several tries to tighten my corset enough to zip up my dress! I sneak out into the cold lightly falling rain, hating myself and everything about me. *God is better off without me.* But I know that's silly. I rage at God. *God, I hate you for loving me!* I don't know where I am; she is soaking wet. I am lost and don't care, and she keeps walking in the rain. Her feet are killing her. I see I-81.

Misery lures her to her former life. I'll go back until I recover. I'll turn to God later. *God! I'm turning to you now! Save me...I'm not worth saving. Don't do it for me, do it for your sake! Do whatever you have to—salvage me from myself!—As if!—I am not worth salvaging.*" Anger—anger at God, herself, the rotten stinking world—overflows into tears that mix with the heavy rain.

Shivering, wretched physically and emotionally, she reflects: *I give up on God and especially myself. God's good—I'm not.* Thoughts race on without resistance: *I'm not good enough for God. I'll only fail God and myself if I keep trying. I might as well turn back...*" But when this thought runs through her head, she resists. Distracted by her thoughts, she doesn't see a truck and is sprayed with cold water from the street. The shock throws her off balance, and she steps off the shoulder of the road. I twist my ankle and slide down a muddy slope face first; then I fall a few feet. The wind is knocked out of me. I tumble several feet and fall hard on my back in deep mud. I pass out. It stops raining. Dawn comes. I'm chilled to the bone. I don't stir for hours. I wake up—it's morning. My recovery, moving, and getting back to the road are complicated by the tight corset and skirt and impossible heels in the mud. I struggle up the muddy hill and limp into town.

I see my reflection in a window. My face, hair, and clothes are caked with mud. I look dreadful, feel dreadful, and am dreadful.

In an instance, the deed is done. I spew out spells that remove the mud, dry my hair and clothes, warm me, and heal my ankle and headache. I see women in the store shocked by my sudden makeover. I cast a spell of amnesia on them, and anyone else that saw me changes from trashed to trashy. I also erase the last minute on video cameras that recorded it. I linger to admire my alluring image in the window. I invoke my inner knowledge—good! I'm neither pregnant nor infected.

My cell rings as it begins to drizzle. I duck under a gazebo to answer it. The police found my car. I can pick it up at the Mount Jackson Police Station at 5901 Main Street. Uncanny! I can pick it up across the street.

I enter the station with confidence. I flirt with the officers. The eyes of a female officer send jealous daggers at me. I cause her period to start with terrible cramps and a sudden heavy flow. She runs to the bathroom in horror. I laugh with delight. The guy who is yakking thinks I'm laughing at his inane joke. He is enthralled with me and will do my bidding—Janet wakens to what she is doing.

"O God," slips from her lips as despair swallows her alive. I toy with their affections and capture their hearts. An officer takes me my car. I chuckle as I hear, "Now we're firmly back in control!" I hear, savor, and suffer a riotous celebration within me. I buckle in and turn the key.

E-mails from Janet update Francine and the others of the whirlwind of events of the next few weeks. She met a wonderful guy who is going to do mission work in the jungles of Brazil. She confides to Francine that he is probably her solution. She joins his team. They leave soon and have to prepare. There are no e-mails for days and then one as she is about to fly out of Dulles. A crisis required they leave immediately. She gives details for prayer.

Sporadic e-mails from Brazil update her plans. Harold proposed. She thanks her dear friends individually and her acquaintances generally. She informs them that she arranged for everything to be sold. Then the e-mails stop.

Janet Awakens

Janet awakens. She is rested and comfortable. Lying on the grass that pampers her body stirs memories of the dream of pampering. Smells of something more luscious than honeysuckle charm her. The pungent aromas ignite mouthwatering tastes. She hears exceptionally beautiful songs from birds. Opening her eyes to see a lush green valley ringed with beautiful mountains capped with snow expands her sense of well-being. *The mountains must be very high. Snow is covering most of the mountain and the valley is in the full bloom of spring*, she concludes.

The richness, beauty, and magnificence of the mountains and the incredible sweet freshness of the air energize her spirit, and the blue of the sky is richer, more saturated and satisfying, its expanse vast and the clouds inviting so she feels a strong longing to fly and almost believes she can. That desire, though unfulfilled, adds to her assent out of herself. She wanders through a grove of fruit trees and satisfies her hunger and thirst. The familiar fruits are far better than she recalls. She samples unfamiliar fruits, and the transport of taste and satisfaction convinces her that they must be unknown. Fruits this good could never stay a secret.

Abiding calm and peace settle into her. Everywhere she looks, everything she hears or smells, all she touches, and everything she tastes—all her experiences—raise in her an unmistakable sense that this is the way it is supposed to be. Wave upon wave of beauty, pleasure, and rapture come to her senses. Tastes and aromas linger until replaced by another delight. The senses don't habituate to the staggering, phenomenal onslaught of delights. Each moment has its enchantments, undiminished by familiarity or exhaustion of her sensory neurons. *It can't be better than this*, this thought springs from the depths of her soul.

Her soul is at perfect rest; she gives no thought to where she is or when. She doesn't think of herself at all. Her senses take in the surroundings, and, she, in turn, is taken out of herself into this wondrous world. Everything fits perfectly.

Janet begins to explore. Her hands dig in the soil and finds it richer than potting soil. She searches in vain for anything resembling a weed. Everything grows in harmony rather than competition. She runs without fatigue, her body relishes the exercise; she runs her fastest leisurely unable to wind herself. *I can run like this forever!*

She climbs a tree in a flash to survey the valley. She revels in picking her way up the branches. Her senses take in more than she imagined. *Am I dreaming or dead?* she wonders. From the heights, she spies an expanse of tall hedges that intrigues her. The descent delights her instead of giving her a sense of danger looking down from that height.

Noticing mosses and grasses, experiencing their different textures with her feet, hands, and then by rolling her body on them, Janet unites with nature. Her soul overflows. Her senses seem bionic; she focuses on a high-flying eagle and sees the feathers and hears the wings beating the air. She does acrobatics on the grasses. Her abilities are heightened; she does ever more difficult aerobatics until she crashes onto the grasses. She laughs heartily—no pain.

Running at full speed toward the hedges, she reaches them in an hour. She ran a half marathon. She has the gratification of perspiration dripping from her, her lungs working hard and of exertion. *Better*, she muses.

Spotting fruit trees nearby (about a mile), she sprints over for refreshment; she returns to explore the hedges. *I've never been this alive! So robust, potent...substantial! My capacities are at a zenith.* She pauses, then amends her thinking. *No, that's not it at all. I've never been so blessed!* She sings an aria, "Senta's Ballad" from *The Flying Dutchman*. She fell in love with it the one time she heard it. She sings it perfectly. She tests her memory, her ability to do complex calculations, and composes a challenging sonnet in her head. Everything she could ever do, she does immeasurably better now.

Janet, returning to explore the network of hedges, estimates that they are as high as a basketball rim. She can normally touch the rim. Here and now? She jumps well above the "rim" and could easily dunk. While briefly above the hedge, she spies a face. She races through the labyrinth of hedges to locate that face.

A Grand Face

A grand face is famed by the hedges below and leaves above. The grandness of that bronzed face intrigues her. It is lit by sunlight and not at all handsome. It is grand, a bit like the Grand Canyon—big and broad with a wild full beard, big bulging nose, and piercing dark eyes that are jovial and attentively darting back and forth like a watchful warrior. It is too grand to take in, too imposing for even her sharpened senses and capacities. It is simply too much for her. The eyes pierce and permeate her for a moment—they seem to take her in, understand, and Master her, even to overwhelm her, but then seem to take no note of her. She wants to matter to the owner of those eyes.

The beard changes her view about beards. She detested beards before. It's wild, unruly, overgrown. It is curly and colorful; the random intricacies of myriad curved hairs draw her in. Each hair, each hair segment, has its own blend of color, sheen, luster, and curvature. There is no order, no pattern—yet, it is an elegant chaos. The beard is ablaze with fiery crimson scattered through a sea of chocolate, silver, and gold with rare jet-black accents. It puffs out from the face and increases its width. It completely obscures the neck.

The eyes—watchful jovial eyes—are surrounded by a host of lines deeply etched by smiles. The eyes draw her in; they give the clearest cues about their owner since the mouth is hidden. The fiery eyes impose extraordinary love and permission on her. The "giant" seems to await her permission as a servant stands patiently waiting for instructions.

"Come on over," she bids. She hears the sound of horse hoofs. She makes sense of the height of the face. "He's on horseback, an enormous horse," she surmises. "But how did he get so close to the hedge." The answer rounds the hedge. The face belongs to a large centaur.

Janet is silenced, not by surprise, fear, or awkwardness—none of those matter. Nothing matters compared to his being there. His presence is daunting, overpowering; he is the epitome of liveliness. His size, piercing gaze, grandeur, and even (or was it especially?) his fierce beard and hair impose on her cravings for permission, assurance, and, most of all, to be noticed by him, approved, and allowed to share in his vivacity. He is in on some secret or penultimate joke of life itself. His presence challenges her to enter in. The warmth of the joyously smiling eyes grants massive permission or she could not endure his presence. The horse portion is much larger than a Clydesdale, pure white, and almost dazzling. But as it rounds the hedge, his nimble spirited gait resembles a restless young colt's prancing as it is led to the starting gate. His flanks look out of place, odd, unexpected; she cannot make sense of what she sees.

The man portion is virile—excessively so—hairy, wild, muscular, unpredictable, the skin bronzed and weather-beaten. He belongs in places wild and free. He liberates this place, perhaps every place he goes. From the massive expanse of chest hang powerful arms. Janet remembers myths about centaurs—their wisdom, strength, and expertise with magical powers. His presence imposes on her the reality that she is weak, insignificant, inadequate, and pale by comparison—almost transparent.

He stops a dozen feet from her, his face far above her. She is undone. Her knees buckle; her gaze falls. The grass around his hoofs grows thicker and greener. The air about him is enhanced—fresher, more aromatic and invigorating, brighter in an effervescent manner, as though the air glows.

The centaur speaks, "Janet!" The warmth, wonder, and welcome in his voice strengthen her—and the way he speaks her name! She wishes her name could always be spoken with that blend of wonder and welcome. He said her name with zest, with a passionate pursuit of her; his voice, face, (especially his eyes—oh, the eyes), and his entire body in harmony. Hearing him say her name was better than a love poem enhanced by soulful cellos. "Do you want to talk?" he asks. "That's why you're here—to listen, learn"—and after a pause—"and heal."

The warmth of his words heartens her further; she can look at his face and ask, "How do you know me? Who are you?"

After a pause he replies, "I am." Janet waits for him to finish, but then, as quick as lightning, a shocking realization strikes. She flings herself—or more like collapses—onto the ground, her face buried in the thick grasses. She is crushed and burdened by the realization that she saw God and is in his presence. He comes to her, bends over, and picks her up as an adult picks up a small stuffed animal. "It's okay to see me here," he assures her. "That's what this place is for."

His touch fortifies her; after a long pause, she splutters out with humbled awe. "Why do you favor me so?"

His hearty laugh gladdens her. For moments after, while he laughs, everything grows before her eyes—grass and trees, buds forming and blossoming and adding their fragrance to the air, and a baby rabbit. As his laugh saturates her, he declares, "I favor all. I love you. You slay me." He hoots with delight for her.

His words charm, enchant, and are potent; they compose new possibilities, masterpieces of superb art. "I love you" embraces her with warmth, depth, and…and eternality. Grand inclusive love, always—ever, for her this moment—every moment. That is his love for her. This love created all, sent Jesus, was present in his every move and utterance and breath, including his last. Love conquers death—even the death entwined with her soul. Reality roots in her soul: *He is for me more than I or anyone could ever be for me.* Love and desire overflow into a compulsion, a new genus of desire. *I'd do anything, give, or suffer anything to love like that!* Love so inclusive, love for God, love for the least of her sisters and brothers, and love for each at his or her greatest offensive. A reality rocks her: *I can't possibly love like that.* Voices within: *I will pour God's love into you. When you see me as I am, you will be like me—will love like me. I am living in you.* Joy and tears erupt from her soul, overflowing into her body.

All this and more resound in her soul from his words: I love you. His Word of creation resonates in quarks, vibrates the strings of the universe, sustains the existence of matter—energy—so his Word spoken to her sustains and enables her to grow, develop, and love.

After love settles her soul, she asks, "Am I dead? What is this place?"

He replies, "No, your body is in a coma. You are fully alive. I call this 'The Soul's Eden.' Here anyone can walk in my presence, naked and unashamed. Hiding from me starves the soul. The valley becomes a desert."

"I could never hide from you," Janet asserts.

"Until several months ago, all you did was hide from me, from others, and from yourself. Your valley was barren until you started having friends," he affirms kindly. "Even after you put on my Son, you kept slipping back into hiding. It was destroying you," he says with a quivering voice and tears moistening his eyes and cheeks. His display of intense tenderness and compassion about her flaws and his caring about her weaknesses from this all-powerful presence awe her to depths of humility and dignity. She is keenly aware of her obvious and silly defensiveness against this all-knowing, loving presence.

She is pierced and pained by an awareness that she willfully evaded God for years until it hardened into a habit. It was her default strategy; even now, it is hard to break free from it. She realizes she is defenseless and without excuses—yet fully at peace; it puzzles her. "I have so many questions!"

Allow Me to Orient You First

"Allow me to orient you first so you will understand how you come to be here." God breathes on her. As his breath settles on her, it stirs her memories and a vision.

"O my," she says. Janet remembers what they did to her from a dual perspective—from her experience and as though she is watching a detailed documentary. An officer escorts her to her car—it was prepared to disable her. As she starts the car, shocks and chemicals enter her, stopping her heart and paralyzing her. They restart her heart, encase her in a stiff wetsuit with tubes and wires through which they introduce chemicals and currents at will, and put her in an iron lung that breathes for her.

When her mind clears, they begin their interrogation—torture—conditioning. Recalling a bit of it elsewhere would traumatize her. Their diabolical ingenuity made her give passwords, access to her finances, almost anything. Her sole resistance was in regard to magic. She refused to invoke magic to help her. A humiliating recall of her failures, her inability to keep her promises to God, to Francine, and to herself, of deliberately plunging back into unbridled sexuality and magic—those fiascos steeled her dependence on God and her conviction to resist giving in to magic or giving them information about it. Finally, as the torture and conditioning grew more intense, she went into a coma. She was in silent prayers constantly during her ordeal, wondering how God could help her. She wonders now why he hadn't. Anger at God erupts.

God whispers, "Janet, Janet, I want to hear what's in your heart and mind." She is lost in her thoughts; the whisper was so still that it takes time for it to register. She puzzles within; God knows what I think: that it is absurd. The whisper harkens her back to God, revealing himself to Elijah in a whisper. *What did he say?* "I want to hear" *Oh! He wants me to talk to him—he already knows what I'm thinking better than I do! I'm not keeping anything secret from him. God, what am I doing?*

"Precious Janet, you are keeping yourself from me again," he responds. She knows it is true and could see its reality. The valley has changed. The colors are less vibrant, her senses slightly dulled, the fragrances less aromatic, and he seems farther away, although neither had moved.

Again, God whispers something but this time so softly that she could tell he is whispering only by the movement of his beard; she couldn't possibly hear it. She pleads, "I want to know what you said. I want—you said, 'Return to me. Want me.' I do, I do." The valley's vibrancy increases.

Janet, in tune again with reality because she is opening herself to God instead of hiding, realizes that the valley reflects her soul. Thinking it is impressive, she notices things rapidly decomposing and smells a rancid odor. In an instant, she is full again of herself, becoming less alive and vibrant. Bursting into tears, she begs, "Help me, have mercy on me! Save me from myself!"

"O, dearest Janet," God sighs with poignancy; it breaks her heart. "Helping you grow requires tenderness and care. They broke you. They stole your freedom. You would do whatever they asked if I hadn't put you in a coma." Her memories of the torturous conditioning fully make sense.

Yes, she thinks, *I would have thought, done, or willed whatever they wanted*. It sinks in deeper. She loses heart as she says, "I still would. I'll do anything anybody wants, or even suggests, eagerly." God embraces and rocks her to sleep.

Janet's sleep is restful and undisturbed; even dreams do not disturb her sleep for this is the place of dreams. She awakes refreshed and with new hope. She cries out, "Abba Lord, command me to follow you with all my heart, soul, mind, and strength!" Though he is unseen, she knows he hears. The possibility of being freed from the tyranny and weakness of her self by being controlled fully by God makes her giddy.

Janet didn't care about the valley. Her desires are solely for God. She calls, searches, and strains her senses for him. She hears faint hoof beats from a great distance coming closer quickly. She runs full speed toward the sound, and soon they are together. She blurts out, "I won't resist anything you ask, so this is actually a great—"

"Janet," he interrupts. "I won't have you a puppet, even my puppet. I will free you—in time."

Janet is disappointed in his unwillingness to override her, angry that God deals with her so that she remains free to think, act, or even be angry with him. She challenges, "Why won't you save me once and for all from myself?" Inwardly, she is making an ultimatum that God must satisfy if she is to…but it's no good. "I need you!" He is this Rock, and she is hard and stubborn. This can never work, but it must. "I'm trapped by my own…" She struggles to think of an adequate description of her need, her weakness, this cancer of her soul, this being chained to her own malignant rotting self. Mercifully, God frees her.

"I answer what you can't ask, but you will not remember when you wake from your coma," he declares.

"Well, that's not fair," she complains. God is silent; she bellows, "So no answer! Too hard for you! Don't make promises you won't keep!" Her anger at God seethes.

"Yes! You needn't hide from me," he says with delight. "You may show me your worst!" His face increases in radiance, his eyes twinkle with fiery joy, and he chuckles. "Do you have a question or request? Or else, I will listen to your complaints and anger. That can start healing. I'd love for you to go deeper."

Embolden by the I am, she doesn't consider whether her rage is appropriate. Angrily, she protests, "You let my parents be murdered and Helena and Frank do terrible things to me. I couldn't remember turning my life over to you after I saw Jesus! Why? All that hardship and humiliation you put me through!"

God breathes a song. The magnificently indescribable occurs. He exhales, she inhales and breathes the song that she hears, sees, tastes, and stirs every bit of her. The richness of nature explodes a billionfold, transforming into its destiny. Eternity transforms quarks; she sees them clearly. The beauty would annihilate her nervous system, her self. She's unmade, remade, and now briefly endures a tiny cross-section of the mind of the Lord God and his perception of reality. Reality is clear to her.

Janet has answers. Fatigue overtakes her. Dreamingly, words stumble out. "You loved us into your image, destined us to obtain your image, emptied yourself of your power, limiting your power with your love so that we can become like your Son, dependant yet eternal." She swoons from the overload—exhausted.

When Janet awakes, the effects of God's "song" are gone. All she remembers is to trust God and that something indescribably incredible awaits her.

He explains why she and the others couldn't remember their "encounters" that reshaped them on an unconscious level. What satisfied her was that he did not permit her to remember the encounters with Jesus to spare her crushing despair.

It satisfies because despair crushed her when she tried to live for God. She reflects: "I was crushed by despair as my habi—"

He interrupts: "Far worse if you were fully convinced and committed to Jesus without any good habits."

"But, but..." she's still troubled. "I saw, experienced, felt passionately, and was won over—converted to your Son. How can that not be enough?"

I Gave You a Body

"I gave you a body—a body not much different from the body of an animal. Habits, to be real, must be practiced by your body, by you. That's a privileged challenge angels don't enjoy," God declares. "The gift of a body, an animal body in essence, is what makes you and your kind a little lower than angels"—he pauses—"for now. One day, it makes your ascent to bear the likeness of my Son possible. You are a mere animal made in my image, destined to bear the likeness of my Son. The difficulties and agonies you suffer, I suffer. The joys and glories coming to you, I share in my eternal now."

As he bares meaning, everything changes. She is transported to intoxicating joy. "If the body's not a prison but a transport, then I don't get it. Why did you make me—" she breaks off in an effort to restrain her seething anger—"forget?"

The Almighty smiles at her. She forgets her anger—for a moment. He grants that she forget herself until another gift of his—her freedom to stand apart—stirs. Her bitter anger opens a gulf between her and God, exploding into a screaming stream of speech.

"Why do you make it so hard for us—for me? Why are you hateful, hating me, treating me so badly? How can you—" Coughing interrupts, her throat is raw, and she chokes as she tries to continue. Tears flow. He gives her a drink to soothe her throat. She rails on more intently and intensely. "You didn't let me remember I was a spiritual whore, was possessed, a mere puppet, and that I was a lie in motion. You made me forget my resolve to trust you, to make my life right, to depend on you. You let me stir up all that trouble with Grunde's awful people. You're to blame for their torture, for all they did to me, for my desperate turn back to magic. You...you...you...if you let me remember, none of that would have happened!"

"Anything else?" he inquires. She struggles with her anger and thoughts, with admitting her need for the one in whom she is disappointed. She thinks, *What do I do? How do I...I'm furious with someone I need and love?* Then seeing his grand face looming large before her, she whispers, "Oh," with pangs of realization intending for the next word to be "he." Instead, she continues with a subdued and sheepish voice, "You hear everything. All my thoughts—how do you stand me?" Recalling some of her thoughts, some of the worst ones, she is overcome with awe and asks incredulously, "How do you love me? Any of us? We're fickle...unreliable...predictably vacillating—"

He interrupts mercifully again. "Yes you are. I made you that way—a hybrid of animal and spirit made in my likeness but also changing in flux, holding to a path approximately and then only with great effort and frequent corrections. That makes it possible for you, but not the angels, to be transformed into the likeness of my Son. If you will but keep working with me, putting your trust in me and putting in your two cents' worth, I will make you like my Son. For that I created everything."

Silenced by awe, Janet's jumbled thinking is stilled. She isn't seeking, searching, thinking, and figuring—she has never been this rational, this at rest. She tastes life before the eating of the forbidden fruit—free of thoughts between her and the "not me," awash in full consciousness, fabulously free of self, of control, of any restraints, embracing exactly what is coming, full, and free.

"Didn't you answer me twice?" she asks. "Or more?"

"Yes, and I continue to," he states. "One answer was for your unconscious, another for your conscious mind."

"What?"

"This is the place of the unconscious, of the hidden. Your conscious self is conquered. I brought it here by putting you in a coma to protect you. Different types of answers suit the conscious and unconscious."

"Oh! Will I have to stay in a coma?"

"No, I have a plan," he promises.

"Ah, like I'm a sleeping beauty," she concludes.

"No." He asks if she wants to explore.

"Oh, yes!" she replies. "I can run full speed forever! I…"

He asks if she wants to ride on his back. She stammers out nervously, "I'm…I'm terrified of horses."

"Your aunt and uncle made you afraid of horses because you loved riding as a child."

Janet realizes she isn't afraid now. *How can I be afraid of riding on the back of God? ?* she ponders. She leaps on his back. He gallops, jumps, and flies. Wings unfold from his body (she remembers seeing them but couldn't see them for what they are) and rapidly carry them above the snow-covered mountains. She sees countless valleys surrounded by mountains. The scene reminds her of a fullerene, a buckyball—a giant soccer ball.

The physics here and on earth must be radically different, she reasons, carried by God at incredible acceleration and speed to an incredible height that produced a gentle cool breeze and only a pleasant sense of acceleration. She should have been torn from her mount by a ferocious wind or tremendous g-force. This high, the air should be frigid and too thin to breathe. But all is well.

"Each valley is a soul of some person living on earth," he explains. "Or, at least, the unconscious part of a soul."

"At least?" she queries.

"Oh, yes, most people rigidly divide the conscious and unconscious. Little of the conscious self is seen here."

"Why is that?"

"People are intent on hiding from me and from themselves," he clarifies. Things spill back and forth though. That's how myths develop."

She ponders silently. She sees how she was determined to deceive herself. Self-recriminations begin.

"You are forgiven," he interrupts her thoughts.

"Thank you for interrupting my twisted thinking. Always do so! Please! I beg you," she says.

"No, I'd be interrupting all the time. It wouldn't be respectful. You'd be a puppet, not a person."

"So…being loved by you is not easy for us or…you," she marvels.

"It wouldn't be good for you if it was easy for you."

"Are all atheists unconsciously motivated to disbelieve like I was? And all agnostics also?" she asks.

"Each person is different, most generalities mislead," he states. "Every human commitment, whether to a person, an idea or even for or against me, has elements of stubbornness and unconscious motivations. People aren't playing with a full deck, and they cheat. A few realize they don't have a full deck. More are aware they cheat—at first—but sadly too many successfully rationalize unreality. Atheists and religionists do so about equally."

"What do I do?" she asks. "Do I tell oth—"

"Apply it to yourself! Let me work in others. Stop hiding from yourself and me. Don't mess with what others hide," he cautions. "Besides, you won't remember any of this when you awake, not consciously."

Perturbed, she asks, "Why not?"

"You aren't better than others," he answers warmly. "It wouldn't do. Your pride would trip you up."

"How can I do better? Even a little," she pleads.

"Love me, seek and hold onto me above all else...then keep at it until it becomes a habit," he says. After a pause, he adds, "Keep coming back to it again and again."

She contemplates that as they fly over hundreds of valleys—all the same shape and size but each unique. Some are fertile, some desert, some in between.

Janet Spies a Beautiful Valley

Janet spies a beautiful valley, one that rivals or exceeds hers. She comments, "That one's spectacular!"

"Look closer," he instructs. She focuses on a blade of what she thought was grass. She gasps. She quickly inspects flowers, leaves, fruits, and the flowing river.

"It's all fake—every bit of it!" she exclaims.

"Yes," he sighs, shaking his head. "He's one of the worst hypocrites. He's got everyone fooled—even himself. Tragic. He's almost impervious to my influence."

"Was I difficult? What was my valley like?" she inquires.

"Your valley was a wasteland and filled with disgusting beasts," he states. "I want to prepare you. Terrible storms will darken your life. You'll wander in wastelands, and, at times, your waking life will be a nightmare. Remember to look for me here—deep within. Only by seeing me here often will you endure. Your trouble will be terrible and long. Open up to fellow travelers, fellow sufferers. Strive to press into consciousness what you are learning here."

While he said this, he plucks her off his back and holds her in his arms, gazing into her eyes. She sees tears in his eyes and agony on his face, doubtless for her. He flies over her valley, its beauty and splendor sparkle; she is mesmerized. Something touches and shakes her shoulder; she looks, but nothing is there. Something tickles her palm; she twitches her hand. It's definite—a hand caresses her face, shakes her shoulder more firmly, and finger spells in her hand. The shock and surprise, this unexpected message from an invisible someone, perplexes her; she misses the message. It repeats. There is a finger spelling a word, and then "I love you." She focuses on her hand, closing her eyes. The message, slower this time, she gets: "A-D-A-M here. I love you." She feels the hand saying "I love you" in her hand and grasps it tightly. It grasps her and holds on.

Janet falls toward her valley. The invisible messenger holds her hand as she falls faster and faster. She looks down—she is miles up. She looks up expecting to see God swooping down to catch her, but, to her dismay, he flies away. She screeches, but God takes no notice. Her only comfort and companion is the hand holding hers. She falls further and faster, headed for enormous trees. A thought terrorizes her. *I'll be torn apart by the branches.* The hand grips hers. She isn't facing death alone—Adam is with her. *But my Adam? It couldn't be*, she reflects.

She is racing, plummeting toward the trees, helpless and hopeless, when she hears God's voice whisper, "Janet, you can wake up if you want." The valley and her memory of it fade as she awakes.

She is in a dark room, lying on a bed with a man kneeling holding her hand. Only faint light from medical equipment interrupts the dark, and she is shielded from its direct light. She tries to move her left hand to his, but her hand is stiff and hard to move, and an IV restrains her.

She croaks, "Adam, is that you?" Her voice shocks her; it's strange, and speaking is an effort.

"Yes," he responds slowly with both voice and by signing in her hand. Janet hears a delightful sound. It's Adam, her Adam. Memories of her torture and grilling flood her, and then there were no memories until the signed "Adam here, I love you." She knows she's safe. He bends over and hugs her gently and kisses her on the cheek. She doesn't register his beard touching her face. That simple kiss becomes the most precious kiss in her memory—simple, innocent, welcomed friendly affection.

She speaks coarsely, "Water—please!" He releases her hand to get it. She asks, "Adam, how did you find me?"

He says haltingly, "You're not my aunt then?" He hands her a container with a straw. She greedily takes three sips.

"I'm Janet. Didn't you know?" she says with a slightly improved voice.

"Janet?" He pauses. "Janet who?" She is irritated that he doesn't recognize her even in the low light and responds a bit tersely, "Janet Stubbs, of course! You haven't forgotten me, have you?"

"I could never forget her—you," Adam replies. He then adds in explanation, "I wasn't expecting you. But you…don't look like yourself. What are you doing in a nursing facility? I thought you went to Brazil—got engaged and were having a great time. Actually, I came here to see my favorite great auntie. She must be in the other bed."

"Brazil? Engaged? Hardly! I was kidnapped, interrogated, and tortured—I remember that," she explains. "I guess they dumped me here. Where are we?"

"We are in Issaquah, Washington." Then remembering that he never heard of it until recently, he adds, "near Seattle. But…" He pauses to make sense of what she just said. "You were kidnapped, interrogated, and tortured? Why?"

"Remember I told you that I was a power-whoring magician before following Jesus? Well, they—some secret group—knew of my power and wanted the secrets or to control me," she clarifies.

"That's awful," he states angrily. "They must have been really hard on you."

"It was awful, painful, and terrifying," she says, recalling a bit of what they did. She is overwhelmed and starts to cry. "But how did you know they were hard on me?" Tears flow. He hands her tissues.

Before Adam replies, a doctor comes in and commands, "Sir, come with me immediately!" Adam leaves with her.

Janet's terror crescendos to panic. She recognizes the doctor's voice. It's Detective Grunde. She tries to get up, but her body is too weak. Exhausted by her efforts, the panic, and a tsunami of emotions, sleep overcomes her.

Adam wakes Janet by gently shaking her and then hushes her. He orders her, "Do exactly what I say. Don't listen to what anyone else says for now. Don't even hear anything but my voice until I tell you otherwise." All becomes silent; she hears only his voice. He continues, "I'm going to turn on a light so you can read some names. You will not feel pain. Your skin won't react to the light." He turns on a light, and her eyes adjust. He hands her a list of names. He tells her, "Pick one of these for your new name. It may be your name for the rest of your life. Choose well."

She picks Eve Marie Smith because Eve is already her middle name and Smith is the name of her great-grandmother from London. "I'll be Eve," she tells Adam.

"Fine, respond to 'Eve' instead of 'Janet'," he replies.

Eve sees her face reflected in a mirror—it's ghastly, shriveled, rough, and blotchy with red and black spots. It looks like she is in her nineties. Her once long thick luxuriant hair is brittle, frizzy, and less than an inch long. She tries to raise her body for a better look. He helps her up. Her arms are skinny and have the same shriveled, rough, and blotchy look. Her breasts are unnoticeable. Her lips and cheeks tremble, grief grips her stomach and chest. Tears gush. She blubbers, "What happened to me?"

Adam hugs and holds her, gently rocking her, and replies, "This is due to the torture and chemicals they used on you." He adds, "I'm so sorry. We have to get you out of here quick. I'll explain later." He turns off the light and says, "Your skin will react again to the light, but you won't feel pain. Oh, I hate this. We have to pretend you're still in a coma. You will have no control of your body, no tears until I return and speak to you again or until tomorrow if I can't come back."

She goes limp, and her eyes close. He squeezes her limp body with his arms, gently rubbing and scratching the center of her back (it feels good and comforting!), and lays her back on the bed. He kisses her cheek. She feels warm tears fall on her cheek.

"I'll be back soon. We'll get you back your life," he promises.

Eve Wants to Die

Eve wants to die. She wants to scream and curse but can't. She can't even cry. Her bowels move. The grief is more unbearable since she can't express and release it. She misses her body now—even her current pathetic body.

Life—what a joke. Get me back my life? What life? Who wants a life of torture, my life, the only life I can have? Everything's taken—nothing to live for. She is reminded she can return to magic and all will be well. In her grief and weakness, the appeal is too great. She has to, but Adam's voice interrupts her thoughts.

"Eve, fill your heart and mind with God. Review the Bible, good dreams, memories of God, and what he did for you. 'Think about these things…so the God of peace will be with you'." The silence returns, but my spirit soars, transcending my condition, dwelling on God and with God.

Eve sleeps soundly, dreams well, and wakens eagerly to Adam's voice. "Wake up, Eve, it's me. You've had hours of physical therapy. Doctor Dye ordered it, and she loaded you with painkillers and drugs to help you move better," he says rapidly. "She'll come soon to help get you out of here. We have to act quickly to keep you safe. Cooperate the best way you can." The IV was gone. Only the faint light of medical devices lights the room.

He helps her sit on the bed and gives her a thick drink. "Sip on this as much as you can," Adam instructs. It is sweet in her mouth but turns her stomach. She almost throws up. "Try to keep it down and keep sipping on it," he implores. You need it for strength." Tiny sips are all she manages though.

"I have to undress you and put some lotion on your skin to lubricate it. I'm sorry that I can't…uh…your privacy," Adam apologizes, stumbling over his words. I say nothing but want to protest as he gingerly takes off the hospital gown. Shame at my body, my once strong beautiful body, my greatest pride, now horrid and helpless, my greatest shame and regret—I would fight to prevent anyone from seeing or touching it. I disowned it at that instant; it is no part of me! It is a prison far worse than that cramped cage in that dream. I wish—but I'm interrupted by the cool soothing cream being gently rubbed on my body. I can't remember feeling a greater physical relief. The taut aching dryness of my skin, an itching burning sensation on its surface and also beneath it, gives way to relief as the lotion is rubbed in. Only the pampering in the dream of the kindly master compares to this pleasure and relief. Adam rubs copious amounts of this wonderful cream over every part of my body, and even gently massages it into my scalp. She is transported by the pleasure and relief. It eases her motion by loosening the skin.

Adam slips cushioned shoes on her feet and tightens the laces for support. He helps her up, and she is able to shuffle across the room with his support. Abruptly, there are several rapid taps at the door, and it opens. Faint light floods in from the hall. Eve sees someone covered by a sheet. When she makes sense of it, she sees a woman clad in a loose-fitting black full-length burqa with her face covered, except for a small slit for the eyes, which is covered by fine mesh. Eve notices extra fabric near the waist.

The woman closes the door and whispers, "Adam, can she walk?"

Alarm at the familiar voice sends Eve into a panic attack. Her heart and her thoughts race; she gasps for air and sweats profusely, and the tears gush. Her mind races. *It's Grunde! She's come for me. I can't take more torture! I've got to warn Adam to save himself. I'm doomed!* Adam catches her as her legs give way. She passes out.

Adam gently shakes Eve and whispers to command and assure her. "Wake up! Be calm! Doctor Dye is on our side. I'll explain later. Pull yourself together so we can get you out of here safely." There is authority and urgency in his voice. Somehow, she manages to obey. In a few minutes, they clothe Eve in the burqa with her face veiled. It is the correct length for her height. Doctor Dye, Grunde, and Adam sneak her out of her room, down the hall, and, after the doctor enters a code on a door, they exit into the cool night air. While in the hall, Eve notes that it's 1:52 a.m.

Eve is tiring rapidly—she lacks energy and stamina. She continues sipping intermittently on the shake. Before they got through the parking lot to the woods, she faints, and they carry her. Again, Adam whispers in her ear to wake and encourage her. She misses the first part of what he said but feels his breath on her ear and hears, "So wake up, stay alert, and keep sipping on the drink for energy." She obeys. With a few minutes of rest, several more sips, and time for the calories to get into her system, she is ready to proceed—until she sees them.

She Sees Two Horses

She sees two horses and remembers her terror of horses. She thinks she can't do this but feels no fear.

Adam explains, "We have to ride to my car to avoid checkpoints on the road. The doctor had me park on the other side of the checkpoints. We have several hours of easy riding through the woods." He puts goggles on her so she can see in the dark. He helps her climb a step ladder and mount her horse. He braces her body with supports and secures her on the horse. He puts a bladder filled with the shake over her saddle and guides a straw to her mouth. He says, "Sip as you can. On a scale of one to ten, ten being unbearable discomfort, what is your current discomfort?"

"About three or four," she replies.

"Good, good!" he responds. "Tell me when it gets to about an eight. And what is your current level of fatigue?"

"I guess about a five or six," she answers.

"Okay. Ah…tell me if it gets to a seven. I don't want you falling. Oh, and tell me if you need anything," he instructs.

Adam puts on goggles and mounts his horse. "Obey my orders immediately and exactly," he commands. "If I say stop, go, silence—do exactly what I say. Follow my gestures," he insists. "Will you obey?"

Taken aback by his tone, Eve replies angrily, "Okay."

He is not satisfied and requires a stronger response. "Say you will obey my every word and gesture. Obey them all. Want to do it as though your life depends on it."

Shocked and offended by his demands, she can't believe she says, "I will obey you—every word and gesture. I want to." She wants to tell him off, to rebel, to tell him not to be bossy, but, to her dismay, all that is swallowed up by an even greater desire to do exactly as he wishes.

He has the upper hand; he'll use it to the max. Men can't be trusted, even a man like him. But then what can he possibly want with me? I have nothing. I gave them my passwords, so I'm sure I have nothing. No money, no beauty, nothing to want. Aha! He owes me money for the cabin! The pain gets more intense. The cheap bas…Adam hears her breathe harder and orders her, interrupting her thoughts, "Forget about yourself and me. Think only of good things, of God, unless you need to tell me about your pain or tiredness or something you need." She does so, and the pain subsides.

They ride in silence for an hour. The horses and her sips from the shakes break the silence of the woods long before dawn. Eve suddenly speaks, "The pain is an eight."

Adam gets her off the horse (the pressure of his hands hurts when he helps her dismount). He speaks tenderly to her, "Doctor Dye explained you'll need the lotion rubbed in frequently. Ah…I'll help you undress and, um, I'll take care of that." He undresses her, has her go to the bathroom, and rubs the lotion all over her. He dresses her. He kneels by the horse and has her use his hand and shoulder as steps to mount the horse. In her weakened condition, she barely manages. Throughout, he has her sip on the milkshake.

Almost an hour has passed. As he gets on his horse, Eve states, "I'm tired…a seven."

Adam sighs. He gets her down and sets up a hammock from his pack for her to sleep on. He directs, "Sleep soundly and dream of God and good things."

She sleeps soundly for hours, and he snoozes. Out of a dead sleep, Eve suddenly says, "The pain is an eight. I'm starved!" It's early morning.

Eve greedily finishes her milkshake and asks for solid food. Adam gives her some, and she eats most of their food. He eats sparingly to conserve the remainder. He suspects, based on what Doctor Dye told him, that she can apply the lotion herself mostly.

He tells her, "Do as much as you can. Ask help if you want to."

She does most of it, needing help only because of the stiffness of her body. They are both surprised at how much better her skin looks. The blotches faded, and the skin isn't nearly as wrinkled, dried out, and shrunken tight to her body. Light still hurt, so Adam holds up the burqa to shield her from the sun. Even so, the indirect light smites her hard; by the time she is dressed again, she needs another nap.

Adam wakes her after six hours. It is afternoon. She needs the lotion again, and she eats the rest of the solid food and drinks more milkshakes. There are only a few left. He orders her to put the lotion on while keeping the burqa on as much as possible. He has to help more due to the challenge of applying the lotion under the burqa. He notices her skin has improved.

They remount the horses and ride two hours and reach the campsite where he left his car. Adam did his best to make their travel by stealth to avoid people who might react strongly or violently to Muslims, since they would assume Eve was one. He had her go to the bathroom and update him on her pain ("it's almost six"), while he secures the horses. He tells her to follow him to the car. She walks much more steadily than at the nursing facility.

Get in the Trunk

"Get in the trunk," Adam orders suddenly. "Stay there and don't make a sound." She obeys without reaction. He closes it—her unconscious fears of being confined, the deep unconscious fears planted by the torture—panic ensues. The panic is more terrible because she obeys and doesn't make a sound. Overwhelmed, she cries out inwardly to God, alternately pleading for relief and cursing Adam—even cursing God and then struggling to confess and plead for forgiveness. The pain passes eight and then nine, and then it reaches and stays at an unremitting ten. She passes out.

Adam ordered her in the trunk because he saw three men coming whom he overheard talking the previous day at the campground about their hatred for Muslims. They might have attacked her based on what he heard them say. He wasn't sure he could convince them to leave her alone. He never felt more awful about anything he did.

He has to explain to them why he has two horses. Adam tells them that he and a woman he likes rode in the woods, but she got very mad at him for how he treated her. They laugh and congratulate him, assuming that he took advantage of her sexually. They insist he drink with them. After he has a beer with them, he begs off due to his urgency to return the horses.

After returning the horses about two miles away, Adam runs back as fast as he can. Making sure of privacy, he opens the trunk. Eve had taken off the burqa before she passed out. He sees that the beauty of her body is nearly restored, though she is still too skinny. He tells her to wake up and get dressed. She obeys without hesitation.

Once she's dressed, Adam stumbles over himself apologizing for leaving her in the trunk. "Ja—Eve, please, please forgive me," he implores. Eve genuinely forgives him with an ease that surprises her.

"Tell me about your pain, fatigue, whatever you need," Adam instructs. "There is almost no pain, no fatigue. I'm starving though!" she reports. "Oh, I need to wash up and put on clean clothes. And I need a good massage. My body's still stiff." He gets a towel for her to shower. She adds, "Oh, I also want a really good cry. May I?"

Without thinking, Adam says, "Of course!" and the waterworks start. She's grieving her beauty, her life, her identity, her loss of self. She wails, and he does not have the heart to stop her. He cries with her and holds her.

He gives her a clean burqa and supplies to wash up and takes her to the showers. "Eve, call me if you want anything. I'll wait here," he says.

A minute later, she cries out, "Adam, come quick!"

He rushes in to be assaulted again with her beauty fully restored (but far too skinny). But this is different than the cabin. She is soaking wet standing in the open shower, her stance open and expansive and filled with innocent joy. She cries out for him to share her joy.

"Look at me! Look at me!" she squeals with delight, pirouetting a full circle. "I'm okay, my body's back! I still need to gain weight. I'm sure my breasts will fill out when I do. Oh, thank you, God, thank you!" Lust is not a factor; there is no temptation for him at that moment. He rejoices with her. His love and joy for her are overpowering.

He departs, remembering to tell her, "Call me if you want anything." He hears the water stop. Minutes later, she calls for him. He walks in as she is drying what's left of her hair with the towel. "I'd like different clothes, not that prison." She was indicating the burqa with her hand. Her face, though a bit gaunt, radiates beauty and joy. "Please don't have me put that on," she pleads.

"Use my bathrobe until we get you clothes," he suggests.

Across the road is "the community mall." Before they walk over, she, obeying his invitation to tell him what she wants, asks him to massage her back, legs, and arms. Only her need, the innocence of her request, and his desire to serve her enable him to endure through his torturous desires.

At the mall are buildings filled with used clothing. Eve picks out three outfits with his approval. She puts on a blue pencil dress with a white fringe. It matches her blue eyes. She finds black flats and a hat to hide her horrendous hair.

"Anything else?" he asks.

"A wig! As I gain weight, I'll need a bra. My breasts were bigger when I was ten!"

"Oh," he suddenly remembers to add, "Wear a scarf over your hair and face to hide from facial recognition whenever you are in the open."

She obeys and locates a few scarves, putting one on to cover her head and face. She looks at him for approval, inwardly hating that he matters to her. She sees he is pensive and must ask, "What's on your mind?"

He pauses, sighs, ponders a while and finally orders her, "Except when we are in the car together, hear nothing but the sound of my voice. Ignore everyone but me. Only I matter." All becomes silent for her. She is terrified by his power over her and how zealously he is protecting it. She lets out a faint gasp. He adds, "Oh, and except when we are in the car together don't—with the windows up and no one nearby—don't make a sound. Use sign language only."

She stifles a sob and signs, "Yes." Her attention is now riveted on him—no one else matters. Despair overwhelms her. He sees her shoulders sag and parts her scarf to look at her face. He says tenderly, "Be joyful," and she is.

He invites her to eat at a decrepit hut at the camp. She signs, "Yes," because he asked, and she is focused on what he wants. He loads the car; they'll leave after dinner. She notices that he is still deep in thought. She must know what he is thinking. She signs to ask him, but he doesn't notice her; she is desolated. She waves frantically to get his attention to no avail. She grabs his arm in desperation to get his attention and know what he is thinking. He looks at her but doesn't attend to her at all.

After brooding a long time, he says while still not looking at her, "If someone uses sign language, you better not be able to understand it, other than me. Understand me, or ask what I mean."

She is doubly crushed that she doesn't matter to him and that she cares whether she does at all. Again, he notices and tells her, "Fill with joy." She obeys with no effort. She eats like she's starved. The meat is marbled with fat, but her obsession against fat is now a craving for it. Her body needs calories, fats, to replenish it.

Her beauty, unadorned with makeup or jewelry, contrasts with the surroundings. Her beauty and radiant joy mesmerizes. Many wonder how he, a plain guy, holds the rapt attention of this beauty with no apparent effort.

They finish their meals, and she asks Adam for a take-out meal. She eats as he drives. Soon, they are on I-90. He tells her that while they are riding in the car together, she can relax and speak freely. She sings for him, does anything she can for him. She hates that she is obsessed with pleasing him. Inwardly, she is fearful and rebellious. She fears his control and resents him and his decisions. She especially fears that he will force her to share his dull dreary life.

As he drives, I study his beard. When it catches the light, its colors, curves, and fullness fascinate me. I recall why beards infuriated and disgusted me. I despise his control and him, yet am drawn to his beard by, what, its appearance, intricacies, multifaceted variety? I often lose myself in it; I'd love to plunge into it.

It's Time to Talk

It's time to talk Adam muses. Adam explains that the torture created a disassociated identity that would obey their every whim. Doctor Dye, also known as Grunde designed the process of torture and conditioning. A change of heart started when Janet called her at the ER to assure her she would be okay.

"When she visited you, the changes in your appearance and actions struck her. After you knelt and wiped her dirty shoes with a dish rag, she gradually shifted to trying to protect you."

"She—Ann is a doctor in both neurology and electrical engineering. She saw you watch the videos of time travel—she bugged your house but kept it to herself," Adam explains.

Eventually, Ann became a follower of Jesus—secretly due to the others. "Unable to protect you, she offered to watch you at the nursing facility, hoping for an opportunity to help you. When I arrived and you woke up, she seized the opportunity. They may kill her," he says.

"I understand," Eve replies calmly; inwardly, she knows she'll eagerly do anything he hints at. Waves of fear, self-pity, and doubt flood her soul. Within, she is losing hope, melting into despair, falling apart. The realization that she can do nothing to free herself feeds her despair. I'll be his puppet. *I guess I'm paying for embracing inhumanity—losing mine*, she anguishes. *I'd like to cry. I thought crying women, except to manipulate, were weak. Now I'm supremely weak, what I always despised.*

Adam explains that Ann told him that Eve's best chance was for him to be the only one who gave her orders until she imprinted on him. She will be under his control only and immune to others. She will no longer accept other controllers a day after her body heals fully. She listens to his every word, watches every gesture.

Her mind is on a dual track, alert to him and bemoaning her lot. My beauty and health returned, but now I belong to Adam. *What will he do with me?* I wonder. It can't be good. He was taken with me but knew his place, so he didn't pursue me. Now he has me. He'll make me his wife, his chattel, his puppet. He's a good man, so he won't do terrible things to me—except make me marry and submit to him. I wish I could die!

"So," he concludes. "Ann—the doctor—said I have to let this gel before you'll be immune from others' control." He needn't remind me who Ann is; my memory's intact—I'm not a dummy! Well, I was, and horribly so. Smart yet foolish!

"Things will be irrevocable soon. Once they are, *I will give you* your marching *orders for* the rest of *your life*," Adam proclaims ominously. Dread and disgust fill her; she hears the embedded hypnotic command and knows her unconscious will absorb and obey it. "Prepare yourself! Eagerly anticipate what I will order. *Desire to do what I want* of you!" he orders. He's lousy at embedding hypnotic statements, but I can't resist or even want to. I eagerly want and dread what he tells me to do. I despise Adam because I'm bound to him.

She can't safely drive. He drives stopping for breaks to sleep, eat, gas up, and use the bathroom, even for showers. We eat in the car, stop every few hours so I can stretch my limbs (I'm still stiff). Our progress is slow. I'm desperate to gain weight, so I eat as much as I can. I also want fuller breasts. I figure Adam wants my beauty restored to enjoy. I want to look good for him, even though I now hate him.

We had driven about one thousand miles since leaving the campground in Washington. Still on I-90, we're about one hundred miles west of Rapid City, South Dakota. Adam continually peppers me with probing questions. I tell him all. He mines truth from me. He knows me better than I ever knew myself. His questions indicate he understands me better than I do. He has an outsider's view and my deeply honest view, more honest than I've ever been with myself. I'm naked before him and unashamed. His inquiries prompt deep thought and introspection that distract me from and relieve some of my dread.

Riding with Adam

Riding with Adam under his control and fearing his total control, I'm terrified of losing my freedom, of being his plaything, his toy, his slave. I'm powerless to resist, unable to want to resist, conditioned to pleasing him above all else. Hour by hour, he bends me further, transitioning me from submission to him to desperately needing his approval of every action, thought, and desire. I will eagerly conform and become exactly what he wants. I see the inevitable aim and outcome of his use of language, of the embedded premises I fully accept, of the radical reorientation of binding and bending my will to his. When he's done, I'll be his puppet, geisha, or Stepford-wife. I won't be a "who" at all, no self, just a what.

God, why let this happen? Is this loving? Does this serve anything remotely worthy of you? This reeks of Satan. Why rescue me from their control, yet allow this? I see, I see. You protect your interests, your kingdom, and I'm a mere pawn. You want me to be a dutiful wife? Not to him, he's so...plain, unattractive. Not that. Millions of women have no choice, no power—do I have to be one of them? I'm angry at you and...and hurt—hurt horribly by you! You should have let them kill me or done it yourself. Do the right thing! Don't make me his! Kill me, but don't make me his slave.

Images, compelling enticing snippets from the dream of slavery, the hardships, and pampering to prepare me to be your Son's bride intrude—is this part of that? They are right. To be favored by you isn't easy; I wonder if it's good. Jeremiah was right to complain about you overpowering him. But how can I please you if I have no choice? Are you a rogue and scoundrel?

His voice interrupts, and I must attend. Slowly and deliberately, he says, "Do you want to do anything I ask?"

"Of course," I reply. I wish I could rebel.

"Are you eager to know what I want so you can want it also?" His voice emphasizes "you want it also" as a direct command.

"Yes, I'm eager to know what you want so I can want it."

"Eve, do you desperately want exactly and only what I want?"

"Oh, yes! I desperately want exactly and only what you want."

"Eve, do you have no reservations?"

"I have no reservations."

"Then, Eve, listen to what I say after we pass under the next overpass. I will tell you exactly what you will want to do."

"Adam, I eagerly listen for what I will want and do." My desire for freedom goes out.

"Eve, each foot we travel until I tell you will intensify your desire for what you will want to do for the rest of your life."

It's nearly midnight, cloudy; the only light is from his car. I can't see the next overpass. It might be miles away. My desire for what he wants grows moment by moment.

"I'm finished. I wish I could resist," Eve despairs. Her growing obsession is: "I want to do his will perfectly. I can't wait to begin willing and doing his will." The pangs of desire are unbearable. Yet, they grow.

Finally, after what seems an eternity of growing and consuming desire, she sees an overpass in the distance. As they approach it, her desire for her purpose, my reason for being, reaches a fever pitch. I'd beg him to tell me now, but that is not what he wants. I overflow with desire; I pant, sobbing with desire.

They pass under the overpass. He takes a leisurely sip. The delay is unbearable. Finally, he speaks far too slowly and deliberately. "Eve, what I deeply want from you more than anything else is that after you sleep deeply, dream of your desires, and awake you decide each moment for the rest of your life what you want."

Eve falls asleep and dreams sweet restful dreams. She dreams of her desires—freely and fully chosen. It's good rest. She's exhausted by the stress and strain of the last days, by the intensity of the desires kindled and stoked higher and higher into a consuming fire. It is one of the best sleeps of her life.

A New Day Dawns

A new day dawns for Eve; she awakes. She is in a tent and sees a patch of crimson sky through the flap. As she stirs, she becomes aware of stiffness, hunger, and incredible thirst. She feels lethargic, almost drugged from the sleep, and struggles to get up. As she stumbles out of the tent, weak and dizzy, she catches a glimpse of a beautiful sky moments before sunrise with the eastern sky flirting with color and the western sky still cloaked in darkness, except for the enormous reddening full moon. She falls onto the mat outside the tent. Things seemed dreamlike, surreal, otherworldly, too good to be real, more real than she remembers. Overwhelmed by beauty and joy, she lies, drinking it in for a moment and almost falls back asleep.

Pain of hunger, thirst, and her uncomfortable position rouse her. Waist up, she is out of the tent; her hips are in the opening, but something heavy inside the tent pins her thighs.

Oh, bother! I'm stuck and need help, she thinks. She's about to call for Adam when she remembers that she wants nothing to do with him. Her frustration builds as she thrashes about to free herself and can't. *I can't stand being helpless! I can't, I won't ask him for help!* she promises herself. But her discomfort and anger grows. Her head is lower than her body; her right arm is pinned under her. Attempts to move strain her arm. She finally screams, "Adam! Get over here!"

He asks, "Are you all right?" He frees her and seats her on a picnic bench with her back to the table. Again, she notices the beauty of the pre-dawn sky, minutes before sunrise.

"Adam, get me something to eat and drink! I need something for my throat—it's parched and sore. Quick! Don't just sit there grinning at me!" Her tone and manner are extremely demanding.

Adam hands her a canteen. She drinks but then spits out, "I need something better than warm water!"

"Okay," he replies, grinning, and does nothing.

She'd attack or slap him if she had the strength. She continues her tirade, "You're unfair! Stop grinning! Stop bossing me around, you're enjoying controlling me. I need something to eat and drink—not warm water!" She stands up to swing at him, gets dizzy, loses her balance, and falls forward, but he catches her and places her gently back on the bench.

Nonchalantly, he says, "I thought I pack up, get a shower, and then drive a few hours before we have breakfast."

"No!" she bellows. "Take care of me first!"

"Why are you being so disagreeable with me?" he asks. "And by the way, you're beautiful when you're mad."

"Don't change the topic! Me being disagreeable?" She shrieks. "You're ignoring me, you—"

She stops, suddenly realizing that she's arguing with him, openly angry at him, asserting her will against his. Abruptly, her anger inverts, and she is giddy with joy. "I'm free! You're not in control! I'm making my own decisions!" Eve says between roars of laughter. "Oh, thank you, God! Thank you, thank you!" She exults. She sees him grinning at her, overjoyed with her freedom. "That's why you were grinning while I—," she says out loud. "Oh," she whispers and then pauses as she contemplates what he did for her and what she thought of him. She vows to herself not to judge others, especially not him. He saved her life, fought off her attack, and wore himself out to keep her alive. He put up with her ignoring his requests about the mortgage. He's been kind, gentle, and comforting about her loss of beauty, and now this—setting her free. Humbled, she lowers her gaze and voice and says, "Thank you, Adam."

"You're welcome," he responds. He adds, "Would you like some sausage and eggs for breakfast? I've also got teas and cold orange juice. How about hot tea flavored with OJ?"

She's beaming, overjoyed, smiling broadly and warmly as she exclaims, "Oh, yes, indeed, inde—"

A sunbeam suddenly ignites her face with light. Her face burns, and he sees it contort in pain and rapidly change color and its surface contract and shrivel. Sweat and oil ooze from her pores. The assault of pain and fear that her beauty is again stripped from her dissolves her into tears. Adam tries in vain to comfort her. She responds with hostility to him, to everything. Locating the burqa and the last of the lotion, he massages it into her skin and helps her put on protection from the light. In minutes, the physical crisis is ended, but she's desolated. She has no interest in food or drink; she despairs of life.

Adam forces Eve to eat and drink something. He prays for her. In minutes, the car is packed up, and he gently invites her to get in. She slaps him hard and then collapses into his arms. She weeps uncontrollably.

Oil from her skin soaks through the burqa, and Adam is wet with oil and her tears. She clutches him tight, her body shaking from the sobbing. By the time she lets go, they both need a shower and a change of clothes.

"Eve," he says, "Ann told me that the tor—treatment left you allergic to chlorine. I'm guessing you are again, since you're back to—now that you're..."

"My hideous self," she interrupts angrily. "How long, how long, how long?" She pleads between sobs. He has no idea and says nothing. She demands, "Did that damn doctor say how long I'd be like this?" She clutches him tight and holds on for dear life.

"No," he responds. "She said your health would return once you were a mere puppet...," he states and then pauses. He hears his heart pounding hard. "Oh"—he sighs before continuing—"unless I gain sole control of you myself. I hoped I..."—again pausing, he struggles for words—"could set you free but didn't dream this would be the result. Ann said they conditioned a dissociative split, a compliant identity. By my freeing you, I guess—I probably resurfaced what they tortured and conditioned. I'm to blame. Hate me if you like. I'm sorry."

There is a pause; it is silent, except for their heartbeats and her labored breathing. Finally, she speaks haltingly, gasping when she pauses, "Well...if this...is the price...of freedom...I'll fight...to accept it."

Adam witnesses a momentous event. He is awed by her fledgling acceptance of this terrible loss for her.

Eve is spent and leans into his chest. He supports her. They need to clean up. Without releasing her, he checks with his phone and says, "There is a campground with well water an hour from here. Let's check if you're allergic to chlorine and decide whether we clean up here or there."

Eve is allergic; they head for the other campground. She talks as he drives. "Adam, when I was under your control, you asked probing questions. I didn't—couldn't hide anything. I assume you hoped details might help you free me. Oh! Thank you! I'm forever indebted."

"You're welcome," he murmurs.

"Ahh,"—she says with increasing energy—"you still blame yourself. I won't stand for that. I forgive you. Please forgive yourself. Who knows how God will use this?"

"Oh, okay. Okay. Thank you," he replies with little conviction.

"I want to ask you to be open and honest with me. I have things about you I want to know."

"Of course," he says flatly.

"No, no, no. I want your promise," she emphasizes.

Adam agrees, "Okay, okay, I promise!"

"First, even before the last few days, you knew more about me than I knew about you. How come?"

"Well, ah…," he says slowly, as if weighing his words.

"Fully open and honest—you promised," she reminds.

"You always spoke so much, there were few opportunities for me to say much, and you never asked," he says softly.

"Oh!" she says and pauses. "Yes, that makes sense. I was dreadful—really. I was afraid so." Eve admits more to herself. She recalls the lengthy conversation with her brother and how her hands ached, but he was the one who said he was tired. She did almost all the talking then too. He got tired of being shut out. And it's been the same with Francine and just about everyone, she realizes.

After a pause, Eve pleads, "Forgive me. Please. Please give me a chance. I want to get to know you. You are an enigma I want to understand." There is silence. She looks at Adam and sees a tear roll from his eye; his face struggles to hide emotion. She asks, "What's wrong?"

"I can't talk about it and drive," he replies. "Later."

"Okay," she says. "Can I change the subject?"

"Please do," he rejoins. "It will help me focus on driving."

"Okay," she agrees. "I was impressed that you realized I was out of reach when we met. Everyone is out of reach for me now. I couldn't believe you weren't tempted when I tried to seduce you. I guess I was, oops, honestly, I was hurt that you weren't tempted. I can't fathom that you weren't tempted when my beauty returned and you had control of me. Am I so…"

Shut Up!

"Shut up!" he roars. "You don't know anything about me."

"I've never seen you angry like—oh. Oh! I'm so sorry. I didn't mean…"

"Shut up already!" he bellows.

Eve realizes she again misjudged him and had deeply hurt him. She whispers in hushed tones, "I want to hear every detail. I want to listen to you when you're ready." She feels terrible and prays for God to comfort, soothe, and heal him.

They ride in silence until he parks. Adam reconnoiters the showers, finding that the showers are private. Eve gulps and says, "You go ahead. I'll get one later."

"No, no," he responds. "You stink. Take a shower."

"Not now," she baulks. "I'm not up to it."

"Okay. I promised I'd be honest. We'll talk first," he states.

"Clearing the air before we clean up makes sense," Adam says aloud as he gets back in the car. "You were beautiful the day we met and more attractive to me almost every moment I've spent with you since."

"Present excluded, of course," she adds.

"Not necessarily, no. Not at all," he corrects. "I withstood your physical beauty because you were so far above me that I didn't want to torture myself. But I couldn't resist that first conversation.

I fell hard for you. I fought being obsessed with your mind. And your spirit—free, new, something I can't describe. You're bright and quick. You understand what I'm interested in and challenge me. I put you out of my mind and heart—a thousand times. Then the cabin—it was hard being with you again, giving you mouth-to-mouth, seeing and resisting you and crucifying my own desires. I survived that. I survived thinking you got engaged. Actually, that was a relief. I won't desire an engaged woman. When Ann explained that your beauty would return as you became a 'slave' either to me or everyone, I faced a dilemma. I could have you—your body—but a mere shell of the free, stubborn, challenging you. The other horn of the dilemma was that if I succeeded in freeing you, I'd lose you for good. But I'd…"

"Oh! I've been ghastly!" she admits. Eve sees he's about to speak. She insists, "Wait!" She deliberates this new narrative about him. "I've terribly underestimated you. You're an exceptional man, and I missed it." she confesses. Shame burns. She can't look at his face, so she stares at the ground. The words seep out with a sigh, "Please. Forget all I've done to you." Her heart's broken for him.

"Now, about that shower. You need one," he insists.

"But I can't manage one now," she retorts. "I don't have the strength. That blast of sunlight did me in. I can't."

"I'll help you," he offers. "We need to get you to Virginia. I can't stand driving with you smelling like you do."

"What?" she says with mock indignation. I promise myself to do anything for him—too bad I can't. I ask, "Why Virginia? I've nothing. I have to hide, lest my tormentors find me. I can't drink tap water. I've got nothing. Anywhere is as good or bad for me."

"You have friends," he assures. "God, and you have me."

"Okay, so I can't give up!" she admits. "All right. God help me, God help us."

"I insist you shower," Adam persists. "You'll feel better. I'll help because you need it."

"I hate to put you through that temptation, to put you through more discomfort," she replies.

"Honestly, your body now isn't tempting," he admits.

"Of course! What was I thinking?" She wonders. "I wish you were still attracted to me."

"Really?" he asks. "Let's get you that shower and talk more when we're back on the road."

They shower. She needs the special lotion. They find some and spent the rest of the cash Ann gave him.

Eve can only ride a few hours before her discomfort becomes intolerable. Her skin is damaged to the sub-dermal layer; it retains little fat or moisture, provides no cushion and is brittle. She frequently stops to re-apply lotion and for Adam to sleep and fix meals and re-supply their drinks, slowing their progress.

Eve thinks, prays, and engages in soul-searching. She listens to Adam, peppering him with questions that encourage him to speak at length. He tells her everything about himself. He is worn out by the turmoil and intrigue and the demands of taking care of her. The next day, he only drives four hours before needing a break.

He says, "I'm exhausted—I need a break. I want a sandwich and beer on a comfortable chair in air conditioning." Previously, except for that first meal at the campground, they always ate in the car.

Letting Down His Guard

Letting down his guard due to his exhaustion, Adam stops at a restaurant and reminds Eve to say nothing. He asks for a booth and plans a leisurely simple meal. Though most of the tables are empty, they are taken to stools at the counter.

"Oh, I'm really tired and need a booth," he protests slightly.

The waiter's surly reply, "Tables reserved. Take it or leave it," surprises them.

They agreed she wouldn't speak in public, lest a security device pick up her voice and, perhaps, alert her tormentors where she was. The burqa, fully and loosely covering her face, prevents face recognition. Silence prevents voice recognition. Eve taps his arm and signs, "Let's go."

Adam hesitates due to fatigue and desperation for rest and relief. A voice shouts from across the restaurant, "Put them on the back patio. I don't want to be in the same room with terrorist lovers." He takes her hand and heads for the front door with renewed energy.

The man who spoke jumps up and signals others, and four men suddenly block their path. One man walks briskly toward them and says, "So your slave"—he emphasizes—"isn't even allowed to talk in front of real men." He spits in her face.

Adam, thinking fast, grabs a napkin and, handing it to Eve, addresses her in Greek, "Προσεύχεσθε ὑπὲρ τῶν διωκόντων ὑμᾶς (pray for those who persecute you)."

It stops her from reacting and starts her praying. Behind them, a voice shouts, "Hey! No trouble in my place. Let them leave in their car." The emphasis he threw into "in their car" makes them uneasy. The men let them pass and follow them out.

Before they reach Adam's car, one of them snatches his phone. They block the door back into the restaurant. In exasperation, he says, "I'm an American and a Christian and—"

"But she sure isn't!" Someone interrupts. Someone else says, "That sure wasn't English you spoke to her!"

Adam pleads, "Let us leave like the owner said." They do, but one of them hits the windshield with something and cracks it. After Eve closes her door, he kicks her door hard a few times, badly denting the door. The men go to their cars.

Once inside his Corolla, Eve cautions, "They're not going to let us just leave. They'll run us off the road or something."

Adam replies as he puts the car in gear, "I'm sure they—we'll follow that police car out of town."

Adam pulls his car onto the road followed by two pickups and an SUV. Adam pulls as close to the police car as he thinks wise. He follows the police car west two hours before he is sure the pursuers gave up. The stress throws Eve into a panic attack. She passes out after twenty minutes. Her susceptibility to anxiety and panic is another consequence of the torture. He drives west another hour to a campsite with well water. They spend the night. He uses someone's laptop to make notes for the trip to Virginia.

After a long sleep, Eve wakes him for help, putting on the lotion. He fixes breakfast, and they get back on the road. She commends his fast thinking the previous night. He confesses, "I was terrified you'd be hurt." Eve frequently prods Adam to talk with an inquiry or statement.

"'Wives, submit to your husbands,' say, what about that? Isn't it just a cultural thing?" she wonders aloud.

"I don't think so," Adam replies.

"Oh," she says with disdain, "How could you think women are inferior and ought to submit to their husbands?"

"It's not a matter of inferiority," he offers. "Remember that the passage starts with 'Being submissive to one another: wives to your husbands.' Later in the same paragraph, husbands also are commanded to love their wives and lay down their lives for them. That's how husbands submit to their wives. People don't argue that's cultural."

"But surely a woman shouldn't have to pretend she is mindless and incompetent just to indulge the male ego!" She retorts with irritation. She is getting worked up over what she perceives as an affront to all women.

"Oh, my. Patience, patience!" he whispers under his breath. "Yes, culture is involved—ours. It's distorting your view of this and its positive meaning," he states gently in normal conversational tone and volume.

"That's judgmental of you!" she roars. "How dare you accuse me of distortion? Positive meaning? Ha! Positive for chauvinists maybe." Sarcasm is dripping from her words.

"Do you want to hear what I think?" he asks softly.

"I don't think so," she says with fury in a staccato voice with pauses between each word. They ride in silence for about an hour. She feels awful for the way she just treated him. "Such prejudiced stupidity doesn't suit you," she says pleasantly. "You're better than that—a lot. I guess you act a lot better than you believe." She pauses before adding, "Unless you're just too cowardly to live your convictions."

"Oh, Eve, Eve," he says, shaking his head. He sighs.

"What?" she yells. His head shakes. "You're maddening, impossible, pig-headed," she bellows. He does nothing. "Caught you without an answer, huh?" she prods.

He parries, "I thought you didn't want to hear what I think. Now it seems you are angry at me for being silent. I'm confused." His tone is genuine and pleasant.

Eve is prepared for battle, but not this. She can't provoke him; she can't destroy his case if he won't contend for it. She meant to write him off and the topic with the thought that he's a hapless lamb, but that one word stirs her in a different and deeper direction. She replays his words and his manner of saying them in her mind. She contrasts them with her own. She concludes that if he is the innocent lamb, she is the fierce wolf. He's been submissive to me; I've been pushy and aggressive to him.

"I don't know what to say or do," she confesses. "Please forgive me and help me understand your point of view," she implores. "I'll still disagree!" she states.

"I forgive you eagerly and gladly," he replies. "I'll try to help you understand if you want."

I Do Want To

"I do want to. Go on," she says as she moves her hand to pantomime zipping her lips and then cups her hands on her ears to show that she is all ears. Adam chuckles.

"Jesus taught to not resist one who is evil—husbands are sometimes evil," he says with a grin. "We are to overcome evil with good, return good for ill. In the story of the fall, the consequences of sin include shame for being naked, hiding from God, and a power struggle between man and woman."

"How'd you get the last bit?" she asks.

Adam explains that God told the woman that she would desire to master her husband but that the husband would rule her—usually men win. "That's the beginning of the battle of the sexes," he adds. "Relationships got messed up. They hid from God, were ashamed of their bodies, and based their relationships on power and struggle with their relationship with the ground."

"Oh, yeah," she recalls. "Both the New Living and the New English translations have Genesis 3:16, 'You will desire to control your husband.' Another translation says the word *desire* means desire to control and refers to Genesis 4:7 where sin desires to control Cain."

"Right," he says while shaking his head in amazement. "Your memory is a marvel."

"So they fight for power," she observes.

"God wants relationships based on love, not power. Jesus defines his and spiritual authority in terms of service, not lording it over others," he states. "The way to escape the power struggle is to not struggle for power—but it's hard. When we submit to each other 'out of reverence for Christ,' women submitting to their husbands, and husbands laying down their lives for their wives in daily service, then the power struggle wilts. Love can flourish."

"I'd want an egalitarian relationship if I marry—no chance of that," Eve asserts. "Actually, I hate to admit I want to be in control. It's wrong and it's messed me and everything up."

"I'd want an egalitarian relationship too," Adam agrees. "Marriage researchers found that hierarchical and egalitarian marriages work equally well if a couple agrees—if they don't have a power struggle over it."

"So love and service are the way to go—ha!" Eve concludes. Then she confesses, "Oh, I badly misjudged you—I have every reason to trust you. You could have had total control of me—no, you actually did but worked hard to set me free. And to think I called you a chauvinist. I've promised myself over and over I'd stop judging people, especially you—not doing too well with that. Please forgive me yet again. How many times is that today?"

"If I keep count, I'm not forgiving!" he rejoins with a laugh. "Oh, delighted to forgive you!" he says with a lilt.

"Thanks again," she says. A minute later, she says out loud, "I'm pretty sure that whenever I have one of my rages, my skin burns and hurts a lot more. Could you put lotion on me?" After he puts lotion on her, they ride in silence for hours due to fatigue, taking some breaks for lotion and lunch, and drive into Pennsylvania.

She leans harder and harder on him and likes it. She wants to talk through everything with him and get his take on things. She wants to hear his voice. She has nothing, no money, and no place to live. He reminds her that he has a few thousand dollars mortgage money for her. She admits she didn't file a mortgage, so legally he doesn't owe her anything. She can't file now. The property is his.

"No, no, no!" he retorts. "Of course, I'll pay you," he insists. There is anger in his voice as he emphasizes, "I won't cheat anyone, especially someone in need."

It is the second time Eve remembers seeing him angry. She sighs long, deep, and wistfully. Her mind races to how blind she was to Adam, to his character, to the things that she now sees matter most. He knows me better than even Francine does, has seen my worst, yet still is kind and loves me as a friend. A desire pierces her sharply, a desire for him, to be his, intensely sexual, yet far beyond. Mere seconds later, a sobbing gasp breaks free from her control—a sobbing gasp of desire, irresistible yet impossible. Her desire for Adam to be his, for God to grant that impossibility somehow, resounds in the depths of her unconscious and transforms the wellspring of her will. There is fusion of her deepest desires and will—a release of tremendous energy. She wants more than anything to be worthy of God's gifts, to be a gift to others, especially Adam, in any way possible no matter what it costs her. It will take years of persistent practice, failures, false starts, and starting over again and again for that new unconscious species of desire, will, understanding to permeate her outer behavior as a consistent habit.

With all the lightness (and deniability) she can put into her voice, Eve jokes, "Wouldn't it be a hoot if we were married—Adam and Eve? My last name is already Smith, so it wouldn't change."

Adam chuckles, responding, "Yeah, it sounds funny, but…" She listens for what's next, imagining the worst. After a long pause, he continues. "It's just too ridiculous."

Eve Is Down

Eve is down from his response.

"Absurd," he adds.

"I was only kidding!" she protests.

Adam goes on, "Well, it's impossible, unworkable—"

She breaks in with irritation increasing, "All right already. Enough!" He catches the irritation and says, "Sorry." She responds, lying, "The thought's funny. I don't want to be married. Not at all. I'm not really sure…" They ride in silence.

In an attempt to save face, she adds, "Besides, I could never get through all that brush to your cabin—not like this."

"Oh, not at all," he corrects. "My dad is a…well, he was an environmental Nazi when I grew up. When he saw the property, he was incensed with my trampling through the woods daily and persuaded the environmental committee that a hand crank cable car had less environmental impact. They approved. Now I get to the cabin by cranking an elevator up the side of an oak and then ride in a metal cage down to the cabin. He's a genius with mechanical things, a skilled machinist. It's five minutes from the shed to the cabin, even with groceries. Working together on that repaired our relationship and led to his coming to faith."

A flicker of fascination dies away quickly as clouds of anger and despair fill her. She hides herself to avoid hurt. They ride in silence after Eve says without enthusiasm, "Oh, how interesting. I need to rest." She closes her eyes.

Half an hour later, Adam notices tears soaking her veil. "Do you need to stop to stretch or for lotion?" he asks.

She merely sighs, "No!"

The irritation in her voice is clear and inexplicable. He wants to dismiss it, give her space, and let it be. "Am I wanting what's right or what's easier?" he says to himself. "No way to know, so let it go." Then he offers, "I'd like to hear what's on your mind, if you want to talk."

"No way!" she screams.

Now he knows she needs to talk but does not want to. *How'd I get messed up in this?* The thought tempts him to self-pity. Thoughts of the extra expenses he could not afford, the danger, the extra time and wear-and-tear on his car and himself, the loss of his phone, and the burden of dealing with the drama flood his thinking and work up a good self-pitying glance at his misfortune.

"This can't be right!" he asserts. Fatigue and strong emotions fog his mind. "This isn't right!" He concludes and prays to do right.

After a while, he ventures, "Eve, are you hiding…"

"Not one bit!" she denies with vehemence.

He wants to drop it. The thought occurs, "If she's like that, then I'm done!" A gnawing sense of unease and a new quest to do the right thing reassert themselves. "'I fear thou dost protest too much, dear lady,'" he hazards.

She explodes into tears and erupts in a geyser of sobbing, blubbering speech only partially intelligible. "Oh, I wish…how much I wish…erring me—ving you, doing someth—anything for you…—gladly die…thousand de…too late!"

Adam turns off the highway and parks as soon as he can. "Eve," he says tenderly, "I love you." He's shocked that he said it openly, though he knows it's true.

"Then, why did you mock my proposal of marriage?" Eve asks with a mixture of hurt and anger, between sobs.

"What? I didn't hear anything like that," he rejoins.

A spirited fight ensues with unruly emotional overtones first from her but eventually from him also. Her themes are her desperate straits, her regrets for being blind to his attractive qualities, her despair of living without him, and how he and the cabin are the best solution for her. The issues for him are practical: concerns for safety after her wildness at the cabin, his inability to provide for her, and his concern that when her beauty returns or her desperation abates, he couldn't possibly hold her interest.

They're preoccupied and don't notice a storm coming, until suddenly it's dark; it interrupts their heart-to-heart combat. In a blink, hail pelts the car with deafening effect. Adam sees golf ball-size hail dimpling the hood and enlarging the crack in the windshield. He drives across the grass to a slab of concrete under a pavilion. Before he reaches it, the windshield is breaking, and hail and glass are bouncing off the dashboard. He pulls under the pavilion. The deafening noise subsides. The bottom half of the windshield is broken out. In the next few minutes, the hail increases to the size of baseballs and then to softballs. Just as quickly, the hail size decreases. In minutes, the hail stops, and sheets of rain pour down. It's pitch dark.

The radio weather report predicts rain all night for the area and warns of flash floods. Adam recalls that the pavilion is on a hill. They wait there until the rain stops.

Dreams free the mind to sort through events and emotions. Both have vivid dreams that night that are interrupted about midnight by lightning striking nearby and loud roaring thunder. They share their dreams and huddle together to share warmth, falling asleep in each other's embrace. Again and again, they dream together and are woken by flashes of light and thunder. Before dawn, Eve pleads with him to marry her—he gets on his knees and proposes. They agree that her life and their marriage will be tough for both of them.

For safety and economy, they agree to be married before God with no marriage license or public ceremony. They want to keep her out of any databases that might expose her identity. They drive out of their way to a town where dear friends of his are ministers.

Renee opens the door, "Welcome, Gabriele," she exclaims. She delights in calling him by his first name.

Her husband Paul runs and embraces him. Seeing a tall figure in a burqa with a thick veil standing by him, Paul asks, "Gabriele, what's this?"

Adam introduces Eve and tells them, "We want to get married—before God—but without a license. People are looking for her, so we can't take any chances."

Eve greets them and, seeing their quizzical looks at each other, says, "Jesus claimed me recently and—well, this"—she indicates her burqa and veil—"is a result of my previous life." The four of them chat a while before Adam explains his need to have the windshield replaced, to get a new cell, and to stay with them until the car is ready. They agree readily, even though puzzled; they trust him deeply.

While Paul and Renee prepare, Eve probes, "Gabriele?"

He sighs and replies, "Yes, yes. My mother was Swedish but grew up in Italy. Gabriele is a good Italian boy's name. Dad was drunk when she went into labor, so she got herself to the hospital. He didn't show up until she was back from the hospital. Her revenge was to name me Gabriele."

Eve chuckles, "Gabriele—I like it. Gabriele Adam Smith. What a gas!" She hoots.

He says, "I was teased about it—please don't call me that or spread it around."

She stops chuckling and pledges, "I'll never mention it again."

After Adam applies the lotion, long overdue, he and Paul leave to get a cell, pick up a few items, and drop off the car. When they return, the news isn't good. It will be a week until a windshield for a Corolla that old will arrive. Paul insists Gabriele use their car to return to Virginia. Adam has to be back in four days to teach class.

Eve wants Francine and others to be part of her wedding. They agree to have another private ceremony for friends when they return to Virginia.

Renee conducts a pre-marital counseling session. The four of them talk for hours. She gives them marriage workbooks, two books to share, and a bibliography of marriage resources. They discuss the ceremony.

They are ready to make their covenant of marriage before God. Adam and Eve fight about the vows each wrote. She insists on vowing "to submit fully to you, to respect even your whims and wishes, and to keep nothing hidden from you." Adam disagrees—he didn't want a pushover but a partner: "I want your input, your intellect and opinions, your wishes, and—"

Eve breaks in, "You'll have them. I'll hide nothing. But when you want me to keep my peace, I will. I know I can trust you to never take advantage of me. I want to give you myself totally, my trust. I commit myself to not battling for control. I repudiate control in our relationship. Oh, how I wish you or God would take away my rebelliousness!"

Paul and Renee watch a heated argument at the threshold of this marriage. Eve gives an ultimatum: "The marriage is off, unless I can make the vows I want"—adding with a tease in her voice—"unless you order me to make different vows." She smiles under her veil; they only see her put her hands on her hips and take a stance of mock defiance.

Adam chuckles, "You've got me. I won't do that." After an awkward pause, he says, "I want to marry you. I'll improve my vows." He rewrites his vows and takes his place.

The Wedding Begins

The wedding begins. Paul and Renee point out that marriage is God-given, a wonderful blessing, a challenge and opportunity for love, and a covenant before God. They each say "I do." They are invited to say their vows.

Adam is opening his mouth when Eve begins saying. "Adam, I relinquish myself to God and you. I belong to God, you, and lastly to myself. I will submit fully to you, respect your whims and wishes, and keep nothing hidden from you. I will stay with you through thick and thin, up and down, easy and hard. I will never leave you. All I have and am forever, I give to you. Thank you, Adam, for loving me ever and always, and even now."

Adam recites, "My precious Eve, I will always love you. I will lay down my life for you moment by moment and serve you. I will pursue you, your thoughts and desires, and what is good for you. I will protect your freedom, cherishing and respecting who you are and are becoming. I will never stop loving you. I will never leave you. Thank you for being my companion in life."

Paul and Renee pronounce them husband and wife before God. Renee says, "Kiss!"

Adam enfolds Eve in his arms and holds her close. They whisper to each other and gently rock back and forth. Renee, who is near Adam, hears him whisper, "Are you sure?!" Paul and Renee hear Eve respond, "Yes!"

Eve lifts the veil. Paul and Renee gasp. Her face is rough, shriveled, and blotchy with red and black spots. They kiss tenderly. She throws her arms around him and grips him tightly. A rash appears on her skin, turning it fiery red with what looks like huge pimples erupting on her face. Eve covers herself with the veil and is sobbing wildly in a mishmash of incredible joy, intense pain, and shame. She faints from pain; Adam catches her. He carries her into their room.

Adam covers the windows and door—the room is dark. He applies the lotion to her, undresses, and waits.

Sex is difficult and disappointing. Her condition limits their enjoyment. He is extremely gentle. She is used to aggressive intense sex and laments his lack of passion. She accepts his lack of passion in view of her appearance and determines that she will never mention it, lest she hurt him. Still, she deeply longs for that consuming desire.

Eve wakes at three with horrible cramps. Her period sneaks up on her. She could always anticipate its coming, and the cramps and bleeding were never like this. She wakes him, "I started my period and need supplies—now." This is now her new normal. In her current condition, her periods will be irregular, unpredictable, and harsh, and her hormonal and emotional shifts will be much more severe. Waiting for Adam to return, the thought *From a charmed life to a cursed existence* repeatedly haunts her.

Eve wakes in the foulest mood. The night's discomforts, disappointments, and her lack of sleep aggravate the misery of her skin. She is on fire. The lotion barely helps. She struggles to manage her reactions with little success. She confesses her struggle to Adam, prays for God's help, and apologizes in advance to Paul and Renee.

Renee calls out, "Gabriele, join us for breakfast. Eve—"

Eve explodes, yelling, "Adam doesn't like to be called that. Why do you persist in tormenting him? Why—"

Adam interrupts calmly, "Eve, don't defend me."

"But"—she bellows and then, recovering herself, lowers her voice, "I'm so sorry. I am a sorry excuse for—"

"Eve! You're forgiven. I'm not sure I could deal with half of what you are." Adam interjects. "I love you!"

Eve bursts into tears and runs back to their room. Adam follows, calming, stroking her, and assuring her that he loves her. After breakfast and thanking Paul and Renee, they head for Virginia in the Brown's Focus. It's Friday and his first classes are Monday.

There's no honeymoon. Her hormones are raging, her misery magnified, and her emotions unruly. They settle into the cabin. He does everything, and she doesn't leave the cabin, except to walk naked in the garden in the dark. She exults in freedom from the suffocating burqa, unburdened from the weight of the thick cloth on her shoulders, air circulating near her skin to cool it, and, as her eyes adjust to the delicious darkness, gazing into the heavens to bathe in the glory of God. On awakening, Adam joins her. Silently holding her, they commune together naked before God. These walks in the garden in the naked presence of God became her routine and his. Treasuring together that garden sanctuary of nakedness before God and each other helps safeguard their love, commitment, marriage, and sanity.

He shows Eve the cabin during her more lucid and calm moments. Besides the elevator and cable car, he and his father rigged up a bike generator to charge a bank of batteries. His parents planted a garden with vegetables and herbs and located rhubarb and asparagus beds established by the previous owner. Adam made contracts with cell and internet companies for antennas on some trees in exchange for fast free internet. He discovered a passage behind a shelf in the cellar to the shed. There were even rooms off the passage. There was a trapdoor in the shed with a ladder. His fighting the storm to bring wood from the shed had been unnecessary!

On hearing that, Eve responds, "Ah—but that's when I started loving you."

Wonderful healing conversations ensue. They discover each other in greater depth. They talk about everything; she deliberately listens more than she speaks. She takes great care to understanding him. He is already a careful listener and very attentive to her.

While he teaches, she reads. By the end of the week, she memorizes all his books (and his notes in them) he had at the cabin. They have stimulating conversations during lulls in her stormy emotions.

She avoids speaking in public or on the phone, lest she be discovered. Eve texts brief messages to him often. She calls him only in emergencies. Her distinctive ring signals him to read her texts immediately. She lives as if she is mute, except around close friends in private.

Medical care is an issue. She can't risk using Adam's insurance or going to just any doctor, lest she be entered into a database that flags her. Dr. Blanke, Eric, helps them locate doctors who are discrete and give her work to do in exchange for their services.

He takes her to visit Francine. Francine doesn't know Adam and hesitates agreeing to his visit. Eve is eager to rekindle their friendship. Eve's last contact with her was to sneak out, and then there was no contact for months. The reunion is sweet, tearful, and joyous. Francine weeps and wails with Eve. They explain what happened to Janet and how she became Eve and married Adam.

Francine surprises Eve with her laptop and iPad. "I thought the people who kidnapped me would have gotten them," Eve remarks.

Francine explains that a boy saw her sneak out the window and came in and stole the laptop, iPad, and a few other things. "I noticed and reported the theft to the police," Francine recalls.

"While I was waiting for them to come, an email saying you were sending a guy to get your things arrived. A policeman came and took a report. I think that guy came while the officer was here but never came in. Something seemed wrong, so I prayed for you constantly." The boy had a change of heart and returned them a few days later.

"Well," Eve exclaims, "that worked out. I don't think we could have afforded to replace them. I mean, they're better than we need—and expensive!"

Eve's Attitude

Eve's attitude is changing. Before she lost everything, she wouldn't have hesitated to replace or spend for whatever she wanted. She hadn't thought in terms of what she needed but only what she wanted.

The next Saturday, they drive to Pennsylvania to return the Brown's car and pick up his Corolla. Worshipping with them Sunday was awkward; at first glance, everyone assumed she was a conservative Muslim. When they saw her signing songs and worshipping, they were pleasantly confused. A few attempted conversations with her. Even those adept at signing had difficulty understanding Eve without facial clues, unless she signed very slowly.

They talk on the way to and from Pennsylvania. They talk about God, literature, and how to better their life together. They agree to find a small house church. It crushes Eve to give up the church she has many friends at and where she was on the deaf praise team and helped interpret.

"There's no limit to what I lose," she complains. She cries bitterly. "I hate being out of control emotionally! And so weak," she sobs.

Once her period ends, Eve functions better and does more. She tends the garden, fixes meals, and does their laundry at a friend's house in exchange for Greek lessons. She washes her clothes, the sheets, and Adam's night clothes in the well water at the cabin. More than brief contact with cloth washed in chlorinated water enflames her skin.

Her hands limit what she can do, devoid of fat, and her fingers are thin spindles that can't endure pressure or time in water. She wears padded mittens to drive. She can't cut all her own food or type for long. On her worst days, she can't feed herself. He feeds her, does whatever she needs to preserve her dignity (well, some anyway).

Eve discovers that stress before her period greatly worsens it. In time, she manages her period—lessens its severity. Exposures of her skin to light for even a moment or exposure to chlorinated water (or worse, drinking it) were the worse stressors. But even anger, prolonged irritation, or worrying caused pain to her skin, stressed her, and worsened her period and might make it start earlier. This realization spurs her to learn to cope; her rages, for instance, caused her intense and immediate discomfort. If prolonged, her rage causes her intense pain and effectively debilitates her. Her periods at worst debilitate her for about a third of the month—Adam would do everything, and she would stay at the cabin and, perhaps, have a friend visit.

Eve read voraciously. She devours books of spiritual disciplines and growth, about coping with emotions, how to communicate and resolve conflict, and leans heavily on Adam, Francine, and select friends. She endeavors to live an open life, full of confession and devoid of hiding. Hiding negative emotions, even negative thoughts, stresses her, causing her pain; it spurs candor.

The unremitting pain, her daily despair of physical relief, her inability to manage her stress, her emotion, or even her own life, and her far deeper despair that she cannot live up to her growing understanding of God's goodness drive her to despair of herself. Despairing of herself (and her ability to live how she desperately wants to) frees her from depending on herself to depend on God. Despite perfect recall of the Bible, many spiritual classics and other good literature, her knowledge and practice of spiritual disciplines are mere stage props. God's gifts, a tiny germ of a childlike acceptance of them, and her destitute spirit are center stage. It is a rehab for her soul leading to gradual awakenings.

Most of her life is dark and difficult, painfully picking her way over sharp stones in the dark. Once in a while, a passing car lights her way. She cannot get over the fence to the road but did, as best she could, memorize the next few feet of path that was made briefly visible.

The very daily grind of her life, her constant humiliation, the pain and futility, grinding inexorably, inescapably, and relentlessly on her soul for years without relief, frees her. There is no mere easing of the situation. Abandoning hope repeatedly, gradually, and imperceptibly, renders her situation, any situation, irrelevant—freedom. Even her own self, with its tangle of weaknesses, sabotaging unconscious, and desire for preeminence and importance, becomes irrelevant. Daily loving and serving others and living and breathing God's presence become her reality.

Despairing of hope, and especially of self, grants hints of hope and freedom. Transcending self and situation yields living (occasionally) with irrepressible love, joy, and faith that sees possibilities in the problems of living.

Her constant failures, her inability to manage her temper, her pride, and self-focused pity drive her to greater depths of despair but also of an awareness of her desperate needs for the suffering redeeming love of Jesus (and also of Adam), for his cross, his dying for her and with her.

Eve catches occasional glimpses of the beauties and wonders in nature, in Adam, in her friends, in every person she meets, and, even amazingly, in herself—her!—and something begins to dawn on her, something unimaginably incredible. She notices each blade of identical grass, each of the myriad blades in a patch of quite ordinary grass—every blade is uniquely different and beautiful. Each day, each moment as she endures it, her senses are flooded with beauties as relentless as the ocean waves and her soul caressed by glories as refreshing as a steady gentle breeze on a hot day. The joy overcomes thoughts of self, emptying her of garbage and filling her with gifts of joy—gifts from the One who loves her.

Gradually, the crescendoing glory lights her soul, lifting her burdened soul and buoying her up to regions of light. All manner of things are put right, turned right side up and right side out; all shall be well. Confidence in God burns bright in Eve—sometimes.

A far greater dawning starts imperceptivity for her. Gradually, bit by bit, the former brilliance of beauty pales in the presence of this rising sun. The contrast: a dim point of ember at the tip of a recently extinguished wick of a candle—just barely glowing—compared to the full noon day sun. The beauties are still magnificently blazing but are of no account. What matters most, what matters solely, is that God makes all beauty possible, makes all love and loveliness possible, and makes everything good and all goodness possible. Nothing else counts; everyone and everything count precisely due to him.

Uncertainty is deeply engrained into her soul and became a vital foundation for her faith. She knows the Bible, theology, and church history backward and forward but remains gloriously uncertain about herself. Socrates would have been pleased with her embracing uncertainty. God is pleased with the resulting humility; he is pleased with her.

Eve can no longer imagine any release from her pain, discomfort, and humiliation of how she has to dress. Her impotency to stop her rages against God and Adam flood her with guilt that eats her alive. God, of course, but Adam also deserves far better from her. She can't deliver nor can she imagine how she ever will.

The pull of her past, her idealized and superficially wonderful past, fills her vision with promises that all would be better not only for her but also for God, Adam, and her friends, if she turned back to magic, if she gave in to the control of the dragon. Spiritual suicide tempts her gravely. She confesses its pull to God, Adam, and to friends often; it is vital to her continued stumble forward.

Prayer and Fasting for Eve

Prayer and fasting for Eve and by her, the embarrassing abundance of patience, forgiveness, and love showered on her by many during her first year of marriage help immeasurably—and not at all. Neither she nor the situation changes the first year. Despair grows, desperation deepens. She spirals into a black hole.

Francine relates her situation with the dream of pampering and hardships; Eve's intrigued. A new desire sprouts in her soul's desolation—she wants to despair of herself. A tantalizing thought comes to mind—going through the black hole to emerge in another reality from a wellspring spewing life—doing God's will in him. She, taking heart by embracing despair of herself, puts her hope in God. Giving thanks seasons complaining, even for hardships and her weaknesses. She loves and often prays the laments of the Psalms. Often at the cabin alone, almost always in times of misery, she bawls out her complaints to God from those precious Psalms or the complaints of Jeremiah, Job, or another saintly sufferer. The intensity and volume of her laments give her release and comfort her soul.

Yet, the strain of the insistent pull of the black hole weighs heavily on Eve. She can't escape, and its pull increases day by dreary day. Adam is an incredible help. He serves her, is mostly patient, and creatively assures her of his love and devotion. But she sees that it—no, that she—wears him down. He encourages her to hide nothing from God, him, and his close friends. Her intense constant laments comfort and humiliate her. She desperately needs others to help with her emotions, to listen to her despair deeply long enough to plumb its depths (is it bottomless?) so that she, not them, wrings out a scrap of hope, faith, or love.

Eve prays to accept Adam as he is rather than as she wishes he was. Daily, she prays fervently for God to assist her, to give her great mercy and grace to resign herself to accepting Adam—her good, safe, solid, serving husband with a few minor flaws. He is patient, wonderfully practical and frugal, but it too often trumps romance, and he's tightfisted with money. And even thinking about it makes her wistful, *He lacks passion for me, but anyone would now. Still, he loves me deeply. I wish he were capable of real passion.* It didn't seem right to Eve to tell anyone these things, or to even think further about them.

The first year is hard on Eve and Adam too. Pain and shame are near constant companions. Their relationship is stormy due to her whirlwind of emotions. Her need for the lotion adds to the financial strain. By the end of the year, they spent the mortgage nest egg. They borrow from Adam's father to pay taxes on the cabin. Eve discovers that all their clothes, everything in the cabin, have to be washed without chlorine in the water. So Eve and Adam together (but Adam does almost all the real work) wash not only all their clothes by hand but also some of Francine's and other friends that Eve spends time with. Life is tough, but joys and wonders mix in seasoning the course of their daily life together and individually. Eve sometimes finds it unbearable, but, for the new perspectives, she gains. She is living to awakening.

PART 4

LIVING

Living Becomes Gradually Ordinary

Living becomes gradually ordinary and mundane, the dull routine of her daily life. Discomfort wakes Eve before dawn. She stretches to regain use of her body and walks in the garden. If cold keeps or drives her in before Adam joins her, she meditates, prays, and sings softly inside. He joins her before dawn. Whispering, touching, and embracing each other start their day together.

Adam helps her bathe, put on lotion, and dress before riding the stationary bike to recharge the batteries. Then he gets ready. Eve checks their e-mails, responding or alerting him if any requires his immediate knowledge or response. She prepares breakfast, mixing the milk, making the tea, preparing the fruit and whatever else she can manage. He fixes lunches for them. They can't afford to eat out, and she has to avoid chemicals and many spices.

After breakfast, Adam cleans up the dishes and completes his grooming. Her only grooming is brushing her teeth in the dark. The burqa covers all but a slit around her eyes; her skin won't tolerate makeup or perfume, and her hair breaks off at about two inches. Most mornings, unless debilitated by her period, she prepares dinner to cook in a crock pot. She slices vegetables, adds spices, and leaves the rest for him to cut and put in the crock pot. He cranks the cable car and elevator to get to their car.

The rare exceptions to their routine of leaving together are if they both stay at the cabin, or if Eve stays there because she is sick (rare), or because her period is too severe (at least a day or two per month). She goes with him when he drives to speaking engagements, unless her "health" doesn't permit. He almost never flies—she can't (to avoid the security screenings)—and rarely is he away from her overnight. That she needs him, or anyone, vexes her. He acts as if anything he does for her is a privilege and frequently says so; it makes her dependency tolerable. That he gladly depends on her gives her a sense of balance and dignity.

While he drives, Eve recites his e-mail to him and memorizes his replies for later entry. Adam either drives to campus, and she takes the car or he rarely keeps the car and drops her at Francine's. Her routine varies, usually including time with friends—Francine mostly—answering his and her e-mails, reading, taking much-needed brief naps, lunch, serving people, and tutoring in Greek or something else. Then she drives to pick up Adam or waits for him to pick her up. Each day, she memorizes his e-mails to recite while he drives.

The aroma of dinner welcomes them to the cabin. Eve changes in the dark into a simple dress, while Adam sets the table and lights a single candle. He signals when all is ready. Eve relishes dinner in near dark, and they prolong it; she is freed from her "prison" and is spared from pain and shame. They talk about their day, selves, and everything; they laugh and thrash out their life together.

After dinner, Adam cleans up while Eve changes, gets his help with the lotion, and puts her safe house/prison back on. The rest of the day varies. As the routine takes root, her stress lessens; she looks forward to simple things. Routine comforts wean her from her addiction to exhilaration. The unbearably ordinary and boring become delightful comforts.

Her options are few. She was a good interpreter for the deaf, but no longer is. Her mouth and facial expressions are hidden. Also, she wears loose mittens on her hands; her hands are too sensitive for gloves. She can't converse fluidly with the deaf due to her mittens and her hidden facial cues. She's too hard to understand. She misses that and being part of a deaf praise team. She misses participating in group discussions—she only speaks in private with close friends. Wearing mittens to spare her hands from light requires her to use a stylus for her iPad in public. In private, she uses her voice to type. Even typing under her burqa with the mittens off hurts her hands before long; everything is hard for her.

Mobility and comfort are constant challenges. She keeps lotion and water safe for her in the car but also carries water, lotion, and a cushion to sit on. Her body has almost no padding. She can't wear a backpack—even the weight of a coat on her shoulders is only tolerated briefly. She can't sit nor stand for long. Walking is easiest. Hours of sleep are only possible on a hammock.

Eve settles into routines that are as comfortable as they can make them. She quickly realizes that being outwardly focused is better than being focused on her misery or her limitations. The more she thinks about herself, the more she suffers.

She wants to make a difference, but her limitations frustrate that. She dares not speak in public or on the phone. She dares not submit her name or social security number for anything, lest she be flagged. Her discomfort and lack of physical stamina disqualify her from even volunteer work. She can't be a greeter, and soup kitchens turn her down as a server due to the negative reactions to her appearance. If only she didn't have to wear that burqa!

Day by dreary day, the burqa and her limitations wound her narcissism (and keeps the wound raw). People spit on her. A man knocked her down and kicked her. The car is keyed repeatedly, dents appear, and someone wrote "pig" in blood on the hood. Insults are hurled at her often, mainly when shopping; she and Adam decide to avoid her shopping alone when possible. But then Adam, or a friend, has to go with her—it's inconvenient, feeds fears that she's inept, and another humiliation. She muses the irony, "I believed I was powerful—how fitting!" It raises a root of bitterness, until Francine uproots it before it grows.

"Don't you want that old self put to death?" Francine asks. The question hurts but removes a painful barb. The relief is palpable. Eve knows in her depths that practicing spiritual disciplines and Biblical and theological knowledge benefits her little compared to her daily hardships. She knows relevant passages in the Bible and literature, but it is enduring the hardships that bit by bit reform her. She rejoices (the words often the reality sometimes) and complains often to God in her laments and to Francine, Adam, and select friends in confession. Going a day without lamenting to God or confessing her distress to others overburdens her.

Francine's mind, even at 110, is quick, incisive, and inventive. She encourages and challenges Eve to new paradigms and radically different ways of thinking. "Being poor in spirit and persecuted are the only beatitudes," Francine often observes (sometimes as though reminding herself) "that the blessings are rooted in the present instead of the future." She encourages Eve to "brainstorm in the Spirit," to pray for God to muse and inspire her. Eve spends as much time as she can with Francine. Their time is filled with conversation, laughter, prayer, worship, confession, verbal sparring, and...play. Time with Francine transports Eve to forgetting herself. Her pain recedes from awareness.

Time with Francine is a relief in another way to Eve. Though Francine's mind is strong and nimble, her body is weak, frail, and gradually wasting away. Eve is of real benefit to her. Eve helps and serves Francine with zest and eagerness.

One day, Francine remarks, "I don't think I'll live to 111."

Eve (and the scared little girl inside) wants to scream and run and hide. Yearning to avoid this topic, this possibility, this inevitable reality, overwhelms Eve. Only her love for Francine enables her to coax out, "I'll hold your hand to and through the portal of death." Though she tries not to, Eve bursts into tears. She didn't want Francine to have to comfort her. Once Eve regains composure, they have their first tearful and wonderful heart-to-heart exchange about death. It helps that Francine does not fear death but looks forward to her rebirth after it.

Brainstorming in the Spirit

Brainstorming in the Spirit with Francine after the car was damaged and Eve cursed and spat on has them caught up in what to do. In worship, they forget themselves, turning their bodies (Francine gets out of her wheelchair and prostrates herself), minds, and wills to God, singing and praying aloud and quoting Scriptures—having their emotions, thoughts, and wills incited to God. A fresh breeze takes them an unexpected direction. They are convicted that they resent what is happening to Eve and her current condition. They are convicted to give thanks for and make use of the hardships rather than resent them.

They ask, "How do we make the most of what is happening?" It isn't a rhetorical or an idle question. They want answers to the depths of their unconscious so strongly that unconscious reservations are negligible. It is passionate prayer, though not worded as a prayer at all. Answers form in the depths and bubbled up in unexpected forms.

One answer is that Eve makes friends with conservative Muslim women. Eve learns Aramaic and memorizes the Qumran in English and Aramaic. They converse about many things, but especially about how to finesse love in a power relationship. They even talk about

Jesus. Those conversations help Eve and other women to be better and more loving wives and to have better marriages. Some couples meet with Adam and Eve for coffee or tea and conversation.

Another answer is Eve confesses to Francine her failings as a wife, her temper and her aversion to her Spartan way of life with Adam. "I snap at him, complain far too much, I'm irritable," she admits. "But he still gives me everything he can and more," she affirms. "I can tell him anything, absolutely anything and he responds well." A thought makes her giddy, and she laughs. "Adam is good to me and for me. He never insists on getting his way. He's given me freedom—" Tears fill her eyes, and she pauses to compose herself. "He's given me all the freedom I've got. Everything good in my life is due to him," she tells Francine and also herself something she finally realizes. She sighs and continues her soliloquy of confession and realization. "He is God's gift to me." She murmurs in hushed awe, "I would never have considered him for marriage. Never! But he is better for me than anyone I could have cooked up. If I hadn't lost everything, then I'd never have known his love." The tears grew into sobs that rack her body. Francine comforts her. Minutes later, an exhausted Eve declares, "I needed this to happen to me."

The next summer, Eve concocts a much better and cheaper lotion. It soothes her skin better and longer and with less soaking of her clothing with oils. The financial strain is relieved, but the damage was done. They have debts they can't pay without more income.

They celebrate their first anniversary. Eve makes progress with her temper; she isn't as miserable and in as much pain, and relishes snatches of bliss: time in the garden alone and with Adam, dinner and conversation with Adam freed from wearing her prison, and times with Francine and friends.

The financial situation is desperate. Adam would mortgage the cabin, but interest rates are too high. The car needs repairs.

His parents visit for several weeks in the fall. The visit is pleasant, but Eve loses time alone in the garden and her special dinners with Adam. When they leave, she doesn't have time to return to her routine before Francine enters hospice care at her apartment. They decide Eve will stay with Francine. Eve stays with her precious friend for ten days until Francine dies.

Time with Francine in decline is hard on Eve. Seeing Francine tired, in pain, and confused most of the time weighs heavily on her. Francine sleeps most of the time, and they have only brief snatches of surface conversations. Still, she's glad to serve and be with Francine. Eve doesn't sleep well. Adam comes for breakfast some days and dinner every day. He brings 'safe' water for her to drink and use.

The night before death, Francine is in great pain, which prevents either from sleeping much. She refuses to eat. She groans and doesn't speak to Eve, or even seem to recognize her. Francine struggles to open her eyes even a tiny bit, and the lids tremble briefly before they close again. Adam texts to check on them. Eve resents his intrusion into her limited time with Francine and texts back a terse reply. He calls and speaks tenderly and lovingly to her. She resents him further for the guilt that assaults her.

Eve watches Francine's breathing get slower and more labored. Eve removes her mittens and holds her hands under the covers. She kisses Francine on the forehead, whispering, "I love you."

Francine opens her eyes and looks intently at Eve. Her eyes are big and bright and pour forth love. After a few seconds, the eyelids droop back to a slit. "Francine, you are true to your word," Eve says while choking back emotion. "You've always been true during the all-too-brief time I've known you. You won't make it to your next birthday. You don't have to make tomorrow. You can go. I'll miss you. I love you. I want you to go to the one who loves you most and will give you relief—and glory."

Almost at once, her eyes open wide, and Francine sits up looking around the room with wonder in her eyes and face and exclaims, "Wow!" Her head sinks back onto the pillow, her eyes gradually close, and she breathes her last.

Eve Wails

Eve wails. Everything is a blur. She cries copiously. It's lonely and long before she can text Adam to tell him Francine died and asking him to come. He doesn't respond. While she waits exhausted, she falls asleep. She wakes hours later. She feels abandoned, totally alone, desolate. She rages.

Adam texts her, finally saying he's had a busy day and asking how she is dealing with losing Francine. She is enraged that he took so long and responds so casually about Francine dying. She tells herself, *He's jealous of our relationship! He doesn't really give a damn!* Her hidden self vows revenge.

She texts Adam telling her to get her; Francine is dead. He calls her and tells her he is on the way and expresses his sorrow for her. On the way, he notifies the mortuary that she died. Someone from the mortuary is there when he arrives. He thinks nothing of Eve's silence since strangers are around. He tries to comfort her, but she is cold and withdrawn. He assumes she's grieving.

In the car, Eve asks pointedly, "Why didn't you text when I told you she'd died?"

Puzzled, Adam responds, "I called." She unleashed a tirade against him for not responding to her earlier text. He explains, "I-I never got it."

Overwhelmed with grief and emotion, she thinks, *He's lying! He knew!* All she says is, "Oh, okay. Let me rest." She pretends to fall asleep. She wants nothing to do with someone who lies to her at her darkest hour.

Eve is withdrawn and hardly talks. He prays for her, tries to comfort her, listen or do anything to ease her grief. When he offers to hold her (something she always welcomed), he is surprised that she says, "No, not now." He offers her neck, back, feet rubs, and help with her lotion. She turns every offer down.

He attends the funeral with her. Adam did not know that Eve wrote a eulogy for Francine that is read by Mary. It's wonderful! It isn't like her to keep that from him. He sits by Eve and pats her arm to approve of her eulogy, but she pulls away from him. He'd heard of women who withdrew when grieved. He is saddened that he might be shut out of going through her grief with her.

Back at the cabin, it gets worse. Adam pleads with her, "Talk to me. Let me be with you through this. Let—"

Eve interrupts, "I don't want your help!" Her tone alerts Adam that something far more than grief is going on.

Calmly and in hushed tones, he says, "You seem to be hiding—some…"

She lies, "I'm just grieving—give me a break!" He's confused and doesn't know what to think or do. She has her moods, but he has never been given so much of the silent treatment. Every day, he gingerly reaches out to her and every day she rejects his overtures. Weeks pass.

Adam's uncle has a stroke and needs a place to recover when he leaves the hospital. A plea goes out to family to help; he will pay some. Eve volunteers to care for him at the cabin to help with finances. She assures Adam that she wants to (she does), but she also wants an excuse to ignore Adam. After talking about it, arrangements are made.

The day Francine died, Eve turned off her phone and hid it, telling Adam she misplaced it. Their only contact during the day is by e-mail, his phone to her laptop, which she ignores at will. The day before his uncle and aunt move in, she announces she found it. When she turns it on, she discovers that the first text she thought she sent Adam about Francine's death never was sent. She feels awful, too awful and ashamed to say anything about that. She stops giving him silent treatments, but she kept so much hidden from him that their former spark and warmth are missing. She tells herself she will make it up to Adam; she promises herself their special times together will return. Her promise proves barren.

Fred and Helen move in the next day. Fred, like Adam's father, loves the cabin and finds it charming. Fred is difficult due to the stroke—he's demanding, has difficulty controlling his body, his bowels, and his temper. Helen is far worse. She is controlling, whiney, and no help. She rearranges things in the kitchen and elsewhere as she pleases. She censors no thought that comes into her head. She talks incessantly about absolutely nothing, except to complain. Eve resents them and also Adam for his low pay.

Eve has no time for the garden, and it's too cold. A cold winter is predicted. She has no time with Adam, except when she is too exhausted to enjoy it. She misses him. After three months, Fred and Helen move out and finances are okay. Eve is excited for the opportunity to reconnect with Adam, but something eclipses that.

Adam and Eve are reconnecting, and she is recovering from the stress of tending to Fred and Helen. A month after, they leave Eve, with her body in a stance and a lilt in her voice that he recognizes as exhilaration. She announces to Adam after dinner by candlelight, "I have a wonderful surprise."

If he could see her face, he'd see a smile so broad that it almost divides her face in two. He is not surprised, knowing how much she likes riddles and guessing games that she wants him to guess. After a dozen questions, he is close enough for her to spill her news: "My skin is healing, my hair is growing longer, and I've managed to gain seven pounds!"

They celebrate with words and hoots, with music and dancing and frolicking together, with their minds, emotions, and bodies. They worship and thank God together. Their joy spills over into making love the rest of the day. *He is so gentle*, Eve thinks.

Eve credits her improvement to the lotion she developed, her coping better with stress, and, of course, God's help. She keeps careful records, figures how to measure progress with all her afflictions, and plots the various measures. She states to Adam, "Extrapolating from the data and my current rate of improvement, I'll be able to tolerate moderate indoor lighting in three to seven years." Her hopes are dashed—she was hoping for a quicker recovery.

Adam comforts Eve. She becomes obsessed with their making love as often as possible. Seeds of discontent are sown in her. She makes excuses to stay at the cabin often to research how to speed up her recovery.

After two weeks of this, Eve is shopping at a food market when she notes a strikingly handsome and virile-looking man working behind the counter. He is taller and far more muscular than Adam—much more attractive. Unconsciously, she thrusts out her breasts as if to offer them. She lingers to watch him. She returns to his area frequently that day. She longs to interact with him. She asks him questions about his wares by writing notes. She loves to hear his voice. She returns the next three days. She can tell that he notices her, is intrigued by her. She stops going to that market. She doesn't like what she's thinking.

She tells Adam that she accepted that her recovery is going to be slow but that "It's still faster than I thought just months ago." Lying and deceiving him is a habit; she considers him a fool for being so easily duped. She is careful to continue her routines with him so he won't notice changes. She acts engaged and interested to prevent his knowing that she's changing.

Winter passes into spring and then into summer. They celebrate their second anniversary. In the fall, Eve returns to the market. Her guy is still there. She notices that he is glad to see her and speaks to her warmly, "I missed seeing you—glad you're back." She allows herself to go weekly to watch him work.

In mid-November, he whispers to Eve, "I'll bet there's a beautiful woman hidden under that." She wants that to be true again. She needs to be beautiful again. She reasons that she can just dabble in magic to speed up the natural processes of her recovery. She does so, and, by mid-December, her beauty is restored.

Starting mid-November, Eve no longer lets Adam see or touch her naked skin, even in dim light. She tells him that she convinced that any exposure to light or his skin oils slows down her recovery and that she is no longer going to expose herself. She also tells him that she is going to be clothed for a few months when they have sex to cut down on irritation to her skin.

Eve shops for clothes for the first time in years. She keeps back money for her plans. She buys makeup and perfume. Her opportunity comes when friends asks her to look after their house and pets while they are out of the country for a month. The day they leave, she rearranges a room for herself and her things (just a few outfits). The next day, she whispers to her guy, "I'd love to provide a feast for you sometime. Text me a good day and time." She slips him her cell number.

So Begins Her Affair

So begins her affair. She loves his compliments of her beauty and his obvious worship of her. His sexual passion, his out-of-control passion for her, is a tonic for her. She is careful to use protection, but his out-of-control passion for her that she stokes finally overwhelms her precautions. After three wonderful weeks, he disappears. He doesn't respond to her texts. She inquires and is told that he suddenly returned to Iran to marry.

She and Adam were trying to get pregnant, and now she is. She is due in late August. She's uncertain who the father is. She conceives her future: she lived through August at the cabin—the heat, no air conditioning, and then the added heat of pregnancy. *No, I can't go through that and the shame.* She nauseates herself, thinking, *I promised I'd hide nothing from Adam, and now I hide everything!* The urge to vomit is sudden and strong; she doesn't make it to the bathroom before she does.

Eve ponders what to do; she gets checked for STDs. She's clean. She decides, *I don't have to tell him about the affair. I couldn't bear to see his reaction. I can't. I won't.* The guilt at her decision strikes her down. *Damn me! He deserves better than me. I won't go back.* She wants to believe she is leaving for him; she knows better. The guilt paralyzes her. *I can't go back*, she reasons, *so I'll have to go forward.* Her friends are coming back in five days, so she rushes past her reluctance, rationalizing that "I have to act quickly while I have a chance." Going forward means finding a rich guy who'll be suitable. Within a few hours of searching on the web, she has three candidates. She contacts her first choice and, after telling him her cover story, invites him to dinner at her friends' house. On Monday, she texts Adam that she has a contagious flu and that, to spare him, she'll stay at their friends' house a few days. After she assures him that she is fine, she persuades him to pick up his car without coming in.

She times it for her guest to arrive after she is sure Adam would be gone. She overwhelms her guest. She hates using the role of a damsel in distress, but it is her surest route to success. He arrives and has a doctor check her for STDs. Only after receiving a text that she is clean does he have sexual contact with her. He is enchanted by her beauty, charm, her melodious voice, and her story. They eat, drink, dance, talk, and have passionate sex. She abandons herself to wow him and succeeds beyond his wildest dreams. She proves to him that she is the perfect date for his many social and professional affairs. Her cunning, memory, and her ability to manipulate others indicate to him that she can "work a room" even better than he can.

Before morning, he is determined to rescue her from her pursuers. He has her sign legal papers to fully specify his commitment to her; after a year together, he will give her one million dollars. He arranges an identity and a full facial mask with voice alteration technology built in, so she can go about freely in public. He assures her that he will arrange plastic surgery and a permanent change to her voice from the best surgeons later.

By the end of Tuesday, she has her identity papers, mask, and new voice. She realizes, *I can go in public for all to see my beauty.* She is buoyant. Years of pent-up desires and tensions are released; she bursts into tears and is catapulted into overwhelming gratitude for Steve. She loses control of herself and flings herself at him passionately. The passion of her gratitude satisfies Steve; he likes having the upper hand. She moves to his bedroom at his estate. He promises to buy her an entire wardrobe and a car. Vanquished by his generosity and the magnitude of her long unfulfilled desires, her identity, already confused—Susan/Eve/Janet—begins to turn into, at an unconscious level, Steve's. She abandons herself to him without reservation.

Steve asks, "How about a corset?"

She responds, "I've worn them, but…" She is planning to say that she will never do so again when she catches a flash of unbridled desire on Steve's face. Her resolve crumbles. He wants her corseted. She reshapes her desires. "What do you want?"

Steve describes his fascination with corsets. A desire from the depths to please him prompts her to say, "Let's get me one." His reaction steels her determination. They leave for an upscale corset boutique. The women are impressed with her twenty-four inch waist and stoke her desire to make it smaller. She tells herself she is only doing it for Steve. His reaction as he watches and comes over to put his hands on her compels her to demand "tighter" again and again. Finally, after about two hours of tightening and resting, the women comments that her waist is as small as it can get "for today." She can scarcely breathe; her only comfort is Steve's reaction. She notes a hint of disappointment in Steve's face. His disappointment crushes her spirit. She wants it smaller for him. She inquires about what can make it smaller. After a detailed description of the process and results and watching Steve's reactions, she is obsessed with submitting to rigorous corset training—part of her rebels. Forces within crush the rebellion, and she is compelled to plead with Steve to let her do so. She persuades him. It is planned and determined for her that she will submit to his every whim aided by hidden desires.

Steve Takes Her

Steve takes her shopping with relentless abandon the next three days. The more he lavishes her with, the more her unconscious bonds to him grow. She doesn't realize what is happening—but likes it more and more. More and more, she needs to please him. The more she pleases him, the more he does for her. More and more, she wants to be possessed by him. This romantic love is new to her, and she gladly bends herself to Steve. She fantasizes about him and about being his almost constantly. *This is true love*, she ponders. Sex is often and passionate.

Shopping for clothes that Steve wants her to wear provokes a brief crisis for her. Steve wants all her clothes to require a corset. He doesn't even know that he wants that, but she discovers it. She again rebels inwardly. Her memories provoke fears of discomfort, of having her freedom to breathe naturally crushed out of her, of loss of mobility, of aching pains. Her determination to never be squeeze-wrapped for consumption dissolves in her desire to excel in meeting Steve's every desire. Seduced and spurred by Steve's delight, she enlists aid to crush all rebellion within. As she watches Steve's reactions to her being fitted, she is compelled to insist that all her clothes be tailored to fit her corseted waist. Steve likes her in extremely high heels. She rebels briefly against being his "Barbie doll" but crushes that rebellion also due to her compulsion to be Steve's.

On Friday, Steve takes her to get the Porsche they picked out for her. It's a Ruby Red Metallic 911 Turbo S Cabriolet. She drives it to Steve's! She delights in shifting through the gears, revving its engine; her desire for Steve also revs up. She doesn't hear Adam's text arrive or hear him call. By the time she gets into his bedroom, she is desperate and frantic with desire—she wants to do absolutely anything to please Steve. He deftly makes full advantage of her eagerness—an eagerness magnified greatly by the multitude she invited back by dabbling in magic.

After feasting on her, Steve tells her they have a formal social engagement that evening. "While you shower, do you want me to pick out something for you to wear?" he inquires.

"Please do," she pleads. His choice reflects the familiar cleavage, curves, lots of leg, and five-inch spike heels. She is laced in with the help of two maids. When they are done, though she can scarcely breathe, her heart is pounding with desire. Dizzy with desire and unable to function, she needs to lie down. He takes advantage of her and ravishes her. She couldn't resist if she wanted to; she couldn't want to resist. He helps her dress. Her body and will conform, and she can breathe enough to function. She is splendid in a tight long red strapless formal dress with long side slits.

Steve and Susan are a smashing success and the talk of the party. She barely remembers to abstain from alcohol; she explains to Steve that she wants to be at her sharpest to work his contacts. Dancing in those heels (she had become unaccustomed to heels) and dress and socializing with his contacts to the wee hours of the morning leave her exhausted. She falls asleep on the way back to Steve's.

He carries her to bed, and she wakes to the delight of Steve ravishing her. She surmises that he is excited by her being in her corset and initially passive. He wants her passion to be a response to his. She determines to provide anything he wants. She sleeps in her corset and is elated repeatedly by Steve ravishing her.

Steve ravishes her again at noon and gets up. She drifts to sleep, unconsciously motivated by hope for a repeat. He wakes her and tells her to get ready. They are going to Philadelphia. As she heads for the bathroom to undress, Steve invites her to eat first. She accedes. After a few bites, she is full; the corset limits her meals. She heads for the bathroom when he seizes her and throws her roughly on the bed and, much to her now unbridled glee, overpowers her. Passions stirs in her powerfully—she struggles mightily against him to be barely overpowered by him. The climax of pleasure and exhaustion coincide.

She asks Steve to pick out something for her to wear. She showers. Her mask makes makeup quick and easy. It is another formal affair, so she is similarly dressed, except that she has herself laced even tighter, desperate for his approval. She hates how it feels. He says she looks even sexier. He clearly likes her in it, so she needs to look like that for him. Steve asks her to tell her all she gleaned from the previous night. He commends her perceptiveness; Steve intersperses remarks about how beautiful she is. His comments about her breasts and figure, especially her small waist, and her legs are poetic and erotic. Years of hungering for praise deepen her commitments to please Steve above all else.

Her feet are killing her in the car; she asks, "How do you feel about my taking off my heels for a while?"

He replies, "Sure," flatly. She knows he prefers she keep them on. Her bonds to him determine that she will wear them when possible.

"I'd rather keep them on," she says; she is surprised that she means it.

The Event in Philly

The event in Philly goes well. She is a smashing success both in attracting attention (tonic for her) and working contacts for him. Her obsession to please him enables her to excel for Steve.

Late in the evening, she heads for the ladies' room. She aches from the corset and heels. She rounds a corner and hears a familiar voice say, "Come home." She sees Adam before her.

"How'd you find me? Why?" she asks. She stares away from him.

"When you disappeared, I was frantic. Are you okay?" Adam inquires with obvious concern.

"I'm fine," she responds tersely.

"Come home," he repeats.

Her head is bowed, and she looks at her feet. After a pause, she sighs. "Sorry, I forgot to tell you I'm not coming back." She is frozen in place, waiting for him. After nearly a minute, the fullness of her bladder feeds an impatience to be done with him once and for all. Without looking up, she controls her emotion and states flatly, "I'm never coming back to you." When he doesn't respond or leave, she adds, "Ever." She waits. "I can't." She wants him to go away. "Look," she says sharply, "I'm pregnant, and it's not yours." When he still doesn't leave, she walks past him on the far side of the hall, stating, "I'll never set foot in that cabin again." She walks as quickly as she is able toward the bathroom.

The urgency for relief, for her bladder, and to escape Adam makes her try to run, but she can't. She is barely seated on the toilet when she loses control. It's minutes before she can stop the flow of tears. She turns off the tracking on her phone and barely keeps herself from destroying it. She composes herself and fixes her appearance. She leaves with a group of women, hoping to get back to Steve without seeing Adam.

When Steve sees her, he says, "Susan, come meet Paul Johnson."

They worked the room separately, but now she clings to Steve. Her appetite for relief, distraction, to avoid further thoughts of Adam, stokes her desire to be ravished by Steve. She brings him several drinks, so he is in no shape to drive. She begs off driving. "I'm too tried to drive. Can't we get a room here?" She presses her body to his and feeds his appetite for her.

They leave the next morning for Virginia after a very satisfying night. She wants to keep Adam out of her thoughts, but riding from Pennsylvania to Virginia forces memories on her that even attempting to repress sharpens. She loses her battle to avoid them. Adam deserves better than to find out that way. If only he had yelled at her or attacked her. *Why didn't I text or e-mail him? I would have spared myself and him the humiliation in that hall.* That hall haunts her. The memory of that floor, that floor she bored her eyes into, which she would have burrowed under to hide, tears at her. *I need help to put those memories to death.* She promises to accept any help she can get, at whatever price, to put those memories to death. A cacophony of motivations overwhelms her to cry out inwardly. *Help me eradicate any and all memories associated with Adam!*

Over and over, she cycles through guilt and shame, plunging deeper into self-despair. *I am a coward. Me! Afraid of that puny, gentle man! Afraid of his goodness.* Each cycle strengthens her desire to do anything to be freed from her shame, her weakness.

She wants to be drunk with power, but then her tormentors would find her. *I need Steve to gain power. I need Steve for all the distraction he is for me, I need his protection.* She is taken over by desires and needs that are foreign to her—needs and desires that, though pursued by her now, pursue and consume her.

She is desperate for relief. She wants to get drunk to forget. *I can't—I'm pregnant! That's easy to solve.* Or not so easy now. *If I was sure this thing isn't Adam's, I'd evict it in a heartbeat*, she bargains. *Damn him! He has me trapped!* A plan is accepted.

By the time they reach Steve's estate, she is obsessed with relief that she no longer conceives of apart from Steve. Her independence plucked from her, she is hooked on Steve. She abandons herself to Steve and throws herself at him. He obliges her need for escape, ravishing her several times that afternoon. She clings to him resolutely. As she drifts to sleep, drained yet full of Steve, this thought embeds in her soul: *I'm Steve's.* He is her only possibility, her only life, her only escape. *You're his slave!* I reinterpret the dream; the kindly master is Steve.

When she awakes and Steve is gone, she is forlorn. She aches for him and for relief. She cries out, "Steve!" She waits briefly. "Where are you?" When there is no reply, she calls him while she desperately searches for him. He is gone and not answering! She finds a sweet note from him promising he'll be back or call her at eight.

"It's only a little after four!" she pouts with disappointment. She orbits Steve and is lost without him.

She Obsesses About Steve

She obsesses about Steve and how he wants her to look. She keeps herself corseted. She asks herself how he wants her dressed. She sits to wait for him. She is up in a minute, pacing back and forth and alternately checking the entrances to the estate. She is in constant motion—difficult, painful, and tiring in the stilettos, tight pencil skirt, and corset. She walks faster and faster in her eagerness to catch sight of him and meet him as he arrives. She dismisses her discomfort due to being engrossed with him. She is increasingly out of breath and perspiring. As eight nears, her need for him reaches a fever pitch; she is anxious and perspiring profusely. By 8:05, she is in a panic and working herself into a panic attack. It begins minutes later.

She is miserable—alone, empty without Steve. Before that day, she was horrified that anyone could be desperate for another person. She is doubly horrified and repulsed that she is so weak, desperate, and dependent. But, earlier that day, with a few nudges, she accepted and resolved that she would do anything to escape the shame that she richly deserved. This horrific contrived unreality was offered and unconsciously accepted as a welcome alternative to the pure reality of shame with a clear but difficult escape. She prefers the unreality. She is an eager prisoner of it and tortured by it.

By the time her phone rings at 8:11, she has been wailing, sobbing, and gasping for breath for minutes. It's Steve! She is relieved that it is not him in person because he might think less of her if he saw her like this. A resolution is made to henceforth turn everything inward that he might dislike, even at peril to self or sanity. Her panic, sobbing, and tears stop suddenly. She catches her breath and answers in a calm melodious voice, "Steve dearest, hello!"

What happens next would throw her into panic without her previous resolution. Steve speaks rapidly, apologizing that he has to go to China on short notice for a few weeks on business. He promises he will call when he can. He asks her to take care of things for him. She is eager to. First, she's to tell the staff to stay away from the house with full pay until he gets back so she can supply what he needs in China. He needs documents scanned that he won't trust anyone to do but her. He tells her how to open the safe, retrieve the documents, and a myriad of details to take care of. All this has to be done in the next eight hours. "You won't have a minute to waste," he tells her. He is adamant that nobody else know about any of this. She begs to be allowed to have two maids come daily just to lace her for her corset training. He agrees. He ends the call with, "Don't let me down. Love ya. Thanks for doing this for me. I'll talk to you when I can. Gotta run," and hangs up. His dependence on her fixes her resolve on him.

All the pain and uncertainty of not knowing when she'll hear from Steve next and the certainty that she wouldn't see him or be ravished by him for weeks turn inward; she springs into action and gets all he asked for done minutes before the deadline. He e-mails her thanks and love and, what is tonic to her, a short message, "I owe you big time." He then gives more instructions of what he wants.

She lives for Steve now, delighted to have no time for thoughts of herself. She rarely takes time to eat or sleep—she barely can with the corset. Each morning, she undresses, showers, and has the maids corset herself as tightly as they can. Then she dresses—obsessing to please Steve. He is pleased by her daily videos of herself she sends. She has no freedom to move or to think, except about Steve and what he wants. He stays busy and keeps her busy for two weeks. He announces he'll be back in two weeks and that they will vacation together. She will have less to do, but he wants her to always be available. She's obsessed to do what he wants.

Her inner self rapidly turns from wasteland to desert, and then the desert sands gradually turn into layers of glass. Communication from her unconscious to her conscious is cut—more and more her motives, desires, and preferences don't matter. She is losing herself to Steve—and loving the relief. She forgets she is pregnant, until morning sickness hits her hard two days before Steve returns. She wants to take care of it before Steve returns but can't quite bring herself to get the abortion.

Preparing for Steve's arrival consumes her once he heads back. Every moment, every thought is focused on getting herself, the bedroom, and the house ready. Steve arrives late in the day, their reunion is wonderful, and he ravishes her repeatedly all night.

She awakens early to attend to morning sickness. She returns to Steve's side—she doesn't know what else to do. When he wakes, he ravishes her again, rewarding her for waiting on him. She clings and cuddles with him, captive to seeking any hints to his whims. Breathing and whispering in his ear, she asks him, "Steve, is there anything, anything at all you'd like?"

Smiling broadly and warmly, his dimples and eyes secure her attention. Steve composes a one-word symphony for her soul, saying, "You!" Then she ravishes him.

During their breakfast together, Steve continues his praise of all she did for him while he was in China and can't take his eyes off her. The delight of his smiling at her binds her closer and closer to him. He loves all she had done, he loves how she looks, and he loves her. "You are by far the best thing, the very, very best that has ever happened to me," he says while grasping her hands, pulling her up out of her chair and into his arms. He holds her close, stroking her back and whispering endearments of love. She is drunk and giddy with Steve. He touches, kisses, and appreciates her often. He feasts his eyes on her, blesses her with his voice and touch, and inhales her fragrance.

Steve tells her the plans for their day together and wants to know how she likes them. She is delighted with them all.

She is delighted Steve wants to be with her, to watch her dress, to be with her while she gets ready. He comments, not at all unkindly, "Oh, you're getting a bit of a belly."

She confesses, "I'm pregnant." Ever attentive to his every reaction, she adds, "And, no, it's not yours." She assures him, "It's from before we even met."

She loves his reaction. Steve walks over to her, embracing and holding her close, and says tenderly, "We'll take care of it as soon as you want." She melts into his embrace and is relieved that he isn't angry at her. He senses her relaxation and comforts her with assurances of love. He whispers warmly, "If you want, but, only if you want, we'll take care of it today."

She did want to but can't, until she makes sure it isn't Adam's. She resents his intrusion into her life, this tender and wonderful moment. *Just do it anyway*, she thinks. But, even with all the anger at Adam that she can muster and all her sense of entitlement of doing whatever she wants with her own body, she can't commit to it. "Steve," she whispers back, pausing to passionately kiss him, "let's just enjoy being together today."

The next days together are great. She is inseparable from Steve. On the third day, she researches where to have Adam go for genetic testing for paternity and sends him a terse e-mail on her old phone. It reads, "I will have an abortion in a few weeks, unless you prove you are the father." The rest of the e-mail directs him where to go for the testing and demands a reply the next day.

After a wonderful night with Steve, she checks for a reply from Adam. His reply infuriates her. He wrote, "I won't submit to testing. I will NOT give implied consent for the abortion of a child not mine." The plan works. She is now angry and determined to do what she wants and be done with Adam. *I'll tell Steve I want to get that abortion*, she vows. But then she notices that there are scores of unread text messages from Adam. An urgent compulsion to delete them almost has the deed done. *I'll just check one*, she decides. It reads, "Come home." It was sent the day after Adam invited her home in Philly, and, she notes, it was sent at 3:21 a.m. She checks the next one. It also reads "Come home" and was sent at 3:21 p.m. She checks each messages. Each reads, "Come home," and all were sent at 3:21 a.m. or p.m. He didn't miss a single 3:21 since that Saturday.

This...3-21 is my birthday, she reflects. *How sw—how Adam.* She ponders that he sent each message himself: he would not have automated them but took great pains to not—she could hear and see him say it—"miss a single opportunity." She can't abort this child; it might be his. The resentment that he is limiting her freedom didn't survive the implications of what he's doing.

A Glass-Shattering Sound

A glass-shattering sound is heard in the soul's Eden; it resounds in each unconscious. What myths will it spin? The glass in her valley reduces to powdery sand. Her unconscious unblocks; she is free to make her own decisions again as herself rather than as Steve's.

She tells Steve she isn't going to abort. He asks, "Is someone controlling your decision?"

"Of course not, I mean..." She starts to say but has second thoughts and doubts. She is profoundly confused. As she thinks, her resolve crumbles. "I...I don't know." A desire for Steve to decide for her trumps in. "Steve, what do you want me to do?" She embraces him; she needs him to take control.

"Well," he says slowly and wistfully, pausing between phrases, "I prefer...you abort...but only if..."

She stops listening after he says "abort" and desires to obey. She feels compelled to say, "Let's do it now!" It is an all but overwhelming compulsion, but then a thought slips through the fog. *Why can't I take others into account?* There is an urgency to ignore, to dismiss, to ridicule that pesky thought, but she embraces it. *I want to consider others in my decisions, especially this one*, she realizes.

She relaxes her embrace of Steve and states, "Thanks for your concern. I want to keep this child or…I couldn't feel right about aborting it. Yes, I'm considering others—I want to. Oh—I need to get new clothes and shoes. I won't be wearing a corset again."

"Well, okay then," Steve responds with attempted enthusiasm. They hold each other close. Steve suddenly holds her tight and starts to cry. "I didn't realize how much I love you," he confesses. "I would have thought nothing of kicking anyone else to the curb, or even you at first. But you've conquered my heart." Steve and Susan enjoy the week.

For her birthday, they fly to Paris in his jet. Her morning sickness is over, and they have a delightful time. He lavishes her with presents, romantic meals, and drives in the French countryside.

Flying into Dulles, seeing the winter wonderland of Virginia countryside under fresh snow, stirs good memories in her. She hadn't checked the iPhone Adam got her in weeks. *He's cancelled it by now to pare expenses*, she thinks. Then abruptly, the thought "He's so cheap!" erupts into her thoughts. When they arrive at his estate, they ravish each other before falling asleep.

The next day, she wants to check her old phone and then recycle it, since it probably doesn't have service anymore. Dread rises in fearsome waves at the thought of turning it on. *I'll recycle it*, she thinks. Curiosity prompts her to turn it on as she descends the staircase. A panic attack hits hard, and she drops the phone. It should have shattered on the marble stairs, but she also lost her balance and her left leg kicks out, and the phone is caught in the opening of her boot. She is too preoccupied with falling backward on the stairs and with the panic attack to notice.

After a terrifying struggle with panic, she crawls to safety. The panic attack made her feel out of control and exhausted. She passes out in the hall. She wakes up feeling sick and drained. She desperately wants to get drunk and almost forgets the pregnancy.

"Why not?" she asks aloud. She knows—and doesn't want to. *I need a stiff drink*, she thinks as she pours a large glass of brandy. *One won't hurt*, I think and raise the glass to take a drink. I see something swimming in the brandy. It looks like one of those cute reptilian creatures in my dream. *Wow, I really need a few! And power.* Suddenly, images from my dreams flash through my mind and rescue her. She whimpers, "Help!" She pours out the brandy and flops on the bed for a nap.

She notices discomfort in her left boot. She finds the iPhone and checks for service. There are a multitude of text messages from Adam. "The fool!" she screeches. "He's wasting his time and money. I can't go back. I can't!" A strong desire to throw the phone almost wins. "I suppose they won't let me go back," she says with resignation. As that realization settled in, she thinks, *Good! I won't be tempted to do anything stupid.*

What she does is stupid. She reads each of his text messages—"I'll torture myself, I'll gorge on guilt, I must." Each day he sends that same message at 3:21 in the morning and afternoon. *Why is he so intent on torturing me? He's destroying any feeling I ever had for him*, I determine. On my birthday, he sent another text at noon. It reads, "I want time with OUR child but wont take u to court. I wont risk exposing u." I hoot. *What an ignorant little boy! He'll never see this child*, I gloat.

I'll beat him at his game. I write at app to send him a text message on his birth date: 8:08. It reads: "NEVER! I live at an estate now." The first refers him to a link (Iwishwenevermet), which reads: "You will NEVER see this child. If you make ANY trouble I'll abort it." After seconds, it will vanish. *That will stop him.*

I am obsessed with Steve, sex, and with defeating Adam. I help Steve with his work, revolving myself around his friends, contacts, and associates—and, of course, exceed his fantasies! I check daily for whether Adam has finally given up. The fool must be wearing himself out, making himself sick. I relish my revenge and feed my anger and disdain for him. Days turn into months, and still he refuses to stop—he has no self-respect.

I Am in My Ninth Month

I am in my ninth month. She kicks and wakes me often. My doctor will deliver my baby in two weeks on August 28 if she hasn't come before. I'm really, really big—and uncomfortable and tired. I'm glad I'm not at that cabin—it'd be unbearable.

Steve leaves, and I check for that obnoxious text. It isn't there. I think, *Great!*—but then—I feel bereft, empty—and alone. I hear "The idiot finally gave up," but tears well up. "I'm relieved," comes out of my mouth, but inwardly I'm desolate, abandoned, and convinced, "No one could ever love me." It settles on my soul like thick ice. I'm guilty of being unlovable. Out of my depths, I overhear myself repeating, "Yes, you can take over. I have nothing to fight back with and no reason to resist." Suddenly, I'm very, very cold. I'm beyond tears, hope, and certainly of love.

I struggle and lose the struggle and myself. I want to go back, to beg for forgiveness, even though it can't be given. I want, but it's no use. I can't do this, can't go home, can't return to him—to him who loves me. I hear, "It's too late," and I must agree, "Yes. It is certainly too late for me." I sink into a stupor, losing my ability to feel, think, will, or act. My emotions die, my thinking is a dimly burning wick, and my abilities to will and act ebb away.

"Soon you will be powerful beyond your wildest dreams."

I'd...rather...be...powerless. "Abba," erupts from her soul's center, her unconscious, "have mercy and grant me to will and do whatever pleases you. Hell? Definitely—especially that if it pleases you." Her conscious mind cannot consider asking for help from God due to her extreme sense of unworthiness and guilt.

She pants, is hot, perspiring, and determined to go to Adam and beg for his forgiveness. When he doesn't forgive her—she is sure he won't—she'll ask for the next step, and then the one after that. She has to leave quickly before something stops her. The walls already seem to close in on her. By the time she waddles to the front door, it almost seems too small for her immense belly. It is unbearably hot and humid, even with the sun behind the clouds. She waddles to the Porsche and plops into the seat, barely squeezing behind the wheel. Falling into the seat and behind the wheel stuns her; in moments, she recovers enough to drive off.

"Thank you, thank you, thank you for helping me escape!" she sings. Joy makes her forget herself; guilt and unworthiness are irrelevant. The rays of the sun pierce through the clouds and strike her skin. Her skin boils, wrinkles, discolors, and the pain almost knocks her out. Losing control, she drives off the road, spinning around in a grassy area. She's unprotected in her sleeveless top and shorts. She has to go back and cover up; she knows the magic she "dabbled" with, or rather that toys with her, no longer protects her. She speeds back to his estate, hoping she can make it before crashing.

In seconds, the pain and reactivity to light subside; she knows she will have no trouble getting back safely. It's clear she will never again get this close to escaping them. She can sense them gloating. She would dismiss it when she disbelieved in the possibility of their existence. But now, she spins the car around, racing as fast as she dares to an area she and Adam went for picnics. It's heavily shaded by trees. I'll drive off the road above it and drive down the grassy hill and across a field to get into the shade. They always walked in from the other side.

Instantly, my skin begins again to boil, burn, and hurt. In seconds, it swells, and I rip off the mask to breath. I have doubts I'll be able to make it. I start to mouth a prayer for help but can't speak. I think it instead. She's also pleading from the depth of her soul, even from its hidden center in her unconscious, for help and to be granted a chance to try to make it back to Adam.

She uses Lamaze breathing, focusing intensely away from the pain, begging for mercy. Somehow, she is able to endure. She drives off the road and careens down the hill, but the Porsche bogs down in the mud about fifty yards from the shaded area. She has to make it on foot. She runs ten or fifteen yards as fast as her pregnant body can, until a foot sinks in the mud and she falls face first hard into the mud. The rays of the sun beat her down, and her body swells. She struggles to her feet and walks carefully toward the shade. Suddenly, she can't see—her eyes have swollen shut.

Waves of self-pity wash over her. The light saps her strength. She falls to her knees and is unable to rise. She doesn't have a moment to waste. She crawls on her hands and knees through the mud toward the shade. The mud gets deeper, and her progress slows.

You can't make it. Without our help your baby will die. We'll keep you alive as an invalid. You know our terms. Surrender!

All will be lost if she surrenders to them, or if she simply reacts with stubbornness, or if she tries to endure and crawl by force of will to the shade. "Abba, help! Dearest Abba Father, inspire me, muse me for your glory," she cries out from the depths of her unconscious.

The demons answer with mocking, "You're a fat pig stuck in the mud—ready for slaughter," followed with scorn, name-calling, a chaotic cacophony of hoots, and fiendish laughter. The image of her and her big belly wallowing in the mud is all she envisions. Rolling back and forth in the mud as best she can, she coats herself with mud. Now protected from the sun's rays, the torture and draining of her last ounce of strength ceases.

Her unconscious converses with her Abba Father. Over the next quarter hour (though it seems like an eternity of hard labor), she crawls to the shade dragging her pregnant belly through the mud. She has no use of her legs and continually calls on God for help.

The following takes place in the depths of her soul, in her valley—the soul's Eden:

"Abba, how will you send someone? No one knows I'm here."

Call Adam.

"Abba, I can't see. I can't speak."

Pry open your left eye so you can see to call Adam.

Her soul cries out in desperate urgency as she pries open her eye to call Adam, "Abba, how can I communicate?"

Tap out 'SOS, dit, dit, dit, dah, dah, dah, dit, dit, dit.' Use one finger for a short tap and drum three fingers for a dash.

"Abba, I can't hear!"

Call and keep tapping out SOS.

She calls and taps out three short taps, three triple drummings of her fingers, then three more short taps. She repeats over and over, until she loses consciousness.

She dreams she is crossing a desert—heat—thirst—lost—no sense of direction, no hope. She continues to plod along, one foot in front of the other, step by step by step. Sometimes, she crawls up steep mountains of sand, sliding or tumbling or rolling down the other side. Everything is parched, including her. Her strength evaporates.

Suddenly in her dream, she feels drops of water from above. She opens her mouth to catch drops. Even a few drops are delicious relief. The drops keep coming! She swallows once, twice, several more times. She is awakening—someone is with her. She knows it's Adam, though her connection with her body is 'unplugged.'

Adam has two friends with him—Jeff, a police officer on crutches, and Sue, a nurse practitioner. Jeff proved invaluable in locating Eve's position from her cell because the GPS is off. Sue examines Eve and tells Adam that Eve needs rehydration, her special lotion, rest, and, as her strength returns, food. Adam swore them to secrecy after explaining about Eve.

Adam cleans up Eve's body as Sue continued to dribble water into her mouth. Then Adam wraps her in sheets and carries her several hundred yards to his car. Sue can't help due to a bad back.

On the Way Home

On the way home, Adam stops for supplies Sue asked for, and Jeff's wife picks him up. Sue will spend the night to help Eve. Her husband meets them with a suitcase filled with medical supplies and changes of clothing she asked him to bring.

Sue is fascinated with the elevator, cable car, and the cabin. Adam washes Eve and carries her downstairs so she can be cooler. Sue starts a drip IV. Adam applies the lotion and massages it into her body. Eve drifts in and out of consciousness. Each time she awakes, her body is more responsive. The swelling subsides.

Adam is exhausted from the joy of having Eve home and the ordeal of carrying her with all the added weight of her pregnancy. Sue is well-rested. Sue insists that she sleep in a chair by Eve's bedside. Adam sleeps across the hall.

Eve wakes up several times. Each time, despite his weariness, Adam is at her bedside before Sue stirs. The third time Eve wakes, she sees his face for the first time in months. Even in dim light, she sees clearly that his beautiful beard is now pure white. His face is gaunt and aged but filled with a magnificent smile. She inspects his body. He lost weight and is fifteen or twenty pounds too skinny. She tries to speak but only croaks.

He paid dearly for her behavior. The width of his smile and its…its depth—intensity—tell her that he paid it gladly. She determines to bind herself closely to God so she can pay any price, bear anything God approves for Adam. She will, with God's help, return and pass on this intolerable compliment. The image of his eyes—loving, forgiving, rejoicing at her—assures her that forgiveness has long been granted. "Lord Abba, grant me worthiness of his forgiveness and of your greater forgiveness."

When Eve wakes, Adam is at her side in a flash. She croaks out, "I love you. I've starved without you. Hold me!" Adam holds and kisses her; they weep together.

After reconnecting with Adam, Eve asks him to fix her some of his cheesy scrambled eggs.

"How many do you want?" he asks.

"I feel like I want a dozen," she said with a laugh. "But I'll take two for me and one for our daughter."

"Coming right up!" he responds as he heads out. He asks Sue if she wants breakfast. She agrees to one or two eggs. He serves two to Sue, three to Eve, and three to himself. Thirty minutes later, he gives Eve another two eggs.

Eve is back on her feet—and overjoyed. Sue informs them that her husband will pick her up and bring lunch for them. She asks what they want and if her four kids (ages three to nine) can ride the elevator and cable car to the cabin to see it. Adam and Eve eagerly agree and beg them to stay for lunch.

The kids love the "rides" and the cabin. The youngest asks about her burqa. She tells them, "I was vain about my beauty. I have to wear this to save me from my pride." She wonders as she says it if that is the true reason, the deeper reality, she suffered all this.

When they leave, Eve addresses Adam. "I want to apologize—"

Adam interrupts, "That isn't necessary, you—"

"I know, I know. You've forgiven me. I can tell," she declares. She settles her emotions and wipes a tear. "But I want to tell you how much I love you and how sorry I've hurt you."

She stops him from breaking in. "There is no excuse for anything I did over the last years," she states vehemently. Anger is in her voice, she feels the indignation powerfully—she is furious at herself and all the lies she told herself and believed.

"Years?" he asks.

"Yes," she confesses, "all the way back to when Francine died. Oh, and recently I've come to realize it—all the way back to our wedding night."

"Really? How so?" he queries.

"Yes, yes, I planted the seeds of my own self-destruction back on our wedding night," she admits. "I even fooled myself that I was being kind to you by not bothering to bring it up," she says.

"Wow! What was it?" he wonders.

"You were so gentle about sex—I didn't feel any passion. I fooled myself into thinking it didn't matter to me, but it tripped…"

Adam interrupts, "Now I'm mad! I've been riding wild stallions of desire—wild lusty stallions of desire for you. I've struggled to control them all because you needed me to be gentle." His voice gets louder and faster. "And…and you hid your disappoint—oops! I also hid my struggle from you."

"Oh…yeah," she concedes. "But my hiding my frustration and not dealing with my desires fermented into a terrible affair…and tore you up. I feel awful. I want to do better. I trust God and you more than I trust myself. Help me with what to do," she implores.

They talk, weep, and argue for hours with Eve frequently getting up, shifting, walking around, and struggling to stay comfortable. The renewed pain of her skin, her huge belly, episodic discomfort from Braxton Hicks contractions—and she is too hot for comfort.

He is heartbroken for her, "I'm sorry you lost your beauty again."

"I'm not sure I am," she reflects. "Nope! Being loved by you is better—I'd rather be loved by you than be beautiful."

Eve finds e-mails from Steve. The first was sent before she left. He wrote that he enjoyed her. He confessed that he is not fond of small children and planed to give her and her daughter their own suite. The e-mails after she left show concern and wanting to know she is okay, and the last one mentions that it is probably best that she left. He states that he would miss what they had but that with her focus on her daughter, there is no recovering that, unless she turns care of her daughter over to someone else. He tells her "Thank you!" and offers her a million dollars as her share of the profits she earned him.

Eve isn't interested in the money but tells Adam about the offer. He agrees they should decline. She agonizes over an appropriate apology by e-mail. She thanks him for all he had done and his generous offer but declines it. She tells him where he can find the Porsche and sends the e-mail. He never replies.

She's Kicking

"She's kicking," Eve says. "Feel and talk to her," she invites.

He kneels by her and puts his hand on her belly. "That's a strong kick!" he exclaims. "What do you want to name her?"

"Well, I like Sarah Ohanna," she replies. "Sarah for my great, great-grandmother and Ohanna means 'God is gracious'... though I'm open to calling her Adam," she jokes. "But, most of all, I want us to call her something you like."

"Sarah Ohanna Smith or Sarah Adam Smith? I don't know," he jokes. "I can't decide. You choose."

"Do you like Sarah Ohanna Smith?"

"I love her, the name, and I especially love you," Adam assures.

"Oh, that I know, I know so well. Why did you stop sending the texts to me? 'Come home' was beautiful. It is beautiful. Perfect! This is the only home I remember. You gave me—home."

"I never stopped, nor would I ever," he declares.

"I didn't get one yesterday morning," Eve maintains. "It shocked me and made me realize what I threw away. That's why I came back." She takes out her phone to check.

"I know I..." he begins to say.

"Here it is! It did arrive..."

"Well, it's the best..."

"Oh! It arrived hours late. I thought…"

"Possible anniversary present," he says with a smile.

"Ouch! Another confession. I forgot, but I don't forget things like that," she ponders.

"Was it…them?" he offers.

"Oh, my, yes," she states with disgust. "I wanted to be beautiful and free of this…this prison," she says, indicating the burqa. "I thought I could handle dabbling in magic. Foolish, foolish, foolish! Dumb, dumb…"

"Stop it!" he bellows. "You're playing into their hands. Forgiven, forgiven, forgive. Say it, 'I'm forgiven" and "Thank you, Lord!'"

"You're right, you're right. I'm forgiven. I'm grateful. Thank you, Adam, for helping and forgiving me. Thank you, Lord, for forgiving me and for granting me Adam in my life."

They talk, pray, hug, take walks when it's cooler, and hold each other in bed that night with a fan blowing on Eve.

Craving to worship God, Eve begs Adam to worship on Sunday with the group led by the deaf pastor. "I'm desperate to worship God. I haven't in almost a year," she explains.

"Sure. Just curious—why there?" he inquires.

"I'm not sure," she replies. Then thoughtfully, she adds, "I yearn for abandoning myself to God. There is a spirited worship there. I can sign and sing. They have a deaf praise team."

"Sounds good to me," he agrees. "Oh," he adds after a pause, "I'll pack a lunch for us in case we need to go to the birthing center. Bring a bag with whatever you'll want if you go into labor."

"But we can't take a chance that those people might find me—especially not with baby Sarah," she objects.

"It's arranged," he assures. "It's safe."

"Oh! Were you that sure I'd come back?" she marvels.

"No, but I never lost hope," he rejoins. "I hoped, I prepared."

"I'm impressed," she says in hushed tones. After pausing, she continues, "I do so love you! You are the best—Oh! I haven't got anything to pack."

"I think you'll find everything you need in our bedroom in your closet or the top drawer," he offers.

She checks and is thrilled that he was so thoughtful, even though he had no guarantee she'd be back. "A pink and a blue burqa!" she exclaims. "Why blue?"

"I never knew whether we were having a boy or girl," he replies.

"Oh, I didn't tell you much. I'm so sor—"

"Forgiven!" he interrupts.

"Right," she replies. She pauses to compose herself. *But what are all the snaps for?* she wonders.

"To nurse Sarah. Unsnap, pull her in, cover her and yourself up with the extra fabric, and you'll be face-to-face with her under the burqa," he explains.

"Wonderful!" she giggles. A thought occurs to her; she snickers and bursts into joyous laughter.

"What's so funny?" he wonders.

Eve could barely contain her laughter and joy and glee enough to utter, "This is better than being ravished! An orgasm of the soul?"

He's with her in her delight and mirth but clueless to her meaning. "You're different," he observes as her mood returns to the lower stratosphere. "Better."

"Oh, I—I certainly hope so," she says wistfully.

"It's clear to me," he vows. "Any idea how come?

"Well," she begins, "I think it may be that I finally realize what love is, or what the best love really is. Steve loved me. He was generous, considerate, supportive, loving, romantic, passionate—he treated me great. He is rich, powerful, influential—everything I wanted to possess. I could maneuver him in ways I've never been able to maneuver you. We owned each other. He was perfect—for the person I used to be," Eve confesses. "I don't want to be her anymore—it won't do, it doesn't work."

"But now—," he offers.

"Yes, your love and God's inspire me," she says in reverent tones. "Love—persistent, gentle," she contemplates. "Freeing, respectful, enlarging…Steve and my love were possessive—I was his, and he was mine. But your love and God's—though I saw it easier in yours—they're the opposite. It's not possession of and power over but abandonment to and laying down one's self for. We don't possess each other. We give ourselves to each other. I can't say it well. I haven't lived it at all, but, with everything I can ever be, I want to love like that." She bursts into tears—tears of insatiable yearning to give herself to Adam.

Adam comforts her, embracing, stroking her back and hair, and whispering tokens of his love to her. Then he asks her, "May I massage your feet?"

Eve considers herself unworthy of such love but also unworthy to decline a request that is genuine by him.

Worship Is Wonderful

Worship is wonderful. Many are at a loss and concerned when they see Eve, six feet tall and hugely pregnant, fully covered with a large pink burqa. As they see her worshipping with signing, singing, and her entire body, misgivings are banished by joy. Some hear her beautiful voice; many see her praise and worship with abandon. Worshipping from the inside out without inhibition heals and restores Eve. She is mindful, from her unconscious core, that translating worship into living heals her entire self.

After worship, many greet them. She converses by signing always (she wears gloves) and uses her voice when those greeting her speak to her without signing. Gerald, the pastor, and his wife, Stephanie, invite them for lunch. Having occasional contractions all morning ("more of those Braxton Hicks things" she tells herself), she does her best to ignore them to worship and visit with people without distraction. A delightful lunch and conversations with Gerald and Stephanie make for a full day. They leave at two.

Eve is sapped and desperate for a nap. While she naps, Sue calls and wants to stop by with her family later. Adam invites them to come between five and six.

Sue, her husband, Sam, and their kids arrive after five. They bring presents for the baby. Eve wakes to a wonderful surprise. Sam goes back for additional presents. They brought diapers, baby clothes, a baby bed, an infant car seat/carrier, and, when Sam returns, a baby carriage and other items. Sam rushes the carriage into the cabin; it is starting to rain.

Sue brings refreshments; they have a baby shower with the eight of them. It starts to storm outside, complete with flashes of lightning and instantaneous peals of thunder. The wind howls outside, and heavy rain pelts the cabin. The storm is right over them. It's pitch dark out, except when the lightning flashes.

A few minutes later, Eve interrupts, "These contractions," she says haltingly, "are getting hard to take. I'm really uncomfortable." Sue checks her out and takes charge.

"You are about to have your baby now!" she exclaims. The storm, lightning, and the start of labor prevent leaving. Three hours later, Sarah breathes on her own. Adam hands Sarah to Eve. Eve lifts her veil and kisses Sarah. Adam and Sue see that the light is cruel to Eve's face and witness pain mingling with the joy on her face.

"You need to cover up..." Adam begins to say.

"Sarah needs to see my face," she states with calm resolution.

"But..."

"I embrace this for her—I welcome it. Let it be," Eve pleads.

Adam is humbled. He strokes her hair. Eve holds Sarah until she succumbs to sleep. When he picks up Sarah, he covers her face.

After thanking Sue, Sam, and the children for the gifts and help, Adam sees them to the door. Sue promises to return Tuesday.

Adam Is Excited

Adam is excited and busy that night. He sets up two nursery monitors, one by Sarah and one by Eve; he naps in between his wife or daughter needing his attention. Whenever he takes Sarah to Eve, she lifts her veil so Sarah sees her face. The mixture of joy, wonder, and pain on her face becomes familiar to Adam.

They enjoy talking and tender moments between tending to needs. Adam calls his parents with the news and sends e-mails.

"I miss having parents at a time like this," Eve laments.

"Oh—that must be hard," Adam agrees.

"Yes! It's hard to be cut off from any relatives, to have to hide all the time," she says with energy.

"Uh-huh, aw! Ouch!" he cries, feeling a bit of her pain with her. "You can't ever even share news with people who care about you as—'Janet.' Agh! That's got to be hard!"

"Yes, yes, yes!" she agrees, with each repetition more emphatic. She leaps to her feet. "The happiest moments of my life—from my becoming a follower—marrying you and having Sarah—oh! And your taking me back, you wanting me back, your ever so faithful 'come home.' I want to tell everyone about those." The energy, angst, and passion are expressed in her voice, her entire body, her gestures, and her pacing the floor. "But, no, I have to be careful, guarded…" she bursts into tears.

Adam holds her close and firmly. She sobs, her body shaking. He joins her—his body shaking with hers, his spirit quivering with hers.

She reflects, "I'm the most blessed, fortunate person in the world. I can't imagine being happier with my life. Loved"—she breathes in awe and exaltation—"I won't risk changing anything about my life—except my silly unfaithfulness both to you and to God."

"Nothing?"

"Well, nothing external, none of the details in my life. I mean, I…I…" she stammers out, "I want to be better in a million and one ways, but I'm not sure I want beauty—my former beauty—back. I worshipped it! I'm still too tempted to…to misuse it… Insanity! I know better by now! I gave up you and God for my vanity and pleasure. I did it easily and was happy in a sick way."

"You don't seem finished," he offers after a pause.

"No, no, I'm not. This is hard to say—especially to you. It's also hard for me to admit to myself that I'm this shallow."

Adam waits for her to go on. "So?"

"If I haven't lost everything I had—everything! My wealth, my health, and especially my beauty—even my freedom…" she stops. She bites her lip. She starts coughing and can't stop. He holds her hand; she squeezes his. "My throat's dry," she croaks between coughs, "and I need something—do we have any OJ?"

"I'll get you some," he says as he jumps up. "Do you want it plain or heated with tea?" He dashes for the kitchen.

"Oh! Heavenly!" She struggles to get out. "Both. Some now and more when the water's hot."

"Coming right up," he says. He returns with two glasses of orange juice. "The water's on. I'll jump up when it whistles."

She sips orange juice and swishes it to clear her mouth. She finishes hers. "May I have some of yours?" she asks"Sure, all you want."They sit in comfortable silence holding hands while Adam rubs her back. The kettle whistles. Adam returns in a jiffy with the kettle, a tea bag, and two mugs.

"Do your tea and fill mine half-full with hot water," Eve directs.

Adam bobs his tea bag to strengthen his tea. He likes his strong; she likes hers weak. They share a tea bag with him using it first. When he's done, he lifts the bag from his mug and says, "Here's your tea"—he pauses to correct himself—"bag."

She reacts in mock anger, "Now I'm a bag?" They laugh together.

"You were saying..." Adam prompts a few minutes later.

"Oh, yes. Hmm. Now where was I?"

"Something hard to confess"—Adam pauses—"hard to admit, even to yourself."

"Ah. Confession is supposed to be good for the soul, isn't it?"

"But not always easy," Adam rejoins.

"Here goes," she determines. "I needed to lose everyth—"

Sarah cries. They're both up in an instant. "I'll check her," he says. "You stay put. Relax." Returning with her in a few minutes, he says, "She's been changed. But I think she's hungry."

Eve exposes her face to suffer the cruel light and Sarah's gaze. He hands her to Eve and begins to close the curtains.

"No, no, no," she corrects. He leaves them open. He sits with her quietly, gazing at her, fixated on her face. It looks painful—raw, reddening by the moment, and pained—yet filled with joy.

He Takes Sarah to Make Her Burp

He takes Sarah to make her burp. She asks him to let Sarah watch her face. He wants Eve to cover up. He pats and rocks her, and Eve coos, "Sarah, Daddy has you. Daddy and Mommy love you." She sings, "Daddy loves Sarah, Mommy loves Sarah too." Sarah burps.

Eve taps him. He turns around; she takes Sarah and sits down.

Adam asks, "Isn't that Lara's song from Dr. Zhivago?"

"Oh, is that what it's from?" she responds. "My parents used to sing it to me. I forgot about it until a minute ago."

"You've never seen the movie?" Adam asks.

"I didn't know there was one. Once Helen and Frank began to funnel me to magic and evil, I never watched anything that wasn't intended to condition or harden me."

"That's awful!" he protests.

"And—" Sarah falls asleep; she puts her veil on and takes deep breaths. She continues after sighing in relief, "They blocked good memories of my parents and planted terrible ones. The good memories are starting to come back—some." She gently rocks. "What a relief to have my veil back on. I love my veil! I need a nap." She hands him Sarah.

Eve spends the day relaxing, feeding Sarah, and cuddling with Adam. They enjoy Sarah, conversation, and being together.

Sue visits the next day. She checks out Eve and Sarah. Adam tries to pay her, but she refuses. Eve interrupts, "Let me give you some earrings. Wait." She returns with earrings with an S at the end of a gold-braided chain.

"Oh, my! These are lovely! Is that gold? And diamonds?" Sue exclaims, "I can't…"

Eve interrupts, "They were given to me by a man that I—that I had an affair with. I don't dare return them, and I won't sell them. Please take them."

"You could keep them for Sar—" she begins to reply.

"Absolutely not!" Eve retorts. "Take them. Please. Give it to the poor, if you like."

"Okay, okay. Thank you. I may do that," Sue agrees.

"Oh—and please keep it quiet because I'm in hiding," Eve pleads.

"Adam told me about that. I'm so sorry you have to go thro—"

"Don't be," she remarks. She speaks lyrically, "I'm richer because of this. Adam is better than anyone I'd choose." She sighs. Tears of joy stream down behind her veil. She ponders, "Absolutely everything that has happened to me has had good results."

After Sue left, she wraps her arms tightly around Adam. Without releasing him, she declares, "I said it. I had to lose everything to gain you. I needed God to give you to me so I could find myself."

Baby Sarah keeps them busy. Adam takes care of Sarah, except for feeding her. His parents and then friends visit to help. They snatch precious time with each other when they can.

Those first three weeks flew by. Eve wants to keep the car without having to drive him both ways. After prayer and discussion, they plan for him to catch a ride most days.

Eve arranges to work about thirty hours a week. She cleans houses, helps with child care, and tutors. She works some for businesses. Each job allows her to tend Sarah and pay her "cash off the books." Adam is adamant that they pay the taxes for her income. They do that by never claiming Eve on his returns.

Eve exposes her face only when nursing and tending to Sarah. She suffers greatly and gladly for it. Usually, she does it in private, more so when men were present. Some occasionally witness the violent reaction of her skin to light and her "painful joy." Eve asks permission and explains before unveiling.

She works at the house of a wealthy Muslim family. After six weeks, she leads a discussion at the Muslim house with several Muslim women. They study the Quran. Eve knew Arabic and memorized the original Arabic Quran and an English translation favored by Muslims. Eve repeats at each study that "our goal is to help us become better people, better women." She also leads groups at Christian and secular households.

Her knowledge of Scriptures (the Bible and the Quran) and literature would impress if she let it be known. She asks incisive questions; she makes observations about life and confessions about herself. Her buoyant cheerfulness (despite her obvious difficulties) and her courtesy to each, even pets, are noticed. But that pales compared to her obvious interest and care for all the women and children she meets. She acts as though each person is more valuable than herself. She seems to be the "mother of all living" in its best sense.

Her passion for each of us, the intensity of her listening to my words, emotions, and hidden sense and how she gently shows me my hidden longing for healing and freedom from self forge a trust and love for Eve that entices us to openness. She sees hidden shame. and yet she loves. She zealously protects privacy—she doesn't expose or force anyone. The appeal of liberation and healing singing unmistakably out of her covered face and body attracts us each to reveal more of our hidden soul, hidden even to ourselves.

A problem develops from the discussions. She has work to do, but we want more of her time. In a few weeks, we do her work for a while, so we can have more of her time. Wealthy women, like me, who were "above housework" eagerly do it.

Eve incites an eager emptying of the self that gives a taste of freedom. She explains: emptying of the self gives freedom; the emptying is endless freedom moment by moment. Straining to do so, tasting the reward, impels me to say, "I gladly suffer it."

Eve devotes herself to Sarah and caring for children (they find her enchanting)—nothing could induce us to deprive the children of her once we saw the glee of infants and toddlers around Eve.

Eve persuades us against the pursuit of power, especially in relationships. "I was a power whore," she confesses. "and became a puppet to powers I didn't admit existed nor understand. Back then"—she sighs—"I wouldn't admit anything controlled me. I deluded myself that I was in total control. I hardened myself for control flinging my humanity away." She tells of her affair and its results. "I lost my identity. Neither God nor Adam gave up on me, even when I willfully gave them and myself up."

Eve often cautions, "It is not enough to reject power. Empty yourself of power. We must love in actions when it's hardest." She states forcefully, "Power corrupts, and the pursuit of power corrodes the human spirit." She pauses to stress her coup d'état, her overthrow of the rebellious Prince of this world, and then continues. "Hu-man-ity is allergic to power and its pursuit. We break out in suffering, despair, and destruction—especially of ordinary people who are powerless—and children. Animals and the earth also suffer from our pursuit of power." She is emboldened by our response. The more we follow the better, the more profoundly she leads.

Often, she advocates, "Creatively exceed demands—give more than what is demanded, accept less than what you are due. Go a third mile when expected to go one." None of us welcome this application, but she won many of us over. "Love your husbands, don't merely pander to them. If they demand sex, coach them to win your passion. Train them to conquer you—body, soul, spirit, and heart—and reward them richly with yourself, and a better himself, for his efforts."

Eve Teaches Us to Respect

Eve teaches us to respect everyone, especially our husbands. Her most profound inducement to respect others is her respect of us. She delights—joy rings in her voice and is palpable in her movements—in listening to us. Often, her listening clarifies me. She helps me understand what I mean or what I think. She does that but much more. The way she listens draws me out of myself; she helps me understand and appreciate myself. How she treats me enables me to love more. I want to be better and willingly embrace what God makes available. I'm more a person. My husband loves it—after some adjustments for him.

She adamantly refuses to use her understanding of us to manipulate us or allow us to commit ourselves with hidden motives. She challenges us to "whole-hearted decisions." This liberation is often painful; it is always worthwhile, and she makes sure it is freely chosen.

The respect she trains us to pursue for our husbands is profound. That doesn't do it justice. I bristled at the thought of going beyond pretending to go along with my husband. She struggles to help us understand and be blessed by doing something far better. She models with us what she hopes for us to do for both ourselves and our husbands. She convinces us, trains, and drills us to pursue understanding our husbands with compassion and depth that forms respect for them in us. I gradually grew to understand my husband's thoughts, feelings, actions, and values, and even his inconsistencies. I'm now qualified to appreciate his peculiar blend of gifts and greatness. Our love blossomed.

Often, Eve passionately warns us not to use our deepening understanding of our husbands to gain power. She confesses in great detail and sorrow how she misused power to immunize herself against love. She told us she misused it to gain the upper hand. But inadvertently she also consigned herself to loneliness, and fed an emptiness inside that demanded power to assuage itself. "I fed the demons my humanity, my self," she declares. "The more I pursued power and the illusion of being in control"—she pauses to gather passion and conviction—"no! Pursuing power pulled me into the delusion of control, into an insanity of me, me, me!" The force of her words—multiplied a hundredfold by her life, the transformation of her past into such an attractive presence, her appeal and assurance in her person, even more than by her words—convicts me to flee the delusion of self, "me," and learn to embrace whatever reality sustains her.

She primes me to give up the insanity of me to pursue loving, not power or knowledge. "The paradox," she explained, "is that knowledge is as vital as food. Don't disparage it." She convinced me with, "Eating isn't the purpose of eating. Living well is the purpose." Her voice rang with rhythm and cadence and, most of all, with passionate care for each of us. "Power…knowledge…living…the goal, above all, is loving!"

Eve entices and persuades us to use our increasing knowledge and appreciation of our husband to serve, respect, and exalt them. "Put to death any expectation of a positive response. Build a better you and invite the possibility of better relationships," she directs. My relationships became better beyond my wildest dreams, loving beyond my wildest dreams.

The early responses of my husband were typical. He cycled through suspicion, welcoming, and using the changes he saw for his own selfish ends. Sometimes, he treated me better, sometimes worse. Occasionally, he treated me much worse. I wanted to retaliate, to tell him he was throwing away my love. I wanted him to suffer and regret not appreciating my efforts and that I was having some success. Eve counseled all of us, "The best revenge is loving long and well." Some gave up. I'm glad I didn't.

In six months, his devotion to Allah deepened, and his treatment of me improved. He was drawn to the loving side of our faith. He began to value my opinion and to consult with me. He valued and trusted my insight into him and wanted my help. We gradually became companions. Giving him respect became a joyful privilege. He began to love me, even though I had been confident that he was incapable of loving. We searched together for a mosque that practiced the loving side of our faith better. We were partners and were happier than ever. Most of the Muslim couples stopped there or before. We continued on to study the words of Jesus. In about three years, we became his followers.

Several Muslim men demand to meet her in December. "What have you done to our wives?" They press. They crowd in close; their tone is stern, their bodies taut, fist clenched, and jaw set. There are five of them. She steps back into the snow-covered grass. Their wives watch from a distance.

"Are you displeased with your wives?" Eve entreats with her head bowed. Then she lays down flat in the snow with her arms extended above her head. "Tell me what displeases you, and I will try to correct them," she invites. Their stance relaxes.

The leader responds, "No, no! Get up!" He steps forward and awkwardly helps her up by offering her an end of his whip. He bellows for his wife to get her a towel. He continues, "My wife—our wives—have never treated us this good." But then angrily, he says, "Too good! What's the trick?"

Eve bows at the waist and replies meekly, "They wanted to be trained to love their husband as I love mine—freely and in reality." There is silence. The towel arrives, and Akmal's wife hands it to her husband. He hands it to Eve. This lion of a man begins to weep.

"I have never"—he exhales deeply—"never been loved like this." He wipes away tears and exclaims, "Thank you!"

Eve bows from the waist again and replies, "I'm honored by your speaking with me."

Akmal confers with the others. When he returns, he bows to Eve and entreats her, "We would be greatly honored if you and your husband would be our guests at my house for a meal."

Eve sinks to both knees and bows herself far lower than he was and replies, "We are honored. I will ask my husband."

A man whistles and says, "You're a good woman! And a Chris—"

Eve interrupts, "We are unworthy followers of Jesus."

Another man says, "We want to hear more about what he teaches that makes for loving wives!"

They exchange cell numbers (Adam's and Akmal's), and the men leave. Eve enters the house and relieves her fear in the bathroom with a brief prayer and a cry.

Eve is eager to tell Adam and watches for him. He arrives long after dark. She hears the familiar sound of the cable car, and her heart jumps. She realizes something is wrong. Today, his approach is slower. When he walks through the door, she sees his face etched with disappointment. She flings her arms around him. They rock and hold each other. He exhales deeply and says, "I've been laid off—no job after exams."

They were saving for a used car and to repair the Corolla. That would wait. They would live on savings and her income. Eve readies his meal and sits with him to eat the last part of hers. She waits for Adam to bring it up.

"Officially, I was laid off to save money."

"So there's more?"

"Yes, I'm afraid so."

"What?"

"Well, one of the Board—Marvin—likes me and respects me enough that he wanted me to know the truth."

"So the full truth is—"

"That," Adam interrupts, "a rich donor persuaded other big supporters to withdraw their support unless I was let go."

"Oh, that sounds personal and…"

"Yeah," he pauses. Eve suspects from the pause that he is uncertain how to tell her. He hides nothing from her. "He thinks I'm married to a Muslim, that I love Muslims and shouldn't teach at a"—he gestures with his hands to make quote signs—"'Christian' University."

"He is part right," she quips.

"What?" he says in mock surprise. "You've become a Muslim?"

"You silly goose, no, I…"

"You think I shouldn't teach at a Christian University?" he teases.

"No, I…"

"Et tu, Brute?" he says at he slides out of his chair and fell at her feet clutching his heart. He lifts her burqa, kisses her feet, and proceeds up her leg.

She squeals with delight as he lifts her over his shoulder and carries her to their bedroom. They share passion and pillow talk.

I Could Have Been Like God

"I could have been like God," Eve mentions over breakfast the next morning. A foot of snow had fallen, and they had a snow day.

"How so?" he asks.

"Remember how God regards Abraham's faith as righteousness?"

"Yeah," Adam says as he sips his tea and watches large flakes of snow gently drifting down. "So?"

"I could have done the same with your gentleness," she says wistfully. "Francine made me aware of this intent of God's."

"I'm…not getting…"

"You were gentle when I needed it"—she pauses—"because you were passionate for me. If I had regarded your gentleness as rooted in your passion for me I, I…"

"Don't let your past mistakes mess with the present and future, with God's present and future, with…"

"You are good to me and for me!" she says, snuggling into his lap.

His comment is healing for her soul because she knows his story. He bears the responsibility for deaths of people he loved deeply. He willingly, with great anguish, told her his painful story before they married. He was shattered and despaired of himself. He wanted to die. He accepted God's forgiveness only as obedience due God. He was unmade; God recreated him. She reasons that his past qualifies him to be merciful to her. She marvels that God brought two broken people together to heal each other.

Sarah is fed, changed, burped, and bundled up to take her out for her first snowfall. They come back in, and she tends to Sarah, while Adam stokes the fire, hangs up their wet things to dry, and fixes mulled cider and lunch. They talk. Eve tells him about the invitation from Akmal and gives him his number. Adam calls to make arrangements.

"Let's bake pies," Adam suggests.

His face and tone tell Eve he has a plan. "Okay—how come?"

"Well, we are not going anywhere and can use the extra heat."

"And?"

"I was thinking," he says slowly.

"You've given it lots of thought, you…"

"You know me well," he beams. He holds her. "I was wondering how we could serve that guy who got me fired."

"Let me guess," Eve entreats. "You were thinking, praying—"

"Aren't they the same?" Adam interjects.

"About how to show love to the guy who got you fired and…"

"You're almost there."

"Pies came to mind," she concludes. "What kind?"

"Cherry!" he responds. "He loves cherries."

"Let's do it," Eve agrees. "And the rest of the plan?"

"I know how you can deliver them in person to him and to two of the other supporters he stirred up against us," he admits.

They bake several pies that day. The kitchen is filled with warmth, laughter, and wonderful aromas.

Eve delivers the pies in person the next day and writes notes to the three men and their wives. They each insist she have a piece of pie with them. "I'd love to, but I can't with the veil," she writes. Noting their hesitancy about the pies, she texts Adam to join the couples for a piece of pie.

When he arrives, Johann asks Adam privately, "How did you come to marry—her?"

A difficult conversation follows because Johann jumps to conclusions. Adam untangles his thinking and asks Eve, "Describe what you were before you started following Jesus."

Adam interprets her signing. "She was an atheist—a power-crazed manipulative sexpot—a materialist magician puppet for demons she denied existed and filled with foolishness."

Johann's mouth opens, frozen in place. His face shows shock, surprise, fear, and disgust. Recovering himself, he probes, "Aren't you ashamed of yourself?"

"Should I be?" Eve signs and adds. "I'm not strong enough to think of myself and honor my Redeemer. I had to give up myself."

"Isn't that a miserable existence?" he says harshly.

After a pause, Eve signs, "Jesus is the hardest and kindest Master. I want to be his slave—it's my liberation, my only option."

"Why dishonor him by dressing like a Muslim?" he asks angrily.

"Oh, this?" she signs and pinches the fabric with her gloved fingers and pirouettes around. She moves her body as if skipping, conveying energy and joy. "I hated that I had to wear it."

"So don't!" he demands. His face is stern, his brow furrowed.

"My skin is allergic to light. It's ironic. Once I insisted on the limelight, now I shrink from light. Oh! My skin literally shrinks and sort of boils when light hits it."

"Oh, I'm sorry," he mumbles.

"Don't be!" she signs with lightness, enthusiasm, and…and something that heals his sour and sorry mood for the moment.

"I-I-I," he stammers while trying to smile broadly.

"Oh, oh…oh," she signs with descending animation and energy. "My vanity was destroying me. In my heart of hearts, I was at the center of my universe. The demons created a black hole of hurt and conditioning and pride that I couldn't escape."

"That's—it's—terrible," he says. She motions him close, closer.

"But," Eve whispers in a tone and timbre that Johann believes must be the tenor of heaven, "God outmaneuvered them. Oh, and me. He grants me the unspeakable privilege of having Adam, pain and ugliness, and him over myself. Though I was the worst, Jesus is the best Redeemer and God the best Father."

"Ah..." he says before lapsing into silence, his mouth half-open. In an instant, a smile explodes across his face, and, in gratitude, he grasps her hands and squeezes them in enthusiastic joy.

She yelps in pain. He releases her hands, saying, "Oops—ouch! Sorry! So you're one of us!"

"I'd have to live the guilt without Jesus, I couldn't," Eve states.

He looks down and begins to confess, "I've made a mess of—"

"May I challenge you, Mr. Schmidt?" she interrupts, whispering.

"Of course," he replies flatly.

"You thought I was the enemy. How does Jesus want us to treat our enemies?"

Brusquely turning away, he replies angrily, "Far better than I've treated you and your husband!" He grabs his wife's hand with his left hand and pulls her after him for a few steps and then abruptly turns back dragging his wife back to confront Eve. He comes within inches of her face and bellows, "Damn you! I was prepared to get your husband his job back, but then you—"

"But we didn't come to try to change your mind but to bless you with a changed heart." She interrupts his tirade.

He is raging, his body shaking. His hand crushes his wife's, and she struggles to retain her balance as he jerks her off balance. "Arghh—he'll"—he looks at Adam, shaking both his fists (jerking his wife out balance)—"never work at my university. Never!" He storms off after smashing a pie into Eve face with such force that he knocks her over.

Adam and Eve return home, comforting each other. They are saddened by his response. They pray for him and his wife.

Dinner at Akmal's House

Dinner at Akmal's House starts wonderfully. Six couples welcome Adam and Eve. All the men have full beards; Adam's is the only one completely white. Adam sits next to Akmal. Eve is next to Akmal's wife in the kitchen. The meal is wonderful.

The conversation of the men is pleasant; Akmal is a good host. That is, it's pleasant until Akmal asks Adam to explain how Eve convinced the woman to love their husbands. Adam's response sparks discord. Adam says, "What Jesus lives and says about love and power is not only for women but also men. God lays aside his power to love."

The discussion got heated, and Adam rarely spoke without being interrupted. Occasionally, a lull in the dispute allows Adam to complete a thought. Twice during their hour-long argument, the men hear the women laughing in the other room.

Adam explains that Jesus corrected his disciples, all men, for wanting to be preeminent. Jesus told them that if they want to be great, they should be the slave of all, and he cited himself as an example. "I came not to be served but to serve and to give my life as a ransom." Jesus washed their feet and taught them to do likewise. The men with Adam that day refuse to turn from power to "become weaklings."

The men reject Adam and all he said and dispatch him differently—cold and impersonal—from the welcome. There is no discussion of further contact. The women remain warm and responsive to Eve until their husbands prevent that.

The outcome of that evening is drastic and immediate. Eve is fired before she leaves Akmal's house. One husband beat his wife badly and was arrested. Akmal calls Adam the next day and speaks with him privately. He and his wife later become followers of Jesus. Akmal becomes gentle as a lamb with his wife.

Eve receives an e-mail asking her to "train my wife to love me like you trained the others." He offers to pay. She talks and prays about it with Adam. She proposes to work with his wife to clean their house and talk while they work. For the next two years, Eve works with several Muslim women under that arrangement.

Weeks later, Adam finds a part-time position at another college. It's closer, but the pay and responsibilities aren't as good as before. They couldn't afford a second car but wouldn't need one.

Eve is irrepressible. Her moods still have ups and downs, but she wears them well, and even her down times are attractive. She is sought after and has to limit her time with others to have time with her daughter and Adam. Their love deepens like a mighty river and sweeps everything with it. They are carried by it.

Sarah walks and talks before Adam finds a full-time position. The job pays less than his original full time position; they make do with the Corolla. There is no progress with her skin; daily exposure to light aggravates it. When Sarah is present, Eve endures light.

After Sarah's second birthday, Adam and Eve agree to have another child. They conceive easily. During the pregnancy, as her body floods with hormones, her skin gradually heals. By the seventh month of pregnancy, her skin is no longer sensitive to light. Her beauty seems greater to Adam than he had ever seen. In public, she still conceals her identity.

Rather than guilt for seizing control of healing herself, Eve fully enjoys the gift of healing and forgiveness. She rarely thinks of herself. Her heart, mind, and life are too full enjoying others, the daily gifts though nature, and her daily privileges of duty.

Life races by after the birth of Samuel Adam Smith. Sam is colicky; Eve is barely able to leave the house for six months. Adam's parents are in poor health and unable to visit. Visitors bring meals often and, when possible, share a meal and conversation with Eve. Extra meals are usually brought for her, Adam, and Sarah to share. Her friends watch the children to help her get sleep. They marvel at her bright spirit, even when fatigued.

Eve "returns to working" six months after Sam's birth. Adam prepares to present five major papers in six months at conferences in Philadelphia, Atlanta, D.C., and New York.

Sam's first year flies by full of challenges. Sam is like Adam was as an infant—an active curious explorer, who rebels at being confined and has to be watched closely. They survive to his third birthday with frequent trips to the emergency room.

Sam consumes all the time and attention Eve can give. Adam and Eve struggle to maintain their relationship. Talking, doing things together, and relaxing times are becoming rarer. They snatch opportunities for a kiss, touch, quick embrace, or a comment over the children's heads to prevent drifting apart.

The twenty-eight-year-old Corolla has to be replaced. It has over three hundred thousand miles. Its demise was hastened by a pick-up bumping them off the road. Adam's father had his license pulled and sold them his small SUV for what they could afford.

Sarah Starts Kindergarten

Sarah starts kindergarten when she is five and Sam three. A new routine begins. They leave early, drop Adam at work, Sarah at school, and then Eve takes Sam with her to work until time to pick up Sarah. She then either takes the children back with her to work or does errands and visits with the children until time to pick up Adam. Some days, she takes the children to a playground.

Eve makes it a delightful routine for the children and herself. They laugh and talk, skip and run, and snack together. She trains them to obey her eagerly. Eve dresses in modest slacks and top with only a small area around her eyes showing. She wears a scarf to hide her identity.

Adam leaves work early on Tuesdays. As a result, after school they always take a brief walk to a park to snack and play and then back to the car to "go pick up Daddy."

The first Tuesday in October is a beautiful day, sunny and slightly breezy. They are walking and skipping back from the park. Eve receives a priority message on her phone. It is a coded message from Ann, Doctor Dye. Eve prays and becomes doubly vigilant. Scanning for any hint of trouble, she quickly whispers directions to the children and broadcasts an alert to Adam, her brother, and a few select friends. The only people in sight are a couple jogging with a stroller and a dog and two women jogging from the opposite direction. She had seen all of them more than once before.

They make their way back to the car, avoiding coming close to anyone. When the couple is about ten yards away, the dog bolts for Eve and is chased by his surprised master. The dog leaps at Eve and would have knocked her down had she not swept her arms to block him away from her body to her left and angling her body to the right. She notes that his master continues to run directly at her and is cupping something in his right hand. The dog turns back toward her. She kicks the dog's windpipe and incapacitates him and then sweeps her legs to take the man's legs out from under him. He reacts like an expert and removes doubt in her mind as to what is at stake.

He isn't using his right hand properly, so Eve incapacitates him as his partner arrives and the women are running at them. "Scatter to five!" she yells. The children run in opposite directions. The children's reaction distracts the women, so Eve incapacitates the closest one.

Eve pulls off her scarf and engages the two women in hand-to-hand combat. They are well-trained but have not expected skilled resistance. They probably would eventually win, but only if they allow both children to escape. Eve hears a dreaded sound—motorcycles revving their engines—and sees motorcycles heading for each of the children. She prays to quickly defeat these women and have a chance to protect her children. She defeats them, but it's too late. She sees their two children pirated away by motorcycle into the trailer of an eighteen wheeler.

Adam is on their VPN with her brother and friends when she joins them. They prepared an encrypted way to share private communication for this possibility. They would have, at least, a few minutes of private communication before their encryption could be broken. Adam has already decoded Ann's message.

"Sound is their new weapon." Adam reports. "Ann wrote that they use sound as a carrier wave to disrupt the brain and, in your case, Eve, to re-establish your conditioning. They want to control you and through you establish control of others." They designed the sound to get to the auditory cortex through bone conductance, so hearing protection is useless. Once the sound reaches the auditory cortex, it activates extreme suggestibility and heightened ESP so they can control others through Eve.

Eve informs Adam that they have both kids. She heard the revving of motorcycles and sees four of them. She had positioned herself near a tall fence and was on the other side before they reached her. She gave a good chase until they tasered her.

An unseen witness to Eve's capture got her phone and followed them to a warehouse. He's an ex-Marine and avoids detection. He told the police and Adam via the VPN of her location.

They reactivate Eve's programming with their sonic blaster. She promptly goes into a coma.

"This isn't supposed to happen," their chief bellows. "Not this time!" He orders, "Secure her body and hook her up. Call me when she's prepped." The chief medical officer walks away but then turns to order, "Bring her children. Make sure she can hear them crying."

Eve is hooked to IVs, electrodes are attached all over her body and head, and she is encased in a rigid wet suit with wires and hoses all over it. Doctor Moser and the chief are summoned.

Eve is secured to a table. Doctor Moser walks over and speaks to her, "Janet," she says warmly, "welcome. You've evaded us a long time. Make her children cry and inform me of her brain activity." A moment later, both children are bawling. "She's responding."

"Good, good," she says, rubbing her hands together. "Watch her responses," she orders. "Now, Janet"—she leans over—

"unless you wake up within ten minutes, we will cut off your daughter's hand."

The technician reports, "She's reacting."

"I thought she might," the doctor replies. The children are screaming in pain. "Get them out of here! Put them in one of the quiet rooms," she orders.

"She's beginning to come out of the coma," the technician reports.

"Great, great. Perfect. No escape this time, Janet," she gloats, and Eve grunts.

"You will obey me," Moser states with strong emphasis on "me."

Eve tries to say "No" but can't.

"Still have some fight in you? You are amazing," she says. "Tell me when you are ready to obey."

Eve is fully awake, her eyes open. She says, "I'm ready to obey."

"Let's test your obedience," Moser counters. "When you press this button, you will experience great pain. The pain will stop when you stop pressing the button. Press and release the button only on my command." She hands the control to Eve. "Will you obey?"

"Of course," Eve replies.

"This will be fun!" the doctor exclaims with a devilish smile across her face. "Press the button," she whispers.

Eve does, and her body is racked with pain; she screams in agony.

Moser waits and then whispers, "Stop."

Eve stops and tries to catch her breath.

"Hold your breath," she suggests. She waits a minute before saying, "Now, without taking in a breath or making a sound, press the button again."

Eve obeys. Her body twitches violently, her face contorts in pain.

Moser tells the technician, "Tell me when she's about to pass out."

Several moments later, he says, "We're about to lose her."

"Okay then," Moser states at a leisurely pace. "Stop and breathe."

Eve gasps for air and sobs.

"No more of that!" she orders. "Totally control your reaction to the pain. Feel it more intensely than ever but show no distress."

"As you wish," Eve agrees.

With a hearty laugh, she orders, "Press the button!"

Eve did, but nothing seems to happen. Moser looks at the technician while raising her eyebrows.

"She's experiencing severe pain," he reports. "All the autonomic signs of distress are present."

After several minutes, Eve faints. She continues to push the button. Moser leaves and takes her time returning; Eve still pushes the button. Moser finally orders her to release the button.

"We are about to be attacked," the loudspeaker blares. "A SWAT team supplemented with Special Forces approaches. All personal to isolation rooms." The chief yells at Moser because Janet lost consciousness.

Moser defends herself, "I had to make sure she's under our control!"

Two men strip the suit off Eve. They fasten a helmet on her with built-in headphones and microphone. They lock her in a small room made of bulletproof glass. Dr. Moser stays with her to wake her. Without Eve, the sonic blaster only incapacitates. When she awakes, they will control them through Eve.

THE ATTACK STARTS

The attack starts with scores of SWAT personnel entering the warehouse. The blaster is played through speakers capable of carrying its wave. The effect is immediate on the SWAT team. They slow to a standstill; their bodies, formerly taut and in rapid motion, become limp and still.

Dr. Moser finally wakes Eve. "Janet," she orders, "tell them to shoot anyone entering the building."

Eve replies, "I obey."

One by one, the SWAT team members fall to the ground asleep. "What's wrong?" Moser shouts. She attacks Eve. Eve knocks her out.

Twenty heavily armed Special Forces enter the building. The blaster activates, and the same thing happens to them. Eve is ordered to have them defend the building from attack, but they also fall asleep.

"Turn on the speaker," the chief orders. "And blast Janet with it to reassert control of—"

"But Dr. Moser is in there!"

"Blast her too," the chief snaps.

"Yes, sir."

The blaster hits Eve; she slips into a coma.

Four others enter. They are lightly armed. They are blasted with the sound. Nothing happens. They pick up heavy weapons from the Special Forces and, in a few minutes, blow the doors and secure the isolation rooms. They capture everyone with no casualties.

They are aided by the blaster still being on when they blow the doors on the isolation rooms. The sound incapacitates everyone inside. Also, after seeing the effectiveness of the blaster on the previous intruders, all are unprepared for anyone immune to it.

When the blaster is turned off, the members of the SWAT team and Special Forces begin to wake. A few minutes later, they free Eve and arrest Moser. EMS personnel check out Eve and put her on a stretcher. She is unresponsive.

As they take her to the ambulance, Adam arrives. He finds Eve and asks the EMS people to see his wife. "She's in a coma," one replies.

He grasps her hand and squeezes it. "Eve," he says, "it's..."

She opens her eyes; her face radiates with joy rapidly mixing with pain as she exclaims in a whisper, "I remember." When she opens her eyes, her skin reacts to the light. Adam covers her with a blanket.

"Daddy, Daddy, Daddy," Sarah and Samuel squeal as they run to him. Eve immediately tries to throw off the blanket and, on her third try, succeeds.

"Sarah! Sam!" she whispers.

Sarah exclaims, "Mommy, Mommy!" and Samuel starts to cry. He had never seen his mother look like she does at that moment.

Sarah comforts him, hugging him close. "Sam, look at Mommy's face closely to see how much she loves us."

Samuel looks at her face, frightened and fascinated by what he sees. The pain and boiling of her skin he sees repulse and scare him, but the welcoming joy, the invitation radiating out of the pain and ugliness, overcomes him. After a pause, he runs to the joy of suffering love—his mother. Adam lifts them both onto the cot.

Adam makes a covering like a tent from two blankets he puts over Eve and the children. He wants to shield her from the light, yet allow her and the children to enjoy each other.

Adam looks up and shouts, "James! What are you doing here?"

Samuel yells, "Uncle James!" while waving his arms.

"My brother?" Eve asks, still barely under the blankets.

"Yes," Adam says, but before he can continue, she throws off the blankets and converses with James in ASL. They sign back and forth so quickly Adam can't keep up.

Two EMS attendants stare at Eve. They are transfixed by her—her face and arms reacting to the light, her signing, mouthing, and gesturing with her face at a dizzying rate—the overwhelming impression made is that they've never seen such joy.

Adam shields Eve from direct light with a blanket. He knows better than to try to cover her completely—she is determined to communicate with James. The children snuggle close to her.

The EMS personnel insist on taking Eve to the hospital. She is loaded into a military ambulance. When Adam asks the general in charge where they are taking her, he gets no answer.

Eve is missing for three frantic days. Adam tries to locate her and is warned to cease. Late on the third day, he receives a text where to pick her up. He wakes the children to go get her.

They celebrate her being back. It is midnight before the children are back asleep. Eve confesses exhaustion but doesn't look it.

"I've never seen you look so radiant with…" Adam begins but can't find an adequate word.

"I've never been like this," Eve affirms. Her voice has a cadence and harmony with a beauty like a song. Seeing her reacting violently to dim light, he marvels that signs of pain are trumped by her—her rapture of love and joy (but that fails to do it justice). She tells him she wants to speak with him face-to-face.

"How? Why?" Adam entreats. "And what did you mean, 'I remember' when you woke?"

"Later," she coos. "Could you fix some herbal tea with OJ?"

He jumps up, "Which tea?"

"Aphrodite," she replies. Then she added, "And make some for yourself also."

"I don't really need it," he guffaws. He puts the kettle on.

"Neither do I. I want to tell you just a little now, and the rest—that will take the rest of our lives together."

"May I put out all the light, except for a candle?"

"Wonderful," she agrees. "Yes, let's make it intimate." That's their code word. "How'd you know that what I want to say—"

"Are you kidding?" he teases. "Your face, voice, your whole body sing it out. You have a symphony in you, an epic, a—" But again, he is at a loss for words.

They prepare. They strip to their underwear and sit opposite at a small table. His inner thighs caress her outer thighs, skin-to-skin, and they intertwine their legs. They hold each other's elbows and gaze into each other's eyes. Occasionally, they sip their tea.

She Begins Her Symphony

She begins her symphony with this overture: "Jesus let me choose," pausing to recompose herself, her radiance swells with this phrase: "To suffer in place of the children."

"How?"

"I was in a coma. They hurt the children, but I didn't know it, until Jesus told me I could awake and suffer far worse than I ever had—that made me shudder—or let the children suffer."

Adam knew how she had suffered; he says, "Rough choice."

"Not at all!" she exclaims, enunciating each word in staccato for emphasis. "I would eagerly die a thousand deaths for them or you but especially to please him. I asked him what he wanted me to do." Tears and joy flow from her eyes.

"I wish I could have suffered it for them and for you," Adam says, "I wish I could have helped."

"Ah, but you did! When I woke, their technology had stripped me of my will—for a small part of a second. You rescued me."

"Huh?" he utters, perplexed. "How?"

"I was back under your control. I suppose since you weren't there in the vacuum, I would have fallen under their control. But you gave me my orders for the rest of my life—to make my own decisions. I obeyed you and was free again."

"Wow!"

"I played along with them to protect the children and to defeat them and their goal. They made me inflict pain on myself, yet keep a smile on my face. It's the hardest thing I will ever do"—she pauses then continues—"eagerly." That word climaxes her ode to joy.

He is speechless.

Moments later, she continues. "One more thing tonight," she says in a manner that broadens his anticipation.

"What?" he asks eagerly.

"I gladly suffer. Still"—there is a pregnant pause—"I want to start healing my body tonight by trying to have another child."

"Your wish is my command!" He carries her to their room.

Later, Eve informs him about the last few days and answers his questions. Some in the military detained her to test using her and the sonic weapon to control others. "They probably would have kept me indefinitely if my obedience to you—freeing me—hadn't made me immune to control. It was worse and longer torture than the others put me through."

"How'd you bear it?"

"God helped, and I wanted to come home. I'm not sure they'd let me go as long as they thought they could make it work. Dr. Dye showed up and convinced them that it couldn't work. She's very respected by them. God played his hand masterfully!"

Adam explains that James was accepted by Special Forces. Being deaf from birth makes him immune to sound weapons like that.

Eve was distressed by the torture; her beautiful black hair grew from its roots snow white. Adam grieves the loss harder than Eve. "We'll match—both prematurely gray because we suffered for each other," Eve concludes.

Eve laughs, "I'll be pregnant through the heat of August!" Nothing got her down for long. It was a good thing. The pregnancy was extremely difficult—pregnant with active twins, debilitating morning sickness, enforced bed rest for much of the pregnancy.

Sleeping on her back with her hips higher than her heart was difficult. She had no relief from the light hitting her skin.

Several things cause moments of despair to Eve. A freeze kills her carefully cultivated plants for the production of her lotion. A woman helping accidentally broke several bottles of the lotion, and she ran out. The lotion she used formerly had been reformulated; she is allergic to it. She concocts an inferior substitute.

Eve is far from stoic—far beyond it. She confesses weaknesses; she suffers greatly and gladly. She cries, laughs, and lives inside out. A fear grows that the pregnancy would not heal her skin. Despair hits hard when the fear becomes reality. Eve wears the despair like a garment that conceals her inner joy. For days, the shroud of despair hides her joy. The shroud thins, and joy shines through.

Eve removes her veil around children. Seeing her face like that a first time evokes revulsion—for a moment. The grandeur of her smile and her joyful eyes especially amend that first reaction. Many agree, "I love seeing the beauty of her joy."

Eve gives birth to Nathan and Nancy after difficult labor. Gifts for the twins include the normal assortment and all the disposable diapers needed. Several Muslims and former Muslim friends provide several solar panels for the cabin.

A year after her kidnapping, the first seven inches of her hair are white as snow. Over the next years, her hair turns snow white, and her skin heals. She remains sensitive to chlorine and chemicals, but her reaction is less severe. Makeup and perfume are not possible.

Wrinkles add character. Eve looks much older than her age—joy is deeply etched in her face. Flashes of displeasure or anger don't eclipse the love and joy singing from her face. Her eyes show attentive joy throughout the range of her emotions. Her piercing eyes show almost perpetual delight and mirth in the deeply etched crow's feet around them. She wears a scarf over part of her face in public to lessen distractions from her joyous smile—it arrests people's attention. It might distract a driver.

Johann calls Adam to apologize. Johann and Rita bring dinner and their fifteen-year-old daughter to watch the children. Johann, normally very poised, stumbles over himself in making an apology and confession to Eve.

The welcome, love, and joy singing out of her face move him to tears. He thanks her "for drawing me back to following Jesus rather than just playing church politics. You've saved my marriage and my life."

Frustration and difficulties skyrocket when Samuel starts kindergarten. He has severe behavior problems at school. Eve picks him up from school early daily. School upsets him and drains her. She needs a break and time with Adam to recharge.

Eve fights a losing battle with the school. They can't handle him. He's diagnosed with Attention-Deficit/Hyperactivity Disorder (ADHD) and starts on medication. His behavior improves, but he becomes an emotional zombie. They don't find a medication without unacceptable side effects. Only special education classes for Samuel or schooling by Eve are options. They decide, after advice, prayer, and discussion, for Eve to teach Samuel herself.

Eve prizes spontaneity—it slips out of reach. Managing everything requires routine and structure. She embraces it. She teaches Samuel for three hours daily—in twelve-minute bursts—that's all he stays focused. Eve lives around the children's needs.

Adam takes the twins to the pediatrician. The twins are "wild as March hares." The contrast from when the twins are with Eve is striking. They are manageable only with Eve present. A child behavioral specialist, Dr. Watts, concludes after observation and evaluation that all of the children, and even Adam, have ADHD.

Sarah needs medication when she entered a demanding program for the Gifted and Talented. Medication was a great success for her. Years later, the twins benefit from the same medication.

Dr. Watts notes the children show no signs of ADHD with Eve. She gives off a riveting stream of positive emotional rewards. Consequences bypass the areas of the brain affected by ADHD. He compares it to Carl Rogers's "unconditional positive regard." Unconsciously, like Rogers, Eve modifies behavior with the warmth and joy radiating from her.

EVE STRIVES TO MAKE LIFE ORDINARY

Eve strikes to make life ordinary for her family. Life is busy, simple, and mundane. Her life is entrenched in the consistently ordinary mass of habits. Worship is continuous, often unconscious, and routine. Time with God, lamenting, conversing, and giving thanks is incessant. Her delight in everything is habitual. She delights with and benefits others with a willing heart.

Freed from ego, Eve rarely competes. Many benefit from her kind driving. Liberated by love, her generosity is uninhibited. She gives time, a cheery greeting or note, and herself freely. She is free from being manipulated by her concern to please her Abba Father.

Eve leaves early to have time to meet needs that arise. She enlists the eager cooperation of Sarah and Samuel. Their reward is that when they arrive early, their mother entertains them with stories enlivened by her face and body. She tells stories about Cassie the dog, the enchanting dress, and the rewards of hard work. She also tells stories from literature and the wonders of Eden.

Her generosity shows daily. One day, she notices a woman and her son clashing. Both are angry, loud, and disrespectful. With Eve are her children, who are bonded to her by firm kindness and the joy radiating from her. Eve asks the woman if she wants help. The woman redirects her anger at Eve and retorts harshly. Eve counters sweetly. She takes no offense. She has no need to rescue. She desires to simply follow Jesus.

This woman, overwhelmed with her son and the kindness of a stranger, pleads for help. Eve spends thirty minutes showing the woman how to re-establish a firm and kind bond with her son backed by realistic consequences. The woman and her son, about six, continue their day holding hands.

Eve rarely wastes a moment; she has few to spare. She doesn't hurry or rush others—living is too precious. She brings a refreshing atmosphere with her.

First impressions of Eve are of her joy and interest in people. Those who know her better fathoms the depths of her struggles and paradoxes. She hides almost nothing, even from herself. She is free from herself, someone who found her true self—secure and serene, passionately obsessed with loving God and others—bringing stability and hints of radical possibilities for living. Many are attracted to the possibilities; some become hostile.

Days flow, and she rides the waves. Benefits scatter freely from her conferring good on all. Love lights her way, mirth leavens it, and joy seasons her. Loving, serving, dying to herself, enjoying the bounties and beauties of nature—all are inexpressible privilege—only living and enjoying it does it justice.

Her routine—the dull, the mundane and ordinary, gradually becomes living.